Gillian White is a journalist and lives in Devon. She has four children.

Critical acclaim for Gillian White:

'A rich and wonderful tale of conspiracy and domestic infamy' FAY WELDON

'Here is a marvellously exciting new writer. She tingles one's spine. She makes you think about people. She's marvellously literate and the similes really bring the writing to life' JILLY COOPER

'A gripping read' *Today*

'A novelist of the highest quality ... an intense and vividly-written novel which takes you by the throat and won't let go' *Sunday Independent*

Rich Deceiver

GILLIAN WHITE

PHŒNIX

A PHOENIX PAPERBACK

First published in Great Britain
by Orion in 1992
This paperback edition published in 1995
by Phoenix,
a division of Orion Books Ltd,
Orion House, 5 Upper St Martin's Lane,
London WC2H 9EA

A CIP catalogue record for this book is available
from the British Library.

ISBN: 1 85799 256 3

Printed in Great Britain by
The Guernsey Press Co. Ltd,
Guernsey, C.I.

Dedication

For Juliet, with love and thanks for all sorts of things,
including the three magic words 'frankly rather repellent'.

1

Another dawn comes to Nelson Street. See how it drifts off the gentle green domes of the glass Arcade, giving it the look of a ghostly mosque, before dropping with a flop and spiking itself on the aerialed chimneys. It slinks to the door of number nine, it rests on the step, it wets one edge of the *Mirror* with an amber tongue.

Habit tugs Ellie Freeman from room to room, drawing back curtains. She is a woman with dishevelled hair, wrapped in a dressing-gown the colour of a cornflake. Everything in her humble home has kept to its shape and form in the night: every picture is straight, every piece of furniture in position, no matter that she's been to sleep and abandoned it for the last seven hours.

She picks up yesterday's paper with the crossword puzzle half-done and puts it beside the bin, wincing slightly at the sticky mess on the lino. Doesn't matter, she tells herself, she can sort that out later. Today is her day off and she will clean the house because she always cleans the house on a Wednesday.

The gurgle of the sink upstairs reminds her of a straw sucking lazily in the dregs of a carton. That's all right, he's up then. She plods past the letterbox three times, not even eyeing the paper lest she be tempted, and the buff envelopes crammed in beside it stick out, rear up where they bend and crease and touch the hem of Malc's raincoat. They are the same colour exactly, apart from the stamps which are crisscrossed and old-looking, like the lining. She is deliberately leaving the paper as a treat for later. She'll start the crossword and Malc will finish it this evening.

'Anything worth having?' The sound of the lavatory chain wafts out behind him, and she hears the flump of the towel on the landing. Wednesday . . . washday . . . even Malc knows that.

1

So she moves to collect the mail and the paper, glancing at it casually as she heads for the kettle in the kitchen. Without really thinking she slits the only envelope addressed to her; without really reading she reads it.

And then she knows what people mean about being dead and floating high in one corner, observing themselves, *because the same thing is happening to her.* She is watching herself from behind. It *is* her – Ellie Freeman – she knows because she's seen herself from that angle only just last week on video. Surprised at her own rear view, she had told the Dixons man, who blinked up at her without interest, 'Think of all those people going through life only knowing about half of themselves.'

'Well, there's not an awful lot you can do about the back,' the Dixons man said, bored. 'And nobody takes any notice of people's backs, anyway.'

Ellie does. Ellie takes notice of people's backs, since she is often not brave enough to stare at their fronts. No, backs are important . . . yet ignored.

So she watches her own head come up from the letter, tight as a cork in a bottle neck, and sees it going down again to check. She is even able to look out of the kitchen window at the strip of back yard, the wall at the end and the scuffed old sunflower beside the dustbin. She watches her neck stretch and her shoulders sag – the tension before the explosion – how she moves her weight from one leg to the other and how her dressing-gown cord is twisted and misses one of the waist loops so that the heavy towelling drags down at one side.

From behind, with her blue dress on, she'd looked like a Domestos bottle, that's what had shocked her in Dixons.

And then she is suddenly back inside her own body again, and her brain is screaming, *'How much? How much?'* And here she is, shaking the paper because it refuses to tell her . . . either that, or she is refusing to believe it!

The road to riches is laid out before her.

'One million, five hundred and twenty-five thousand pounds.' And the letter says quite a lot else, only she hasn't time to read it all, about somebody calling this morning, investment advice, very many sincere congratulations . . . It reads like a

2

birthday card, or one to someone who has come through a dangerous operation and she knows that flowers will inevitably follow. It also asks if she would like to change her mind and accept the publicity, and says that they would have telephoned but were unable to get through.

That is polite of them, because she doesn't have a telephone. They sound excited, as if they might well do something silly. She'll have to ring them and stop them coming – she'll have to convince them to leave her alone.

She doesn't have a telephone and she hasn't got a car.

She flaps round the kitchen in a perfect oval, following the edge of the old rush mat.

She hasn't even got a bank account. 'It's never worth it for what we've got and those bastards just want to get you in trouble for the sake of the interest,' Malc says. Malcolm stopped doing the pools last New Year after twenty years at it. 'Bloody waste of time, and they say here they reckon you're more likely to get struck by lightning than win. That's what they reckon and that's what it says here.'

But Malc tells lies easily. Ellie knows he tells lies because of the one he lays on her constantly, the one that says that their lives are finished. He tells her flatly as if there's no arguing about it, 'We've had all the chances we're going to get and we've missed them.' The way he says it makes it sound as if she is to blame. But Ellie looks forward to every day just as she always did, hoping that something nice will happen, and the suspicion that it won't makes no difference . . . she isn't being silly, it's just that she cannot continue to live without pleasurable expectations of some sort. So Ellie carried on doing the pools, secretly, in her own name, a forecast by postal order, while Malc watched the football from deep in his chair, angrily, and checked the results automatically. Since he'd thrown in his hand Ellie had lived in dread that one day Malc's numbers might come up. It would finish him. She'd changed the numbers. She'd never dreamed that she'd win, but still, she'd changed the numbers on her coupon.

Funny really, because she isn't normally a secretive person. Well, there is nothing about her to hide. Thoughts don't count.

3

She stuffs the letter and cheque deep in her dressing-gown pocket, beneath a wad of tissues as though it is a dirty little packet, a shameful, personal thing that will have to be carried away and burnt afterwards.

'Dear God, what have I gone and done now?'

And why isn't she leaping up the stairs, shouting her head off and telling Malc the news, proving to him that they're not finished, that it is only just beginning?

Well, she doesn't do that because she just can't bear to hear him saying, 'You bloody fool, it's a trick or some sales promotion. Read the small print, you soft sod. You get caught every time, don't you, you and all the other idiots like you.' She knows he'll say that. She knows she'll stand and watch his hope gathering fright, so like a child fearing the worst, begging for contradiction. Oh, she understands why he's so angry and she knows why he's hurt, why he has turned into a sullen man, and frightened, why his sole preoccupation in life is himself. Life, as he tells her again and again, has not been fair. Well, she's contradicted him for his own sake so many times now that she is tired of it. He is not a child.

And then the moment for action is gone, and her behaviour is secretive, and the fact that she is being so sly soon explodes into a massive act of betrayal. She lays the kitchen table for breakfast, trying not to shake.

'One million, five hundred and twenty-five thousand pounds.' It is no good whispering it, either. It sounds just as unreal as it looks. Maybe Malc's cynicism is apt ... maybe it *is* some trick. She stifles the urge to closet herself away with the letter, she makes herself wait.

When she hears the plodding, socky sound of his feet on the stairs Ellie realises with amazement that she is gasping, and that this is nothing to do with the letter, that she always gasps when he first comes down – before she knows what mood he'll be in. She lowers two eggs into boiling water with her stomach firmly pulled in, and her breath is still doing more of a gasp than a hold. The two eggs float down into the water leaving uneasy streaks of white behind them.

Ellie Freeman twists her head round to look at her husband. It is a long time since she's really seen him, taken any notice of what he *looks* like, not what he *feels* like. To a stranger, she supposes, Malc would look like a man with a bad hangover, but that is just the way he comes down with his hair unbrushed and the way his eyes bag underneath first thing in the morning giving him the dull, challenging stare of the drinker. The tie drooping low round his open-neck shirt does not help. He is a forty year old warehouseman and overweight, trying to be all brave in front, with nothing behind except sagging. The clout has gone out of his smile: it's still there sometimes, but shy, and his hair is the same as it always was, curly-tight and crinkled to his head. Some of the handsomeness of him remains too, firming him up, if you look hard. She feels a brief flash of love for what he has been, and for mornings, years ago, which she has forgotten now.

'I'm not going to have time to eat those, not if you're only just putting them in.'

The toast is fringing on burning. She reaches into the fridge for the orange juice and puts it down in front of him. He is reading the headlines and feeling his way across the table to the tea, pouring it. She watches his hand. He only pours out one cup, although her empty one is set right beside it.

'Will you be late back, Malc?'

As he doesn't answer she has to repeat the question, and then he grunts, and says impatiently, 'It's only Wednesday,' and so she knows he will not be late. On a Wednesday, he is home by five, if not five-thirty. He is lucky to have a job at all, with unemployment round here as it is, although the job that he's had for twenty years is constantly under threat. Oh yes, she knows why he's bitter and frightened. So many men round here have become like that lately.

He rustles the paper and says of the rattling eggs, 'I'll not have time for those.' Then he asks, 'Was there anything?'

What is her lie going to sound like? 'No post, other than the usual.'

He rustles again. 'Bills, I suppose,' as if she's sent them.

She wants to rest her hand on his arm and ask, 'Malc, when did you start hating me?'

Ellie spoons the eggs into a double-armed eggcup, a white,

porcelain thing which makes her think of a hospital feeder, before sitting down opposite him. She thinks she hears her letter crinkle, she thinks she blushes. She will not remind him that the eggs are there, for if she mentions them at all he will not eat them. If he discovers them by accident, of his own accord, there is a chance that he might.

Sulphurous eggs and a million pounds for breakfast this morning. Oh Malc, when did we die? Was there one, specific moment when we closed our eyes? And who died first, you or me?

What does she care if he eats the eggs or not? But she does care. She cares very badly. And so a game is happening between them, with two contestants playing it, only up until this morning she hasn't quite realised how long it's been going on.

He always leaves home before she does, for on the days Ellie works she has to be at the Arcade to open the shop by nine. Malc has further to go, a twenty-minute bus ride, and he starts at eight. If she tells him about her pools win he will not go to work. For the first time in twenty years, apart from the few days of illness, she knows that he would not go to work.

And what would they do instead? How would they share the great news together? She tries to imagine as she stares out of the window and watches him disappear off down the street in his mac. Her heart sinks – even now she could call him back and take that shuffle out of his step, straighten his back for him, light up his eyes. Her hands grip the windowsill and the ends of her fingers are white with the pressure. They'd go down to the pub and make the announcement . . . drinks for the boys all round. And then what? Go round the garages looking for THE CAR – the convertible Merc, oh yes, he has his dreams – with Malc getting louder and louder? He would want the whole world to know. For him, Ellie knew, it would be part of the winning. He would want to take advantage of the special weekend in London, the celebrity celebration at the posh hotel, the theatre trip and all those sequinned models posing.

That's what he thinks enjoyment is now. He gets it from the papers he reads, he gets it off the telly.

And who does she think she is to deprive him of any of that? Doesn't she owe him that much?

They could even live in London now, she supposes, if they wanted to, and move south.

Ellie draws the cheque out of her pocket and spreads it on the kitchen table before her. It is real, it is every bit as real as the remains of her husband's breakfast. Malc has eaten his eggs and now just the broken shells, the smell, and the smokey toast crumbs remain.

She plays the old game of turning the eggshell over so that it doesn't look broken. She smashes it with a teaspoon. The excitement of winning is bursting inside her. She longs to tell someone, even climb to the rooftops, cling to the chimney and shout out the news to the world, swinging Malc's football rattle. 'Poor people don't win the pools,' she remembers Malc telling her. Well, she is poor and she's won. It is just another of his lies. She'd felt like this when Mandy was born . . . she'd pushed the new pram up the street and expected everyone to look in it. They had, and with great pride she'd pulled the bunny rabbit cover down to show them. It was that sort of neighbourhood. In those days women were at home, cleaning and looking after children, but now everyone works. Now, after half-past nine, almost every house in the street is empty.

She has made a secret, and if she isn't going to tell Malc then she mustn't tell anyone. If he finds out she has not shared this with him, she knows he will never forgive her, never begin to understand. He'd be hurt and bewildered. So she can't tell Mandy and she can't tell Kev, but can she do it? Is she good at keeping secrets? Ellie doesn't know. This is the first proper secret she's ever had – and she wonders why she didn't consider this when she first decided to go ahead with filling in the pools. The thought that she might react like this had never crossed her mind. All she'd imagined – when she'd given it any thought – was champagne, party-poppers and paper hats. And THE CAR, she supposes, oh yes, the car. And sending for those holiday brochures she used to get so that Mandy and Kev could cut them out, but this time with a view to actually going somewhere!

7

The furthest she and Malc had ever travelled was to a caravan site by the sea near Harlech.

'One million . . .'

She supposes, with her money, she'll attract men now . . . men of a particular type who want that kind of life-style and who use silver cigarette cases and wear brogues. Ellie Freeman gets up and, after pushing her hair back from her face, tightens her dressing-gown around her, needing the warmth and the bulk of it, wanting protection. She'll be forty next March, a forty year old millionairess who wants a pee, who works in a gift shop in the Arcade and whose husband has lost his pride. She shakes her head wonderingly. The truth is so simple really that it comes like a pain, and the pain is sweet though it cuts her chest sharply. She doesn't want to be rich and free with Malc like he is. She doesn't want to sit and sip rum and cokes on some soulless beach in Majorca with her toenails painted orange, her body wrinkled with that awful, freckly brown of middle age. She doesn't want Malc's plastic palms, his dyspepsia, his lethargic, grunting sex, his oblique kind of blind fury, nor the loud-voiced friends he would choose. He'd make friends with some drunk old barman, a loser like himself, and they'd swop losers' jokes about sex and mother-in-laws, being comical together. It was not because he wanted to be like that, it didn't come naturally to him, but that was the way all his friends behaved and so Malc thought he had to, too. But Ellie doesn't want him to be comical in that tragic, self-destructive, old man's way, and she doesn't want to be rich without him, either.

Well, she loves him, of course she does. She knows him better than anyone else in the world and she can't be bothered to start knowing anyone else. She'd looked, and as far as Ellie could see, no one else could hold a candle to him . . . that's the expression, isn't it?

She puts the dishes in the sink to soak and clears and wipes the kitchen table. She'll have to move quickly to get everything done by this afternoon. She goes upstairs, the cheque gripped between finger and thumb, playing with it. In the bathroom, the windows are misted. She holds the cheque out over the flushing lavatory, toying with it, enjoying the

8

many possibilities of it – she could throw it away, or give it to some deserving cause, only she knows she won't. She clutches it far too tightly for that.

Cars start up in the street outside and a milk-float whirrs bumpily by. The morning light that says summer is ending silvers her favourite trinkets. She sits before her kidney-shaped dressing table with the double mirrors which allow her to see one half of her head at a time. Not behind, though. Never behind, and what good is one half without the other? What good is a front without a back? What a fright she is now without make-up, sort of raw ... She beams at herself insanely, refusing to be absorbed by her eyes this morning. Is she homely? Ordinary? *Common?* People used to say she looked a bit round-faced and straight-haired, like the American singer Connie Francis – but who would say that now? Her skin is firm, her brown eyes are bright and her hair is thick and shiny with hardly any grey in it. People have already started commenting on this: 'You've hardly any grey in your hair yet, have you, Ellie?'

And Malc, who has hardly any grey in his, either, tells them, 'What's she ever had to worry about?'

Her hands still shake, her breath halts and quickens and she feels a hunger in her throat that is almost a sickness. Something has happened, as she'd always known, had always believed that it would! Is it possible that all she has ever wanted is going to be granted? Is it possible that she can take time back, and change it? She feels young again, and powerful, and all swelled up with hope. She sprays away the smell of herself. She brings her lips down on her lipstick. Between every blusher stroke she glances at the cheque. She puts it on the unmade bed then takes her navy suit from the wardrobe and picks off the old dandruff. She doesn't have grey in her hair and she doesn't have veiny legs but she is getting plump, she is sagging. She takes out a pair of new tights and carefully pulls them on – such wild extravagance!

When she's finished with herself she stands back and stares at her image in the full-length wardrobe mirror. She shares the wardrobe with Malc and her husband's slightly woody body smell comes off his two suits and sturdy brown shoes,

9

breathing on the mirror with its aroma and fading her. Well, she looks like everyone else, of course she does. She's spent a lifetime trying to do that, hasn't she? Ellie smiles, steps back and picks up the cheque. Before she ties on her headscarf and pulls on her clear plastic mac, she checks in her handbag for change, because she'll be needing to make a longish telephone call.

And she needs the bus-fare to get to the bank . . . the exact bus-fare, if possible, if she doesn't want the driver to moan at her. And she doesn't. Ellie Freeman is a woman who can't bear anything like that.

2

She hesitates at the door of the bank and allows annoyed people to push past her. She has never been in a bank in her life, for when she and Malc had savings they put them in the post office. Now, from where she stands gazing in, the bank looks like the foyer of the public baths . . . all rubber plants and plush, baggy seating in soft brown leather – the sort of seats you have to fall back on, briefly losing control – and the low, square tables are covered in forms. Perhaps she ought to have made an appointment? Perhaps no one will be available to see her? Someone has been busy polishing the glass because the whole place smells of Windolene.

She edges her way over the smooth beige carpet and sidles up to the nearest counter. She waits. She keeps her head down and she waits.

She'd rung the pools people on the way over. The woman who answered had been sternly helpful, and had put her straight through to someone who knew all about it . . . Caroline Plunket-Kirby. Ellie had launched straight in. 'Is it true?' She'd gone red in the face holding her breath, waiting for the reply, wanting it to be yes so badly.

'I am extremely pleased to be able to tell you that yes, it is true, Mrs Freeman. I have been trying to trace your telephone number to confirm the good news for two days without success. Of course arrangements have already been made for you and your husband to come down here as soon as possible to discuss the practicalities . . .'

'I don't want him to know.'

There was a brief pause, then, 'That has to be your decision.'

'Yes, I know, and I've already taken it.'

'Perhaps it would be wise to talk this over first with someone who has experience . . .'

'It's too late now. I have already decided.'

'There might well be difficulties.'

'I know there will be difficulties, but I'll just have to cope with them as they arise.'

'How long have you been married, Mrs Freeman?'

'Twenty years,' Ellie shouted into the phone, to reach smooth-speaking Ms Plunket-Kirby above the rumble of throbbing traffic. She prodded her bag to keep it from slipping off the tiny, metallic shelf.

'Twenty years is a long time to suddenly squeeze somebody out. I really do feel that this is a matter which should be discussed face to face, far better than like this ... two strangers in a hurry. Won't you give me your number, Mrs Freeman, so that when we're cut off I can call you back?'

And Ellie defiantly gave the number, rammed up hard as she was against the phone booth door to avoid the dark puddle of water in the concrete centre. 'And I don't want publicity, or flowers, or any kind of interviews. I don't want anything like that.'

It sounded like a funeral, but what a relief it was to be talking about it with someone who knew.

'Well, I can see that that would be unwise, given the circumstances. And when do you intend to leave your husband, Mrs Freeman, or have you already left? We can help you in all areas of your life, you know, not just the financial aspects of it. In fact we like to help, we prefer to be involved. We are not merely money distributing machines, you see.'

For goodness sake, this was extremely personal stuff! Ellie had never before in her life spoken so freely to a stranger like this. 'Leave him?' She was shocked. The thought had never occurred to her. 'Who said anything about leaving him? I've been married to Malcolm for twenty years and I wouldn't dream of leaving him.'

'I see. Then it's just the money you're keen to keep secret?'

'I can do that if I want to, can't I?' She thought she'd feel different with her money behind her but she didn't.

'It's your money, my dear. And most certainly you can do what you like with it, but sound financial advice is urgently necessary.'

My dear?

Ellie said, 'I'm on my way to the bank now, with the cheque. I've got the cheque with me now, in my bag, on the side here. It's not too soon, is it? I'm not too early?' She prodded at the softness of her handbag once again, annoyed at being made to feel like a mutinous child.

'Can I be of any help by ringing your bank first, discussing the situation with the manager, maybe . . . paving the way, as it were?'

She might as well be frank. 'I'm not sure yet which bank I'm taking it to. I don't want to use the one in the Arcade near my house because I don't want to be spotted going in, all dolled up to the nines like this on a Wednesday.'

There was another slight pause. Anyone would think that Ellie was about to cash the whole lot in and dash off and spend it – and what if she was, eh? That was her business, wasn't it? And then Ms Plunket-Kirby said smoothly, 'Of course, but may I suggest that you give the manager my number when you do get to see him, as it does tend to make things easier.'

You can suggest what you jolly well like, *my dear*. Ellie feared they might gang up together to try and influence her decision. Money people . . . huh, she knew what Malc used to say about them. It was beginning to sound as if he might have been right.

Ellie imagined exactly what Caroline must look like and what car she drove and what house she probably lived in. Even what programmes she watched on the telly. Ellie felt squashed, but was that her own fault she wondered quickly as she stood there trying to hold her ground, wobbling dangerously on those heels, terrified of manipulation at so early a stage in her newly-found independence. Her skirt was too tight and it made her arse stick out. Malc always said so, and she knew it. She could stand up to the women round here all right, she'd never had any trouble doing that, but Caroline Plunket-Kirby made her feel ignorant and small. She'd never been able to handle women like that, women of power, not since school when such women went into teaching. Slow, silly old Ellie, riddled with uneasy emotions and not too good at anything, only cookery. At Nelson Street School, whenever one of those quick-witted women turned to speak to her she

13

always seemed to have one finger up her nose, or be cheating or something. But she was the one with the money, wasn't she? She was the one with the riches! Sod Caroline Plunket-Kirby and everyone else with plums in their mouths.

Bloody snobs.

If she had a fag on her she'd light it, just like she used to sneak behind the bike sheds waving two fingers in the air and wishing she wasn't so dim as she was. Wishing she could be a star pupil, and liked. But she had run out of fags and she was nearly forty.

'I will give the manager your telephone number, if and when I get to see one, but my decision is made and it's too late to go back on it now,' said Ellie rather shortly, pulling at her headscarf. It was then that she suddenly realised exactly why it was she felt small, because to Caroline Plunket-Kirby a million pounds was probably nothing at all. Her house probably cost more than that . . . and Ellie's over-excitement and her little bit of rebellion possibly sounded quite pitiful. Why, the director of the pools personnel department even considered she was qualified to delve into Ellie's private life in her well-meaning efforts to guide her!

So here she is inside Barclays, the Avery Road branch. And it is stripped of her new feelings of powerful size that Ellie stands at the chequebook counter, still a pawn in a life-sized game, waiting for attention with a million pounds in her hand but unable to attract it, and her mettle is up. Malc's views are quite right. She fidgets, moving her handbag from one hand to the other, bending to ease her ankle from the ungiving heel. She can already feel the blister forming; it is at the burning, itchy stage. It will sting like hell in the bath tonight.

'Can I help you?'

She stares directly at the girl. 'I would like to see the manager.'

'Let me check. Have you made an appointment?'

'No,' says Ellie, 'this is an emergency.' She should take her rayon scarf off. She is the only customer wearing one, and it is snagged, and why has she put on her mac when it isn't even raining? Habit, really, for wearing it saves carrying it. Her suit

14

is meant for club nights out, frilled as it is round the waist like this, and no one wears such high heels in the daytime. She's overdone the make-up, too; in her excited exuberance she's overdone it completely. She looks like an ancient tart, a woman of the streets. You see people like her in shadows tottering across pavements towards kerb-crawlers. If she had a voice like Caroline Plunket-Kirby this girl would not be looking her up and down . . . nor if she was got up like Caroline Plunket-Kirby with silky hair, not permed, and wore a man's jacket and trousers and a long silk scarf and a big belt with a buckle.

Or at her age, probably a camel hair jacket would be more appropriate, and flat shoes with holes in the sides and flaps. Well, Ellie reminds herself, she can afford to dress like that now. She can afford to, but she won't. Not just yet.

The girl goes to check in a book which has a pen on a chain on a crystal pyramid beside it. 'Mr Bradshaw, the under-manager, can see you in half an hour if you'd care to wait.' She pushes back a fetlock of hair which is as smooth and beige as the carpet she treads on, tucking it behind one jewelled ear that looks intricate as an ivory carving.

Ellie sniffs. The road to riches is not at all as she'd dreamed it would be, but then she had never dreamed this part of it.

'I'll wait,' she says, patting her headscarf, and the girl eyes one of the clumps of chairs beside which a percolator bubbles.

Ellie doesn't think, 'Wait till they know what I've got in my bag!' any more, because she now realises it isn't very much . . . not to them, anyhow. She's not about to impress anyone here. They'll smile and congratulate her and pat her on the back but all they'll want to do is get it out of her stupid hands, and control it. And they'll all insist that she shares it with her husband.

She's not the sort of woman to be trusted on her own with it . . . well, look at her eye-shadow! She is ignorant, and she lives in a rented back-to-back down Nelson Street. No phone, no car. Very wobbly in the monetary sense – very wobbly in *every* sense. Her hands shake when she pours her coffee and then she sits too far back to reach it. She is yards away from it, trying to wrench down her skirt because her knees look knobbly when she sits like this, holding a glossy magazine on her lap.

Never has Ellie Freeman felt so foolish or inadequate.

She's never given money a thought before, but already she knows that a million pounds is a long, long way from real riches. It's beginning to feel all spoilt, and she hasn't even been able to tell anyone yet.

Staring around her guiltily she puts her coffee cup down, replaces the magazine neatly and then, fighting down panic, leaps up and runs out of the bank before she can be spotted, before anyone can call out and stop her.

3

Oh, Malc!

The bus nudges its way towards the city centre and Ellie feels every shudder of it, every roll and every sigh of it because her face is pressed hard against the grimy window. Leaving the bank in a hurry like that, in despair, defeated . . . she had felt as though she had committed a crime and that everyone who'd seen her hastening away would think so, too.

Ellie wants to know just how rich she is. All my life, she thinks, I have waited for something like this to happen. The chance to be happy, the chance to make a new start! But what if somebody stole her handbag? They couldn't go and cash the cheque, could they? It is just a piece of paper, and worthless until she makes a decision. Presumably, if that's what she wanted, she could leave it dormant for ever . . . like those boring bits of bark they sell as plants which will never do anything unless they are tended and watered. Ellie must keep her money dry, or water it. Kill it, or let it live. She cannot give it back . . . she can't possibly do that. She has to keep it, even if she never touches a penny of it.

But she doesn't want to do that, either.

It is only a piece of paper. She feels an urge to thrust her handbag under her mac in case there's an aura coming off it which people might see and recognise . . . people who know about money and what it smells like. Her eyes flicker round the bus, suspiciously seeking, but her fellow passengers stare straight ahead, letting themselves flop about with the move-ment . . . bored, listless, pulling themselves in as tight as they can so as not to touch their bus-fellows.

She peels her ticket to shreds. What colour is the aura of money . . . what colour would she see if it sweated as she suspects that it might? She turns her troubled eyes towards her handbag and rests them there for a moment before replacing her forehead on the window. Was it blue or gold?

17

What about red? Or maybe all the colours of the rainbow mixed up together to make a fuming, raging purple.

Or the dull brown of a child's badly-used paintbox.

'Ta, love.' Ellie hops off the bus. She is going to do her secret thing . . . a thing she never tells Malc, has never confessed even to Di and Margot. Perhaps Ellie is a more secretive person than she herself supposes.

She is going to finger the furs.

Oh, she disapproves of fur coats just as much as anyone else. Of course wild animals should not be killed in order to make women feel better but even so . . . it's not just the furs themselves, it is the thick carpeting and the silence in there. The fur department at Lendels gives Ellie exactly the opposite feeling from the one she gets when she goes to sit in the Cathedral. The Cathedral is full of space and magnificence and she goes there to absorb the sense of wonder and of her own goodness, while the fur department at Lendels smacks of sensual wickedness and unhealthy eroticism, of the ways you could be if you wanted to be, if you had the money to be, if you were wild enough to be . . .

The only thing that spoils the fur department for Ellie is the way the assistants sidle up and watch her.

'Can I be of any help to you, madam?'

Normally, at this point, Ellie Freeman would snivel and slink away. It is always so hot in here, how can people work in this heat? Ellie looks round. The assistant is dressed all in black and her lips pout into a cartoon kiss, stickily. Ellie turns back to the black sable which is under wraps but there is enough of the hem showing for her to bend down and feel it. With her face turned away from the anxious assistant, Ellie says, 'I was just wondering about the price. I have looked, but I cannot find it.'

'Well you won't find it, I'm afraid madam, because here at Lendels we do not staple prices on to our furs.'

Ellie reads the woman's little label. 'Well, Mrs Gilman, would you mind telling me how much this coat costs?'

What a bore, says Mrs Gilman's attitude, wearily forbearing, and her voice is laden with sarcasm when she tells Ellie, 'If you would mind coming to the desk.'

18

Ellie doesn't mind.

'Now that particular coat . . .'

Ellie can tell that this Mrs Gilman is savouring the bombshell she's about to drop while she flicks through her dockets and chitties. In effect, she is going to be able to say to this person, 'Piss off.'

'Now let me see, that particular coat . . .'

The cheque burns. Funnily enough it is bright green.

'The sable you were looking at . . .'

They are both enjoying this. Mrs Gilman is going to flatten this jumped-up creature in the tatty headscarf and the plastic mac – it ruins the whole charisma of the department for women like this to be seen wandering about – and the figures she is about to squeeze through her lips will soften them for just a moment. And Ellie is going to know . . . or she hopes she is . . . that if she wanted to she could reserve this sable and probably come back to pick it up this afternoon. Hah!

Mrs Gilman's hard blue eyes focus on Ellie. 'Ten thousand five hundred and twenty-five pounds.' And her lips relax into the smallest of smiles.

Ellie beams. It is hers if she wants it and everything that that wicked black sable promises is hers . . . *if she wants it*. Ellie is the slinky black cat with the power of the vanquisher, while Mrs Gilman is the slow old warthog wandering about piggily in the watering hole.

Ellie pounces. She looks at her watch. 'I think I have time to try it on.'

Mrs Gilman's carefully contrived accent slips with her face. 'Look love, I honestly haven't the time or the inclination . . .'

'I said that I thought I'd have time to try it on.'

'Well, really!'

Ellie stands before the mirror with the fur wrapped round her. She swings a little to the right and then to the left. The luxurious feeling hangs from the shoulders and kind of spreads out from there like a bell. Ellie sways, trying to block Mrs Gilman's cross face from the right-hand corner of the mirror. It's like a smudge and she wants to walk forward and wipe it off.

Wild and mysterious, sensual and erotic. Ellie tries for the right expression.

'If you don't mind me saying so, I think it might look better without the headscarf.'

Ellie laughs. 'I could buy this, you know,' she says. 'I could buy this, spend ten grand and I wouldn't even miss it.'

Mrs Gilman is wary now. She casts worried glances over her shoulder when she agrees with Ellie quickly. 'I am sure you can, madam. And I must say it does look very nice.'

A fur coat – expensive restaurants, theatres, high heels tapping along river-side pavilions, cities at night and limousines. How much of this would her money buy and what about afterwards?

And Malc in a suit beside her, handing her the ballet programme with a rose and a kiss?

Hardly.

Ellie sags, takes off the coat and hands it back to Mrs Gilman. She watches it like you'd watch the departure of a friend at a station, staying until the train pulled out and only the sad vibrations were left. With little bits of fur on her fingers.

'It's just not me,' she says. And then, 'Is it? Be honest.'

Mrs Gilman looks suddenly sad as if the make-up has cracked and they are women together, treading on a dream. Aching legs, tight shoes, the demoralisation of a job that's depressing and the knowledge that somewhere out there the whole, rich panoply of life is going on without them. She does not believe that Ellie has any money at all.

'You looked very lovely in that coat, madam. It suited you perfectly. I have never seen it sitting quite so right on anyone else before.'

Neither admits to acting. Both keep very proud.

'Well, maybe I will return when I have looked around a bit,' says Ellie, dragging on her mac.

'Certainly, madam,' and then the store's motto, 'We are here expressly to please.'

Haberdashery? No, and what a ridiculous word. And then Ellie gives a similar performance at the jewellery department, trying on diamond earrings and even a tiny tiara – well, she could take that home in her bag and hide it away in a drawer.

She loiters before estate agents' windows, she lingers on garage forecourts – she sees Malc's car, the very one – until she is saturated, gorged, indulged to the point of nausea, with dreams dreams dreams.

But all lonely dreams, because every time she wakes up and asks, like a frightened child, 'Where's Malc?'

Maybe she should have told him immediately. This secret fortune is wearing her down and her handbag feels almost too heavy to carry.

It is one o'clock and she walks about trying to absorb the stolid structure of Liverpool, the magnificent sadness, the pride, but all around her men in suits rush for their lunches, waving umbrellas importantly. They come out of buildings which have grand stone steps and columns, they swarm through arches . . . they are positive men who know where they're going but look . . . Ellie has disappeared into the pavement and no one can see that she's even there.

Perhaps she should wave her handbag . . .

Perhaps her dreams could come true with one of these men . . . Who are they? She tries to see them as individuals, tries to grab something from them as they march past but it is as impossible and as ridiculous as it would be to reach out and grab at their balls. Do they have balls? Do they dress to the right or the left? Ellie stares at their pin-striped crutches. They are a marching army and nothing will defeat them. Their suits and their newspapers, their briefcases and their rushing intentions seem to be all that they are.

And if Malc was standing here with her, he would disappear into the pavement, too . . . in his working overall or his shower-proof brown mac. Even if Ellie and Malc stood here dressed in designer gear with the most up-to-the-minute hairstyles, even if they scurried and hurried along with the rest brandishing umbrellas, they would still feel they had disappeared.

Pride!
Purpose!
Excellence!

Money alone is not going to do it, thinks Ellie, close to despair.

And yet she must spend it! She can't keep it hidden away for ever – well, of course she can't, she's not that odd!

She buys a packet of cigarettes from a kiosk in order to hear her own voice.

Deep in a trance of confused thought Ellie disappears off the street and heads up the formal steps into one of the restaurants. She doesn't make a choice but she seems to be swept there. It is like a hotel inside, and she is the only woman. There is a pause in the sipping of soup as she enters the room: hands poise over bread rolls and eyes appraise her. Never dreaming she'd feel quite so stark she makes for a table by the window but it is reserved. An elderly, stooping waiter hurries towards her and ushers her to a more suitable position tucked behind a column.

Some men are smoking. It'll probably be okay to light up a fag, so Ellie noisily opens the packet, cursing crackling cellophane.

This is the first time that Ellie has been anywhere for lunch other than the Littlewoods canteen or the Woolies Serve Yourself. She should have stuck with the rest of the shoppers in Bold Street, but she seems to have lost her bearings because otherwise, how on earth could she have wandered in here and what is she doing in this very male place? What would Malc say if he could see her now? What would he say if he knew what was happening?

Ellie doesn't know who she is any more.

Nobody stopped her coming in here, though, did they? Still, the waiter knows and he helps her with paternal condescension. Dressed in a black suit done up to the neck, and with his white hair in that straightest of fringes, he looks like an ancient Beatle. He suggests the set menu, which is soup and lamb chops, and she can have chocolate pudding afterwards if she wants to, with chocolate sauce or custard. Or both if she chooses, and she smiles like a child at a party. He brings her a glass of house wine.

This is nice and peaceful. This is tasteful, thinks Ellie. No chips and greasy eggs, no sticky sauce bottles on the table, no, certainly not. There are no paper napkins, either, but white cotton pyramids and proper little minty-green bowls with tiny spoons for the sauce. No music, just sensible talking. What if she climbed on to one of those tables in the middle of the room and took off her knickers?

She'd love to be here with Malc . . . with Malc fitting in, not different from everyone else and awkwardly demanding his chips. And he would know he was doing well if he came to have lunch in here. Everyone would know he was doing well, wouldn't they just? But how can you buy your way into this and how can you enjoy the rest of a book when you haven't read the beginning?

They were going to pull Nelson Street down once, but they ran out of money just as the bulldozers began to move in. The contractors had to be paid compensation.

When Ellie finally reaches home she feels as if she has woken up from a dream, bewildered and cold, as though her blanket has fallen off in the night. She ought to have braved the bank because she's absolutely terrified of this cheque. At least if she'd stayed she could have deposited it and then it wouldn't have preyed on her quite so intensively.

One million, five hundred and twenty-five thousand pounds.

She washes up the breakfast dishes, pulls out the washing machine and fills it before she starts preparing the tea. She's got to hurry and get it all done before Malc comes home or he might guess she's been out. But that doesn't matter, she tells herself again and again. He's never complained about her going out, having a wander round the shops on her day off. Well, why would he? It doesn't matter to him.

It is the lies she is so frightened of.

It is the enormity of her deceit

But she can right it, can't she? Surely there is still time? She stands at the sink peeling the spuds and rehearsing what she might say.

Ellie fixes her expression and finds she has barred her teeth. 'I couldn't tell you at once, Malc, because I was in shock.'

She lifts her voice. 'I didn't tell you because I was too excited.'

She is quiet and serious. 'I wanted to keep the news to myself for a bit, you know, digest it.'

'I wanted some time on my own to think.'

And the truth – she tried that out to see what it would sound like. *'I wanted to keep control, Malc. I wanted to discover what my dreams were before you swamped me with yours.'*

And even worse than that, 'I am terrified about what having money might do to us, Malc, as we are at the moment.'

And then with desperation, as she pushes back the washing machine, 'I am sorry I am sorry I am so very very sorry.'

She hears the key in the lock and panics, feeling herself going bright red. Then the door closes and here she is holding her breath again – but why would he go and look behind the immersion? He's got absolutely no reason in the world to go scratching about up there so the cheque is quite safe.

Tiredly he comes to sit down at the table and grunts a muted greeting.

'Malc,' says Ellie, with her back to him, staring hard at the pink sink plug, 'I got the jackpot on the pools this morning.'

He shrugs off her words. 'Oh Ellie, please, for God's sake. I've only just got in and I'm not in the mood.'

'It's true.' There is no expression at all in her voice and his is laden and weary.

'You don't even do the pools, you daft cow. Have I got time to have a bath before tea?'

'I didn't know what to do with the money, Malc.'

He raises his eyebrows tiredly when he notices the basket of washing. 'Have you used all the hot water? I wish you wouldn't use all the water . . .'

'There'll be enough water, Malc,' she tells him. 'There always is.'

I have been and looked and I have seen this other world today, Malc.

She longs to put her trust in this human being, sometimes crying, sometimes drunk, sometimes a stranger, and she watches him dumbly with tears in her eyes.

Malcolm Freeman picks up the newspaper and, pulling his shirt over his head with most of the buttons still done up, tramps up the stairs. And the indignation that Ellie feels on his behalf is so fierce it is hard to believe that her heart is capable of accommodating even half of it.

4

Three times – sod it!

Three times now she has got this far, standing like a cretin at the door of the bank before backing out in a kind of confused exhaustion, but this time it is different. This time she has to go in or her new idea is going to explode inside her head and burst it right open.

The cheque is a little dusty and crispy from its sojourn behind the immersion but that's all right, that won't matter, surely.

Her fears turn out to be groundless. It's just that silly old lack of self-confidence thing of hers again.

She's shocked by the youth of the manager. Yes, she's going to see the manager himself – Beasely, E. R. she reads on the plaque – because this time the under-manager is busy. He is not much older than Kevin and wears the sort of suits Kevin chooses, smooth yet whiskery, with wide lapels and very few buttons. Not a trustworthy suit, she thinks as she perches herself on the edge of the chair, afraid to sink back into it. Not a moneyed suit. She undresses him because she is nervous and wants him naked and at his most vulnerable. She slips off his tie with her eyes, and pushes off his shirt. She unclips his belt and his trousers fall down, followed by the polka-dot boxer shorts.

But he isn't quite as ridiculous as she would have liked him to be.

'Mrs . . . er . . . Freeman,' he says, raising his eyebrows and pulling his chair nearer to the desk where a file is laid out with an empty foolscap page inside it. His voice is mannerly and friendly, the one used by the young men who come to the gift shop to buy cuddly toys for their wives, romantic cards, and jokes. He is a smooth-shaven man, round-faced and fair, with friendly blue eyes that twinkle. Disarming, she thinks, that's what he's being – disarming.

And Ellie is grateful for that.

She nods yes to her name, and he flicks back the file and writes it in blue on a label, in tidy writing, while Ellie glances at the peephole in the door behind her and wonders at the courage and desperation it would take to come in here with a sawn-off shotgun and hold up the bank. She thinks that if someone did come in here and do that, Beasely, E. R. would continue to be nice, to be calm and polite while he pressed his hidden button.

'How can I help you, Mrs Freeman?'

And he doesn't seem bored to see her, distracted by other business or aloof, as the young girl had been.

Ellie begins to feel better but she is very aware of her naked knees and the shortness of her skirt. Still what else had she got to wear for such a special occasion? What else could she find in her wardrobe that was remotely suitable? Nothing! So she covers her knees with her handbag and places her legs very close together. She keeps her scarf on.

'I have won some money,' she says, 'on the pools. The cheque came in the post almost two weeks ago and I think I want to deposit it here in the bank.'

'Well, Mrs Freeman, congratulations are obviously in order. I am absolutely delighted for you. You are not already a customer of ours, I take it?'

'No, we never had anything to hand over before. If any money is left over we tend to keep it in the kitchen drawer, in an envelope wrapped in a rubber band. We had a post office account once but that never really worked very well. Malcolm likes to see the notes, you see. If he can touch them he knows they're real. And he's never trusted money people, banks and the like.'

'But now Malcolm, your husband I take it, has changed his mind?'

'Malcolm knows nothing about it. This is my win, entered in my name, and the cheque I have here is made out to me.' And Ellie unclips her handbag, delves in the back silk pocket and stretches to put the cheque on the desk.

He leans forward to read the amount, sits back and appraises her. 'This is a very great deal of money,' he says.

'You must be over the moon. Why on earth did it take you so long to come in?'

Mr Beasely carries on talking but Ellie does not hear him. She is being drenched by the joy of telling someone, sharing the cheque with someone, smiling broadly, unaware of anything else but the sharp shot of pleasure which trickles pure happiness into every vein in her body. She sits back in her chair, happy to be in that relaxed position, quite unaware of her knees any more, or her skirt, or her over-done make-up or the fierce perfume she has chosen this morning which is cloying the room.

'Yes,' says Mr Beasely, finishing off, 'I can see that you are over the moon.'

'Well, I am really, yes,' says Ellie. She leans forward confidentially. 'It is more money than I ever dreamed of . . .'

'But it isn't a dream, is it?' he says. 'It's real. And it's yours.'

'Yes,' says Ellie.

'And when you've got over all the celebrating and all the excitement you're going to have to decide what you want to do with it,' he says, seeming to share in her wild excitement, his pen long ago flung down.

There is a little pause, a happy one, they are both happy with it. He looks into her eyes and she looks into his and they smile in that knowing way, in the pause, together. She puts his clothes back on for him because she doesn't mind him being dressed any more. She is glad she waited and got to see this Mr Beasely and not his assistant. He might not have been so nice.

'And when are you going to tell your husband?' he asks her. 'Are you saving it up as a surprise? Are you going to set up a special occasion, dinner perhaps, or a family party? Or are you going to buy him a car and have it left outside the house?'

'Yes,' says Ellie breathlessly, remembering Caroline Plunket-Kirby and slightly fearful. 'Yes, that's what happens, isn't it? That's what I'm supposed to do, but I don't want to do it that way, Mr Beasely. I always thought that's what I'd do, but the minute I opened that envelope and saw this cheque I knew it would have to be different. I have other ideas, other plans, that's why it took me so long to come in. I was busy working things out – and I'm going to need someone to help me do them.'

How can she possibly explain to this fresh-faced, enthusiastic young man how it really is? If she brought Malc into the bank to meet him Ellie knows what Mr Beasely would see . . . a gruff, slightly grumpy nobody who would deliberately clown around. He would make himself look like a clod and, if pushed, if threatened, would try to show off and only succeed in being rude and unpleasant. He'd start criticising everything around him, and everyone. Hiding every bit of his natural fun, his charm, he'd come over vulgar and crude.

Oh yes.

Caroline of the personnel department had assumed that Ellie was planning to leave him – and yes, if that was all Malc was, all he was capable of being, that would be easy. Now she has money, leaving him would be easy.

But Ellie knows Malc. You can't live with someone for twenty years and not know them. Young love, oh no, Ellie is not so naive as to believe they can go back to that. They're not those two young people any more with the world at their feet and the wings of love on their heels. She doesn't want that back, anyway – that is unrealistic and silly. Scrimping and scraping and hammering away at the same job, year after year, has turned Malc into what he is now, has humiliated and demeaned him. Hope has slowly dripped away until it is too far off to see any more, until it no longer exists. The way they lived their life . . . well, it was nothing like how they'd planned it.

Heart beating hard, Ellie launches herself, knowing that Mr Beasely's attitude to this is the only one that will matter. 'As we are at the moment,' she explains painfully, 'we have no future. Even rich, we have no future. Years ago, when we began, we were going to save up and get a mortgage. We planned to buy one of those new bungalows on the estate up at Triptree. Malc was going to stay at Watt & Wyatt – they paid good money then – for a while and move on, work his way up to the top. He went to night-school, you know, Mr Beasely. Malc was never a stupid man. Just because he's been a warehouseman all his life doesn't mean to say he's stupid.'

29

Ellie pauses for breath. What must she look like from behind, huddled here like this, being so fervent? A bit like a turtle in a headscarf in a choppy sea, frantically trying to bump its way over that barrier desk. She sits back slightly and puts down her hands. 'We used to have such fun making plans. He had a motor bike then, Mr Beasely, and at weekends when he wasn't working, we used to ride out to West Kirby, take a picnic up Caldy Hill by the beacon or go over to Hilbre Island if the tide was out. We'd have a bottle of wine and two glasses and sandwiches and angel cake, and we used to dream how it would be. We were determined to have a home of our own and get away from his mum and dad. We'd both grown up in Nelson Street, four doors away from each other you see, and we were determined not to bring up our kids there.'

She stops, clears her throat and tugs at her skirt. She knows she is hurrying, cutting out the important bits, putting it far too crudely. Mr Beasely is hardly reacting, but he is listening, tapping his pen on the table now and then, turning it over between his fingers, but he is listening.

'Well, we did bring them up in Nelson Street, and that was okay. I've got a daughter, Mandy, of twenty-two, she's training to be a hotel manageress and she's working up in Scotland now. And Kevin's bright, like Malc. He's at Cardiff University and he wants to be an architect.' The turtle is pounding its flippers now, pathetically trying to scuff over its eggs with sand. She has to go on and tell it. 'It took money to bring them up and pay the rent and heat the house . . . and it happened that there was never a time when Malc could risk changing his job, even though it was obvious that Watt & Wyatt weren't ever going to promote him. And then, after Malc's mother died, we had his dad to cope with and that wasn't easy. It took away a lot of our energy. So we just sort of stuck . . . you know, it happens so easily. And then we were in this kind of rut. I accepted it, I suppose, that's how I helped to diminish Malc, by accepting it. And so he got angry and bitter with all the futility of it. For the last ten years the job he's hated has never even been safe, and he's gone to work looking over his shoulder.'

'Ah, romance has gone,' says Mr Beasely glibly.

And Ellie reproves him quickly. 'I'm talking about a damn sight more than romance here,' she says.

'Other people made it,' says the manager. 'Other people with the same problems that you had got out. They took risks, they made it.'

'Oh, we know that! Do you think that fact helps Malc? We're the only original ones left in Nelson Street, as everyone else has moved on. Don't think I'm feeling sorry for myself, or pity for Malc. I don't feel that way. I don't look at it that way, not at all. We failed. Malc failed. He could have succeeded, but he didn't. He failed, like thousands of people fail all the time without quite knowing why. And now I have the chance to turn that round, to give him back his pride and dignity and maybe some of those old hopes. And that's the way I want to do it, don't you see? I want him to be able to buy me presents, take out a mortgage, get himself a car. I want him to feel that he's succeeded on his own account, and got back his self-respect. Only then will I have what I truly want, what winning a million pounds could never buy me. I'd have some of Malc back, the man I married, the man who is still there underneath but who is too afraid to show himself any more.'

'And how do you propose to go about this great transformation?'

'I need someone like you to help me.'

'I will certainly help you if I can.'

'Well then. This firm Malc works for, Watt & Wyatt, the animal food people – is there any way I can buy my way in? Is there any way I can buy myself influence without anyone knowing what I'm doing?'

'In order to promote him?'

'Yes, for a start, to promote him.'

'This all sounds dangerously patronising, Mrs Freeman. If your husband should ever find out or even suspect . . .'

'He won't – how could he? And if I sound patronising to you then it's because I haven't talked about myself. Oh, I don't consider myself any prize Mr Beasely, and I don't want you thinking I do. Just look at me – I'm as jaded and battered as Malc is. The only real difference between us is that I keep on dreaming inside. I'm an optimist, that's all, and I think I've turned Malc away, closed myself off from him and been living on dreams for years. That's not very honourable, is it, really? It's just a knack I was born with . . .'

'Are you sure you're not dreaming now?'

She looks at him sharply. 'I don't think I am. I think I am being practical now, and positive.'

'Maybe you won't like the man you turn your husband into. Maybe he won't change, or maybe it's too late for that. His desires may not be your desires any longer, and you could find yourselves poles apart.'

'Even if that should happen, for good or for bad we'll both have grown, not stayed still, decaying and no wiser in that old rut.'

'You know, Mrs Freeman, on a professional level I would have to advise you against this . . .'

'I don't see why,' Ellie objects. 'You would have been perfectly happy for me to invest my money in order to make more. You would have encouraged me to make my money grow. Well, why not a person? What's wrong with investing in a person in order to make them grow?'

'Because your actions might well have the opposite effect.' He is filling in a deposit form for her and asks her to write down her address. He rummages in a drawer and takes out a chequebook.

'Keep it,' she says. 'I don't want any evidence in the house. Keep everything here for me and never ever send me letters or statements. Mr Beasely, in order to have the opposite effect you are suggesting I would have to destroy him.'

'And might you? Have you considered that you might do that?'

'He is destroyed already, Mr Beasely. He was destroyed, as a man, years ago.' And she signs the papers he passes over.

'Sometimes you sound as if you love him, sometimes as if you hate him.'

'Yes, precisely, that't exactly how it is.' Ellie looks at her signature and wishes it was bolder.

Mr Beasely swallows. He sits back. 'You'll have to give me some time to think about all this. I know several small firms which are struggling at the moment and which might well look favourably on an unnamed shareholder or a partner pumping money into their depleting funds. In exchange for the promotion of a man they do not know, however, that's quite another matter . . .'

She interrupts him quickly. 'Malc is a clever, talented man. All he has ever needed has been an opportunity. I am not trying to pass on a moron, a time-waster or a parasite. Wherever Malc goes, given the right chance, he will flourish, he'll pull his weight. I give you my word on that, Mr Beasely, and I promise you that that is something I have never given lightly. When will you know?'

'Give me a week,' says the young man, standing up. 'In the meantime, can I propose that next Wednesday we meet over lunch, a little more informally than this?'

Ellie is surprised. It is such a long time since she's been asked out to lunch that she can't remember the last occasion. Worrying about what she would wear she says, 'That would be nice – but it had better be somewhere out of town. I don't want to be seen . . .'

'I quite understand. You just tell me where you'd like to be picked up.'

She thinks quickly. 'On the top floor of the multi-story carpark behind the Arcade,' she says. 'I'll be beside the exit doors, and if anyone sees me I can say I was helping someone I knew with a parcel.'

'Twelve-thirty then,' he tells her, peering through his spyhole before opening the door – in case there is a raid going on, she supposes.

This is a collusion. They are colluding together and she likes the feeling. She is pleased with herself. She's been frank and open and has touched on the personal feelings she always finds so hard to discuss. Ellie waves away the burrowing little snake of thought that unsettles her, because without quite meaning to do so, she has misled the bank manager. She has allowed him to think she is kind and concerned, tender-hearted and caring, but the bit she's left out is the fact that Malc, as he is, is the greatest threat to her own existence. Whenever she sees him she feels shackled and dragged down to earth. Only by changing Malc can Ellie change herself and that is why she can't leave him, why he has to come with her. No matter – she's said enough to get by.

She isn't sure whether or not to shake Mr Beasely's hand, but he puts his out automatically so she gives him hers quickly. His is a firm hand, and a strong one, not sweaty or clammy or anything and she feels safe holding it. And when they smile they exchange understanding. It is going to be all right. Ellie stands very straight. She might be an unsuitable person to be inside a bank, forced into this spindly walk by those high heels, but when she walks through the plush foyer she wants to shout and clap her hands. She knows why people streak across football grounds, she feels like a millionaire with the world at her feet and she thinks the beige carpet is rather drab. It ought to be scarlet.

5

Two weeks later and it's Friday night so they're all down at the club. 'Go for it, Dad,' says Kevin.

Inwardly Ellie winces, outwardly she nods brightly. She's cut out the advert and brought it along with her tonight. *'Opportunity for quick promotion in small expanding company initially as salesman covering the Merseyside area selling quality garden accessories. Basic salary, commission and good incentives . . .'* And that's enough to be going on with.

Malc delves in his pocket and brings out fifty pence which he contributes to the draw . . . to the 'snowball'. There is over a hundred quid accumulated in it now. He says, 'What's the matter with you, woman? I'm forty. I haven't any experience. I don't even know anything about the product. I won't get it.'

'But just to try, Malc, that wouldn't hurt.'

But even as she says it she knows that to try and fail would hurt . . . agonisingly. Before her big win another rejection for Malc would have hurt her, too, and she can't tell him that he will definitely get the job. She can't tell him that the ad has been put in the local paper expressly with Malcolm Freeman in mind.

Kev is home for the weekend, not for pleasure really, but to pick up his golf clubs. They were second-hand – Malc bought them for him on his eighteenth birthday but the two had never had enough money to join the golf club and the public one was always too full to get near on a weekend. Now he is at university, Kev has a chance to play. He would not normally accompany his parents to the club – he disapproves of the place, as Ellie does – but this evening his mother has encouraged him to come along. Eager to create the perfect atmosphere, she wants Kev's help with the advert, thinking perhaps that mellowed by booze and with Kevin's promptings, her husband might agree to apply in front of his friends and then be unable to draw back.

Malc is playing snooker on one of the three tables in the wooden addition to the otherwise galvanised building. He takes his shot and he shouts across to her, 'Woman, I can't even drive! How d'you think they're going to take on someone who can't even sodding drive!'

Malc might act daft sometimes but he is astute, enough to sense what a sore spot this is for Ellie. Is that why he's flung that fact back so loudly and proudly just now? She's never said it and of course she wouldn't, but secretly she is ashamed that Malc can't drive. She hates herself for her feelings, but she can't help them – she's always felt Malc to be less than other men because he can't drive. She's even heard herself telling people lately that Malc didn't drive on moral grounds, that he despised the motor car, perferred the bus or the train and that if everyone felt this way there'd be less pollution and the country would be a more peaceful, healthier place.

Of course the reasons Malc can't drive are nothing to do with pollution. They are to do with the fact that they've never had the money to pay for driving lessons and a car of their own, even the tattiest second-hand banger, has always been out of the question. Never mind the car, they couldn't have afforded the maintenance, tax or insurance.

It isn't Malc's fault and Ellie has no right to feel the way she does about it.

'They might pay for you to learn to drive, Malc.' Diana Legget's voice is high as it drifts through pieces of ham sandwich and over the fumey paraffin airwaves towards the snooker-tabled area. The Leggets bought their own council house three years ago, and they own a caravanette which they use for foreign holidays. They bring lots of snapshots home with them and they've had one of themselves, almost hidden behind bougainvillaa, enlarged and framed. The photograph, which hangs above their fireplace, had been taken on a hilly slope, with wild goats and a little blue lake peeping out behind them. Now the big, jolly woman nudges Ellie and winks, 'He'll believe anything after half a dozen beers!'

Diana looks exactly as Ellie had looked when she'd gone to the bank. Her hair is out of rollers but you wouldn't know they're not still in; her whole head is covered in tunnels and

36

she's used too much of that purplish blusher. Ellie sits with Diana and Margot Hughes, Bacardi and cokes set on the glassy round table between them and lemon slices wetting the ashtray. Malc plays snooker with his friends Dick Hughes and Dave Legget, and their glasses of beer are balanced on oval shelves built into the pinewood walls and painted ebony. Kevin drifts uneasily from one area of the club to the other, to the bar and back again, wishing, Ellie knows, that he hasn't come. She wants him to go and stand with the men . . . she dreads one of Diana's coarse conversations. If she joins in, her son, hovering there behind her shoulder, will despise her and if she doesn't then Diana and Margot will scoff and call her snooty.

Malc and Ellie have been coming to the club like this on a Friday night for at least fifteen years. Habit, security, are important to both of them, but what part have habit and security played in Malc's failure . . . and in Ellie's?

Ellie turns round and catches Kevin's hand. She catches something else, too, the look he is giving his father, and she winces for the second time that night. 'Go over and talk to him about it, Kev,' she urges, and then turns to Diana and Margot. 'Help me persuade Malc to try. You know what an old stick-in-the-mud he is – and how he likes to show off. Maybe one of you could persuade him where I can't.'

'To be truthful I can't see Malc as a salesman, Ellie,' announces Diana, trying to control the damp ham sandwich which flops between her fingers. Her lips twitch before she continues, 'You've got to possess a certain kind of charm if you want to sell anything. Showing off and being glib and silly isn't going to get you very far with the customers.'

'But Malc can be charming, when he chooses to be. Look how nice he was at Teresa's wedding last year. All he needs is a little encouragement.'

'I think a change of job would do him the world of good,' says Margot, who is thin and delicate-looking in that see-through blouse with a bow at the throat, a speckly black like the roots of her golden hair. They favour black if they want to feel smart. All three of them favour black, and when they want to be really smart they smoke black cigarettes.

Ellie smiles at Margot. 'So do I.'

'But what he says is quite right,' persisted Diana. 'He won't get it, because he's too old and can't drive. It would be a waste of time him applying.'

'Ellie wants him to try, so the least we can do is help her.' It is rare for Margot to come out with so firm an opinion and Ellie feels grateful. The club is never quite full, and never quite empty, although the snooker tables and dartboard are always in use. It is at its fullest tonight because of the accumulated money in the snowball. If you're not here and your ticket comes up you lose it. Your winnings go into the next round and there aren't many folks round here can afford to let that happen. Drinks are cheaper in here than they are in pubs. *Pearl's a Singer* plays on in the background, the sad strains of it tangled up in the gargling money sounds of the gambling machine next to the jukebox, its bright lights flashing like the carousel at New Brighton fairground. A long, lean man in a too-small suit bends down over it, his wrists all bony and white, scooping up the coins in his hands with a fluid, practised gesture as a thirsty man might gather water.

Money and luck. Malc considers himself unlucky, as unlucky as that philosopher guy when an eagle spied his bald head and dropped a tortoise on it, mistaking it for a stone. Now that is bad luck, to die like that.

Betrayal. Not only is Ellie betraying Malc by sitting here like this with her mouth closed tightly round her secret, but, perhaps even worse than that, she is betraying her two closest friends. Normally there is nothing they keep from each other, sitting here, week after week, year after year, 'girl talk' the men call it, laughing. What talk do the men exchange as they stand at the bar with their beer bellies touching, and sometimes the edges of their glasses? What else do they touch? What do they swap but jokes, what other sort of exchanging ever goes on, except a few dubious tips about runners and riders, tirades about poufs, dykes and wogs, and a few mechanical hints.

Ellie is glad she's not a man.

And yet Kevin, in a comfy tracksuit tonight, all woolly-looking except for his nylon turtle-necked sweater, is not like

38

that. Kevin is as uneasy around his father and his friends as any woman would be. And although Malc teases him, gently mocks and discourages him, Ellie knows that secretly he is as proud of their son as she is. She's spent many long hours in the past trying to convince Kevin of that and sometimes she thanks God that Kevin, so academically-minded, so serious and sensitive, has been blessed with a natural ability for sport. It is sport, thinks Ellie, that saved him. And sport has been the one weapon that he's been able to use against his father.

Against his father? Ellie frowns.

Ellie knows how Dick Hughes and Dave Legget perform in bed, and she knows, in spite of that sexy black underwear that shows through Margot's blouse, how fed up those women are with it all. They'd laughed till the tears ran down their faces, they'd laughed till they'd had to go to the loo and wipe that smudged mascara. 'When will it end, that's what I want to know,' Diana had shrieked fatly from behind the leaking partition, pulling off wads of loo roll to dry her weeping eyes.

'Grunt grunt, on on, off off, snore snore.' Margot was slumped beside the hand-drying machine, quite drunk by this time, and it looked as if her tears were not tears of laughter at all.

'If you want it done properly you've got to do it yourself, with a book.' The chain would not pull and Di came out, almost too weak to walk.

'D'you think it's just Englishmen?'

'The cold you mean? Cold bedrooms?'

'A hole in the wall and Dick'd be happy. D'you ever feel anything, Elle?' and Margot pushed herself off the tiles and held herself upright on the edge of a basin. She ran the tap and flapped water towards her mouth. Her see-through blouse got soaked and her bow drooped undone as she asked again, 'D'you actually feel anything down there still? Some-times I think they did something when I had the kids.' She tapped the enamel in a strangely positive way. 'See this! See this basin! Those bastards stitched something up the wrong way round and whatever I had, it's gone in. I could be enamel, down there, I could actually be enamel. Or metal. Or wood.'

'It's all in your head anyway,' said Ellie, just as drunk as they were. 'You've got to get it right in your head and be willing to lose control. You've got to keep your eyes tight closed and lose control. I read that.'

'And dream about somebody else,' said Di.

'Gorbachev, they reckon.'

'Gorby?'

'Gorbachev, or somebody like U Thant. That's what they reckon – power, but I suspect novelty is the answer. The same man gets so fucking boring.'

'Not film stars then . . . not Robert Mitchum or Dudley Moore? And who the hell's U Thant? I thought he was dead.'

Oh yes, Ellie is close to her friends. She loves them in the kind of way she could never love Malc who is always trying, never able to really laugh at himself . . . not in the same kind of way. When he laughs at himself it's a cruel kind of laughter, blaming, blaming her, while Margot and Di blame nothing but life.

The kids, teachers, money, big boobs, small boobs, nose jobs, old prams, head lice, thread worms and washing machines . . . is there anything she and Margot and Di have not discussed? Ellie looks at them now, sitting round the table together, at ease. They'd even talked about winning money and what they would do with it if they did. She had lied then . . . but not knowing it was a lie. 'Big house in the country,' she remembered saying, with such certainty. 'A car for each of us, flats for Mandy and Kev, and a holiday home in Benidorm.'

'Think of the clothes!'

'Nothing in the fridge except M&S dinners . . .'

'No need, you'd have a cook.'

'Would you want servants in your house, then? Listening and watching and probably hating you because you were rich?'

'Everyone'd secretly hate you because you were rich,' said Margot sagely. 'Even us. We'd try not to, but we'd be jealous.'

It was then Ellie realised she was already jealous, of the Leggets' house and caravanette, of the picture on their wall, and jealous because Dave Legget had just been promoted to under-manager of the local branch of Boots.

So what does their friendship mean, then? And all that

honesty – how real is any of it? Wouldn't she like to help her friends out, now that she's able?

Yes, she'd love to take them to London and treat them to a fabulous shopping spree. She'd love to buy a yacht and whisk them off for a year to the Bahamas, or the Greek Islands, lagooning it. They'd have such a laugh . . . a laugh . . . a laugh. She must have drunk too much because tears are stinging her eyes and it isn't the background song this time although she's always loved *She*. She's always been silly and romantic, a fool really. And Malc and Dick and Dave? Where will they be while the women are tanning themselves on deck? Well, they'll be standing at the local bar, landbound, knocking back the local brew, swapping jokes and racing tips and mechanical hints. No doubt bemoaning the fact that their wives are not so hot in bed these days. Ellie wonders if they ever confess that fact to each other sincerely, or do they always wrap up their sorrows in jokes, like dirty books in black jackets?

Malc, with his renewed pride, with his self-respect, will be different. She knows it; as surely as she knows her own name she knows that he only behaves in that way because it is expected of him. She is investing one million, five hundred and twenty-five thousand pounds on the certainty of that in spite of Mr Beasely's unease.

And now everyone is suddenly cheering and clapping Malc on the back because, for the first time in his life, he's won something: he's gone and won the snowball.

6

So it was winning the snowball, really, that gave Malc the courage to say he'd 'go for it' as Kevin so subtly put it; it was not the exhortations of his drunken friends nor the quiet, plodding determination of his wife.

He is sorry the next day. These courageous bouts of Malc's tend not to last long . . . scarcely twenty-four hours, and Ellie bleeds for him on the day of the interview when he shouts at her, red-faced, 'Well, you tell me then. It was your bloody idea, what d'you think I ought to wear? As a potential frigging salesman without a car, what d'you think would be the most fashionable way to go?'

And when she doesn't answer he carries on, 'I've never heard of these damn people anyway,' he curses.

'That's because they're a new company starting off.'

'Oh? And how many other new firms round here have started off, all beaming and pushy in the papers and then gone under? If I get this job I'll be a laughing stock. If they offered it to me on a plate I'd be a damn fool to take it.'

'At twelve thousand a year plus commission, Malc?' She is strangely shy of mentioning the money.

'Well, I could never go back. Watt & Wyatt wouldn't take me on again, you know Elle.'

She longs to tell him it matters not a jot what he wears. As long as he doesn't turn up dressed like a scarecrow the job is guaranteed his. Nor does it matter that he's cut himself shaving, and goes round the house with a tissue dot on his chin, bristling with irritation, discarding his white shirt, demanding the blue one, asking her why she's been married twenty years and has still not learned to iron trousers properly, with the crease where he wants it. 'Not halfway across my arse like this. It makes me look as if I'm walking about with two hot-cross buns hanging on behind me.'

She likes to see him in a fuss, she likes to hear him

concerned again about how he's dressed. It makes her feel all sweet inside. Normally he doesn't care.

She'd thoroughly enjoyed her lunch at the Red Fox with Mr Beasely. He'd certainly not been idle, he'd done some poking about. He'd told her, while pouring the wine, 'Watt & Wyatt have never looked particularly healthy, especially now with the Common Market and the decline in farming expenditure. High protein animal foodstuffs and lethally potent fertilizers are luxuries of the past. Keep it under your hat, but that firm is already in trouble, and even if fate hadn't intervened I think Malcolm would have been made redundent ere long.'

She hadn't dressed up like a tart. She'd dressed in a way that she hoped might complement the young, the trendy Mr Beasely, and just about the first thing that gentleman had said when she'd closed the car door furtively in the charcoal darkness of the echoing carpark had been, 'Why don't you call me Robert?'

'And the E? What does the E stand for?'

He'd blushed when he told her, 'Erskine. It's a silly family tradition. They call all their firstborn sons Erskine.'

'Will you call yours Erskine?'

'I already have a son. He is five years old and his initials are J. P. for James Peter. There's no E anywhere near, not even lurking on the birth certificate. And maybe I can call you Elspeth?'

'Ellie,' she said, settling down to enjoy the journey. He was a good driver. He didn't show off like Dave Legget did in his Cavalier, and the little country pub he chose was just perfect. Perfect for what? Well, for a business lunch, she supposed. Here was she, Ellie Freeman, going for a business lunch, and feeling far more comfortable dressed in her grey Crimplene skirt from Marks with the simple white blouse. She wished Mr Beasely hadn't seen her in her navy suit and high heels.

'How terrible if anyone should see us,' she said.

'It would be hard to invent an excuse,' he agreed. And she wondered then if he'd be appalled if somebody saw them and thought they were having an affair, what with him being so young and she ten years his senior, although she had heard of

43

women having affairs with men much younger than that. She'd read that the arrangement tended to work rather well, what with men wanting mothering like they did and women being willing to mother.

She suddenly imagined Mr Beasely's rather attractive mouth tugging on her left breast and she stared hard out of the car window.

Ellie had had an affair once . . . that's what Di and Margot jokingly called it. In fact it was more of a rude incident. It was at the club, on the shiny little bit of dance floor with the sparkly ball twirling above it, a curiously neglected waste-ground of a place except on disco nights. She'd seen the man stare at her the moment she'd got in the door – a jowly, fleshy man, very dark. She'd nudged Margot who'd compared him to Elvis Presley at his worst time, and the white anorak, if you used your imagination, could have been thought of as leather, with tassles across the chest.

Well, he'd stared at her darkly like that all night, he'd bought her drinks and then, to Di and Margot's delight, he'd put *Are You Lonesome Tonight* on the jukebox and asked her to dance. By this time Ellie had been quite tipsy, and oddly excited – she knew he was, as Margot whispered, 'quite disgusting', but even so. He'd held her tightly, they'd smooched she supposed, and Ellie had used her imagination, vividly, and she'd felt something stir. Until, all of a sudden, without any warning, this man called Marvin had manoeuvred her into the darkest corner, whipped out his prick and tried to stick it between her legs. Which was insane, really, because she was wearing a tight skirt and she'd have to have slipped it right up to her waist for him to succeed. She'd peered helplessly over his shoulder for Malc, but he'd been concentrating on his next snooker shot, sliding the cue up and down between his hands quite sensually, which is just what Marvin was attempting to do. She'd come down to earth in a rush, feeling dirty. Bristling righteously she'd pushed Marvin off and gone to sit down but Marvin had stayed in the club all night, all manly and proud at the bar, still staring, as if nothing had happened. She'd never been able to explain the sadness she felt about this to Margot and Di.

She'd never told Malc.

The Red Fox was dark and beamed and riddled with stone passageways. Every now and then you came upon an alcove, where people sat with candles on their tables. There was something quite secretive about it. It was right that they should be having their business lunch in the Red Fox, and it was ten miles out of town so Ellie felt quite safe.

He took her coat and went to hang it up for her.

She said, 'I suppose you often take clients out for lunch.'

'It's not often I enjoy the experience quite so much,' said Robert Beasely, and she felt like a queen sitting there and hoped that whatever Malc turned out to be as a result of all her plotting, he'd make her feel like Robert Beasely made her feel just then.

'Oh, I can't choose the smoked salmon,' she said, shocked.

'Of course you can. This is on the bank, and you may choose anything you like.'

So she started with the smoked salmon and he chose a beautiful wine to accompany it. She knew she must go steady. She was not used to drink at lunchtime, and Malc was disdainful of wine – 'a sissy's drink', he called it. He meant that poufters drank it, vegetarians and yuppies. Real men drank only spirits or beer.

It was between courses that Robert brought out his briefcase and showed her a glossy brochure, and after she'd glanced at that, he produced the figures. 'These are the predictions for next year, but I personally think the profits are going to far exceed this. It's working capital these two young men Ramon and Murphy are short of.'

To her shame she wasn't really listening. She was watching his face and listening to the nice way he said his words. She was noting how intensely interested he was in his job, how keen he seemed to see this new company succeed, how careful he was to bring to her notice the snags as well as the likely benefits. This is what a man's work should be, she thought to herself. Not just a slog, day after day, that did nothing but knock it out of you, but something you could involve yourself in, something at which you excelled. She tuned in again when she heard him say, 'Basically what they

45

are doing is importing garden furniture from Sweden, and what they want at this stage is someone to make local garden centres and shops aware of their existence, to ensure deliveries are promptly dealt with and to get new samples round on time.'

'That's where Malc would come in?'

'Yes. The basic wage would be paid for by you and he'd receive a percentage of his sales. In exchange for this arrangement you would be made a sleeping partner in the company – in the name of the bank, of course.'

'But what about the future? Malc wouldn't want to stay just a salesman for ever.'

Robert nodded. 'There are already plans for expansion. If this company gets off the ground it'll happen fast and there will be all kinds of opportunities. Quite apart from Malcolm, your investments would quickly multiply. Neither of these young men want to stay in the area . . . so they're going to need a local manager for a start. And if Malcolm's as good as you say he is . . . But Ellie, I have to warn you that even if things go well, this won't be for another year or two. It might take even longer than that.'

'But you think this company – Canonwaits – is the answer?'

'Yes I do. I can't think of anything more promising or suitable.'

She sipped her wine quickly. 'How do we go about it?'

'The only way to do it is to advertise properly.'

'And I've got to convince Malc to apply?'

'I can't see any other way.'

'But what if he refuses? He's long ago given up trying for new jobs.'

'I have total confidence in your ability to persuade him,' said Robert, and Ellie caught his eye. She looked down.

'You must think I'm very odd – doing what I'm doing. Making it all so difficult for myself.' She twiddled the stem of the wine glass before glancing up again. His eyes were still on her but the gleam in them was not for her, it was reflected off the ice bucket on the table in front of him. She wondered if her waistband had rolled over yet, and if that little bit of zip at the top had come open. She'd go to the loo, later on, and check.

He said, 'I think what you're doing is very brave. You're taking a big chance.'

'I'm not being brave really.' She decided to latch on to his stare. 'I suppose that if I was honest I'd admit to being rather cowardly. I could just leave him, find someone else and go off.'

'I would very much like to meet him, this Malcolm of yours. At the moment I'm rather confused about him. You must care a great deal to be taking this trouble, and I don't think you're the sort of person to act impulsively.'

'You don't know me at all,' she said gently, 'so how can you say that? Are you classifying me into a type?'

'Yes, I suppose that I am.' And he leaned back to let the waitress in the black dress and white apron take their plates away. Ellie thought the woman had broken something by stretching across, as if she'd stuck her arm through a cobweb and torn it. She resented the interruption.

'What am I?' she asked him. 'How do you see me?'

'Strong,' he said, picking up the napkin which he hadn't yet unrolled. And Ellie wasn't easy with that. She doubted if Malc would call her strong. Stubborn, probably, but not strong. And she'd been hoping for something a little more feminine.

Into the silence Robert asked, 'What kind of life are you hoping for, Ellie, if this all goes well?'

'Nothing extraordinary. Oh, I'd like to be able to buy nice things when I see them, go out for meals, have cream horns in tea shops and visit the theatre occasionally. I'd like to learn to drive, to have a car, to drive into the country at weekends and maybe stay in some of those lovely hotels they advertise . . . those brochure weekends.'

'What sort of house do you see yourself living in?'

This was lovely. This was sharing a dream, and yet it wasn't as silly as dreaming.

'I'd like one of those Georgian houses in Ridley Place opposite the library. I've always hankered after one of those. And I'd have it all in wood with rugs and huge pictures and those false gas fires which look real, with canopies.' She stared at him suddenly. 'D'you think it'll happen, Robert?'

'It could happen straight away if you decided to change your mind.'

'But it wouldn't be the same. It wouldn't be anything like how I picture it.'

'Because of Malcolm?'

'And me. I'd be different if Malc was different.'

Robert Beasely frowned at her. 'Would you?'

'Well, of course I would. I'd be more confident. I'd know when I looked nice because he'd tell me so, I'd be able to choose my friends knowing that Malc wouldn't grumble, I'd read different books and learn to like classical music. I'd improve myself . . .'

'If you want to do those things, why haven't you done them already?'

It was so difficult to explain. 'There never seems any point. I sound pathetic, don't I? As if I am just a reflection, not real unless Malc says so.'

He didn't answer that, but said, 'And you truly believe that a few lucky breaks are going to change this man?'

'Not change him – no, not change him! It's already there underneath. It's all there, I know because I knew him when he was different. There was a time when he wanted those things, too. He's kind and gentle underneath and I don't think he likes himself as he is any more than I do, but he's seen his dreams crash down around him so many times that he's buried them. He's taken the easy way out, if you like. He's not strange or extraordinary, Robert, he's done what so many people do and he's put a barrier around him.'

'The trouble is, Malcolm's barrier seems to have circled you both.'

Ellie said, 'I'm not angry, or bitter.'

'You don't need to be – Malcolm is carrying it all for you. And isn't there a danger that what you're doing is asking him to carry you again? You've no need to, you know. You're strong enough on your own.'

But she wasn't strong. She didn't want to be strong and she found it slightly annoying, the way he kept insisting that she was. 'I find it very easy to talk to you, Robert,' she stared at her glass, 'or is it the wine? I'm not used to wine at lunchtime, you

48

know. Normally I slip across to the sandwich bar for a cheese and pickle roll.'

'I suppose you're planning to carry on working?'

'I have to,' said Ellie, 'until the plan starts to take shape. I don't mind working – I wouldn't know what to do with myself at home all day.'

'But when Malcolm makes his fortune this, too, will be different?'

Ellie ignored the slight irony in his tone. She was proud to be sitting in here with this striking young man and talking so intimately like this. She had a superior feeling whenever a woman walked by. It was funny, really, what money could buy . . . like this kind of hidden factor that she'd never imagined when she'd filled in that column of numbers over all those years. She was glad the bank manager hadn't been a woman. She knew what sort of woman they'd choose . . . one of the Caroline Plunket-Kirbys of this world who wouldn't have listened in quite the same way. A woman wouldn't have considered her 'interesting' and women were more sensible than men – oh, not women like Di or Margot – but successful women, powerful women . . .

They would talk down to her.

They would see through her, they would know how she was enjoying all this. They might even tell her not to be silly while Robert Beasely thought she was only absorbed in the plan.

'If I had come into your bank and deposited one hundred pounds you wouldn't have given me the time of day, would you?' she asked him now. 'I have never spoken to a bank manager before. I have never been on first-name terms with any professional person before . . . not even the doctor, and we've had him for years. We still call him Doctor Grant. People like you, you know, their eyes slide off those who have nothing, and when enough people's eyes slide off you, in the end you can feel you have disappeared.'

'If you had come into the bank and deposited a hundred pounds you would not have been in need of my help,' he told her. And she shouldn't be accepting more wine, but she was.

'I might have needed help, perhaps with debts, and that need would have been more real, in a way, than this one, which some people would call rather fanciful. You wouldn't have invited me to lunch if I'd come to you weighed down under a load of debts.'

'No, I wouldn't, but then the bank would not stand to profit from you very much if you were in that sort of trouble.'

'So we're only sitting here now, talking and drinking and eating, because I am good for business?'

'That's not strictly true. We needn't have had lunch – we could have discussed all this in my office. I am genuinely interested in what you are trying to do and I am interested enough to involve myself personally, Ellie.'

'I like that,' she said, and then hiccupped and knew she'd drunk too much wine.

'What is it you like?'

'That you are taking a personal interest. It would have been difficult to go through with this, all on my own.'

And she loved the warm smile that he gave her.

It was a sensible decision that they should meet once a month on a Wednesday . . . and that she would ring the bank the day before to confirm.

7

Third time lucky – just as it had been in her own case.

Oh no, Malc had not gone through with it the first time, nor the second, but Ellie pinned all her hopes on this, the third time of trying. She pretended she wasn't hoping at all, and all day long she tried not to think about it.

She wasn't a Catholic, but she'd even been to light a candle in the Cathedral and she'd sat down, closed her eyes and said a little prayer on his behalf.

He let her ring up in response to the ad on the strength of winning the snowball. She was very polite on the telephone but she stated his name very slowly and clearly, spelling out FREEMAN – in case the girl made a mistake.

'He is the one,' she wanted to shout. 'He is the one you are after!'

Back came the application form. It was both formal and formidable, with no humanity in it. They had not amended it in any way, on purpose, Ellie supposed, for it wouldn't do to raise his suspicions. Malc opened it in a hurry before leaving for work, held it at arm's length, frowned then leaned across as if to stuff it straight in the bit bin.

Ellie held up her hand like a traffic cop. 'Malc – don't do that! At least let me see it.'

But his attitude was that of a cross little boy who didn't want his mother to see ... what? Another carefully devised instrument of rejection?

'Let's just look at it and read it. Tonight, perhaps, when we've got more time.'

Malc stood up. 'You do whatever you like, Elle, but don't expect me to take any part in it. They'll have thousands of replies to an ad like that, and look, they want to know everything about me, down to the colour of my frigging underpants. Well, I'm not prepared to get into these kinds of games.'

No! You are not prepared – not because you disapprove of them, but because you are so terrified of losing!

'How would it be if you had nothing to do with it, if I filled it in and sent it back? I'd even forge your signature. You would never need to know anything more about it.'

He stared at her belligerently, suddenly terribly angry. 'I'd sodding well know if they turned me down, and what is this anyway, Elle? What's so great about this job?'

Ellie subsided. 'I just have a feeling about it, that's all.'

'You do what you like, Elle, you always do anyway,' he said as he left the house, banging the door behind him.

So that was the first time he tried to back down, but Ellie ignored it.

She took the application form to work because she knew she had to fill it in when Malc wasn't around. To see her sitting there in the evening with the form on the arm of her chair and a pen in her hand would have been, for Malc, too threatening and too wounding. She filled it in between customers. Even knowing that he'd get the job, she wanted to fill it in correctly. She wanted to give these people a good impression of the man who was her husband – she didn't want to be seen by anyone as some kind of misdirected charity.

Experience. Ellie leaned over the counter, letting her eyes rest on an unpacked box of flashing Christmas tree earrings and tapped her teeth with a pen which had a teddy bear dangling off the end. Twenty years with the same company must count for something! He'd passed his fork-lift truck test, he'd learned to work the computer and he had a basic certificate to prove it. He was strong from all the years of carting sacks, he was loyal, he never took days off and his overalls were always clean – Ellie saw to that.

She put it all down.

Examinations. How stupid of her – she'd gone and put his two certificates down in the *Experience* section. Well of course Malc didn't have any exams. Ellie thought about Kevin, and quite without shame she listed his . . . English language and literature; history; French; maths; geography; sociology; art; physics and chemistry – should she stick down the A-levels, too? She decided against it; for a salesman's job that might have been going too far. She didn't want them to think he was overqualified.

But what was Malc doing in a warehouse with ten GCEs?

Oh, she couldn't bother about that . . . she'd done it now, and anyway, that does happen to people . . . odd people.

Medical History. Well, that was easy. Malc had never had anything seriously wrong with him, apart from the odd broken bone, in his life.

Motivation? She'd been told that the partners were American, and this strange question was surely something that only Americans could understand. But still, it had to be tackled and she knew she couldn't put 'the money'. It had to be something to do with 'getting on' – they wanted to know if Malc was aggressive enough. Twenty years in the same old warehouse was a daunting stumbling block in this particular section, and one for which the company might genuinely want an answer. There was quite a wide space so Ellie filled it with, *'This is the first time in my life when I have been able to think about my own prospects because the children have left home and I don't have that responsibility any more. I am determined to make up for lost time.'* Then she thought for a bit and decided to add, on its own at the bottom, *'For me it is now or never.'*

She hoped she hadn't made him look like a man clutching at straws.

Then there were easy bits like *Religion* and *Driving Experience.* Easy, because Malc had neither of these.

Ellie posted the form on her way home, fairly pleased with her work and not prepared to discuss it, but when he came in that night Malc asked her if she'd sent it. He tried to sound uninterested, as if he didn't really care one way or the other, and Ellie replied in the same vein, with nonchalance.

'Well, that was a bloody waste of a stamp then,' he said, turning on the telly and turning himself off to her and to the whole matter.

The invitation to go for an interview was cleverly done. It was a print-out, with only his name typed differently at the top, so it looked as if the same invitation had gone out to hundreds of applicants.

'But I can't bloody drive,' said Malc, refusing even to look at it.

'Well, what if I ring them up and ask about that?' ventured Ellie, despairing.

Malc stared at her with curiosity. 'Oh, they're going to love that, aren't they? They're going to love having women ringing them up at all hours of the day and night asking damn stupid questions like that.'

'I don't see why they'd mind,' said Ellie weakly.

'You daft bat,' snorted Malc, turning away in disgust.

And then she'd had to tell another of her lies. She discovered she was good at this lying game . . . *she had to be.*

'They were ever so nice on the phone, Malc. Really friendly and helpful. They say that not being able to drive is no problem. It is the right man they are after, and they don't mind paying for driving lessons. They said that naturally they'd *prefer an experienced driver*, but that it was by no means essential.'

Malc looked surprised. 'Well, they must be out of their minds then, and not the sort of set up any right-minded person would want to work for.'

And then Ellie got angry. She stood over his chair and banged clouds of dust out of the top of it. She felt like reaching just a bit further down and bringing her clenched fist on to his head. 'I'm just getting sick and tired and fed up with all this, Malcolm! Here's me, going out of my way to fill in forms and post them off and make phone calls as if I've got nothing better to do with my time, and there's you, sitting there with that stupid look on your face like a great lumbering lout! Okay, okay, all right! You don't think you'll get it, you don't want to make a clown of yourself, but you're not, you fucking feeble sod! Get up off your arse and TRY, Malc, and if you don't get the frigging job then we'll say sod it all, go and have a drink, and forget all about it.' And then she softened. 'But why don't you just go for the interview? After all, you swore you wouldn't get this far but you have.'

'I don't know what's come over you, Elle.' He didn't turn round.

'Well nor do I, but that's just how I feel.' She flumped

across the room and sat down in her own chair, exhausted. She tried to stop but she couldn't . . . she couldn't stop herself crying. She was so near! So bloody near and yet still so far. She almost hated him . . . no, no, she *did* hate him then, just briefly.

He said, 'Don't cry, Elle.'

'Well, what else am I supposed to do?' she sniffed.

She could tell he was thinking it over. 'If I went for the interview I wouldn't want anyone else to know,' he said at last, grudgingly.

'Well, of course not,' agreed Ellie, sniffing again loudly. 'It's nobody else's business, is it?'

'Not Di, or Margot.'

She fluffed herself up in her chair, gasping on hope. 'I wouldn't tell them. I wouldn't dream of telling them.'

He looked at her sharply. He was silent for a while and she didn't break it. Somebody answered the call to 'Come on Down' on the telly, the audience roared and the fire crackled uneasily. 'When do they want me?' Malc asked.

'Next Tuesday.'

'I'd have to take a day off and they'd want to know why.'

'You're going to the doctor's,' said Ellie quickly, 'with your hernia.'

'And taking the whole day about it?'

Oh Malc, she wanted to scream . . . these pissing little issues of life! So much scree had fallen behind him that when he turned round he saw another huge mountain. 'You can tell them you were in too much pain. You won't need a doctor's note for one day!'

The day of the interview finally came along and then they'd gone through the hassle of what he ought to wear and his cut chin. She sorted him out, but at work Ellie was a nervous wreck unable to concentrate on anything. She clutched her hands together at one point and yes, she actually prayed for him. And she squeezed her eyes closed, willing it, willing it, willing it, and saying over and over again, 'Oh dear God let them be nice to him. And let him not go to pieces completely so that they have to come back to Robert and explain that they just can't accept him.'

But her heart was light as she hurried home on a vast billow of hope, soaring. She didn't notice the storm that raged, the rain didn't wet her and the wind didn't buffet her. She floated above such inconsequentials as weather: let others discuss such mundane matters, not her. For this was the moment . . . the beginning of everything! This was like staring at that cheque again, that hysterical excitement when there were no words, only feelings too large to contain on your own. Now they were going to share it at last! This was what winning the jackpot on the pools was really all about!

'I didn't go.'

'You what?'

'I didn't go. The rain started coming through the bedroom ceiling again, there were buckets to fetch and then I had to go down to Leesons to get some plaster . . .'

'Did you ring them up? Did you explain?' The rain was running down her neck and her hair had been blown all over the place. Ellie shivered.

'Didn't think they'd miss me. They must've had plenty of others to interview . . .'

'Bastard.'

'Ellie!'

'Bastard. Bastard. Bastard.'

He tried to approach her with a soft face and soft words. 'Elle, it wouldn't have worked, my love. Calm down and think about it for a moment . . .'

She took off her mac. She didn't look at him, she couldn't. She said, 'I *have* been thinking about it, Malc.'

He flapped, 'How could I have left the bedroom with the carpet getting wet?'

'You have managed to leave the bedroom ceiling for at least five years.'

'The rain hasn't been coming in for that long, Elle, don't exaggerate.'

She stood very stiffly. 'I do not want to hear you say the words "bedroom ceiling", not once more, not ever again, not in my whole life, do you hear me, Malc?'

He gestured helplessly with his hands. He said, 'Ellie!'

She didn't move. 'This means a lot to me, Malc.'

'Well, I realise that. Hell, I can't help but realise that, but I can't arrange the weather just to suit . . .'

'I am going, now, to ring them up.'

'Oh Ellie, why won't you leave it alone?'

'Because I just won't, that's why.'

'But there's a storm out there.'

'I'm not bothered about any sodding storm.' She tried to put her mac back on but he stepped forward to prevent her.

'There won't be anyone there, Elle. It is after six o'clock.'

'Well, I'm going out anyway.' She fought him. They wrestled, fumbling about together for a moment, neither of them knowing what they were doing until Ellie screamed, 'Leave me alone!'

And Malc seemed to collapse. He told her, 'All right, Elle, all right. I will ring them tomorrow and see if I can make another appointment. I will explain about the storm and the damage to the house and ask if they will see me again.'

'And you'll apologise?'

'Yes. All right, I'll apologise.'

'You swear to me, Malc.'

'Yes, I swear to you.'

The next time Malc was due to go for his interview Ellie forced herself to feel nothing. If the thought came into her head then she pushed it aside because it had grown too big for her to cope with. She took an hour and a half off at lunchtime, got on a bus for nowhere and found herself sitting in the Catholic Cathedral staring listlessly at a candle. She couldn't say how she'd got there, she had the strangest feeling of being somebody else. She came home from work in a perfectly ordinary manner and got on with the liver casserole. She arranged the meat, carrots, swede and onions, and was covering the whole lot with a layer of potatoes, sliced very thinly, when he came through the door and stood before her with a smile on his face.

'I got it!'

8

She hopes to God that Robert Beasely is on top of his job. Her heart sinks into her stomach when Malc hands in his notice. His eyes are desperate when they meet hers.

'There's no going back now, Elle. And I blame you for it, you and your feelings.'

'We'll be okay, Malc, whatever happens.'

'Oh yes, on the dole we'll be bloody fine, won't we?'

'I've got my job, remember.'

'Some good that'd do us.'

'But didn't you enjoy saying goodbye, Malc, after all those boring years? Was it a good feeling turning your back on them and walking out? I bet they never dreamed you'd ever do it.'

His expression is hard to define when he picks up the crossword to finish it, leans over to switch on the lamp and confesses, 'It gave them the shock of their lives, and I suppose if nothing else comes of it I'll always have that expression to remember on Willy Wyatt's face. The bugger.'

And Ellie considers that moment as her first real dividend.

She understands how scared he is having to tackle something so new, and she had anticipated how hard he'd find it, learning to drive. It's not so much the learning . . . after all, he's travelled in enough cars throughout his life to be able to go through the motions. No, it's not that, it's having to buckle under to the instructor, to obey orders, to control the bursts of aggression which have become a natural defence against his inadequacy.

And four double lessons a week is quite an intense way to learn.

Ellie overhears him defending his decision to Dick and Dave. 'What had I got to bloody lose – twenty-five more years lugging sacks about if I'm lucky. Of course I had to try.'

'I'm surprised they picked somebody who couldn't drive, what with the advert being for a salesman.'

'Well, my face must have fitted. For once in my sodding life my face must have fitted, mustn't it?'

'Odd though,' says Dave Legget, 'when you come to think about it.'

'Well, it's best not to think about it, mate. It's best not to think about anything. Perhaps my luck's changed and if it has then it's about bloody time.'

But Ellie can tell he is proud.

To begin with he slunk out for his driving lessons without speaking, closing the door quietly behind him as if trying to pretend he wasn't really there, that the person sneaking out was not him. And he used to come home in a mess, angry and mean like a furious child wanting to sob over impossible homework.

'It'll come, Malc, it'll come suddenly. You'll see,' she tried to console him.

'And what do you bloody know about it?'

She rolled on her bedsocks, her head well down and that night he kept to the edge of the bed. He was afraid he'd never be able to do it. He never discussed the driving with Dick or Dave.

And then, gradually, he started looking forward to his lessons, ceased to refer to the friendly instructor as 'the wanker', and if it was Bob Tucker's last job of the evening, Malc might ask him in for a drink. Ellie couldn't remember the last time Malc had invited anyone new home. He despised and suspected strangers. She watched him, smiling over her knitting, and felt as she had when Mandy first learned to read, when Kev had been picked for the school cricket team. And once there was even a moment when she felt tears prick her eyes.

He was growing! Already he was growing!

Ellie was so excited she couldn't keep it to herself and she rang Robert at the bank, singing success over the wires like a yellow canary suddenly uncaged. Robert was suitably impressed.

Mandy rang from Scotland after six o'clock and when she heard about the new job and the driving she said, 'What's got into Dad, then?'

59

'Perhaps it's the male menopause,' said Ellie. 'He's been getting restless just lately.'

'Well, you must be very pleased. After all these years at last he's got off his backside.'

Yes, Ellie was pleased. She felt joyful and proud, as if she'd discovered a dusty old canvas, digging it out of the attic and holding it up to the light, seeing something beautiful there, and new.

Mandy plied for confidences. 'What d'you think, Mum? Is this job going to work out for him or has he bitten off more than he can chew?'

How easy it is for the kids to criticise Malc from their safe, elevated positions. Malc, who has given up his own dreams so that they can realise theirs. How simple it is for Kevin to wrinkle his nose, and for Mandy to bestow her sympathy. Ellie had never asked for it, she'd never complained about their father. So part of the joy of all this, if it works, will be to see him regain their respect. Oh, it's true he'd never done much in the past to earn it, if you could call bringing home a wage packet for twenty years doing nothing. Bringing up the kids had been her job and Ellie had been quite happy with that, but how often she'd wished he could have shown a little more interest.

But men didn't do that much in those days, not the men round Nelson Street anyway, although he'd made Kev a fort, one Christmas, and done up a pram for Mandy. At weekends Malc had gone off with his mates to watch the football. And when they were little Mandy and Kev had been in bed by the time he got home nights, tired. He worked hard, and deserved to sit down in peace with his feet up in front of the telly. There was never much time in the mornings, what with Ellie having to get herself out, as well as the rest of them, iron the clean shirts and fix the packed lunches.

Ellie peers through the curtains, out into the gloom of the November night, disturbed by her daughter's phone call and searching for the lights of the Driving School car. Over the years the house has grown cleaner, not, as you might expect, dirtier. And that was nothing to do with Ellie's efforts. Making the area a smoke-free zone had made a big difference, although fires were never the same after that . . . you don't get that same crackly, homely sound. And the by-pass had diverted the heavy lorries two miles away. You can still hear them rumbling at night, but the windows no longer shake, flakes of plaster no longer fall from the ceiling and it is safer for children to play in the street when they get home from school.

Her own mother had had it much worse. In those days steam from the railway yard a block away used to yellow the windows and crisp up the curtains. You can still hear the goods trains clanking and buckling together on a still evening, but their shunting sounds are no longer so violent, just an electronic purr – deadlier, perhaps, like the dirt is probably deadlier, no longer the smutty kind you used to be able to see and wipe off, brush away in the dustpan, but cunning dirt, stealthy dirt; you wouldn't know it was there unless you read about it in the papers.

So Ellie still cleans, on hands and knees with screwed-up eyes; she gets under beds and into cupboards on a Wednesday, trying to locate it. They used to say that the old soot was good for the garden, and Malc's dad had certainly grown some lovely tomatoes.

At the end of the street is the stark red-brick of Nelson Street School. It has changed out of all recognition since she was a pupil there, and wore plimsolls summer and winter alike, but the sloping wire still strings the tops of the walls, and the two Victorian stone arches, GIRLS and BOYS, have never been taken down although the sexes aren't separated any more. She'd wandered past it, idling by, pushing the pram with her two children in it, and stared up at the windows, wondering why their expressions had not changed. Why did they stare at her sullenly, balefully, like that? She was a mother now, and a married woman! She had in some small way succeeded, hadn't she? In spite of all their predictions. But those windows always stared the same way, making her shiver. They never smiled.

Oh, dear Jesus, it would be so good to get away from here.

Is this Malc now? No, the searching headlights go past the house as if it is something else they are after. They cast themselves into the sky, peeping and seeking, but all they pick up is the looming shadow of Dwarfy Sugden, limping, pushing his laden barrow home.

Somebody ought to do something about that man. Without thinking, Ellie expresses the opinion of everyone in Nelson Street and those who live in the surrounding neighbourhood as well. Disgusting. Pathetic. And even when you know who it is you can't help being frightened to come upon Dwarfy if you're out late at night.

Where's Malc got to? Ellie sighs impatiently. There she'd been then, fourteen or fifteen, spindly thin, with a straight fringe, a tartan ribbon in her hair and a face like Connie Francis, from four doors down, a clean, respectable house, unlike Malc's. She used to carry her pride and joy – a portable gramophone in a case – out into the street and play *Baby Love* over and over. She used to play ball up against the wall for hours, two balls, three balls, over her legs and under, and women used to huddle in the street in those days and cast beady eyes on the Freemans. Well, she was a drunk and he was a thief and was it any wonder the kids were like they were?

They were hardly ever at school, but watching from behind the coke heap for when the other kids came out.

She could tell Malcolm Freeman liked her. She used to walk in a certain way when she saw him and he hit her friends with the sharp little pieces of coke which he threw with such deadly accuracy, but he never hit her.

Gorbachev? U Thant? Well, they had never heard of people like that but if it was power you needed to turn you on then Malcolm Freeman had power.

You didn't do well at school in those days, and how bad you were was just a matter of extremes. It wasn't that Ellie hadn't tried. She'd always felt happier trying to please and she'd been meandering along somewhere in the middle when she'd moved up into Miss Bacon's class – 4A.

She'd fallen in love with Miss Bacon, it was as simple as that. She flirted with Malcolm, and knew that he liked her, but secretly she thought boys were disgusting. Even now, at forty and looking back, she knows it was love – the thought of it still gives her a pang. It was a pure and noble kind of love

62

that asked for nothing in return but a smile and a word of praise. And yet it consumed her, it burned her up so that she couldn't wait to get to school in the morning, and she deliberately arrived late at the beginning of term so she could get a front desk. For the first time in her life she really cared about what she sounded like and looked like, and she remembered feeling ashamed because she came from Nelson Street.

Miss Bacon wore a sheepskin coat and arrived every morning in a little blue Mini. She wore her hair in a pageboy and carried a shoulder bag.

Ellie ditched her best friend, Muriel, because Miss Bacon said she was insolent. Ellie wouldn't let her mother cut her hair, but insisted they pay for her to go to Shirley's down Marley Road for a pageboy. And the worst thing was that she couldn't tell anyone about it because nobody else seemed to share her admiration. They were all at the 'feeling' stage with boys – apart from Susan Mitchell who went all the way. So she kept a secret diary, wrote poems, saved up to buy sad records and drew hearts with only her own initials on the arrow, the second set mysteriously missing.

Ellie smiles. What a little prig she must have looked, sitting up straight in her desk with that worshipping smile on her face, just itching to put her hand up.

No wonder Miss Bacon couldn't stand her. She wasn't interested in goody goodies who were prepared to stay behind and tidy the classroom. She was here to study difficult children and there were plenty of those in 4A. It took Ellie a couple of terms to realise this, writhing in agony as she did so. The holidays were almost too painful to bear and her schoolwork improved astonishingly.

Ellie wasn't clever enough to make an impression in that way; she'd been wasting time trying, and there was only one other. By the time she grasped the true situation it was almost too late. She'd be fifteen next year and moving up . . . *if* she passed the end of term exams. She couldn't bear to be parted from Miss Bacon. She would fail them, and what's more . . .

What sort of passion had driven her? What sort of passion could drive a child to do something so alien to her nature?

Looking back on the incident . . . this small event that had mapped out her life for ever after, Ellie can't help but imagine . . . and this is the strangest thing . . . *that in some peculiar way she had been manipulated*. As if she had no will of her own – but why would Miss Bacon do that? There was nothing in it for her . . . nothing at all! Ellie can feel the same sense of dry, unblinking-eyed terror now as she'd felt when she'd crept between those empty desks, approaching Miss Bacon's shoulder bag. She'd been shocked to discover it was plastic. Should she take the scissors, the purse, or the keys? Ellie groaned. It would have to be the purse. She jumped as a door banged shut in the wind. She rushed out into the playground, almost sobbing with fear and excitement. She'd notice her now, *she'd have to notice her now!*

Back at her desk and sitting to attention, the window cord rattled in the breeze and the taste of ink was in her mouth. Miss Bacon went to her bag twice, once for a pen, when she strapped it shut again, and the second time for her handker-chief. On neither occasion did she notice the missing purse. The afternoon dragged on. They were meant to be copying notes, but Ellie copied nothing, just complicated squiggles, patterns of feeling in heavy black.

Ellie knew that the third time Miss Bacon would make her discovery. And she did. She lifted her face into a superior, surprised expression and swept the classroom with one of her cool glances, gazing at all the drooping heads, at all the writing children who'd stopped so suddenly, pens poised.

She said, 'Someone's been into my bag and taken my purse.'

All heads went up, because even for Nelson Street School this was serious.

Ellie looked down. She was the only one who looked down, desperate to make herself noticed.

Miss Bacon said, 'I shall wait for ten minutes after school, to give the culprit one chance. If they do not come forward then, I shall have no option but to go to the headmaster, and the police will be informed. Now think about that, and get on with your work.'

There were moments during that long afternoon when

Ellie caught flashing glimpses of the thing she had done and longed somehow to obliterate herself completely; there were others when she quite literally quivered with excitement. When chalk squeaked on the board it was in direct answer to the state of her own charged nerves.

The bell rang and everyone trailed noisily out, except Ellie, who sat there blushing from her head to her toes. Would Miss Bacon leave the desk and come down to stand beside her? Or would she have to confess from here, across all that chalky space? She'd heard her teacher's voice turn soft for other people . . . never her . . . would her voice turn soft for her now? *Soft and interested?*

'Well, Ellie?'

Ellie dared not look up. 'I took your purse, Miss Bacon.'

'Right, then. Well, you'd better come along with me and explain yourself directly to the headmaster.'

Footsteps down a long, long passage . . . the last walk of a child. Does everyone remember their own last walk?

And when she'd come out later, much later, under the arch that said GIRLS, when she'd crept out across the empty playground, lonely, humiliated, confused and lost, Malc was there. He'd heard what had happened and he'd been waiting for her in his old position beside the coke pile.

She'd been crying. Her body juddered with every breath.

Miss Bacon's words as she packed up and left her in Mr Wilkins' study – 'I never trusted that child, I always considered her sly' – rang like the wildest peal of bells, like the loudest clamour she'd ever heard in her ears. She thought she'd never get them out of her head and that her heart would go on breaking like this for ever.

What's more, she'd failed her exams and Miss Bacon was leaving – she'd only signed on for a year. The world was bleak, the world was cold; any future Ellie had ever imagined had got all smudged up and kind of toppled over.

Steeped in the deepest misery she had ever known she told Malcolm, 'I've got to go to the copshop. I've got to tell Mum and have her take me down there.'

But even this grimmest of prospects hadn't really reached her.

'Go on, you'll only get a warning. You don't want to get yourself all steamed up about that,' he said, 'but you should never have owned up. Surely you're not so sodding stupid as to go and nick something and then go and own up?'

They'd been born and grown up four doors away from each other, but as far as Ellie can remember that was the first time she'd actually spoken to him.

9

The days tighten up and darken into mid-winter. They drive through lanes full of tired and empty trees.

'Malc is quite impressed by the fact that Ramon and Murphy are American,' Ellie tells Robert Beasely at their December meeting in the Red Fox. 'I think it's thrown him a bit, since he's always admired Americans. And I suspect he's a little bit out of his depth.'

'I heard they took him out for lunch,' says Robert, peeling a prawn and licking his fingers.

'They asked me to go, too, but Malc wouldn't let me.'

Robert raises his eyebrows slightly before squeezing a lemon into the finger-bowl. 'I'd feel far happier about this if you were finding something worthwhile to do, too, not just sitting back and waiting for Malcolm. What about your ego, Ellie, doesn't yours need boosting?'

'Oh, I don't think so,' and Ellie smiles happily at him as she wrestles messily with the tail of a prawn. 'I've always been a contented sort of person,' and she gives a little laugh, 'happy with my lot.' But she has to admit to him how difficult she is finding Christmas shopping this year, 'Knowing I could buy them anything they wanted. It's hard to walk by the glitzy stuff and stick to the market.' Christmas is going to be special this year because Mandy is coming home, just for a few days as she has to be back in Scotland for the New Year. It will probably be the last time they all spend Christmas together; it might be the last Christmas they spend at number nine Nelson Street. If Ellie had used some of her money to buy a grand house she knows the children would come home more often. That's how life works, with more space there is more to do, more room for tolerance and goodwill. In the Nelson Street house they're a bit cramped up. 'I know Mandy would like us to go back with her to spend the New Year in Scotland,' continues Ellie, 'but to be frank, Robert, she knows how Malc would perform once he found himself in a snooty hotel surrounded by what he considers to be the world's privileged few. And she can't risk her job, well, obviously she's not going to do that.'

'In future years then, maybe,' says Robert. 'Once your spell has started to work.'

'It's already started! Malc takes his driving test next week, you know. He's been finding it tedious having to get around by bus all the time. I don't know how he's managed it, but he has. He says that Ramon and Murphy are very pleased with him.'

'That's what I'm hearing, too.'

'Was it hard, Robert? Be honest with me now, did you have trouble getting them to agree?'

'They were looking for an older man, someone with energy and character, and they were desperately in need of capital at the time. A great deal depended on that first meeting, I have to admit. But, as you told me he would before all this started, Malc came up trumps. He really impressed them. He's quite a complicated person this husband of yours, isn't he?'

These few words of praise please Ellie more than she even admits to herself because it is proving difficult, and oh, it's not just the shopping. It is getting harder and harder, when the mornings are dark and that cold wind whips down Nelson Street, when there's frost on the pavements, it is getting much harder to drag herself out of the cosiness of her bed, denying herself even the warmth of the two-bar electric fire, as she always has denied it, 'for economy's sake', and get herself off to work. It is hard now she knows she doesn't really have to.

She is wrapped up tightly in her decision; she is bound in it like a parcel.

And another thing . . . she'd been a little surprised at the strange sense of loss she felt when all that initial excitement, after the planning and the plotting, had died down. She supposes it is a bit like a starving man being led to a banquet and then choosing to go on punishing himself, choosing to leave it till later. No, that's not a good comparison at all. It is not like that, it is much more emotionally depriving than that, because every second of every day, if you care to look, there are ways to spend money in order to buy yourself comfort or respect, even admiration. Yes, there is definitely an aspect of that involved in spending, especially spending carelessly which is what Ellie could do if she chose to. All that bowing and scraping in shops as she went in and pointed to the most expensive shoes, all that intimate woman-talk, envious looks and flattery she'd get if she went into Lendels and bought a posh dress. Receiving love. A certain kind of love, dished up under certain kinds of smiles. She knows it is false, of course she does – she's done it herself in the gift shop to customers. *But Ellie's never had it happen to her.*

And it's still not happening.

'It isn't that I feel I'm lacking in anything,' she explains. 'Good heavens, with your help, Robert, I'm buying exactly what I want since Malc is much happier already and I couldn't have dreamed the effects would be noticeable so quickly. But sometimes I feel insecure about the money, as if it's not really mine yet.' She dips her fingers into the bowl at the same time as Robert; their hands touch and they smile. The little flowers on top of the water, the colours of the ruby in her engagement ring, float along. 'I think it's because the money is so remote from me,' she finishes weakly. 'Robert,' she confesses, 'already I am getting afraid that I might lose it.'

She is used to his hairy suits now, she is used to accidentally feeling his cuff or arm as he stretches over to help her with her seatbelt or, like now, when she sits back and unexpectedly finds his jacket on the seat behind her.

'There is absolutely no chance of that, Ellie,' he reassures her with one of his special smiles. They are in the alcove in which they always sit and now she considers it theirs. He knows this, so he has started to book it beforehand specially. He has got quite a shy smile: he is a little bit like John Major but younger and his hair is dryer and blonder and there is more of it. 'You are using just a tiny proportion of your money at the moment ... twelve thousand or so a year to pay Malcolm's salary and a one hundred thousand injection of capital with a promise of an annual ten percent return. It is not a secure investment, there are no guarantees, that's why Ramon and Murphy had to search so hard for a backer at the

69

outset. But I ought to tell you now, Ellie, that everything about this enterprise is looking good. Let me explain a bit more thoroughly . . .'

Ellie attempts to concentrate for Robert's sake, but he has misunderstood her. Her feelings of insecurity and imminent loss cannot be smoothed away by strong balance sheets or City predictions. She has always trusted Robert's judgement; from the beginning she has felt certain that Canonwaits would succeed . . . Her fear goes deeper than that but he has not understood because he's getting excited, is in his element, and she feels a strange sense of condescension as she listens.

'I saw at once that security was the most important aspect of Ramon and Murphy's likely success . . .'

'Of course, yes, security . . .'

'Have you any idea, Ellie, of the huge leap in reported thefts and burglaries in this country over the last two years?'

'Things are getting worse and cars are being . . .'

'When Ramon and Murphy first came to me with their feasibility study, I mentioned their interlocking internal shutters to a colleague of mine who works at the Mutual Alliance Insurance Group, which is based here in Liverpool. He took it back to the board and they expressed a great deal of interest. Now they have decided to offer cheaper premiums to customers prepared to install these internal shutters to their downstairs windows.'

'Well, that sounds very promising . . .'

'And small market towns.' Robert fiddles with his folder and brings out a newspaper cutting but Ellie does not want to read it. She is sitting back, relaxed and comfortable, enjoying the sound of his voice. 'It is happening all over the country in small market towns. They are using those ugly metal bars to protect shop windows, ruining old high streets – and there has been quite an outcry just lately. Now, some of these Canonwaits shutters will do the trick and still manage to stay sensitive to the environment. I've got a letter here somewhere from the Association of County Councils. . . am I boring you, Ellie?'

Ellie jumps, scalded. 'Oh no, quite the opposite!'

'And that's not to mention fuel conservation. For security

and fuel economy, Canonwaits interior shutters come out better than double glazing in tests that have been done. They cut down noise as well, you see, as unlike double glazing they absorb vibration. They have been cleverly designed to be cheap and easy to install, folding back either on hinges attached to the window-frame or on metal rods. Oh yes, I saw the potential immediately and now the interest being shown in the Canonwaits product is growing considerably. The garden furniture will eventually become nothing but a sideline.'

Ellie sips her drink. She watches him. He is so full of enthusiasm.

Robert goes on, 'Remember that the rest of the money you've got safely invested will pay back that hundred thousand in one year alone. You must never fear you are going to lose your money, Ellie. It's being very well looked after.'

Is this strange hole that has formed inside her anything to do with losing her money? Ellie hates the new thought she has, tries to push it away but it will not go. Is there just a tiny bit of her that resents losing Malc as he was? After all her moanings to Robert, all her blusterings, and her certainty that the change was what she wanted? She is suffering from some kind of insecurity, certainly, but there could be a dozen different reasons for it and she's never been one for self-examination. Apart from being boring she considers it a complete waste of time.

Will she be able to keep up with Malc? Might she fall behind and lose him? The more successful Malc becomes, the more he will want her to stay at home. Time and time again he has cursed the necessity for her to go out to work, he's very old fashioned like that . . . but what would she do at home all day? She would much rather be involved, she would much rather help him. *But how can she?* Between them, now, will always be her deception.

The joy of being able to give – is that what she's missing? And is it being made worse because it is nearly Christmas time?

'I'd like to give you something, you know,' she tells Robert now. 'I'd like to buy you something really nice and expensive for Christmas, and something special for Victoria and James.'

'Whatever for?'

She pleads in her head – oh please let me give, you are the only one who knows and therefore the only one I could give to. She says, 'Just to say thank you.'

'I am only doing my job.'

'You never had any need to do it so nicely.'

'You know that I am enjoying this. Sometimes I think I'm enjoying it all nearly as much as you are.'

Ellie squeezes her hands together under the table. 'It's going to work, isn't it? Malc is going to do well and he's going to change. Already he's different. I notice little things. For instance, this morning he poured the tea and he passed over the paper so that I could read it first. He was busy working out yesterday's figures for Murphy, so he couldn't read it himself, but still, he didn't just shove it aside, he passed it over.'

Robert is sincere when he says, 'I'm glad for you Ellie, but I think you deserve a great deal more than being given the newspaper first and having your tea poured for you.'

'It's nothing to do with the newspaper. Don't you understand – I am there again, in the kitchen, in the morning! I am there and Malc knows I'm there. I have come alive – we are coming alive together!'

'Now you sound silly.'

'I know,' she grins. 'It's the carols in the background. Carols always make me feel sentimental.'

There are more forms to fill in and decisions to be made. When Ellie is here with Robert the money becomes real and she feels safer. She reads about it, she moves it from account to account, and it's only when he drops her back in the carpark and drives off that she gets the pang. It's when she goes home to the empty house and the morning's dishes, when she trails upstairs to make the bed and to think about Malcolm's tea.

But it doesn't last long – she doesn't let it. And she's started looking forward to Malc getting home. Last week he did something he's never done in his life before, he brought home a bottle of wine. She stood back with her hands clasped and exclaimed, 'Oh, Malc!' knowing how disdainful he was about wine.

'Don't get excited. It was given to me today, along with a calendar.'

But he couldn't spoil it for her like that, nothing could spoil it, so she'd got out the two special glasses that Di had given them on their tenth anniversary – she kept them in the scooped out satin shapes in the box – and put them on the table. They were having shepherd's pie, beetroot in white sauce, and Pouilly-Fuisse. She watched while he opened it, but he didn't remove the cork or pour it with the same flair or skill employed by the waiters at the Red Fox. Nor did he taste it first like Robert did. Well, it was hardly worth it with them sitting down in the kitchen like that. It'd come, though. Given time, it'd come.

Ellie asks Robert, 'What are you getting Bella for Christmas?'

'A suede coat, but I'm not choosing it, she's chosen it herself.'

'And what is she getting you?'

'That's a surprise. I won't know that until Christmas morning.'

'And what will you do?'

'On Christmas Day?'

'Yes.' She wants to know all about him. Robert Beasely is like a night-class, her new interest, her new hobby, and from him she is learning. She is never ashamed of asking and he never objects to telling.

'Nothing very exciting. James and Victoria will open their presents and then there'll be a trail of friends in for drinks before lunch. Bella's family are coming this year . . .' Ellie knows all about Robert's wife's family. She's asked. Her brother is something to do with TV . . . something in the background she's never heard of, and her sister is an artist. She wonders if she and Malc will ever get to be one of those friends who call round in the morning, or whether they'll always be too boring, although being a bank manager isn't the most thrilling career she can think of. She wonders if Bella's disappointed in him and if she has ambitions for Robert like

Ellie has for Malc. She thinks all this but obviously she doesn't say it.

She doesn't tell Robert about her Christmas Day. Malc'll be in the pub all morning and they'll go to the club in the evening. There's always a special do on, on Christmas night. They've never missed it, not once during their whole marriage. When the kids were small they took them along, and Ellie left early in order to put them to bed.

But then up until three years ago Malc's dad had been alive and they'd always had to do what he wanted.

'Yes,' she replies to his question. 'Christmas Day's a Monday so I'll have the weekend and two days off. The sales start straight after. They decorated the Arcade a month ago. They've done it Dickensian this year, they're selling hot chestnuts outside the gift shop and they've got an old horse-drawn carriage all decked out. It looks really lovely.'

'How long have you worked at the gift shop, Ellie?'

'Since the Arcade was built in 1984. Quite a time. Before that I worked in Valerie's Boutique, and before that I was in the Liberty's shop, selling material, you know.'

'Have you ever done any other kind of work?'

'I left school at sixteen and went straight into a shop. There was nothing else around here then really, unless you were bright, and then you went to the business college.'

'But when the children were small?'

'Oh, when Mandy and Kev were small I stayed home and we had to manage on Malc's pay. I think that's really when the rot set in. We were so stretched in those days, I look back now and wonder how we coped. And it was hard, with Malc's mum in the state she was and his dad at home all day, and if he wasn't home he was in the nick.'

'Quite a character, eh?'

'No. No, it wasn't like that.' She gets a quick glimpse of Arthur Freeman's face as it pushes itself into her memory, and she winces. Nobody cried when he died, not even Malc. No one stood out in the street or closed their curtains like they still did sometimes out of respect when one of the oldest residents passed away. And yet Ellie admired him in a way. There was something admirable about someone who could be so irredeemably unpleasant throughout their entire life. She's always known why she never found the old TV comedy series *Steptoe and Son* very funny – she'd always felt embarrassed when they all sat down round the telly together to watch it, because it was so obvious it was painful . . . Arthur Freeman *was* old man Steptoe, but without any of his scallywag charm or devilish humour. And years ago everyone in Nelson Street had been nervous of him; he'd been bigger in those days, and a bully. And Ellie has never forgotten the way she went in after Lily died and found Arthur bent over the bed prising the engagement ring off his wife's finger.

She shudders.

Oh, she had not wanted to begin her married life there. Nor had Malc. And they wouldn't have, but for Mandy coming along so suddenly like that. There hadn't been much choice and she'd only been seventeen – she hadn't known anything about abortion, where to go or what to do. And if she had done, well, they'd never have had Mandy. They had not put themselves down on the housing list because it was so long Malc lost his temper and shouted at the woman, pushing Ellie out of the door before him – she can see that door now, yellow glass and wired with studs in – 'Sodding waste of time, you'd be in your wheelchair before they got round to you and needing a ground-floor flat.'

She'd been glad to get him out of the housing office before he made a real scene. As it was he turned over a chair on his way out and left a boot mark on the canvas.

And there'd been the spare bedroom available at number nine while Ellie's house was still full.

Robert Beasely is repeating himself. 'I said, what are you going to give Malcolm for Christmas? You've been miles away. Look, your steak and kidney pie's getting cold.'

Ellie feels as if she's been sound asleep. She even has to rub her eyes since the steam from the pie has fugged them all up and they're gazing into the gravy, unseeing. Robert's got some fishy dish with sauce on. 'New shirts, I can get them cheap off Margot. I normally get him a couple of shirts but this year I've got him a key-ring as well . . . for when he gets the company car.'

'I hope he passes his test after all this,' Robert comments.

They have coffee, and as it's nearly Christmas he suggests a liqueur. She doesn't know what to ask for so she refuses. 'I've had quite enough to drink already. I always feel like going to sleep on a Wednesday afternoon.' As they're leaving Ellie checks and checks again. She feels as if she's left her handbag behind or something else important, but she can't see anything despite her careful peering, nothing tangible or visible remains of their visit.

10

Malc passes his driving test first time.

Swing hammocks like those you see on porches in the American west, twirling gazebos, arbours, kissing benches, Henry Moore donkeys made out of wood, tiny log cabins for children with even tinier wicket fences, and shutters ... ready-made shutters for houses, easy to fix and available on easy terms. Even Ellie, who's normally bored to tears by garden accessories, pores over the brochure with relish and envy. How she'd love a garden like that ...

And the brochure is so nicely done, with none of those garish colours and Bible-thin pages and cheap-looking women posing half-nude. It's like the paper they use for up-market newspaper magazines. Stylish.

'It's the shutters that people are clamouring for now,' says Malc to A. P. Murphy, who has driven round to Nelson Street with the car. It is a black jeep, a Cherokee – huge. Ellie went out and almost cried when she saw it, with its rugged wheels and silver hubcaps. A crowd of neighbourhood children were gathered round it, exclaiming.

She'd been scared to meet Murphy and Ramon. She'd been nervous about them coming to the house, but out in the street, admiring Malc's new car, had been time enough to get used to them. You couldn't be timid with them, and they didn't ask for respect, either. They clapped her on the back when they saw her and shouted 'Hey!' and 'Well!' Ellie could see why Malc liked them. She couldn't remember a time when she'd seen him quite so easy with anyone ... or anyone quite so easy with him.

'So it's mail order now, nationwide,' says Ramon. He's surely too plump for his age, but he carries his fatness well, uses it wealthily, covers it flamboyantly. No one could call him flabby or sissy. It is a hard kind of largeness, thinks Ellie, because everything about him is large – his blue eyes, his nose, his mouth – he smokes large cigars, and he'd look silly thin.

Murphy looks like a dark, lean lumberjack. He wears jeans and boots and padded tartan shirts, and a gold wrist watch drips off his wrist. He is a lumberjack with smooth hands. They sip tea in Ellie's carefully-clean kitchen. She's washed the curtains, had the cooker out and wiped the grease off the sides of it.

These high-flying young men spray excitement and energy. They have come with large presents for everyone. They admire her ancient Christmas tree and she's disguised the broken branch with tinsel. They don't know for sure if she's the one injecting the money into Canonwaits; they've been told by Robert that it is 'a wellwisher, and someone with Malcolm's future at heart', but they must suspect it is her.

To Ellie's undying relief they give nothing away.

'Does this mean that Malc's going to have to work away from home?'

'Certainly not, he's already too indispensable to us here,' shouts Ramon, a teaspoon disappearing into his mighty hand, 'and we've taken on part-time reps up and down the island.'

How on earth does Malc take this compliment? Ellie glances over but he is too engrossed in sales talk with the lean-limbed Murphy, so she doubts he's even heard. Perhaps he doesn't need to hear? He seems to have gone on to another level: he's not in the dungeon any more, knocking his head against rocks, he's floated up into the open air. He's been there ever since he was invited to his first 'meeting'.

'I'm late because I've been at a meeting,' is what Malc said when he came in with the news. Well, that was extraordinary in itself because over all the years he'd been with Watt & Wyatt he'd cursed like hell if he'd had to stay just five minutes over. And then there were meetings every week, and sometimes he and Murphy and Ramon went to eat at the Bunch of Grapes in town. And his tea got burnt.

'You might try and let me know,' said Ellie mildly.

'How can I let you know, love, when we haven't got a phone? And anyway, I'm too busy to be bothering with that sort of nonsense. Good God, d'you want me to get on or don't you?'

'Well, of course I do Malc,' and Ellie smiled inwardly, and her heart glowed from the inside out, a tinfoil steak in the sandwich bar microwave with two great aching crusts around it.

He leaves his mac at home now. She's wondered whether to move it off the hallstand but thinks that might be tempting fate. He wears a suit – it was the first thing Murphy and Ramon insisted on. 'It's a question of image,' they told him. 'You are Canonwaits now, you are our flagship.' And they made him go to Lendels to buy it. They even went with him.

At the time, in a funny sort of a way, Ellie had felt jealous about that, and she thinks she'd have chosen a black one, not brown, but the brown does suit him.

He's wearing it now, and he hasn't loosened his tie.

Murphy and Ramon stay longer than she expected. Ellie moves into the lounge and whispers to Mandy, 'I hope they don't expect food. I didn't think about feeding them. I thought they were only coming to deliver the jeep and they'd go when they'd finished their cup of tea.'

'Warm some sausage rolls up, Mum. What else have you got? No, you stay in here and open your prezzie, I'll move them out of the kitchen and see what I can do.'

Is it warm enough in here for the visitors? Should she ask Kev to build up the fire? She's a little bit embarrassed to be sitting on her sofa opening her present with Murphy drooping over the fireplace which is too small for him – he's going to knock those cards off the mantelpiece in a minute – and Ramon filling Malcolm's chair, making himself hugely at home. Malc comes to sit beside her and he smells of aftershave. She puts a smile on her face, ready. These two young men know nothing about her so how can they have chosen anything suitable? She can tell it's been done up by a shop – ordinary people don't wrap things like this.

It's in a box. *It's a telephone* . . . Her heart sinks, how can she tell them they're not connected? It's not an ordinary telephone, either. It's a gold one, the kind that you see in film stars' bedrooms, and it isn't cheap . . . she knows the price of these telephones.

'Well, what can I say,' she tells them. 'It's really lovely but you shouldn't have!'

Malc leans over and kisses her, just a peck on the cheek, and then he reaches over and takes her hand! She smoothes down her skirt with the other although there are no creases in it. 'The day after Boxing Day we're being wired up,' Malc says, still close, 'and then I won't have any excuse not to ring you when I'm going to be late. The jeep has a phone in it, too.'

There are tears in her eyes when she thanks them again, not because of the golden phone but because of the thought and the kiss and Malc's hand and the way he is smelling tonight. The lights on the Christmas tree blur before her eyes, the star on top could be real. And Mandy, unflustered by getting the tea, has been given a burgundy-coloured cashmere sweater and Kev a briefcase. They are all glutted by receiving, and Murphy and Ramon are cool with the giving. What's Malc got?

It is a cravat. Ellie smiles to herself – he'll never wear it. But he loosens his tie and stands before the mirror, puts it on and laughs at the look of himself. And yet he likes it! Has he lost weight, was he always so tall? Ellie can tell that he likes it! She should have got presents for Murphy and Ramon, Malc should have warned her. She says so. And she should have bought something special for a meal.

Ellie flushes.

This is Christmas Eve, a Sunday this year. Normally Malc would be down at the pub and she'd be fussing in the kitchen making preparations for tomorrow. Wait till she tells Di and Margot about this! Wait till she tells Robert! How she wishes that Robert was here to see it.

She can't wait for everyone to leave so she can go and sit in that Cherokee, quietly by herself. Feel it and sniff it.

The atmosphere in here is warm and relaxed. Ellie can tell that Murphy and Ramon like her. She doesn't know quite what she did right, but she's passed the test she set herself. She hasn't let Malc down, and nor has Mandy because look at that table with the flaps out! Mandy's got a knack of making a table look enticing no matter what's on it – where did she find those little red flowers? – and Kev's chatting away there to

Murphy about golf as if the two have known each other for years. It wouldn't be possible for Malc to start showing off and being crude because, somehow, Murphy and Ramon are just not that kind of people. They wouldn't really know how to respond, they'd think he was joking or something. She feels a rush of gratitude towards Robert Beasely – he could not have chosen two more suitable people, no, not even if he'd spent years searching.

This must have been meant, thinks Ellie.

'To redwood shutters,' shouts Ramon, raising his glass.

'To redwood shutters,' they all reply, searching for their own drinks in the mess of cheese straws.

'Yes, they are nice, aren't they,' she finds herself telling Ramon about Mandy and Kev, speaking about them as if they're not there, but she's always praised them in front of other people. Normally this habit of hers drives Malc mad. He used to say, 'They're both big-headed enough, and pleased with themselves already. They don't need you sticking your oar in.'

But Ellie's always known how important it is to make a big deal of the kids and the detrimental effects of the opposite approach on a growing child. All that nonsense people talk about showing off ... let them show off ... give them something to show off about! From the very beginning she'd been determined to give her children self-confidence, and if a mother couldn't do it who could? So despite Malc's annoyance she'd taught them to read and write before they started school, she'd sellotaped flash-cards up all over the house, she'd read them stories and when they'd watched telly she'd watched with them, so they could talk it over afterwards.

Money was short so she went without but Ellie was used to that. 'They've got to have what the others have got, Malc. They mustn't feel inferior.' And he plodded home from work, grumbling as usual when he saw new socks or vests or toys that she'd bought second-hand.

'Look at you gel, you're exhausted,' he used to say sometimes. 'Give yourself a break. There's more to life than the kids, you can't go back and live your life through them!'

She'd laughed at him, knowing how jealous he was – a

81

naughty, jealous little boy, and Di and Margot, who weren't like that with theirs, encouraged her when she flagged. 'You do what feels right,' said Di, 'never mind him.'

What a wrench it had been when she'd had to go back to work.

She'd conquered her fear of Nelson Street School – she'd had to, for their sakes. If she couldn't be there in person she'd damn well stamp her determination on the place. She'd forced herself to go to every open day and parents' day and lecture, she made herself known there, she put herself up for the PTA. Never mind that every time she pushed through those heavy swing doors she died a little inside, never mind that she had to buy barley sugars to keep her mouth wet or that she stuttered every time she had to confront the headmaster.

Very often she was worn out after a day's work, but still she'd drive herself on in order to take Mandy and Kev on outings, to the park to sail boats on the lake, to the zoo or the cinema, and sometimes they'd buy fish and chips on the way home. She insisted they had a bath every night – 'it's only half an hour for the immersion' – and in the winter the fire's back boiler heated the water anyway.

'You're never in,' moaned Malc.

'Your tea's always in the oven,' she told him brightly, 'and who'd want to be in, anyway, with the place never feeling like ours.'

'Mum and Dad don't interfere,' he said gloomily.

'No, they don't interfere but they're always there, and they're not the most glowing of adult example!'

'Mum can't help it.'

'I know she can't help it, Malc, but that doesn't mean to say I feel happy with the kids being around her.'

Lilian Freeman was a tiny, fairy-like woman with eyes the colour of pale pain, two watery pools with ripple-wrinkles coming off them. Poor Lilian. Actually Ellie always got on very well with Malc's mum, once she'd grown used to her little ways, once she gave up hiding the bottles, marking them, and striving to cure her. She was, as Arthur said, incurable. Too far gone. Something should have been done much earlier but there were no help groups or phone numbers flashed up on the telly for boozers then. For days she'd be perfectly all right, a sweet woman really, very good at telling stories and she loved reading, and then, for no obvious reason, it'd start. She'd go. Her eyes went first and the rest of her dissipated body followed, sort of flowed away after her, treading on the hem of herself. Once, Ellie, furious and dismayed at the lack of concern, had marched Lil up to the doctor's and refused to leave until something was done. And her mother-in-law had been taken away, locked up until she dried out. Ellie had gone to visit and been unable to bear it. She'd signed the forms straight away and taken her out, brought her all the way home on the bus, propping her up with her knee to stop her sliding off the seat and on to the floor as you would with a wayward umbrella.

She should have been firmer. She should have followed the doctor's advice and realised that you had to be cruel to be kind, but if Lilian needed a place to go to escape from reality, then who was Ellie to take it away? How could she, Ellie, insist that Lil confront the reality that was Arthur, that was two of her sons shut up for life, that was Nelson Street and no way out of it? What right had Ellie to pull down the veil from anyone else's eyes?

She missed Lil desperately when she died, even more in a way than she missed her own mother.

'They always loved school,' she tells Ramon now, proudly. 'Unlike me, I detested it. Well, I wasn't too bright and in those days they treated children very differently.'

'It looks like a terrible place,' says Ramon. She's not surprised that he noticed it ... it dominates one end of Nelson Street in the way the Arcade does the other.

'It's the people inside it that make a place terrible,' she tells him, remembering with shame her ignoble exit, caught screwing Malc in the central heating shed. And her mother's face, with her voice rising to a scream behind it, 'A thief and a whore! It's that Malcolm Freeman, isn't it? To have anything at all to do with that family is to court disaster. Everyone knows that, Ellie, so why not you, that's what I want to know!'

'Malcolm's not like the rest of them,' she'd whined.

'I had hopes for you and I'll not deny it,' screamed Freda Thwait, Ellie's mother.

But Ellie hadn't known that. *Oh, she'd never known that.* What with Freda always so busy and everything.

'Going round with those two unpleasant creatures . . .'

'Now you're moaning about my friends!'

'Friends? Those two!' Freda Thwait screwed her finger to her forehead. 'They're daft in the head, the Peters sisters. They're missing up there! I've seen you, skulking in the playground, whispering, drooping about with those two weirdos. Where is your pride, Ellie? What has happened to your pride?'

But Ellie felt strangely comfortable with Fern and Blanche Peters. She was an outsider, as they were. And anyway, Muriel wouldn't have her back after she ditched her while trying to ingratiate herself with Miss Bacon. Ellie wasn't exactly a friend of the Peters sisters, because they didn't have friends in that way. She wanted to explain to Freda but it was too hard to put into words.

Freda Thwait said, 'And now you've gone and let me down.'

'I never had to fear that they'd let me down,' she tells Ramon, watching the paperchains waft in the heat and sipping the first of the Emva Cream. They'll be able to save the petrol coupons and get free glasses now, like Dave Legget does. Funny how easy it is to forget that she is a millionaire. She wonders when it will really sink in. 'I always knew they'd do well and they have.' She smiles up at Mandy who sits on the arm of the sofa. Mandy is on one side, Malc on the other, and Kev is still jawing with Murphy.

'Malcolm has talked a lot about them,' says Ramon. The house smells richly of dusty coke and his lovely cigar. He pats his lips and puffs out smoke rings, and there is cigar ash in Ellie's hearth, a step up from Malc's roll-ups. Is he just saying that to please her, or could it be true? She's never heard Malc doing anything but mocking the kids in that meaning-to-be-joking kind of way.

'Yes, mam,' says Ramon, Malcolm's new boss. 'He's always bragging about his kids but that's nothing to what he says about you.'

'Would you think me terribly rude if I just stepped outside and took another look at that jeep?' says Ellie, not caring if they mind or not but hurrying out through the door before it all gets too much for her.

'Keep your eyes open for the Skinner kids while you're there,' shouts Malc after the closing door. And she hears him explaining to Ramon and Murphy, 'Nothing's safe when you've got families like that on the loose, when there's wild kids like that about.'

But Ellie is alone with the jeep in the darkness. She is thankful for that, and of the terrible Skinners there is no sign.

11

They have built the Arcade on a mound, like they built the Catholic Cathedral. Ellie struggles towards the doors, still bloated and puffing from Christmas. She hasn't felt completely well since Christmas Eve when she drank too much and somehow, although she didn't particularly want to, she had foolishly continued to do so. The wind nips at her heels and blows the tops of the dwarf conifers that have been planted in paving spaces, at regular intervals, beside the iron girders.

They pulled down a tenement to make space for this shopping precinct, and the dust that she'd had to contend with at home during those months of demolition was quite incredible. It got in the food, it got in the beds, an evil-smelling, foul-tasting dust that carried with it something of the despair of the garbage-strewn stairways and the endless, graffiti-covered landings. Ellie had taken up the carpets, then, and tried to bang some of the gloom out of them.

From the tenement dust had surfaced the Skinners, lock stock and every last barrel, motorbikes, prams, broken-down freezers, the lot. They have spread out from the boundaries of number forty-two into the road outside with their ancient sofas and discarded pieces of mouldy carpet. Once the council had to send a skip in order to clear the area. They are the despair of Nelson Street. They are the despair of everyone, and Ellie feels that while the Skinners are there that tenement block has never truly gone.

Inside the Arcade, up the moving staircase beside the waterfall, all is suffused by that eerie green light as if it is always just on the point of raining but never quite manages to succeed. Ancient men and women crab along on their sticks, faces pinched against the cold, and small groups of youngsters are already clustering, taking up their positions on the park-like seats beside the raised brick borders. They have nothing better to do, and it's warmer in here than it is outside. The café downstairs is on the point of opening. Her heels click on the smooth marbled walkway. She knows how easy it is to slip, she's been over herself many times. She's always having to leave the shop and go and pick up distraught old ladies, and she's taken to keeping a chair beside the counter specially for the purpose.

Funorama. She takes out her key. The first thing she must do is take down those old posters and replace them with Sale signs. She hadn't made it to the pantomime ... her secret hope was that Malc might have taken her, but she had gone to the second event advertised on the giftshop window. She'd sat at the ringside quietly on Boxing Day while Margot and Di screamed beside her for Giant Haystacks, the Mighty Chang, El Bandito and Skull Murphy. She's never liked wrestling, but her hopes are high for next year.

Yet she mustn't grumble. Christmas was better than she ever remembered. There were no long sulks from Mandy and no sneering remarks from Kevin, as if everyone seemed to sense there was change in the air. Everyone was slightly excitable and nervous – or was that just Ellie's imagination?

The jeep had shut everyone up. On Christmas morning they had gone for a ride with Malc driving, looking so tall and proud sitting there in the driving seat, his keys clipped to his new keyring that Ellie had found it difficult to keep her eyes off him.

'Where shall we go?'

'Let's go out Bebington way.'

'What for?'

'No reason, except that you asked me and I had to say somewhere.'

Robert Beasely lives out Bebington way. Ellie knows his address off by heart although, of course, she has never used it, never written to him there, never visited. She still doesn't know if they passed his house because they flashed by the road signs too quickly, but she saw cars parked outside an attractive Victorian residence which had an impressive plant in the window and linings to the shop-fitted curtains and scalloped pelmets. There was a small light on in an attic room so Ellie wondered if that was Robert's study.

'Wait until Dave Legget sees this,' said Malc.

'Oh, I know,' said Ellie, knowing exactly. How smoothly the jeep went along, how luxuriously comfortable was the seating. Some people even stared at them and Ellie savoured their envy. Not only were they out in a jeep but they might be calling somewhere for drinks – after all, they were out, looking busy on Christmas morning. For the first time ever, Christmas dinner was late and it didn't matter. The Freemans had better things to be doing with their time . . .

Now Ellie gets out the small step-ladder and carefully moves the goods from the front of the window to make space for herself. She strips down the posters, wetting the edges to loosen them, and starts sticking up the strips marked 'Sale', which are adhesive on the backs. It is important to get the angle right first time because they are difficult to get off once they have gripped the window. She waves to Rita in the dress shop opposite.

She has complicated feelings about Malc's Christmas present to her. She's thrilled, of course, because he had no need to go searching for something so special. It was a bracelet in a velvet case with tiny seed pearls dotted about in the silver. Her wrist didn't look like her own with it on and Mandy had to help her with the safety clasp because her hands were too clumsy to manage it.

'You shouldn't have, Malc.' She'd given him a thank you kiss.

'Why not? I can afford it.'

'But there are other important bills to pay.'

'They can wait their moment, like I have had to.'

And then of course she'd had to give him his shirts with 'special' on the packet, which proved that they came from the factory where Margot worked as a supervisor. That 'special' said there was something wrong with them. You had to look hard to find it, but there was always a flaw. And the keyring, which had looked so nice in the shop, now seemed a bit shoddy and boring.

Ellie's musings are interrupted when the bell clinks. It's Mrs Gogh, looking the worse for wear in spite of her dusty rose Jaeger jacket. 'I just thought I'd pop in to make sure you were coping all right.'

Ellie knows that the popping in has nothing to do with that, and everything to do with the fact that Mrs Gogh thought Ellie would be late, and that she might be propped by the counter, pampering herself with the electric fire on, sipping coffee. They had talked about prices before Christmas and all the bargains are down on the list: Ellie's only got to cross off the old prices with a red pen and replace them with the sale ones.

She continues to lean, quite dangerously, across the display; her arms ache from reaching out for the window and her legs tremble a little. She is out of condition. 'Did you have a good Christmas, Mrs Gogh?'

'Quiet, Ellie, but pleasantly relaxing as always. How about you?'

'Lovely, thank you,' says Ellie, biting her lips with intense concentration. Mrs Gogh doesn't bother her, there are plenty of Mrs Goghs round about here and Ellie has known them all her life. They are rich, they are successful, they are invariably smart in a chain-store-cosmetic-department sort of a way, and yet they are nothing like the Caroline Plunket-Kirbys. They are predictable, and there is only one way of dealing with them – subservience. Ellie learned how to do that long ago, and she's quite happy with it. She neither likes nor dislikes Mrs Gogh, she doesn't have an opinion on the matter. She certainly doesn't want to be like her, for she doesn't envy her or her lifestyle. Mrs Gogh has an unhappy mouth and unhappy, spoilt eyes, and her children have let her down. She's always going on about it.

'Too much too early. We made it too easy for them,' she often complains. And Ellie dunks a Rich Tea biscuit at those confidential times, and sympathises.

Caroline Plunket-Kirby eats people like Mrs Gogh for breakfast.

'Would you like a cup of coffee, Mrs Gogh? It's freezing out there this morning.' And in here, especially with that door open. Come in or out, one of the two, woman, do!

Mrs Gogh hesitates. She would like a cup of coffee but she's reluctant to interrupt Ellie's efforts.

Eventually she says, 'That would be nice, but you carry on, Ellie, I'll get it. And would you like one?'

'If it's no trouble,' says Ellie. 'This is thirsty work. I think it's something they put in the glue.'

'Probably,' says Mrs Gogh, closing the door with a chink and passing, scentily, through to the back room.

Ellie gets back to work. The club is only a ten-minute walk from Nelson Street, but on Christmas Day night they had chosen to go there by jeep. This meant that Malc could not drink and even he admitted that he didn't know if he'd be able to handle it.

'But I'm torn,' he confessed, 'and I think I'd prefer showing off the jeep and sticking to alcohol-free.'

Ellie was pleased by his decision. She sensed a wall about to collapse and this was the first brick. Kevin was pleased, too, and so was Mandy. It was strange how the not-drinking excluded him from other things, too. At the club and without a beer in his hand, Malc seemed vulnerable and naked. Di and Margot recognised this and straightaway jumped on it.

'Good evening, vicar. Where's your dog collar, then?'

'Drop one vice and pick up another, that's what they say.'

'What's going to happen to your beer gut, Malc? You want to watch that it doesn't slip down and crush you where it hurts.'

But they were all impressed by the jeep, and Ellie's bracelet. It was a most wonderful feeling, but even more wonderful than all of this was the way he stayed himself all evening, and didn't go off to the bar and remain for ages, talking. She noticed how he kept picking the car keys up off the table, and weighing them in his hand before replacing them. He danced the spot dance with a giggling Mandy and he had a game of darts with Kevin. Ellie went steady on the rum herself in order to keep him company.

'What's come over your old man then, all of a sudden?' Di asked her, with the perspiration of booze shining her make-up.

'He's got something to show off about, hasn't he, and he's determined to make the most of it,' said Ellie.

'You can't blame him for that,' approved Di. 'That jeep is something else. And fancy him getting you that bracelet! I can't imagine Malc choosing anything so dainty.'

Ellie raised her wrist for the fiftieth time, hardly able to believe it herself.

The youngsters, none of them really wanting to be there but forced into it by responsible feelings of Christmas, formed a small group of their own at another table and made the most of the disco. There were Ellie's two, and Margot's three and Saul, who belonged to Di, and several others who always came. Mandy was flirting with Saul and they danced the waltzes together. Half-past ten came and normally, by now, Malc would be acting the fool on the dance floor, making it quite impossible for his children to dance or be seen in his vicinity, but not this year. This year he'd seemed quite pensive and muted, sitting watching, and much tidier with his hair still in place and no sweat-stained armpits or streamers hanging from his head.

Once, during the evening, Malc caught her eye and held it. But was he enjoying himself, she worried.

When the last waltz came along she felt him standing beside her; he said nothing, but held out his hand. He was just about the only man in the room with his jacket still on, and she realised how nice it was, how safe it was, and how much she'd missed cradling her face against a suit jacket. There is something very sensual about a man's lapel, thinks Ellie . . .

'This is just what the doctor ordered,' she says to Mrs Gogh, after coming down from the step-ladder and resting against the counter to admire her work, a cup in her hand. The steam from the coffee must prove to her employer how chilly the air is in here, stale and damp, but Mrs Gogh does not suggest turning on the fire. If she's cold, then Ellie must find ways to keep herself warm. There are always the shelves to be dusted or goods to be packed away. Mrs Gogh keeps her Jaeger coat on and sits, huddled up, on the only chair. Her hard golden hairstyle is held with a bow at the back of her head, and her rings look heavy on her fingers.

I have probably got more money than you, thinks Ellie. What would you say if you knew that, Mrs Gogh, and how would your attitude change towards me? Ellie knows that Mrs Gogh would think it wrong for people like Ellie to win money. 'Poor things, how can they possibly know how to deal with it?'

she'd ask her coffee-morning friends, and her Chamber of Trade husband. 'They'd squander it on frivolities,' that's what she'd say. 'For people like that, winning money is a sure road to ruin.'

There wasn't much point in opening this morning, the both of them know that. The goods they sell in here are the type of thing customers want before Christmas, not afterwards. Useless things, really – fluffy toys and extraordinary teapots, rude car stickers and pink-framed pictures of teddy bears, posters and cards. Still there are always the sprinkling of meanies who come looking for bargains ready for next year, and the odd child who's been given some money and is desperate to spend it.

The main reason for Ellie being here this morning, apart from Mrs Gogh's own satisfaction, is to prepare for the sale, the response to which will be more of a trickle than a roar.

'We had Mandy and Kev home. We had a full house,' says Ellie, to pass the time.

'Yes, Christmas is hard work, isn't it,' says Mrs Gogh, who has an au pair and goes to an hotel for her Christmas dinner so knows nothing about it. 'It's always nice to get back to normal.'

Is she, Ellie, going to turn into a Mrs Gogh? Bored and bad-tempered with nothing better to do the day after Boxing Day than come to the Arcade? Robert has constantly warned her about being left high and dry with nothing to do, and Ellie supposes that he is afraid she'll turn into someone like this. But no, it won't be the same at all, because she's going to share Malc's success with him. She's going to take an interest in his work and, if Robert's wildest prophecies come true, she'll be busy moving house and getting everything perfect. She'll have to buy herself a car and learn to drive, and she'll go to night-classes to improve herself, to make herself more worthy of Malc.

If Malc's going to be successful then Ellie intends to help him.

She'll learn to cook the sort of meals he's going to need her to cook if he has colleagues home to dinner . . . like Bella Beasely does. They'll learn about opera and ballet together,

92

they'll go for country weekends. They could learn to sail, or take up walking. The possibilities are endless.

Ellie dreams. She might even get friendly with Bella Beasely.

The difference between Ellie and Mrs Gogh, as Ellie sees it, is that she will have novelty on her side, and that she and Malc will enjoy their new riches together. She'll have a new man by her side while poor Mrs Gogh is stuck with her old one.

'Well, time and tide . . .' says Mrs Gogh.

'Yes.' Ellie nudges herself forward off the counter. 'There's plenty to be getting on with this morning.' And then, suddenly, startlingly, she feels such a surge of pity for this woman, this fellow sufferer, sitting so rigidly there on the chair, that Ellie can hardly bear it. She can't think of anything else to say but, 'Would you like to stay and help me out? I could do with a hand this morning.'

'I think not, dear,' says Mrs Gogh, a cross smile tightening her face.

And Ellie stands and listens to the quick clicking of those receding footsteps, worrying in case Mrs Gogh might fall over in her haste to get away.

Ellie shrugs as she picks up her overall. Perhaps she's got it all wrong.

They have not got around to changing the piped music, and suddenly the Arcade is ringing, singing, the whole of the vast green space is full of a sugary, crystallised version of *Jingle Bells*.

12

There are only a certain number of physical types in the western world, thinks Ellie now, sitting at a window table of the Hung Toa in China Town with Malc opposite, talking quietly. No more than twenty really, but it's difficult to categorise those you know well and even harder to place yourself. But if she's forced to do it she would class Malc as a burly Albert Finney with hairy Dennis Healey tendencies, veering dangerously close to Stan Ogden. And herself? Well, leaving Connie Francis aside because that was a long while ago, maybe she's an older, North of England version of Mary Beth in *Cagney and Lacey* – that's just in looks, of course, not temperament. And Ellie approves of the clothes that Mary Beth Lacey wears.

Is Ellie a snob? Is that why she wants to get out and get on and is discontented with her lot? She has thought quite a bit about that just lately but has not been able to come to a conclusion.

What is she going to do about Di and Margot when the Freemans come up in the world? Abandon them? Certainly not, she could not survive without them. She'll just take care who she invites them to dinner with, and where she chooses to take them, that's all. And that's not being nasty, that's being sensible, because certain types of people just don't mix and there's no good pretending they do. They ought to, but they just don't.

Will Di and Margot still want to know *her*?

She knows, now, that she doesn't like Sake. She pushes her glass to one side and says to Malc, 'I just thought it would be nice, on the occasional Wednesday, to come with you on your rounds so that I can see what you do, and learn what it's all about.'

This is the first time they have been out for a meal together. The first time ever. 'Put your hat and coat on, woman,' Malc had said when he arrived home, late again. 'I'm taking you out to dinner.'

Ellie smiled. He had never called 'tea' dinner before. And then she'd panicked because of the state of her hair.

Last night he and Murphy and Ramon had dined at the Adelphi, entertaining prospective clients.

'It wouldn't do anything for my image to have a wife riding along beside me,' says Malc now, very definitely. 'And I'm a different person when I'm out and about – I've got to be. Having you there would just make me feel bloody silly.'

Ellie is hurt but she doesn't show it. Fair enough, she supposes, but how can she be any help to him, how can she even talk about his work with him if she knows nothing about it? Apparently Murphy and Ramon have often asked him to bring her along to their evening sessions in the Bunch of Grapes, but Malc says he's not keen.

'I know that I'm part of your old world,' she tells him now, 'but I don't want to be excluded from the new.'

'You can't help seeing me in a certain way, and that's difficult for me when I'm having to put on this act and be different,' Malc tries to explain.

'Well, d'you think I'm going to laugh at you or something? I'm proud of you, Malc, I'm really, really proud of you.'

'Didn't you think I'd be able to do it?'

'I *knew* you'd be able to do it. That's why I encouraged you to apply, remember?'

They're not sure what to order so they decide on a set meal for two. The burnished dishes arrive and are set on a heated tray.

'Shall we try chopsticks?' asks Malc, and Ellie laughs and shakes her head.

'We don't know what we're doing anyway,' she tells him, 'so don't let's make it worse.' She is amazed that he chose a Chinese restaurant, he who has always scorned foreign food and sworn there were rats and alley cats in it.

But when she's got the food on her plate it is Ellie, not Malc, who eyes that strange bit of bone.

Malc stays silent for a moment, staring across the top of his

95

food, before he says, 'And I won't be doing this job for long so it's not worth you coming anyway, Ellie.'

Ellie pauses in mid-swallow and her heart starts pumping fast. She reaches for a drink before she remembers how much she dislikes it and her hand stays hopelessly wrapped round the glass, making hot fingerprints on the sides. Oh, dear Jesus, she'd thought he was enjoying it! She'd been certain he was coping – everything he came home and told her sounded good. The redwood shutters were selling like hot cakes, since they were cheaper and healthier than double glazing which nobody can afford any more, and Murphy and Ramon have been pressured into taking extra warehouse space. Some of the shutters have been sent straight to America. The last thing she heard was that they were considering borrowing big money in order to try and start producing them here with the help of a government grant. Is this what this meal is all about? Is it a sop, a comforter? But how can he think about going back, and what on earth has he got to go back to?

Malc says, slowly and clearly, 'Elle, they are going to make me a partner.'

Robert never told her! All the breath leaves Ellie's body at the same time.

'Well,' is what she hears herself say while she dabs her brimming eyes. 'Well, whoever would have guessed it? And you've only been there for four months!' And since the day you first started, she thinks, as the tears flow, I feel I have not been able to reach you.

'We mustn't raise our hopes too much because we're still at the stage when anything could happen, but if we sign this new contract next week we'll be in business for the next five years and that's definite. It's going to mean a hell of a lot more money coming in. We can think about getting a house, you'll be able to stop work . . .'

Oh thank God thank God.

Ellie stops listening and watches Malc's face instead. She can remember Malc like this. This isn't new, although in some ways, given all the years that have passed, it is a revelation. Her heart takes her back, oh, more than twenty years; she can smell the warm scent of bracken, she can feel the moss on the backs of her legs. And Malc's voice, much the same, with that note of defiance in it as he strokes her arm with a blade of grass. 'This is my dream, Elle. We won't fall into the poverty trap that happens to everyone else. We won't have kids till we're ready. We'll take it slowly, we'll both keep on working. One day we'll get a house, maybe somewhere round here and I'll commute to work . . .'

And she'd thought of her mother's face, how her mouth went all tight when she spoke his name. 'Malcolm Freeman! Talk about a ne'er do well, talk about a loser! You've picked a right one there, my girl, and that's no mistake! Open your eyes, Ellie, do! All those lads are taking after their father. Warren's already shut up for five years and Mickey's heading in the self-same direction. It's in their blood, Ellie, it's in their gin-soaked, shifty blood, you've only got to look at them to know, and the girls are no better. Karen's on the game and Linda's down that escort agency nights . . .'

'Malcolm is different, Mam.'

That didn't work.

'If you marry that lad then I'm washing my hands of you and I can tell you that now for nothing. You've made mess enough of your own life, fouling up all the chances God gave you. You always had a brain, Ellie, and once I expected, not great things perhaps, but I never imagined you'd end up in a shop no better than that Margery Ducker! Chucked out of school before the term's over, I ask you, honest to God. And what d'you think you're going to live on?'

'Malc's earning, Mam.'

'Huh! What?'

'He's going to night-school. He's doing business studies. He wants to get out as much as I do.'

'For God's sake, Ellie, shut your mouth for once and open your eyes instead.'

She'd been wearing a pale blue cotton dress with white spots on, and she'd felt like the sky with a waspy belt on. As the sea wind blew over Caldy Hill, they rested their love-lorn, aching eyes on the grey Atlantic. Their picnic was ham sandwiches with mustard and crumbly fruit cake, everything smelling ever so slightly of petrol because the bike was playing up. It was all so vast, then. The possibilities and the hopes were all so vast, then.

'I haven't got my johnnies with me, Elle. I didn't think I'd need them.'

'Take a chance, Malc. Take it out, it's a safe time of the month.'

'We can't risk it. I don't want to do that to you, you're so precious to me.' And Malc had almost been crying.

She'd pulled at the St Christopher he'd worn round his neck, the back of his white shirt billowed. Oh God and they'd both been frantic.

And afterwards they'd walked down by the shore, passing all the big houses on the edge of the golf-links. Malc skimmed a stone out across the water. 'One day, Elle, I swear to you, one day . . .'

When they got home in the evening Lily Freeman was lying down in the street outside number nine with a small crowd of disapproval gathered round her.

'They've taken Arthur away again,' sniffed Freda when Ellie got back indoors, swilling the brown teapot with self-righteous energy. 'It's a pity they don't shut him up for good, him and the rest of that filthy lot.'

The Hung Toa waiter hovers intrusively and Ellie wonders if they are doing something oddly. 'We've waited long enough for this moment, haven't we?' she asks Malc now.

'That's why I'm so determined to make it happen.'

'Perhaps we had to go through what we have, maybe that had to happen. I sometimes think that before all this we had lost ourselves. I used to sit and look at you and feel like a total stranger. D'you know what I mean, Malc? And did you sometimes feel that way, too?'

'This could all have happened much earlier. We would have made it if we hadn't gone and crippled ourselves . . .'

'But that's all done with now.'

'Is it, Elle?'

'Of course it is. There are just the two of us now. Nobody else to think about but you and me, nothing to hold us back any more.'

Ellie is almost breathless because the conversation has

taken this unexpected, intimate turn. She feels like a young girl again, almost embarrassed by it, likely to blush. Malc has escaped and she's frightened about what he might say. She has trapped a spider against the sofa and she doesn't know which way it's going to run.

'But we've both changed.' He sounds perplexed.

'Of course we have changed. We are twenty years older and we've been through the mill together. Think of all those ups and downs, but we've triumphed, Malc, and now we're coming out the other side.'

'You make it sound simple. Easy.'

'I know it's not easy. I know that you're working very hard and I can imagine the kind of strain you must be under.'

'But I'm not under a strain. The strain seems to have gone.'

Yes, it's just Ellie who's under a strain, watching for him and worrying.

'I worry,' she says. 'I still worry.'

'With the children gone perhaps you haven't got enough to fill your head. Still doing that same old job every day, still pandering to that bloody daft Gogh woman. Maybe you should look for something else now, Elle, in case this all goes wrong. Maybe you should grab the chance and find something to throw yourself into.' She is shaken by his gentle manner. And it's not just his voice, his face is gentle, too. It's a long time since she's seen that expression.

'I don't need to do that, Malc. You have always been my life, you and the kids, you know that.'

'You were always full of the things you'd like to do. You were for ever going on about how you'd like to join the drama club and the choral society, but that you had too much to do and were too tired and anyway we didn't have the cash. Well, now, with things taking a turn for the better you've got the chance. Why not take it?'

Because I don't want to be on my own, I want us to do things together.

'I was thinking it might be nice if we could find an interest we could share.'

'It's not like that for me, Elle. I haven't got any spare time at the moment, I never know what I'm going to be doing of an evening – and I don't want you to be always waiting for me to get home.'

Oh?

'Well, if we move, if we buy a house, that is something we'd be sharing. The house and the garden and the furnishing of it.'

'I don't think a new house is ever going to mean so much to me as it will to you.'

'I can remember a time when buying a house was important to you, Malc, one of the most important things in your life.'

'For the family, yes, for the children, but that part of our life is all over now.'

'That part's over, but there's a hell of a lot left. We've got years still, Malc, and we want a nice place that we can enjoy together!' Why is she having to remind him of this? And what Malc used to say about Chinese food is quite right, Ellie doesn't like it. She'd rather have popped into Tesco on the way home and bought a nice piece of steak. She would have made a tasty, thick onion gravy.

'I am not saying we don't, I'm just trying to say that I don't think it can ever be something I'll want to take a big part in.'

'You really love this job, don't you, Malc?' Funny, she's never quite realised this before, and it's something she hadn't anticipated, either. Didn't she want him to enjoy his job then, the job she's given him, *the job she's paying for?* She stares at his hands and is shocked to see how clean they are, and how his nails have grown; they are not chipped at the ends and grimy any more. He has nice hands.

He looks even better in this grey suit than he'd looked in that first brown one. Malc is not frightened by any of this! How very extraordinary. Malc is not frightened at all!

And now he is telling her, 'Next Thursday and Friday we have to go to London to talk to a firm of importers. Murphy and Ramon are keen for you to come, but I said I didn't know how you'd feel about that. I told them you'd never liked London.'

'What about you, do you want me to come?' Ellie attempts to keep her voice casual.

'I don't mind either way, but you might find it a little bit daunting and boring, all this Canonwaits talk. It's going to be fairly intensive. Still it's up to you, Ellie. I told them I'd ask you.'

'What sort of people are they? Where will we stay, and what do you think they'll want me to wear? What would I say – I don't know them!'

'That's okay, I'll tell them no.'

'Don't do that! I do want to come but . . .'

'Not if it's all going to be a great fuss.'

'No! No, it won't be a fuss. I'll have to buy something new and see if I can get in for a perm. I can get the shopping done if we get back in time on the Saturday, but don't worry, they'll fit me in if I say it's urgent . . . and London'll be nice in the spring with all the blossom out . . .'

Dare she go to the bank and withdraw some money in order to buy something really smart, or should she wait till she gets to London? But Malc is not listening. He has turned away, and Ellie is left chatting to a rather bored, Albert Finney profile.

When they finally get up to leave she discovers the hem of her skirt has come down and she's trailing white thread behind her.

13

She cannot complain that circumstances are drifting along without change. Changes are taking place frighteningly quickly; sometimes Ellie feels they are happening so fast she can't grasp them.

Malc has given up smoking. He has thrown away his tin, leaving Ellie anxiously dragging away at her forty Silk Cut. And the worst thing about that is that it was Malc who gave Ellie that starter puff in the first place.

Now Ellie has her million she doesn't feel quite so guilty about squandering money on ciggies.

And another thing. It was on the train journey going to London that she glanced down at his feet and realised that Malc was not the sort of man you could give reindeer socks to any more. They all had breakfast on the train . . . she and Murphy, Ramon and Malc. It was incredible, biting your British rail sausage while you watched the world flash by. A pale blue sky arched the land, the rivers were silken ribbons, and the tiny cars and lorries that moved at a slower pace than the train seemed to flow through the stillness of an eternity.

She had to ask for sauce because they didn't provide it, only mustard and she didn't want that . . . not with breakfast. The dining car was a non-smoker. The whole of the journey took place in a non-smoker, and Ellie had to squeeze in the odd fag under cover of going to the toilet. Well, she didn't want Ramon or Murphy to know she was that desperate. It was only when she went to sit down again that she realised they must have known why she'd gone, because she hadn't clicked the lock which informed the whole carriage that the toilet was engaged. That's if they were that interested . . . which she supposed they were probably not.

The three men had a lot to read and a lot to talk about. Ellie slid through *Woman's Own*, and filled in a puzzle book she'd bought on the platform at Lime Street.

London – so much paler than Liverpool, quite wraithlike really, when you compare the two. Not so substantial, not so wise, not so wounded. Just like the people. They check in at the Curzon Hotel, climbing over coachloads of skiers in shiny red and white anoraks who pepper the hotel steps in order to reach the foyer. And when they get to their room she discovers that it is a non-smoker, too, with a plaque on the door sponsored by the British Lung Foundation.

'Take no bloody notice of that,' says Malc, wrestling with the window which takes all his strength to shift it. 'If you want to smoke, you smoke. This window has not been open since this hotel was built,' he complains, sweating as he tries to budge it, and they are both breathless from the incredible heat which sears your throat and parches your mouth so you are forced into buying little drinks from the fridge under the dressing table.

No wonder people wander round with hardly anything on. You can't wear nice woollies, thinks Ellie, if you live in London. You'd have to stick to blouses and cardigans which you could put on and take off easily.

In the afternoon, while the men have a meeting, Ellie goes shopping. She strolls around seeing things she would like but is unable to buy because of her self-imposed circumstances. London pavements are harder than Liverpool ones. She would like to have been with somebody else, especially when she stops for a cup of coffee and a sandwich. She is not used to passing time. She feels so uneasy sitting here on her own that she brings out her puzzle book and pretends to do some but she feels too lonely to concentrate. And she discovers that she is sitting at a no-smoking table.

This is silly, she thinks to herself, pushing aside her great need. Everything is working out exactly as I planned, so why do I feel so miserable? She sits and she waits for the coffee to seep though the holes in that ridiculous manner – it will be cold before she gets her mouth to it – and she thinks that her loneliness has something to do with keeping such a huge secret to herself. It forms a big part of her now, so it is something that, really, she ought to be sharing. But how can she?

She passes a hairdresser's and is tempted – she's not satisfied with what they have done at Shirley's. She hadn't come out with what she'd wanted . . . they hadn't changed her enough, no, not at all. Ellie walks in, and backs straight out when she sees the prices.

Eventually she buys a newpaper and returns, defeated, to lie on her hotel bed. She turns on the telly, feeling a failure and wondering why.

Perhaps she shouldn't have come.

That night they dine in splendour. Ellie wears a dress she's bought in Lendels which cost her £250! Buying it, spending that amount on a dress had actually made her feel sick. She'd had to rest in the ladies powder room afterwards. Malc had given her £50 – he might know about redwood shutters, revolving gazebos and men's suits, but he doesn't know much about women's clothes. She had meant to stick to the fifty, but there'd been nothing in the cocktail department in Lendels anywhere near that amount.

She'd been very careful to throw away the receipt.

It is a simple dress in a black, filmy material with a V going down to her waist at the back and a high, rounded neck with black beads in it which form the shape of delicate petals. To her horror, it doesn't look as if anyone else in the restaurant is wearing an expensive dress. And yet, in some peculiar way, they look as if they've spent more than she has. Ellie just can't figure it out. Here they are, these London women, in skirts with white petticoats showing and fairly simple blouses and yet . . . is it her jewellery that lets her down, or her hair, or her make-up? Miserably she toys with her food, trying to see where it is in the gloom of the candle, trying to work things out. It's not fair. And when Ramon, in a velvet jacket and bow-tie, says, quite sincerely, 'Smashing! Say, man . . . we're dining with the prettiest lady in town tonight,' Ellie does not feel pleased at all. She just wishes he hadn't said anything, partly because of the way she feels and partly because she's noticed that Malc hasn't commented.

It is so much easier for men, somehow. Well Malc looks fine, he looks as if he's been born to the life in his suit and his bright white shirt and his dull gold cufflinks. Even his hair

104

seems to fit, it is successful hair, and she sees that it has a lot to do with the way you carry yourself, how pleased with yourself you are. Well, Malc is obviously pleased with himself, and isn't this exactly what she's wanted?

Surely Malc's success is Ellie's achievement tonight?

They change the conversation from business to pleasure just because she is with them. She knows very well they'd have talked business if she had not been here and that they'd have preferred it; exciting things are happening, very exciting things.

They keep asking her questions politely and politely, she answers. Oh, it is all so stiff and formal, not at all like that first time at Nelson Street. But is this because she's so nervous . . . in this alien environment, trying so hard to please? She realises this, and yet can do nothing about it.

She fixes the smile on her face. She sees the shiny end of her nose and tries to hide her rough red hands.

She sits and she sweats, she eats and she drinks, and then her tummy makes threatening sounds, the pain making her clutch the sides of her chair. She'll have to go to the loo . . . and she might be there for hours. Oh no God oh no God oh no!

'Ellie? Are you okay?'

How she hates Malc for asking. 'Yes, I'll just have to disappear for a moment.' She tries to giggle in a feminine manner but the sound that comes out is more of a hoarse, throaty cry. 'I'll just go and powder my nose.' And she seems to lumber off, blindly through the darkness, and has to ask that snooty waiter where the lavatory is. His eyes slide off her in pain.

She sits on the loo, weeping, spraying expensive scent in the air in case other women coming in and out might be too disgusted to stay, and somehow recognise her when she goes back inside, point her out to their companions, telling them, 'That's the one!' She longs for Margot or Di, Margot's firmly determined chest and Di's comforting floppy one. How they'd laugh if they could see her, how they'll shriek with laughter when she tells them how her posh London meal has gone! But they are two hundred miles away and yet they feel much further than that.

On the Friday, alone again, she makes for the park. The Canonwaits meetings are going well, 'And today we'll clinch it,' says Ramon, tucking into a terrifying breakfast which they have to eat because Malc says, 'We've already paid for it.' And Ellie feels the same way about that.

'We'll import larger quantities at half the prices we're paying at the moment,' says Ramon, still in his velvet jacket. The skiers have disappeared in the night and now the hotel is filled with Japanese tourists carrying raincoats, binoculars, airline bags and umbrellas.

'Go and see something worthwhile while you're here. Go to a gallery or a museum, or how about the Turner Collection? You always said how you'd love to see that,' urges Malc.

'It's a pity we're not here another day and then we could have gone together,' says Ellie wistfully.

And then they are gone and so, mysteriously, is everybody else in the hotel. Alone and wandering about like this she sticks out like a sore thumb, so she picks up a handful of brochures listlessly and starts to read them upstairs in her room. When the chambermaids come in with a trolley she decides to go to the park.

London people aren't ashamed of begging. Ellie clutches her handbag close to her and carefully skirts around them. She's seen them on telly, begging like that and she knows that they sleep under boxes at night. She would be able to help them without even noticing the difference. Perhaps she should go to the bank and draw out a cool fifty thousand, put it in a suitcase and go round distributing it to right and to left.

She'd be liked, if she did that. People would think her important.

And she'd feel important, too, and worthwhile.

She looks directly into a young woman's face and sees the shadows of Lil in it. Giving Lil money would not have helped her at all. Having money makes difficult things easier, but it is not satisfactory in itself. You have to earn it. You have to feel worthy of it. Giving someone an interest, or a talent, or some love they'd lost, now that would be better than handing out money. Nevertheless, when she is 'openly' rich she will give beggars money because you have to have it first in order to work things out. Money is what they want and who is Ellie Freeman to decide for them?

It is pleasantly warm; the sun is shining and the pavements are dappled by railings.

London roads are difficult to cross.

And she doesn't even have bread with her, nothing to feed to the birds.

The girl who comes to sit beside her looks no older than twelve, but she must be, because she is obviously the mother of that baby. She gets it out from its cover, she dangles it on her knee.

'How old is she?' asks Ellie, eager for some conversation.

'Six months.' Obligated to speak, the girl is thin with enormous eyes and long, stringy blond hair. Her boots are scruffy and worn.

'You look far too young to be a mother.' It is out of her mouth before Ellie can prevent it.

'I'm nearly eighteen.' The girl delves into her handbag and brings out a grimy-looking rattle. The infant's eyes light up. 'You're from Liverpool,' says the girl dully. 'I know that accent.'

'Yes, and I don't know London very well. I came here to find some peace and quiet,' Ellie lies, because it is not really peace and quiet she is after. The child gurgles and Ellie leans over to admire it. 'I used to take mine to the park when they were tiny, but ours was a much smaller park, more of a bombsite, really, with old stones and ruins poking up through the grass, not all smart and green like this one.'

'Looks aren't anything. This one's covered in dog turds,' says the girl.

'Yes,' continues Ellie, 'I used to stay out for as long as I could, giving the kids some fresh air in an afternoon before going back to get the tea.'

'You were married then?' says the girl, without interest.

'Yes. Aren't you?'

'Why would I be?'

There is no need for the girl to go on the defensive, not with Ellie. There are enough girls around about Nelson

Street who get themselves in the family way without a man to stand by them for Ellie to know all about that.

'It's easier, with a man. You have to struggle so hard if you're on your own.' Ellie, with nothing better to do, is eager to bestow her sympathy.

The girl sniffs her dissent. 'I get much more help on my own, and they gave me a flat. If I'd married I'd be really stuck, and having to run round some useless sod cleaning and cooking and such like. No,' and she licks a tissue and wipes the baby's milky mouth with it, 'I chose to have Apricot and I chose to stay single. I won't have a man move in with me. For a start they piss all over the place and make the toilet seat messy.'

'What did the father feel about that? Did he want to move in with you and get married?'

'I didn't stop to ask him. I had the baby, it's my body, isn't it? All he did was push and grunt, that's the only part he took in it.'

Ellie is swamped with sadness. She remembers Malc, 'I'll take care of you, I'll never leave you. We're all right together, Elle, you and me, and the kid.'

And her mother again, 'Tramp! Fool! Idiot! There's no room here!'

'All our plans, Malc.'

'One more mouth won't make much difference. It'll only be a little one.' He had held her hand and pressed his own lightly on her stomach. 'We'll get married as soon as we can get the banns read.'

'But where will we live?'

'It'll have to be back home just for now, but it won't take us long to get out.'

Number nine! The scourge of the street! That awful, drunken woman and the shifty-eyed lout of a man. They had married before Mandy was born and Ellie had moved in. It was the evenings when Malc was at night-school that had been so impossible. Often he came home and found her weeping.

'Women do get depressed when they're pregnant,' he said reassuringly. 'I've read all about that.'

108

She used to whine, 'It's just that it's so horrid being here without you, three whole nights a week. What with Lil sitting there glassy-eyed and Arthur shouting his mouth off about this and that and knowing that I can't go home and we haven't got enough money for me to go to the flicks with June.'

'I know it's difficult,' said Malc, 'but it's worth it. We've got to be patient and think about the future.'

'Perhaps you should take a break – just for a little while. Maybe you could pick up the course again after the baby's born.'

'That's not so easy. The places are hard to get and I've only six monthes to go until the exams.'

Oh, she'd been so young, so weak, and so childishly needy! Not at all like this positive child, coping so easily, so sure of herself, sitting on the park seat beside her. When Malc was at home he dealt with Arthur easily, exchanged curse for curse, was bigger and stronger. And he had a sweet way with his mother, too. He was used to her illness, Ellie supposes. He wasn't frightened by it as she was.

She was frightened of having a baby, too.

He brought home his wages from Watt & Wyatt but they only paid for the basics, they never actually got them anywhere! And then there were baby things to buy, and the room really ought to be decorated. Ellie didn't want her first child to be brought up in a slum.

'Don't come moaning to me,' said Freda. 'I warned you!'

Pigeons are scratching around on the path. 'What did your mother say when you decided to go it alone? I bet she's worried about you, isn't she?' Ellie feels ridiculously old, out of touch and inadequate.

'It was nothing to do with her. I'm my own person,' says the girl, giving a thin little smile.

'And won't the child miss out, never knowing its father?'

'I doubt that, very much.'

'And what about money? Getting a job? That must be difficult for you. They don't pay very much . . .'

'Well, I wasn't ever going to be a model, was I, or a company director, or an advertising executive. I'd have been lucky to get work as a ticket collector on British Rail. I didn't get any exams, I didn't bother with school. I just larked about. That's what me and my friends did.'

'But surely it's never too late.'

'What do you know about it?' says the girl, just a little bit angry and Ellie realises she has gone too far. After all, this is none of her business. 'It's all right for people like you,' says the girl, 'come here visiting, staying in skyscraper hotels, pottering along to the park for an airing in between the shopping.'

'It's not like that for me,' says Ellie. 'It's never been like that for me.'

'Well it SOUNDS as if it has,' says the girl, getting up to go. 'That's just what it sounds like. It's time people like you dragged yourselves into the present! Men aren't the answer to everything in life, you know, and nor is money.'

WHAT IS, Ellie feels like screaming! If you know, then for Christ's sake tell me. Instead she crosses her legs and her arms and starts scanning the distance, not wanting the girl to think her so needy, or so poor.

'Here,' says the girl unexpectedly, turning round and offering Ellie a paper bag. 'I haven't the time to be sitting around any longer. Feed this to the birds. It's part of what people do when they come to London. *Don't you even know that?*'

So Ellie sits there and does so.

And then, around about teatime, she wanders back to the hotel.

14

'So it wasn't really my fault that Malc stopped going to nightschool. It was just that everything suddenly got so difficult, and we could never have known that there wouldn't be a second opportunity, nor that he'd change so much that he just stopped wanting to improve himself.' Ellie tells Robert Beasely this during their August meeting. Nearly a year has gone by since her big win and they are sitting outside in the sunshine, at trestle tables beside the river. Dragonflies skim the silvery surface, and old yoghurt cartons and pieces of torn clothing cling to the weeping branches of the willows where they touch the water.

Has Ellie been trying to buy her way out of guilt, an old, knotted guilt all hard and horny inside her? But it was Malc who decided to give up the classes, wasn't it – not she.

She flaps at herself with the menu, against the flies and against the heat. A trapped wasp buzzes in an old coke bottle on the table. Someone has screwed a twist of cardboard down the neck to keep it in. She pulls out the cardboard, drops in her fag end and it sizzles in the moisture next to the wasp. Should she rescue it or shouldn't she? 'And I just can't tell you what a relief it is to be able to come here and explain how things are, to let someone know how I feel and be able to talk about it!'

Robert Beasely is sympathetic. 'I'm glad you feel that way, Ellie. That's what I'm here for, not only to help with the money. It was obvious that there would be problems, but I must admit that my greatest concern when you first spoke to me was believing that Malcolm would make it. He didn't sound much of a proposition, not from what you first told me. Did you ever consider what you'd do if it all went wrong? What would you have done about the pools win if the company had failed, say, or worse than that, if Malcolm had failed?'

'I suppose I would have had to confess in the end, and he wouldn't have been too pleased about that, I can tell you. But it isn't like that at all, is it?'

'No, certainly it isn't.'

Christ, and it's true what they say about money making money. Ellie stares at her accounts with bulging eyes. Robert says, 'And it'll continue to grow like that while you're managing it wisely.'

'It just all seems too easy!'

'I don't think it has been particularly easy. Not for you.'

It is a relief that Robert understands. Sitting here with him like this her burden feels lighter. She has money and she is building it up sensibly, making plans for herself and her husband's future. Robert has never looked at her as if he's thinking she's worthless, or second-rate, or a failure.

'Would you come to our house-warming if I invited you?'

'Well, of course I would come. I would be honoured to be invited.'

'I wonder if I'll ever be able to invite you to anything. I wonder if I'll ever even tell Malc what has happened. And what about Bella, would she come, too?'

'I am certain she would,' Robert smiles, 'but I'd have to ask her. She has her work and I have mine.'

'Work?' A shadow moves over the water, and the dull pewter rushes more urgently over the stones. The wasp makes one more frantic bid for freedom before falling on its back in the purple dregs at the base of the bottle. Ellie picks at the label while she waits for his answer.

'Yes, I'd never have known you, never have become a part of all this if it hadn't been for my work.'

'I feel the same way about you, you know, as I feel about my friends,' she confides.

'Well, that's nice. That's just how it ought to be – and I'm glad.'

'Malc uses Barclays. He asked Murphy which bank was the best and Murphy recommended you.'

'I know nothing about Malcolm's account.'

Ellie picks at her ploughman's platter. Already, in this hot sunshine, the cheese has gone dry. 'What if he called in and asked for your advice? What if we had to come and see the bank manager together, that would be interesting.'

'Malc's account is not a joint one, and neither is yours so the chances of that happening are negligible. And if Malcolm wanted my advice, well then, I'd arrange a meeting, have him in and give it.'

'So you wouldn't feel uneasy with that, knowing what you know? Knowing so much about him and working for me, as it were?'

'I work for many people, Ellie, and in my job you get to know many secrets.'

'Yes, yes, I suppose you must do.'

Ellie likes to feel she's special to Robert. She's always felt important and interesting in Robert's eyes.

'You'd better tell me about your new house, if I'm not going to be able to see it.'

So she tells him quite truthfully how she hadn't been able to prevent herself from feeling just slightly disappointed. Malc didn't want to overdo it, stretch himself too far. 'I don't want to raise your hopes and then have them dashed,' he told her when he brought home the brochures.

'We don't want anything too large and unmanageable. You've got to be able to put your feet up, that's an important factor,' said Malc. He seemed to have set his heart on a bungalow, but Ellie still dreamed about those Georgian houses in the library square. How long would it take them to reach her dream going at this pace? But how could she ask him that?

So they'd gone to view. There'd been many times when she'd made appointments with agents and then had to cancel because Malc rang and said he was sorry but he couldn't get home. While Ellie waited she started gathering stuff together ready for the removal, ancient stuff packed away in the outhouse and the attic; the Freemans had never been a family for throwing things away. Most of the items were broken and useless, anything good and unnecessary would have quickly been sold.

But she had found her old gramophone. She had come across it one Wednesday morning when she'd decided to devote the whole day to the enterprise – yes, she still worked for Mrs Gogh at Funorama . . . but not for much longer now. Just seeing it there under a roll of old carpet like that had made her heart ache. It was more real, more like seeing herself as a girl, than any of those cracked black and white photographs. She couldn't even remember putting it up there. Carefully cradling it she'd brought it downstairs, along with the old 45 record case. It had the same, slightly tacky smell. Would it still work? Had a battery been carelessly left inside, might it be ruined and mouldy?

She'd prised off the back with trembling fingers. Empty. Clean as a whistle. And then she'd hurried up to the corner shop for the batteries, almost running in her haste, in her urgency to settle down on her own and play some of those old songs again.

She sat on the floor beside it, slid the first record down the stem, heard the primitive clack that she'd thought so sophisticated at the time, and prepared herself to listen. *Carolina Moon.* Crackly and tinny and breaking her heart.

Baby Love; Crying in the Chapel; King of the Road; The Carnival is Over; A Whiter Shade of Pale. They stopped around about 1968 . . . the year she and Malc got married, the year Mandy was born – music and all that kind of thing seemed to have stopped for her then. Well, they hadn't the money to go buying records, they hadn't the time and, she supposes, they hadn't those wild, yearning feelings any more.

All day she swam in a wonderland of forgotten emotion. Nothing else mattered but the music and trying to find something, trying to get back. She wondered whether to leave the gramophone out for when Malc got home; he might be interested in spending an evening sitting listening to old songs and reminiscing. They could open a bottle of wine, perhaps, and pore over the photographs.

But she decided against it and put it away for another day when she could listen alone.

'Shouldn't we stay in the area? Do we really want to live out in the country?' she'd asked him. The panic gripped her heart, squeezed it out like an old floorcloth.

'Of course we do. Haven't we always longed for green

spaces, dreamed of getting out of the town? And we can't afford anywhere nice nearer in.'

Ellie considered this move to be temporary, but it was important for Malc's self-esteem that she acted thrilled.

They settled on a bungalow on a new estate at Heswall, and Malc joked, 'The right side of the river at last, eh gel?' It was built out of natural stone and had an oval church window above the porch and a windmill with a bucket on a chain over the goldfish pond on the front bit of lawn. It was easy for Malc to commute from there. He wasn't a rep any more, had only done that for a few months and last month he'd moved to a suite of offices in the city centre. Ellie had wanted to help with the move but Murphy told her it wouldn't look good for it to be done in an amateur way. Canonwaits were using Pickfords.

They took photographs of the house and showed them to Di and Dave, Margot and Dick the next time they went to the club. They rarely went there any more, once a month at the most and Ellie, who never dreamed she would miss it , missed it terribly.

'It's just habit,' said Malc. 'You never liked it, you always complained.'

'We'll never see you, living out there,' objected Di. Everything else might be changing but Di wasn't. She was still bulky and coarse, fiercely direct, downing the rum and cokes as if there was no tomorrow. Di still worked fulltime in the hospital catering department and Margot was still at the shirt factory, so during the day there was going to be no chance for any of them to meet.

'You won't come here any more,' prophesied Margot. 'Why would you bother to drive out here? You wouldn't be able to drink for a start and it's hardly the Ritz.' They all knew that it wasn't the Ritz and Ellie heard the hurt in Margot's voice.

'Perhaps you will come and stay with us at weekends. There'll be plenty of room, there's two spare bedrooms.' Ellie was frightened by the note of desperation she heard in her own voice. 'And when I can drive I'll come over and we'll be able to go shopping on a Saturday. Or other than that I can get here by train.'

But they had never gone shopping together on a Saturday, and they all knew that very well.

They hadn't taken the jeep that night. They'd walked, as they normally did. Perhaps they didn't need to flaunt Malc's success any more. In a strange sort of way, without agreeing to it between themselves, they had started to play it down.

But that way felt worse, more devious – patronising?

What were the men saying to each other over there at the bar? What were they exchanging, what were they swapping? It was as secret and baffling to Ellie as it had always been and she could hear Malc's voice rising importantly. Whatever he was saying was leaving Dick and Dave most impressed, because they stared at their feet with their chins down while he was talking, in the way men do when they're listening intently, their glasses protectively against their chests. Giving him space.

'We'll have to have a farewell party,' Di said brightly in order to cover the silence and filling as much space as she could with her loud voice and her bag of crisps. 'We can't let you go without a bang.'

Oh, how Ellie wished she could tell Di and Margot the truth.

The photographs of the bungalow were pink and blue like the Leggets' holiday snaps; they smiled glossily and rather slyly. Why do people take pink and blue photographs? So they can never forget? Shouldn't that decision be left to the memory where the colours are surely truer? They were lying on the table getting stained. Ellie happily left them there. Oh, if only they'd bought a Georgian house by the library none of this would have had to happen, all of this would have been different.

They moved house – well, Ellie moved house, Malc couldn't get away. He'd had to fly up to Glasgow so Ellie had made the removal men tea, travelled to Heswall in the van and told them where to put the few old pieces of furniture they'd agreed to take with them. They left quite a bit behind. Malc went round the Nelson Street house with a notepad, making a list and striking off anything that wasn't worth the trouble.

Margot said, 'It's one of the most disturbing things that can happen to you after death and divorce.'

Everything's changed.

Now Malc takes Ellie in every day except Wednesday, and on Wednesdays, if she has to meet Robert, she catches the train into town. She is learning to drive in the evenings, and as soon as she's passed her test Malc is going to buy her a second-hand car. Next week she is going to have to hand in her notice to Mrs Gogh who knows something strange is going on but, so far, hasn't mentioned it.

The hot sun sears the top of her head. Robert returns with more drinks in his hand, slopping them as he crosses the road; the ice has already half-melted. He sits down opposite. He wears a short-sleeved blue shirt but he keeps his tie on and his jacket is in the car. It is odd to see his naked arm, it has little blond hairs on it and it is freckled. 'It must have been strange leaving Nelson Street.'

Strange? Was that the accurate word for leaving the area in which she'd been born and brought up, for abandoning the house she had kept clean and lived in for twenty years? Almost empty, stripped naked like that, she'd had to leave it with such a forlorn, lonely feel about it. She hadn't been able to look back when the van moved away and the removal man told her that people often felt like that. Yes, Ellie supposes she could call it strange, but then, was there anything in her life now which was not strange?

'Yes, it was a bit of a wrench.'

'How are you liking it over in Heswall?'

'I can't get used to the silence.' Ellie shreds a lettuce leaf.

'You will,' says Robert sensibly. 'In time. You will find things to get yourself involved in once you've given up work. I can't imagine you being content with nothing to do all day. You've always said how you'd hate that.'

What things? What sort of activities could she get involved in? Ellie's mind is a total blank and she can't imagine, now, what she ever thought she would do all day, given her precious freedom. And yet she used to know, once, didn't she? She used to dream – once. She doesn't know anyone in Heswall and Malc's never home to go out with her. Bebington's not far from Heswall but she notices that Robert does not suggest she contact Bella; he's not offering his wife as a stepping stone or an open doorway into this strange new world. Ellie knows that Bella works, running creative writing courses for prisoners, sex offenders and the like. Bella's a busy woman with probably no time to go visiting.

Ellie can't keep moaning, sounding spoilt and dissatisfied when she's achieving all she set out to achieve and it's all going faster than anyone dreamed.

She pulls herself together. 'I'm just a little bit bewildered by it all, I suppose,' she tells him firmly. 'It will all settle down in time, once I get used to it.'

'It hasn't worked out quite as you imagined it would, Ellie, has it?'

And it is the gentleness in his voice that causes Ellie to burst into tears.

15

New bedroom, new dressing table, new view out of the window across the meadows and over the roofs of the little red farms. *New man.*

She's heard once that love isn't love at all, it is envy. You only love someone you would secretly like to be, or someone who has the traits you'd like for yourself . . . there is so much for you to admire that you give up feeling jealous, Ellie supposes, and it turns into love. Just like that.

Certainly there are aspects of Malc which she envies now. His adaptability, for one, the ease with which he chats to the Williams, their new next-door neighbours, the confident manner with which he treats the pushy furniture salesman in Baring & Willow when they go to purchase the contents of their new home. And his energy, all of a sudden! Where on earth has that come from? He's taken to playing squash with someone called Jarvis, from work, on a Saturday afternoon. Ellie warned him, 'Be careful, you're not as young as you were and squash can be dangerous.'

'You ought to take more exercise, Elle. It makes you feel so good afterwards.' And he smacked his hardening stomach with pride.

But Ellie can't breathe from the smoking.

He isn't content to slump in front of the telly any more; he's either at work or in the garden, digging away there as if he's trying to fork something heavy out of his system.

She lures him indoors with shouts of 'Tea, Malc? Coffee?' He scrapes the mud off his boots and, placidly, he comes.

When he returns to the garden she goes into the sewing room . . . the room that doubles up as a dining room only they don't need a dining room for the two of them . . . and hems some more curtains on her ancient Singer.

It is hard to find dirt in the new bungalow. You can search and search and not find it. 'But it must be here,' she mutters to no one in particular as she moves round the house with a dustpan and brush. 'It can't have just disappeared.'

Sometimes, of a Sunday, having sought yet failed to find it again, she unfolds one of their new garden chairs and sits on the lawn to watch Malc. A mouth-watering smell wafts from Ellie's new oven, but Malc had said earlier, 'It's far too hot for roast potatoes and lamb. Why don't we have a nice fresh salad for a change?' She always gets a joint, well she always made sure they had a joint, even in the leanest times.

'He's ever so nice, isn't he?'

'Sorry?' Ellie is disturbed in her dreamings as Maria Williams' head pops over the garden fence. She lowers her new sunglasses and stares against the glare.

'Your other half! What a pleasant, friendly man. And what a difference he's making in that garden!'

'We've never had a garden before.' She transfers her fag to her other hand and lets it rest, out of sight, on the grass. Malc will be annoyed. He hates stubs, they fluff up like snow when he cuts the lawn and they clog up the blades of the mower. Ellie doesn't know whether to get up and go over or whether to stay sitting down, hardly able to hear and having to shout. She doesn't want to be thought of as pushy, and she doesn't know if she really wants to get too familiar with the neighbours. It wasn't wise, of late, in Nelson Street.

'Why don't you pop over and have a swim and a glass of fresh lemonade? Then we can have a chat and get to know each other.'

Well! That's a shock!

She knows where her costume is. It's in the bottom drawer of her new built-in wardrobe, so old that the seat has worn silvery thin and it smells of mothballs. With the sun behind it you can see right through it. The last time she'd worn it was during the years she plodded along regularly to the Alvington Baths to teach Mandy and Kev to swim. When they'd gone to Harlech on holiday she'd borrowed one of Di's and the top had fallen down in the waves.

Malc's already been over to the Williams'. He's on easy, chatting terms with Maria and pale, spindly Wilfred, and last weekend Maria gave him some of her home-made ginger cobs to try.

'She's nice,' Malc came and told her then. 'You'd get on well with Maria. You'd like her.'

Normally it was always Ellie who made the first approaches and who found friends first. Ellie realises that she needs to know people; it is essential that she makes some friends to counter these feelings of isolation and she doesn't want to be totally dependent on Malc. So this is her chance. It is very important that she succeeds.

Maria is brown and sinewy, athletic and healthy with a fresh, open smile. Her ash-blonde hair is held back from her face with a black and white spotted bow. She wears flowing African prints when she is out in her garden. In the evenings, when they think that no one can see them, Maria and Wilfred swim in their swimming pool naked. Wilfred put the pool in himself, carting all the concrete round the side of the house in a wheelbarrow.

Word has it that Maria, who owns a boutique in Heswall High Street, is having an affair. Ellie overheard that bit of gossip while queuing at the butcher's last Wednesday, and it was also suggested in the same whispered conversation that the Williams' barbecues weren't straightforward picnics at all, but wife-swapping parties.

When she told Malc that he said, 'So what? As long as they don't interfere with us.'

'I don't feel like swimming, but I don't mind trying your lemonade.' And that doesn't come out in the pleasant way Ellie meant it. 'I'll just tell Malc where I've gone in case he wants me.'

'Oh,' says Maria Williams with a gleaming smile, 'ask Malc to come too. The more the merrier!'

Malc says he's too busy, he has to finish the roses, so Ellie finds herself sitting under a green and white striped umbrella beside the startling blue of the Williams' pool.

'I hope you've settled in.' Maria's glass jug has fishes and reeds cut into the sides. And the glasses match.

'It's surprising how long it takes to get everything right.'

'Well, we've been here five years and we're still not

121

straight.' But Ellie knows that Maria Williams is lying. Lots of people talk like that . . . say they're not straight when they are, say they're busy when they're not or that they can't cope when they obviously can. Touching wood. Everything around here is straight, or cut into perfect circles like that little flowerbed, or in line, like those white plastic urns. Out of the corner of her eye she can see that through the french window, the lounge is one of the straightest lounges she has ever seen . . . even down to the *TV Times* and *Radio Times* which sit on the exact centre of that low round table. A bowl full of dried flowers decorates the empty stone fireplace.

Too clean. Too sterile? It is unusual for a couple this age not to have children, but of course Ellie does not ask because there might be a sad reason.

'We were worried about who might buy it. The Mattinglys were such nice people.'

Ellie says, 'Well, that's natural, I suppose, the bungalows being so close like this.' And then she feels she ought to defend herself, prove to Maria that she and Malc are acceptable. 'We live very quietly,' she decides to say. And then she remembers the barbecues, 'And we're easygoing people.'

'Well, that's nice,' says Maria, flashing another bright smile.

'Home has always been very important to Malc and me.'

'And you used to live . . . ?'

'Down Nelson Street, on the edge of the docks. We were there for twenty years. It's our anniversary next month.'

Maria gives a short laugh. 'You're going to find living here very different.'

'I am discovering that already.'

'And Malc? How is he settling in?' Maria's limbs glisten with Ambre Solaire.

'Well, he's not at home much now, because of his work.' Maria raises her careful blonde eyebrows so Ellie has a chance to explain, and she ought to love this part, the praising and the boasting, but funnily enough this perfect opportunity isn't how she's imagined it. She's tempted to dwell on the darker side of life, she's tempted to exaggerate the seamy side of life on Nelson Street, the poverty times, the humiliating times of unpaid bills and scratching about for the last penny so the kids could order their Atlases, or their mapping pens, or that extra French which had seemed so important at the time.

She doesn't give into temptation, though. She sticks to the sort of conversation Maria is keen to have ... the kind of conversation one ought to have while sitting at a pool-side.

And anyway, Maria knows all about it already. 'They featured that company in *The Post* last week. Wilfred read a bit out to me – they say it's quite staggering how well it's gone. They're using it as an example ... trying to lure other new firms into the area.'

'Well, Malc had everything to do with that. He took the job as a lowly salesman and since then he has never looked back.'

'And what did you say he did before?'

'He worked at Watt & Wyatt, in their packing department.' She's not going to say he was a warehouseman. She doesn't want Maria Williams knowing that.

'Don't you swim, then?' People who change topics so quickly like that have always unnerved Ellie. They leave you bumbling along in midflow, feeling boring, when they move their eyes and the subject at the same time.

Ellie sips her drink. 'This is good,' she smiles at Maria. 'Yes, I do swim, but in all the disruption of moving house I've lost my costume.'

'You could always borrow one of mine.'

Ellie smiles again. 'I doubt I'd fit into it.'

And then it's Wilfred's turn for the spotlight, and Ellie learns how bright is the future of the pale man in shorts who is down the garden behind the clumps of lavender with a watering can. How really excellent are his prospects, how they do not intend to stay here for long but are beating time while they wait for the right opportunity. 'Wilfred's in sugar.'

'Is he really?'

'And my boutique is just a little hobby – it keeps me out of trouble, you know,' says Maria. 'You should pop in some time.' Her eyes take in Ellie's old sundress. It is poplin, with an elasticated top. They don't make sundresses like that any more. 'I have some quite nice things hidden away for discerning customers.'

Ellie feels as if she's being offered a porno video or a smutty magazine.

'Oh, I will,' she promises. 'Next time I go by.'

'It's surprising how mean some men can be when it comes to the essentials of life,' laughs Maria, crossing one supple leg over the other. In the heat Ellie's legs have stuck together. She could not do that. Moisture is trickling between her breasts and the backs of her knees are stuck to the white plastic chair.

'Malc's very generous,' Ellie replies, raising one leg gingerly.

'Yes.' Maria's eyes slide towards the fence. 'Yes, he has a generous mouth.'

It does not feel as though it's Malc Ellie is discussing with Maria. It doesn't feel as though it's anyone she knows. Making love to a stranger . . . is that why she's started feeling so different of late? Why she's started to take more care when she goes to bed, leaving off the Oil of Ulay, leaving out the rollers – disguised as beauty aids but surely the first line of defence – putting away the old winceyette along with the swimming costume, deep down in that bottom drawer?

Nothing is said. Well, Ellie and Malc never discuss sex . . . not since those balmy days up on Caldy Hill. The walls were paper-thin in Nelson Street and they often heard Arthur swearing and grunting as he pumped himself into his comatose ghost of a wife. There gradually ceased to be much to say about sex. Sex died with the music. For Ellie and Malc it was on, off and over.

Not any more.

She wants him now. She wants some of that raw energy, some of that driving determination of his to rub off on her. She wants to be touched, to be made alive by it all.

It is Ellie who turns her light off first, it is Malc who stays reading – minutes of meetings, complicated order forms and manufacturers' specifications.

And last night, after he'd put down his notes, he insisted on keeping the light on. 'You're lovely, Elle, d'you know that?

You're very lovely.' Ecstasy was the only word for her happiness then. She'd never imagined it could last so long or that he could transport her to such a delightful place.

'It is so important to mix with the right type of person, we always think.'

'Yes. Yes, I suppose it is, really.'

'It is so easy to be dragged down. You see it everywhere you look.'

Ellie, stuck down Nelson Street for so many years, has never had the time or the inclination to look until now, but she's glad she left her fags behind in her own garden. Ellie is quite confused. She'd imagined that Caroline Plunket-Kirby was a snob, and women like Mrs Gogh, but they were snobs in a covered-up way, not overt about it like Maria Williams: they'd never talk quite like this. Bewildered, Ellie doesn't know where she stands.

'People don't choose to be poor, or down on their luck,' she says bluntly.

Maria's eyes flash. 'Oh, we all know that, but some people just never try, do they?'

'Some people don't get the chance to try.'

'Some people know no better. And yet they are artful enough to make sure they put themselves out of house and home and get nannied by the state while it's left to men like Wilfred and Malcolm to take destiny into their own hands, to create their own chances.'

Who are these 'some people' they are sitting here talking about? Ellie's not sure. This . . . girl . . . Maria, she looks so fresh and young to be talking like this. What on earth has made her so angry, Ellie wonders. And what is she so frightened of? Losing her money – well, the little she has? Losing Wilfred's love?

Ellie's sham smile is wearing her out. She used to like people, used to talk to them easily, but just lately, everyone she meets is making her sad. She is amazed at the depths of her disappointment. She suddenly shivers, feeling confused and lonely, horrified by her strange inertia. Malc said Maria was easy, he said she'd like her and get on with her. Well, it's bloody well not happening like that, Malc, she wants to shout over the fence.

She sighs with relief when she's back in her own kitchen again; it suddenly feels like a refuge. She peers out through the curtains and down the garden. She would like to talk to Malc but he is busy. He is bronzed and tall and energetic and shorts suit him. He puts the puny Wilfred to shame. Even back in his very worst times that twinkle had never quite left his eyes.

'I am not on an island.' She speaks out loud and forcefully, telling herself off. 'It might feel as if I am, but I'm not. There's the phone. I can always ring someone up.'

'Who?' the voice seems to answer back.

'Well, Di's on the phone, and I could ring Mandy.' And what about Robert Beasely? Would she dare ring him up on a Sunday, his day off? No, she's not desperate enough to risk that.

'Go on, then.'

'The trouble is that I am not quite sure what is wrong. Everything is coming up roses and I wouldn't know what I was complaining about.'

'Why don't you make yourself feel better next week by going and spending some of your money? Maybe that's what's wrong. Maybe you're feeling bitter because you've got it there and can't use it. You're all uptight, perhaps that'd loosen you up a bit.'

The voice of temptation – it comes slyly on a high wind from the wilderness places intent on casting her into the abyss. What could she spend her money on, even if she succumbed? She couldn't bring anything home, could she . . . not without the danger of Malc finding it. And anyway, is that the honest answer to her problems?

She remembers that first thrill – she shivers as she feels it again – *one million, five hundred and twenty-five thousand pounds*. Not Malc's, not anything to do with Malc but MINE MINE MINE. But where is it? What is it?

'It is this place,' she tells the niggling voice. 'It's this bungalow, this awful, suburban halfway house. I'll never fit in here. We should have gone all the way . . . Georgian or nothing at all.'

The sweet smell of lamb makes her feel sick. She doesn't

fancy lamb either. Perhaps she'll take it out and let it go cold, make a salad as Malc suggested. 'What do you think about that idea?' she asks the voice.

'I thought I heard you talking to someone,' says Malc, coming in and dropping a kiss on the top of her head so that all her distress flies out of the window with the steam. She catches his soily hand briefly as he passes by.

'I didn't like Maria,' she confesses immediately.

'Well that's okay, why should you? She's a bit grasping and superficial, but I'm sure she means well.'

In the past Malc would have called Maria a cow. It would have been Ellie who added the 'means well'.

'I'm not doing any potatoes.'

'Fine. Fine.' He goes to the sink and rinses his hands. Ellie can smell the soap.

'I thought we'd have a salad as you suggested.'

'That would be nice.'

'And then this evening when it's cooler, we could go for a walk on the shore.'

'If you like , Elle.'

'Malc . . .'

There is a silence while he puts on his shirt, reaches for the comb and positions himself before the mirror to tidy his hair.

'Malc,' she tries again. 'I don't know that I'm going to like living out here.' Is it really this warm in the kitchen? The heat that is coming off Ellie is fire.

Malc turns round abruptly, his comb halfway through his hair. 'What?'

She shifts uneasily in her chair. 'It's just that . . .'

'What are you going to tell me now? That all this has been a waste of time, that you'd rather be back in Nelson Street?'

'No.' She is quick to contradict, she can't bear the pain she sees in his eyes. 'No, Malc, not at all. Nothing like that.'

'We've hardly been here a month, Elle, you've got to give it time. It's bound to be difficult at first, especially for you.'

Especially for me?

'I don't think I'm going to find any friends. I seem to have lost the knack.'

'Don't be silly, Elle. Just because you don't get on with

Maria. You'll have to have Di and Margot over more often, that's all. And when you can drive you can choose where you go.'

'I was thinking, Malc. When I give up at Funorama next week, what about me taking a secretarial course ... then I might get a job with Canonwaits, and I could help you.'

Malc comes over and takes Ellie's face in his hands. 'Hey, steady on. I want you to be a lady of leisure, I want to think you don't have to go out any more to earn your crust. I think you're panicking far too soon. Why don't you just wait a couple of months, see what happens and then, if you find yourself on your own too much, if you're bored, then certainly take a course. But why not do something a little more frivolous, like floristry or brass rubbing.'

'Piss off, Malcolm.'

He kisses her hard on the mouth and she tries to hit him and twist away. 'That's better, Elle. That's my girl!'

See, she silently tells the voice. Leave me alone when I'm being silly! We are going to be all right.

16

'It's a bit twee, Mum, isn't it?'

Ellie does something she's never done before in her life. She reaches across and slaps her daughter's face.

Mandy bites her lip and goes white.

Ellie wants to apologise. She wants to fling her arms round her daughter and hold her tight but she's hit her and she can't. So she wraps her arms round herself instead and stares out of the window, turning her back on the misery.

'Mum, what's the matter?'

Ellie sniffs as her face contorts, as her mouth does strange dances across her face and her nose starts to run. She stretches out for a piece of kitchen roll.

'Mum, I didn't mean it. When I said it I thought you would laugh.' Mandy's voice is quiet and steady, and Ellie knows hers, when she speaks, will not sound like that.

'I've been a bit . . . I've been a bit . . . lately I've been . . .' And she scrubs at herself with the kitchen roll which has scrolls on the border. There seems to be no end to what's trying to come out.

'I didn't mean to insult the house. I didn't mean to sound patronising. If this is what you and Dad want . . . I just never imagined you'd choose somewhere like this. I ought to have done, I am stupid and thoughtless.'

'Your Dad thought it would be more practical, and you know how we've always longed to get out in the country.' Her words feel like Band-Aids, as though she is covering a wound with one of those airtex plasters.

The silence seems very long, and they both keep to protective positions, not moving, not drawing closer, and both of them stay very still as if the shifting of an arm or the angle of a neck might say something dangerous or unmeant.

Mandy breaks it, because it cannot go on and someone has to grasp the nettle. 'I'll put the kettle on.'

So Ellie can let herself go loose and actually move to the table.

Over her shoulder Mandy says, 'I expect you are finding it strange, Mum, not going to work every day any more.'

'Don't make excuses for me, Mandy. I feel bad enough without you doing that.'

'I don't know what else to say, and I have been wondering about you, at home all day.'

'But you didn't ring me.'

'I wasn't sure that you wanted me to. I know how you feel about telephones.'

'That's just a silly aversion.'

'It might well be, but it's real.'

'It's just that, with a telephone, you can't prepare yourself, can you? You never know who is going to be on the other end, or whether you want to talk to them or not.'

Mandy tries to lighten things up. She is unused to wading through her mother's darkness and naturally she is nervous of it. For Mandy, this is new. 'I bet Mrs Gogh was at her most wounded best when you told her.'

Ellie understands what Mandy is doing and she's grateful. She is also quite proud at the maturity of her daughter, a maturity which has taken place in some distant zone, patterned by distant events unknown to Ellie. And look at her now! Quite the young lady in that smart dress and those beads. Even Maria Williams couldn't sniff her snobby disapproval at that sophisticated choice.

'Mrs Gogh was a cinch!' Ellie manages to smile. 'Now it's that terrible woman next door, I have to hide to get away from her. She keeps coming round with things, God knows why she thinks that I want them. And they have these peculiar parties on a Saturday night.' Ellie sniffs again, stares at her hands. 'You'd think she'd have more to do with her time than come meddling over here, peering at everything and criticising.'

Mandy sets a cup of tea on the table before her and Ellie is grateful for the teaspoon with which she can play. She and Mandy seem to have swapped positions, Mandy taking on Ellie's role as the sensible one, the comforter.

Mandy smiles gently when she says, 'I've never known you to have trouble dealing with meddlers before. This is something new!'

'Well, I'm new here. I don't want to appear unfriendly. I don't want to upset anyone.'

'And would you upset this Maria if you told her you wanted to be left alone?'

Ellie feels a flicker of annoyance. 'Of course I would, Mandy. Nobody wants to be told to get lost when they are trying to be nice!'

'It doesn't sound as if this Maria is trying to be particularly nice. Nor does it sound as if she's the kind of person you'd want to know anyway.'

'You soon get a reputation, living out here, for being offish. Christ, I used to think gossip flew down Nelson Steet but that wasn't a patch on what goes on here. In the butcher's. In the newsagent's. In the cleaner's.'

'That sort of thing never seemed to bother you back home.'

'They all knew me back home, Mandy. This is different. Here I am a stranger. Everyone's a stranger. No one's been here long enough, really, to call themselves natives, although people like the Williams do.'

Mandy sips her tea but she keeps her brown eyes fixed on her mother when she says, 'So what does Dad think about all this?'

'Well, I suppose he agrees with me, really, but he's never at home. He doesn't have to put up with it in the same sort of way. You know Malc, he says I shouldn't get myself in a state over it. He's beginning to say it's my age.'

Mandy groans. She is a feminist. Ellie likes the way she's got her hair cropped short like that. Short but curly, it's not an aggressive style, in fact it makes her pleasantly angled face look softer. A bit like Mia Farrow, but more substantial, not so fluttery.

Ellie had driven to the station this morning to pick up Mandy with mixed feelings. Oh, she wanted to see her daughter it's true, but the way she'd been feeling just lately, she wondered whether she'd be able to cope with somebody else in the house all the time. A fortnight suddenly seemed an age and she found herself making plans to pass the time as if it was a total stranger she was expecting, someone who would want every minute of their visit to be full and entertaining. She had to force herself to say, 'This is Mandy! This is Mandy! Mandy won't expect anything from you other than that you be yourself!'

And the voice answered back, 'But you don't know Mandy!'

'Of course I do,' Ellie told it sharply. 'I will always know Mandy and Kev.'

'Is it yourself you don't know any more, then?' asked the voice, unkindly.

The journey home had been easy, the conversation full of the sort of things people want to tell each other when they've been too long apart. And Mandy expressed amazed admiration for her mother's driving, even though Ellie touched several kerbs because she was trying too hard, and took the wrong turning at one stage.

She heard herself giggling in a silly way. It was all the excitement, she supposed, and she was still quite a nervous driver.

'Calm down, Mum! Calm down,' Mandy laughed, 'or you'll be done for dangerous driving in a minute and you'll lose that brand new licence.'

God forbid. God forbid that she be stuck in the bungalow with no way out.

No, everything had gone smoothly until they reached the house. Ellie had manoeuvred the coffee and cream Metro up the steep little drive, kangarooing it slightly, and Mandy just said, 'Is this it?'

What had Ellie expected? What had she wanted this daughter of hers, this honest daughter of hers, to say? This daughter to whom she had always maintained it was stupid and cowardly to lie or to back down in the face of adversity.

'This is it!'

Then Mandy had stood and stared for a moment, giving no reaction, before she opened the boot to get out the cases. Ellie had hurried forward to open the front door, one anxious eye on the bungalow next door in case Maria came out and wanted to know what was going on.

Mandy had dumped her bags in the hall and waited until they reached the kitchen before she made her hurtful comment. Ellie hasn't even shown her the rest of the house yet, and now she doesn't want to, even though she's taken such trouble over Mandy's room, getting it just right.

'And I think that Maria next door is a snob.'

At this Mandy Freeman roared with laughter. 'Well, of course she's a snob! Nobody but a snob could have a pretentious front door like the one she's got, or ornate wrought-iron gates, or two concrete whippets on top of the wall. Of course she's a snob, Mum.' And it is obvious that Mandy doesn't think this fact, so worrying to Ellie, should bother her.

'She's clearly just as much of a snob as that grotesque Mrs Gogh.'

'Poor Mrs Gogh,' says Ellie.

'Yes, poor Mrs Gogh, exactly! So now why can't you feel the same way about Maria? She shouldn't be a threat to someone like you, Mum. You shouldn't be intimidated by a person like that. Good God, just treat her like you treated Mrs Gogh, with calm superiority.'

'But I wasn't trying to be anyone special when I was dealing with Mrs Gogh.' Then Ellie removes her eyes from her daughter, as she can't answer that puzzled frown.

Mrs Gogh had said, 'So you want to leave me, Ellie. After all these years you want to leave me.'

Amazed, Ellie realised that Mrs Gogh and Funorama were one in her own head . . . that she was going to take this personally.

'Is it more money you're asking for?' Mrs Gogh's face was stiff under the make-up. She wore her most dignified expression. Above her was a poster of a half-naked man, before her a pile of little sacks with laughs inside, called 'a bag o' laughs'.

'If it was money I was wanting I would have said so,' said Ellie lightly. 'No, it's nothing like that. It's just that now Malc has this new job . . . he's a director of Canonwaits here in the city . . . and we've moved out to Heswall, it isn't necessary for me to work any more.'

'You are burning your bridges, Ellie.' And the way Mrs Gogh said that made it sound like a matter of life and death.

'I don't think so, Mrs Gogh. We did wait until we were quite certain we could manage without the extra pay packet.'

'And how am I supposed to cope, with this sudden bombshell dropped on my lap with no warning?'

'But I am warning you now. As I said at the start, I am prepared to give a fortnight's notice, or longer if you like.'

'Don't humour me!' said Mrs Gogh. 'I can find a replacement tomorrow. No trouble.'

'That's what I thought,' said Ellie.

'What really hurts me, Ellie, is the little matter you've obviously overlooked, of loyalty.'

'But I have been loyal!' spluttered Ellie.

'And I have been loyal to you,' said Mrs Gogh. 'And then, at the first opportunity, you go and abandon me.'

'I am sorry that you see it like that.'

'How else am I supposed to see it? Fair's fair, Ellie.'

Yes, Mrs Gogh had been easy. Sad, but easy. And it had been awful, because as Mrs Gogh turned away, preparing herself to stalk from the shop with all her dignity gathered together, she had knocked over the tray with the sackfuls of laughter. . .

Ellie had wanted to run after her. She'd wanted to explain something to Mrs Gogh but she didn't know exactly what, so she'd left it. Mrs Gogh wouldn't have wanted to listen anyway.

Ellie is revived by the tea. Mandy has always made a good, strong cup. 'Mandy, I want to say that I'm really sorry . . . Something came over me but I don't know what.'

'No, Mum.' Mandy stretches out her hand and Ellie takes it. Squeezes it, dangerously near to a second collapse. 'Come on, let's have a look at the rest of the place. No nasty comments, honest. And then you and I are going to have lunch at the smartest place in town. On me. I'm rich now so I'm paying.'

What if they ever find out what I've done?

Oh, honesty. Oh, truthfulness. Where have you gone and why did I desert you?

And for what?

17

Ellie has been round and round the word 'money' so much that it feels as if she's sat on it and squashed out the meaning.

'I promise I'll ring you, Mum, and if you're not feeling like talking you're going to have to say so. I won't be hurt. I'll just ring another time.'

Over the last couple of weeks Ellie Freeman and her daughter have travelled around the countryside, exploring, having picnics, swimming and lying in the sun and learning to talk honestly together. However, when Mandy ventured, 'Is everything all right between you and Dad? Is there anything wrong?' Ellie considered this going too far. She had never, and she would never, discuss her marriage with her children. And anyway, there was nothing wrong – things had never been better. It was lovely but Mandy's two-week stay was over too soon as all good things are.

Mandy has gone now, leaving Ellie invigorated and refreshed, and Kevin is sending his news home on extra-large postcards. He is coming back from Greece overland with some friends on what he calls the magic bus. Ellie associates the word magic with drugs, and she hopes that Kevin is not on them. The end of September will soon be here and, prodded into immediate action by Mandy, Ellie has signed herself down for two local classes, 'Cordon Bleu Without Fuss' and 'The Patterns of Poetry'.

Throughout the summer her meetings with Robert Beasely at the Red Fox have taken place regularly, although he went on holiday for a fortnight to the South of France with Bella's lively, rather frightening-sounding family. Ellie, half-expecting, half-hoping for a postcard, had felt unreasonably disappointed when none came. She is even nervous about answering the phone on a Tuesday, now, in case it is Robert cancelling. He has never cancelled yet, but she's terrified that he might. She has become oddly dependent upon these monthly meetings; she relies on the high they give her which carries her along for days.

Last time they met, Robert explained that Canonwaits were now ready to repay her initial investment and that option was open to her if she chose it. 'But I wouldn't advise it,' he said. 'Not with the way that company's going. We should hang on to those shares, Ellie.'

Ellie was surprised that he'd even suggested selling. She wouldn't have dreamed of relinquishing her shares, whatever they were doing.

Ellie had not felt easy with the woman who accepted the poetry money. She was huge, with beaded hair and wearing black robes. Safely outside in the hall again she'd fussed, 'But Mandy, where can I find women like myself? Where do women like me meet and gather?'

'They don't, Mum – that's half the trouble. They're too busy keeping body and soul together, too busy working. You've just got to try and realise that everyone, deep down, is the same underneath. That everyone is frightened and pretending not to be, just wanting to be loved.'

'Some people seem to have a funny way of going about it.'

'Self-defence,' said Mandy dismissively.

'Perhaps I should have signed on for the karate instead.'

She would have known, of course, that in this area there are only certain kinds of people who are free to go to classes in the daytime. Her type – lonely, undirected people desperately searching for ways to fill their time, and mothers with little children who have to be home by three-thirty. There aren't many unemployed round about here . . . down Nelson Street the class would be full of quite a different type of person with quite different needs . . . keeping warm and a free cup of tea for a start.

Still, she's paid her money so she must go and anyway, Mandy will be most annoyed if she finds that Ellie's backed out.

She doesn't feel proud of the little dish she brings home from the Cordon Bleu course to set before Malc at the table. She doesn't feel proud, just pathetic and slightly ashamed, like a child bringing home grimy grey scones from a school cookery class. She could have copied the recipe at home out of any one of her cookbooks and she doesn't want him beaming and commenting like this . . . as if it is praise from him that has driven her to tackle it in the first place.

'You don't have to eat it if you don't like it, you know.'

'But I do like it, Elle.'

She bristles. 'What, you'd rather have food like this all the time?'

He shakes his head in the middle of a hot mouthful. 'No, of course not. But it makes a nice change.'

'Well, I'm not keen,' and she pushes away her plate, watching him carefully, her chin on her hands as he ploughs manfully on.

'It is called "sole en papillote *festa del mare*",' she says, still watching, as a cat watches a bird, and using the broadest scouse accent she has ever used in her life.

Perhaps she shouldn't have cleared the dining room because she feels she has set up some sort of 'occasion' without meaning to do so. It's a cold room which smells of disuse and the paste aroma of wallpaper glue gets into the food. The pattern and colours she'd picked for this room – enormous pastel flowers with complicated stem patterns – do nothing for Ellie's need for security. The surface of the new table is so slippery that every so often they have to retrieve scudding mats. But it's not funny.

They eat their pudding in silence and then Malc gets up and goes to his study to do some more work. 'If you'll be all right,' he says as he departs. And she's not sure what leaves her feeling so wild with anger, because it's not Malc's fault that she decided on the cordon bleu. In fact, he had suggested something slightly more challenging. 'You've always been a good cook,' he'd protested. 'I can't see the point in you learning cookery.'

'It's not just ordinary cookery, Malc,' she remembers insisting. 'It's special.'

So why is she blaming him now?

'And I'm not going again,' she shouts across the hall, furiously, in the middle of clearing the table.

'Fine,' he calls back.

But that's not enough. She wants to go and hit him.

She talks to the voice while she washes up. 'Bastard,' she says.

'You are just disappointed that the afternoon didn't bring you the pleasure you hoped it might.'

'You're quite right for once,' agrees Ellie. 'It was like dishing up a fillet of failure with a sprig of bloody parsley on the side.'

'And you're miserable because you didn't make friends.'

'There was nobody there to be friendly with,' says Ellie. 'They all had their own friends anyway and they weren't about to break ranks for anyone else. Especially not for an elderly newcomer.'

'They would have acted very differently if they'd known about your money,' says the voice slyly.

'Well, I certainly don't want people who'd like me because of that.'

It hadn't been quite as bad as all that, and maybe Ellie's hopes had been too high. The woman who took the class had been quick and keen and no-nonsense, so really it wasn't a suitable place to make friends or to start conversations. It was all a matter of, 'Now take your filleting knife and slice just here . . .' or, 'No, no, brush lightly with the oil!' and, 'I think this crimping could be just a soupçon firmer, don't you?' all said with a brisk, encouraging intake of breath.

The teacher, who was called Vera Bus, had made a little joke at the start. She told them that a certain Lord Houghton had sighed on his deathbed; "My exit is the result of too many entrées", – and we certainly don't want to be blamed for any of that,' said this Mrs Bus. Everyone tittered but Ellie didn't really understand it. And anyway, it certainly wasn't funny enough to make anyone laugh.

Everyone at the class was very 'sweet' and polite. And when they had finished they just kind of wandered out with their various dishes, still smiling.

Perhaps she should give it another chance. After all, she doesn't have anything else to do on a Tuesday, or a Thursday, or a Friday . . . and try as she might she cannot find any more dirt in the house and all Malc's shirts are ironed. She has a race, now, with Maria Williams, to see who can get their washing out first in a morning. When this pathetic little performance first began Ellie had not recognised it for what it was, and by the time she did recognise it she was too involved to pull back. She despised herself for it and told no one. 'Now you are feeling sorry for yourself,' reproves the voice. 'So just stop it!'

'What about joining the WRVS or something like that?' shouts Malc. He's obviously not got down to his work; something about her attitude this evening has disturbed him. Well good, and it's ABOUT TIME.

'Just leave it out, Malc, please,' replies Ellie quietly, viciously wiping the kitchen surfaces.

She is wary now, but her hopes rise again two days later when she approaches the Patterns of Poetry class – surely, on a subject such as this one they will all be forced to communicate and not on any superficial level. Ellie knows nothing at all about poetry, but she wants to. She watched Alan Bennett reading some out on the telly recently and decided it wasn't difficult after all, that the poems he read were speaking to her. He made it so she could understand it – every word of it! She smiles to herself when she thinks about Di and her loud, scornful laugh if she knew Ellie was here. She's glad Di's not with her – if Di were here she'd be nudging her now, and whispering. She climbs up the linoleum stairs of the paint-flaked building, noting the funny little black rubber treads on the ends which put her in mind of the council rent office. The posters on the walls point at her accusingly, trying to involve her in Third-World affairs, petitions and protest marches. And Ellie, who has always dismissed this sort of appeal with, 'I can hardly feed my own family let alone anyone else's,' starts when she realises that now, with her money, that is no longer the case.

She would not miss a few thousand a year. The next time she sees Robert she's going to tell him she wants to give some of her money to charity. She is immediately humbled by the knowledge that she's only prepared to give because she won't miss it.

But how can you win, then?

'Well, that's just the point – you can't,' says the voice, and it sounds like the Malc of the old days.

Ellie is surprised to hear the voice in here, outside her kitchen.

There are unemployed around here after all, and they come out for poetry as they did not come out to the cordon bleu – well, of course they didn't, because how could they afford the ingredients?

Ellie arrives at the top of the house where this course is held. She is slightly doubtful when she sees that she's going to have to sit on a mattress on the floor, embarrassingly close to somebody else. There are no chairs at all in this garret room and only a skylight in the sloping ceiling to let in the daylight. She picks a safe-looking place in one dark corner, but the roof angles meet here, and it's only after she's settled down that she realises she has to half-sit and half-lie to avoid hitting her head. She does not want to move.

One girl with a very straight back is sitting on a cushion with her legs crossed and her eyes closed. The expression on her face is exaggeratedly peaceful. Another of about the same age, just a little older than Mandy, is lying flat on the floor gazing up through the skylight with her arms behind her head. A young man wearing a colourfully knitted Afghan hat and tatty fingerless gloves is rolling a cigarette, and his red silk trousers are tucked into suede tassled boots.

Ellie's going to keep her mac on and she's really glad Di's not here.

Slightly more reassuring are the two middle-aged men who saunter in holding hands and wearing trainers and tracksuits. When they see her they nod and they smile and raise their hands in a stately kind of greeting.

'Hi.'

'Hi,' says Ellie, smiling back and looking away hastily.

Hippies! How often has Malc told her just lately not to categorise people. 'That's half your trouble,' he's pointed out. 'You decide what they are, and it's because of that that you're frightened of them. Look at your response to Maria Williams! Now you think that all women who wear their hair in that way

140

and who rest their sunglasses on their heads are exactly the same.'

'I never used to do that, and if I do it now then it's something new,' she answered him miserably, aware that he was right.

And yet is this new habit of hers so wrong? Well, look . . . she knows without being told how these people vote, what kind of food they eat, their attitudes towards medicine, the state, the poor, the rich, the police, education; she knows what kind of books they read and she knows what kind of cars, if they have cars, they would drive.

They are like children, she thinks, proclaiming themselves while pretending not to be doing so.

And are they doing the same thing to her? Are they summing Ellie up in the same sort of way – and is she unconsciously proclaiming something, too, in her rollneck jumper and flared beige skirt – or is she hiding . . . hiding! How much do they think that they know about her? Well, they certainly don't look as if they are bothering. Nobody, except for the tracksuited men, has even acknowledged her existence. They are all concentrating, very hard indeed, on themselves and for Ellie, this is a new experience. She's used to being greeted with a smile and the offer of a cup of tea. Where Ellie comes from, making people feel at home is thought to be very important. When she lived down Nelson Street and went about in her plastic mac and her headscarf, summing her up might have been slightly easier, or would it? Down at the club the women Ellie knew wore widely individual colours and styles although the garments were mostly chosen from the same catalogue. Mind you, they did drink the same sort of drinks, they liked the same kind of music and they tended to hold their fags in the same way.

But underneath, oh underneath they'd been seething with a million different emotions – yearnings, longings, fantasies, fears . . . as these people must be, too, she thinks as she watches the Afghan-hatted man bring out a mauve crystal and rub it between his horny hands.

'I must give this a chance,' she says sternly to herself, knowing how important it is, just now, for her to feel she has succeeded at something. She just can't go home with another failure under her belt.

'Well, I suppose we might as well start. I don't know who else is coming but it's already two-thirty.'

On the form Ellie took home with her the starting time was two o'clock.

The large woman with the beaded hairstyle is wearing what Ellie calls 'genie' pants and she squats on the floor on a cushion she's brought with gaudy tassles attached to the corners.

'I see we've got somebody new here today. We are glad to have you join us. I will start by telling you that my name is Dawn. Would you like to tell us your name and maybe share something with us?' Almost all of this is spoken on one, calm note.

Share? Ellie panics when she says, 'Ellie Freeman,' quietly and rather abruptly.

Dawn nods deeply and waits there, with her head down for a while, absorbing Ellie's name. She lets her shoulders sag and gives a great sigh before raising her head again with a definite kind of heaviness. Perhaps she doesn't like the name Ellie. There is a pause and the most fleeting of smiles from Dawn as three more people enter the room and glide to the floor, silently.

'Well, Ellie,' says Dawn. 'The rest of us here know each other already; we have been meeting together for some time now.'

You wouldn't know that they knew each other. No communicating has taken place . . .

'Two years,' says the girl on the floor, still staring up at the skylight as if measuring the time by the clouds that drift by.

'And what we like to do first of all is to go round the circle and invite anyone who wants to, to bring something forward. Perhaps, Ellie, you would like to wait and see what we do before deciding if you're ready to contribute yet or not.'

'Yes,' says Ellie. At least she can smoke in here, although she can't see any ashtrays and the man with the roll-up and the crystal seems to be using his hand. 'That might be better.'

There is another big nod, and a long pause which unnerves Ellie but seems to be quite all right for everyone else.

'I'd like to start by sharing something I wrote only last night,' says one of the latecomers, who is elderly and might be mistaken, in any other circumstances, for a bag lady with deep and slightly clouded eyes. Nobody moves or reacts, nobody even looks eager.

In fact they all wear looks of martyred acceptance. Ellie opens her handbag with a loud click. She gives a silly little smile and stays absolutely still, as if that was an accident.

> *'Thoughts of the inevitability of every minute*
> *Enter my head*
> *In this strange house*
> *Which I will leave in a few moments*
> *Never to return.'*

Alan Bennett had not read out anything like that, nor had he used that strange lilting tone. He had been very matter-of-fact with the poems he had recited.

People are nodding softly and thinking deeply.

Eventually Dawn says, 'Would you like to tell us anything more about that, Rosy?'

Rosy the bag lady reaches up and pins some escaping hair to the top of her head. She starts to explain . . . but Ellie loses track, grasps this opportunity to take out a cigarette, draws on it deeply and waits for the next person's turn.

But the next person, the girl lying on the floor, doesn't need to read from a paper and speaks her poem from her position on the floor. It is a very long poem, and Ellie only hears the first line:

'While it lasted it was tremendous, of course, isn't that always the way. . . ?'

To Ellie it doesn't sound like a poem at all. It sounds as if she's just talking in a rather strange kind of way . . . like a caterpillar humping and creeping along a pavement.

Time goes by slowly. She has found a silver cup-cake case on the floor and is using it as an ashtray. It has started to rain and raindrops hit the skylight and trickle down it. The glass starts to steam up. Ellie thinks of the steak and kidney pudding she has left boiling on top of the cooker and her tummy rumbles unpleasantly. She decides to stop at the greengrocer's and buy a swede on the way home. Malc likes a bit of swede mashed into his potatoes.

Some of the members of the group are scribbling away while they listen. Ellie is nearly drifting off; she is very relaxed in this yellowy light with the room fugged up and the rain and the spluttering of the little electric fire. Ellie has brought a notepad with her but so far she has written nothing. And then, before she knows it, it is her turn, and Dawn is turning her moon-like face towards her, not asking for anything directly, but clearly expecting some response.

'Oh,' says Ellie, jerked into the rather dim limelight and unprepared, expecting to have longer. 'I didn't know, actually, that I had to bring anything to read, and I haven't managed to write anything.'

'Fine. Fine,' says Dawn. 'And is there anything you'd like to add about the poetry you have heard so far this afternoon?' Dawn's smile is a sweet one, but vacant, not directed at anyone in particular.

'Oh, I don't know all that much about poetry. I'm kind of new at all this. I've never really done much of it before . . .'

'Fine. Fine,' Dawn's smile has fluttered away and she is staring at her with a curiously sad expression. She understands . . . oh yes, she understands . . . but what? Ellie feels the first prickles of anger.

But the rest of the group moves on.

They have a break for tea. It is herbal, with strange, nutty-tasting biscuits arranged very carefully on a tray. They each drop their ten pence into a white, chipped sugar basin. There is quiet conversation, and quite a lot of stretching and yawning and Ellie senses the peaceful cosiness of a winter's night, but she is excluded, knocking outside, trying to get in.

At the end of the session Dawn picks up a book from the pile she has on the floor before her and says, 'I'm finishing by reading a poem of Stevie Smith's,' and then she smiles at the girl they call Joey who has sat upright all afternoon, 'by special request.'

144

'Oh no, not again,' say two of the others, but smiling placidly as if this is something they often have to endure. 'Can we all join in?'

Dawn smiles broadly as she begins. She is still smiling when she reads the last line, *'And not waving but drowning.'*

Something is coming up . . . something so despairing and so deep Ellie cannot reach it, let alone control it. She needs to speak to someone about the poem she's heard but Dawn won't do and she doesn't want to hear these people say anything about it anyway. She doesn't want to 'share it'. She drags herself up, her face distorted with pain, not even slightly concerned that she disturbs the peaceful person beside her. Gripping her handbag like a weapon and holding it before her, she storms from the room, creating a draught in her haste to be gone, to be out and away from this . . .

Past the wretched posters she goes and down the stairs with her clothes flying around her. She is almost blinded by tears and where can she go and what can she do to dislodge this wedge of misery? She makes a dash for the Metro. She fumbles frantically for her keys, gets in and drives away, not knowing where she is going.

And no longer caring.

18

'He is leaving me behind. I thought I'd be able to keep up with him, Di, but I can't. I haven't got any self-confidence and wherever I go or whatever I try to do seems to be making it worse. It's not as if I haven't tried, for Christ's sake. Even Mandy, when she came to stay, seemed far more capable than me all of a sudden, and although I was glad to see her so mature and able . . . you know, Di . . . it did feel as if my own inadequacies were highlighted.' And Ellie doesn't burst into tears. She'd done that when she'd first come in. Her face is all red and blotched from it.

'Inadequacies, Elle?'

She'd had to come and see Di. She'd been driven to it. Malc wasn't coming home until late and Ellie could not have endured one more evening in that bungalow on her own. She had rung her up on the wave of one desperate surge of misery and Di hadn't even sounded surprised. She'd just told her, 'Get in the car and come straight away.'

And Dave is sitting in the kitchen with a cold cup of tea, banned from the front room and trying not to listen.

'Yes. Inadequacies. I want to be good at something.'

'And you don't think you are?'

'Well, what am I good at then, Di? I'll just sit here quietly and listen while you tell me.' And Ellie stubs her cigarette into the sensible ashtray on a leather strap which lives on the arm of Dave's chair. There is an ironing board in the corner of Di's little lounge and Ellie wishes Di would get up and do the ironing. It would be easier to talk to her sensibly if she wasn't sitting down, deliberately trying to be sympathetic like this. Di has gone blonde and a full inch of dark roots is showing through.

'You are seeing yourself now, you are giving me a picture of someone I have just never seen before and it's taking time to sink in.' Di is dressed in a bright pink tracksuit for aerobics.

She was going to the class tonight but cancelled it immediately when she heard that Ellie was coming. Perhaps Ellie should have put her name down for aerobics . . .

'Don't play for time, Di. You were going to tell me what you thought I was good at.'

'You were a brilliant mother, Elle. I always used to envy the natural way you had with your children and the way they just automatically liked you . . .'

'WERE! We are talking about *now*!'

'Well, you are a good listener. You are patient, considerate, kind, and there are times when you can be extremely funny . . .'

The cuckoo clock on the wall hoots nine. Across Di's wallpaper go shepherds with crooks and milkmaids sit beside their pails. Something has always made Ellie think they are probably gods and goddesses, not ordinary working people at all. She thinks it is possibly the blue in the dye that gives her this idea, for it is a rather mystical eggshell blue. In her despair Ellie picks at her cardigan sleeve and sits silently watching the fire. 'Am I ugly, Di?'

Di laughs. 'Don't be so silly! Of course you're not ugly!'

'Do I look old?'

'How can I tell you that? Do I look old? Does Margot look old? You can't tell when you're with people. They just look exactly the same as they always did.'

'You're saying that when you know someone well, you cease to notice?'

'I suppose I am saying that, yes.' Di speaks slowly. She is being careful, glancing anxiously at Ellie.

'Well, what about Malc then, Di? Does he look exactly the same?'

Di says, 'No, no, he doesn't.'

'What does Malc look like?'

'Well, Malc has changed an awful lot just lately . . .' She leans back in her armchair and calls through the door, 'Stick that kettle on, Dave. And have we got any cheese?' And then they can hear Dave's chair scraping back as he gets up to obey instructions. 'Malc has had to change, I suppose, because of all the new circumstances, because of his job. And I suppose . . . in a way . . .'

147

'Yes?' Ellie sits forward, her inner wretchedness showing in her hunched-up shoulders.

'. . . I suppose you could say that Malc does look younger. But it's not just a matter of looks, is it? It's the clothes he has taken to wearing, and the weight he has lost, and the way he's always hurrying around now as if he's got more on his mind than just passing the time, beating time until Friday night when he can go out and enjoy himself.'

'But that hasn't happened to me, has it, Di?'

'No, Ellie, I don't think it's happened to you, but then why would it?'

'Well, my life's changed.'

'Yes, but not in the same sort of way.'

'So how can I get my life to change like that?'

'We've got some Eccles cakes,' says Dave from the kitchen, 'but I don't know how fresh they are.'

'They're stale,' says Di. 'I meant to throw them away but I forgot. Look in the fridge for the cheese, Dave. No, what you need, love, is a new lease of life, an all-consuming interest, I suppose,' she goes on, settling back thoughtfully, but is it the cheese she is thinking about, and the whereabouts of the crackers? 'After all, that's what seems to have happened to Malc, isn't it? But he seems to be being very nice about it. He doesn't exclude you, Ellie, does he?' And then Di leans forward and whispers, 'Sod it, Elle, I wish something like that'd happen to yours truly.'

'Malc and the kids have always been my all-consuming interest,' whispers Ellie back. 'I have to admit that. I have never, really, had anything else.'

'Well, who has?' Di hisses. 'Perhaps you should not have given up work.'

Ellie snorts. 'That was hardly an all-consuming interest.'

Di shakes her head. 'There must be something you could find to get yourself absorbed in now that Malc's on the up and up.'

So Ellie tells Di about the secretarial course and Dave comes in with a tray. You can tell he is prepared to stay, hoping the confidences are all over, but Di frowns at him hard and he backs out again, taking the third cup with him and a handful of crackers.

Di is not impressed by the idea.

'But I might get a job with Canonwaits.'

'Would Malc want you there in that sort of capacity?' asks Di sagely. 'After all, he is company director now and maybe he wouldn't want his wife working so closely with him. No, Elle,' she says convincingly, 'if you find something it must not be connected with Malc in any way – it has to be something for yourself.'

'I'll just have to sign up for more courses then,' says Ellie, feeling tears prick the backs of her eyes again, 'because I can't think of anything else.'

'How about painting?' asks Di, and Ellie winces. She hasn't told Di about the poetry, only about the cordon bleu and Di laughed loudly and horribly about that.

'Well, what about taking some exams and going to university?'

'Who, me?'

'Why ever not? There's a woman at the hospital, thick as a plank, not a brain in her head, couldn't be trusted to empty a bed-pan but she . . .'

'Thanks a lot, Di.'

Di is serious when she says, 'Have you talked to Malc about this, about these feelings of being excluded and left behind?'

'Of course I have talked to him.'

'And what does he say?'

'Mostly he tells me I am being silly, and I don't like to moan on too much because he is so pleased with himself. I don't want to always be spoiling it, being miserable when he's at home, forever going on about myself. At last he has something for himself . . . something that's changed him and made him happy. I did want that to happen, you know, Di. I wanted that very badly.'

'Well, I know you did, Elle. We would all like that.'

Ellie nibbles at a cream cracker she does not want and cannot taste. She licks her lips before she confides, 'You know, Di, I used to think I was disappointed in Malc, and that he was pulling me down. Now I know different. Now I realise that I was not disappointed in him as much as I was disappointed with myself.'

'Well, you never had any need to feel that way, Elle, and you still don't. Really. And I just wish I could find something to say to convince you. Could it be the place that disagrees with you? Could it be that moving back to the city is the answer? I know that sounds too simple but from what you've told me . . .'

By now both women are desperate for an answer.

'I think you're right!'

Di looks pleased.

'Yep. Yes. I think that you've hit the nail on the head. I was never keen to move out there.'

'Well then,' says Di, stretching with relief. 'There you are.'

'I am going to have to go home and tell Malc that.'

'He has got to be told,' Di agrees with her, 'whether he likes it or not. There is no point in him getting more and more successful if you're going to be unhappy.'

'He doesn't really mind where we live, anyway, although he has worked hard on that garden.'

'Well, buy somewhere with another garden,' shrugs Di.

'And we'll be able to transfer the mortgage, I suppose.'

'That's easily done,' nods Di.

Ellie muses as she sips her tea. She forces herself into believing that Di has hit the nail directly on the head. It might take time to sell the bungalow – sod it, if only she could use her own money – but the knowledge of the move will help her.

There is a bunch of flowers on Di's table. Ellie has stopped putting flowers in her house.

'Some houses have bad effects on people, you know.' Di is rambling on, keen to hammer her triumphant point home and Dave, sensing safety, comes wandering in from the back room where it's cold. Ellie notices the same shuffle in his step that Malc used to have, although Di and Dave have not done badly with their own house like this and their caravanette . . . but that old picture of the goats must be depressing . . . always looking back on that same old snapshot, never able to avoid staring at it. Dave is different at home, much quieter and gentler than he is when he comes to the club.

150

When Ellie's got her Georgian fireplace she won't have a picture over the top, she'll have one of those enormous mirrors. And by then she'll be happy to stand before it, looking straight at herself, because by then all will be well again, she'll feel different. She probably won't even be able to remember this awful time – she and Di will sit back and laugh as they laugh over so many painful things.

Ellie watches Di and Dave together and realises the extent of the change that has taken place in herself. The warm expression in the eyes of her friends which ought to be making her glad is filling her with the stinging anxiety of guilt and a sense of irreparable loss. She is here on false pretences, on the take – she asking for their help and them so readily giving it, but all the time she is deceiving them. She isn't like them any more. She knows very well how they worry, how they struggled to get that caravanette and how heavily the mortgage weighs on their shoulders.

Ellie has been freed from this daily grind and all its debilitating difficulties. She only has to pick up a pen and write a signature in order to buy whatever luxury she can think of and somehow this old familiar friendship, so necessary, so precious, is no longer appropriate, fair or excusable.

She has taken from Di for the last time. And now she can only drink up the rest of her tea, share a few reminiscences for old time's sake, the odd laugh, and go home.

19

A week goes by and Ellie does not mention the move, but keeps herself busy with a dustpan holding unseen germs at bay.

She has also started to make a patchwork quilt.

Tap tap tap – that can be nothing else but the sound of Maria Williams' high-heeled boots tripping across the patio. Ellie lies low, ducking automatically; she's not dressed yet and the dishes are piled all higgledy piggledy on the draining board . . . pans, vegetable dishes, wooden spoons, colanders and the chopping board. Last night's dishes as well as this morning's.

Yes Ellie lies low, balancing in a half-crouch, hanging on to the edge of the sink. Her neck aches from holding her head up so stiffly to listen.

'Hell-oooo.' And there go the boots, clip-clopping round the side of the house with their owner peering in at every window, no doubt noticing last night's unemptied ashtrays in what Malc has started to call the drawing room, the ashy fireplace and the squashed, forlorn morning cushions.

Ellie holds her breath. She feels that her head is about to roll from her shoulders, feels like she used to whenever she played hide and seek as a child – frightened, desperate to reveal herself, and dying to pee. She crosses her legs and blows her tension into the air out of ballooning cheeks, through tight lips.

'Oh God go away woman.'

'Ell . . . ieeeee. Ell . . . ieee. I've got something to show you!'

Don't people's words sound sinister when you are hiding from them? Ellie imagines herself as a child, probably hiding behind a tree, not playing hide and seek now but being pursued by some creepy abuser. The longer she hides herself the more alarmed she feels, as if time itself is her enemy.

You're telling me Maria's boutique is a hobby, because she's never ever there!

Good Lord, what if anyone could see her? And who does she think she is trying to fool, because when Maria gets round to the kitchen window she'll have to be blind not to see Ellie's fags and lighter set on the kitchen table beside the open newspaper, and her coffee cup steaming.

They get the *Telegraph* delivered now. It takes Ellie quite a while to work through it. Malc can do the crossword but Ellie is lucky if she gets one clue. 'It's not that you're thicker than me,' says Malc, 'it's just that your brain has gone rusty.'

Maria is at the kitchen window, not feet away from the top of Ellie's head. This is just bloody daft. Ellie jumps when Maria calls again; she jumps half out of her skin and then starts crawling like an ungainly crab across the kitchen and through to the hall where she can't be seen. And when she reaches this comparative safety she calls back, 'Hang on. Hang on a minute,' because she just can't go through this performance any longer.

She straightens her hair by flattening it down with her hands. It hasn't seen a comb yet this morning and nor has she put on her make-up. Her housecoat, padded and covered in roses and nothing at all like her old dressing-gown, hangs open to reveal a knee-length coral-coloured nylon nightie with ribbons set into the low-cut neckline. She buttons it up as she goes to the back door, sees the fuzzy image of Maria in the rippling glass, and opens it.

'I knew you were in,' says Maria.

'I was just tidying up the bedroom,' explains Ellie. And Maria moves the cigarettes, and folds the newspaper, making room for her elbows as she sits down. It looks as if she's got the start of an eye-infection coming on, or is it just the cold of the morning that has affected her?

'I know you don't get *The Deesider*,' she says, bringing the magazine from the depths of her dufflecoat pocket, 'so I thought I'd bring it straight round so you could see. You didn't tell me that Malc was going to the do at the Grosvenor. Were you there, too? Why on earth didn't you say?'

Ellie eases herself down on her chair, rubbing the sides of

her neck for comfort. 'I didn't go. Malc asked me, but he said it was just some civic do, bound to be boring speeches afterwards, so I thought I'd be happier here by the fire with a book.'

'I'd have gone,' says Maria. 'You should have got him to ask me! I'd have loved to have gone!'

'I think he looked on it as more of a duty, rather than an event to enjoy,' says Ellie complacently.

But Maria's not listening. She places the magazine flat down on the table and flicks through the pages, licking her thumb now and then like tellers used to do at a bank before they thought of sponges.

'Well for someone who considers he's doing his duty he seems to be having a wonderful time!' She twists the magazine until it's facing Ellie, and pushes it forward, right under her nose.

'Get out! Get out!' Ellie screams in her soul while the black wings of fear bat about her.

Ellie smiles, because straight away she recognises bald-headed, tubby, bespectacled Mr Gogh, and in his arms looking surprisingly tiny is Mrs Gogh in a pencil-slim gown with the dazed glaze of too much booze on her face. Her eyes stare at the camera, unfocused, like a statue's eyes. And there is Murphy, looking cooler and leaner than ever in a dinner jacket with Ramon's great face like a summer moon rising, trying to force itself into the picture behind him, and the caption underneath that one says, *'The men who brought Swedish style to Liverpool.'*

'That's them, isn't it?' Maria prods with a finger. 'Wilf says they're a couple of whizzkids. He's sure their success is a phenomenon that can't possibly last. Yuppie types.'

'The city embraces the arts.' And there is Malc, looking very handsome and formal, dancing with this woman in his arms. And the little box caption beneath it explains that Gabriella de Courtney has been living in Liverpool for a year now, running the new Royal Albert Art Gallery in the old dockland.

'That dress,' states Maria, 'that skimpy bit of cloth that woman is wearing cost more than all the creations I've got in my shop added up together. And what's more, you'd travel the world and never see another one like it.'

'It suits her,' says Ellie shortly, aware that she's blinking very hard but unable to stop herself.

'Mind you, anything would suit if you looked like that. You could go round in a sack and still look enticing. But isn't it a good one of Malc? All his charms are emphasized, wouldn't you say? The photographer has obviously caught him just right. You should have been there, Ellie – turning down an opportunity like that! I'd have gone like a shot if anyone'd asked me.' And her voice makes quite clear what a fool she thinks her.

'Perhaps I should have,' says Ellie, staring down at the picture. She is looking at a smiling Robert Beasely who sits at a white, very cleared, after-dinner table, a selection of glasses before him and that must be his wife beside him.

'They're certainly all there, aren't they, all the big-wigs, all the wise-guys.' Maria rubs her hands together. They are stubby little hands, like a child's and flawless – you could almost imagine she's got rubber gloves on. 'Well, I can't hang around here all day. Got to go and open up . . . people are coming in now with an eye on Christmas. I've brought all my ballgowns out to the front, there's some lovely ones this year. Very glam, very Cinderella. Women are wanting to look like women again and I think that's nice, don't you? Ellie, next time you're passing you must come in and look.'

Ellie sighs, lowers her shoulders and stretches a neck that feels painful and sinewy as she promises, 'I will, Maria. And thank you for showing me these.'

'Keep them till Malc comes home,' she says. 'He might not have seen them and I know he'll enjoy them.'

'I will, yes, thanks.' And a cold draught gusts through the door as Maria Williams passes brightly out of it and it feels as if it comes from inside Ellie, as though somebody's walking over her grave.

She smiles to herself, weakly, as she hobbles back to the table to peruse the pictures again. How silly. How very, very stupid and silly . . . this sick feeling, this plummeting of the heart, this terror. What else was Malc meant to do all evening? Huddle at the bar with the men like he used to? Of course he's not going to do that now.

What time did he get home that night?

She doesn't know. She was asleep.

What did he say about it in the morning?

She doesn't know. He was gone before she woke. He left without waking her up.

The tug of pain that comes with the knowledge that Robert is with them . . . one of them . . . part of it all . . . is twitchy, like the start of a toothache. She dabs it with commonsense on a cotton bud of reason, secretly knowing there is nothing you can do to take toothache away – not when it starts at this level of intensity. Of course Robert would attend such functions. He'd have to attend them because of his job, and it's natural that Bella would go with him. Ellie studies Bella hard. She is not quite how she'd imagined, not smooth and sophisticated at all but wirily thin with a narrow, intelligent face, small shoulders and two little knobs of breastbone shining in the photograph. And sitting beside them is the jovial, hearty lady mayoress with a chain, instead of a breastbone twinkling and sparking across her chest.

In the cold, private silence that exists now (even the fridge has stopped its humming and the tap has ceased its dripping), Ellie takes her eyes back to the picture of Malc. Are these the typical fears and reactions of a bored and lonely woman, with nothing better to do but make up situations inside her own head? Oh yes, Ellie knows quite well what's been happening to her state of mind lately, she's not daft. You can't pick up a magazine without reading about it . . . *'Dear Sonia, Help me! What shall I do? I suspect that my husband is having an affair and sometimes I fear I am losing my mind . . .'*

'Dear Anguished of Ipswich. Fear not! Do not give your suspicions the time to flourish. If you fear that your bloke is two-timing you, don't keep it to yourself. The solution is quite simple dear, just ask him!'

As for the danger signals, everyone knows them; everyone knows what they are supposed to be. Is he more gentle than usual? Sweet? Extra attentive?

Yes he is, actually.

More loving than usual, in bed as well as out?

Mind your own business.

Deeply disturbed now, Ellie makes the bed; she's working out in her mind the times he's rung to say he won't be back home until later . . . an unexpected client, or a meeting, a sudden panic at the office . . . urgent messages to be sent . . . they're all working late, not just him.

STOP IT, ELLIE, STOP IT. *'Dear Anguished of Ipswich . . . ASK HIM.'*

On what grounds? She tears her mind apart.

Should she rifle through his suit pockets? Should she open his desk and go through that, too? He's only dancing with a woman, for Christ's sake, in front of a camera for the whole world to see – hardly the kind of behaviour that could be described as furtive. Why the unease then . . . why the unease?

Just a feeling. That's all.

She rushes back to the kitchen along the narrow corridor, almost slipping on the carpet tiles, and clutches the magazine. Her eyes burn into the photograph. Where's his hand where's his hand where's his hand? It is resting demurely on Gabriella de Courtney's waist. He is not even looking into her eyes, he is gazing off over her shoulder.

But she's looking at him.

Freedom is in her stare, in her hair, in her dress and even in her movement which is on paper and therefore quite still. Freedom and daring, those two things are both in her smile. This Gabriella – she is not familiar with Fairy Liquid, or Pledge, or Gumption, she is not on speaking terms with back-breaking, unreachable plugs or the little mats of dust that accumulate on the bottoms of kitchen chair-legs, and the wind has never blown the dust from a carpet back into her face.

She has a cleaner. Some other woman with strong arms thrusts her duvet baggily into its cover, sweating and swearing and wondering whoever thought they were less trouble than sheets and blankets.

Somebody else empties her bit bucket, and keeps that cupboard fresh and clean.

Freda, Ellie's mum, had once been a cleaner. She cleaned offices in the early morning and private houses in the afternoon, and when she got home from work she rolled up her sleeves, put on her slippers, popped on her button-through overall and started on her own house. When Ellie was in love with Miss Bacon she had felt shame that her mother was a cleaner . . . never before that, and never since. Freda Thwait – five kids and her man long since disappeared, 'sailed off on a ship and never came back, the bastard.' Spick and span. 'Lift your legs, Ellie.' 'Put this bundle in the spinner and then hang it out in the yard, my pet.' If everything was spick and span then Freda could cope, she was on top of it. Ellie was the oldest so Ellie had to help; she was ten when her father sailed away and the strongest memory she had of him was his mobile tattooes . . . he could make women dance erotically all the way up and down his arms. That was her memory – and his raw-red, bristly chin.

Like a Jumbly: *'If only we live, we too will go to sea in a sieve'.* Ellie remembers the envy she'd felt when she heard that her father hadn't come home, because she had this ridiculous vision of him sitting eating pineapples beneath a brown mountain while a dusky woman in a grass skirt brought him cranberry tarts and Stilton cheese and covered him with garlands. Why she thought of the Jumblies Ellie could not guess, unless the connection was made because of the *'small tobacco-pipe mast'* and the *'forty bottles of Ring-Bo-Ree'* . . . and he might as well have sailed in a sieve for all that he left behind him.

Apart from the kids.

And they all left home and scattered, except for Ellie of course, who moved out first just four doors down to the life-long disgust of poor Freda. She is on Christmas card terms with her two brothers and two sisters now. They always agreed that they wouldn't send presents.

Freda died in hospital, having everything taken away. She'd been so thin by then that Ellie was concerned about anything solid being removed from her . . . surely she needed whatever she had to fill her out, to keep her standing. But the 'everything' turned out to be riddled with cancer and by the time they got to it, it was far too late. She was only forty.

One of the first things Robert Beasely had advised Ellie to

do was to make a will. 'However you feel about your money, it would be unforgivable not to organise your affairs, and there might be some extra bequests you might like to make.'

An awful realisation hit Ellie. 'When I'm dead everyone's going to know.'

'You'll be dead – you won't care.'

'But they will always know that I have deceived them.'

'Not for any selfish motive.'

'But it is selfish. I am depriving them all of an easy life, deliberately manipulating the people around me. I don't want them to know that, Robert, not even after I'm dead.'

'Well, there's nothing you can do to prevent it. They'll have to know. Now have you any other family with whom you might like to share it?'

She'd had to think very hard about that. She hadn't seen her brothers and sisters for years, but she got the impression they were all doing well: Bobby in Canada, Craig down in Kent, Cara, divorced now but still living in Preston, and the youngest, Libby, in Maida Vale.

If she left them some money she'd feel even more treacherous. No, if she was dead she'd want Malc to have it all, or Mandy and Kev, whatever.

'How about a trust,' Robert suggested, 'if you're worried about how they'll handle it, and then you can more or less control it.'

'No, that wouldn't be fair. I don't believe in control from the grave.'

So Ellie had to accept the possibility of hurting them all posthumously, or perhaps – and this was a rather lame hope – those enormous bequests would soften their attitude towards her. She wrote a letter of explanation, with Robert's help, 'so that they understand how I felt,' she said. And in that letter she was careful to stress her confidence in Malc. She didn't quite beg for forgiveness because Robert wouldn't let her, but she almost did, and she certainly felt the need to do that.

She has not yet mentioned the fact to Malc that she wants to sell the bungalow and move back into the city. After her return from her desperate visit to Di's house last week she had felt much better, until this morning and Maria's visit. But now . . . now . . .

She straightens herself as she sits there in the kitchen chair, and puts a determined expression on her face. A complete overhaul, that's what she needs, both physically and mentally. She glares at her cigarette packet and the one that spirals so foully, so acridly, from the mess which is the ashtray. She picks it up and drags it angrily through the ash. 'You can go for a start!' And Ellie breaks it and kills it and mashes it into threads before getting up and tipping the whole lot into the bit bin. She crumples the packet in a fist that is strengthened by grim resolution, and she throws it away.

She has brought all this pain on herself.

Everything is suddenly startlingly simple. The reason she does not accompany Malc on his various social excursions is because she feels unworthy, and she feels unworthy because she lacks confidence . . . she always has. Being plump and forty and a heavy smoker does nothing to boost the depressing state of her own self-esteem. And what's more, she says to herself, brightening visibly, all my insecurity and neurotic suspicions stem, not from fact, but from my own manufactured fear and I will not dwell or wallow in any of it.

'Fighting, Fit and Forty-Something' – those were the head-lines that had run over an article on Farrah Fawcett last week. Well, Ellie might never compare with Farrah Fawcett with her long golden hair and her hour-glass body and her sexy eyes, but she could do much better than she was doing if she tried . . . especially with money no object!

So she forces herself to get up. Never mind the weight in her mind and her body, she makes herself concentrate hard enough to find the yellow pages beside the phone in the hall, and telephone *'The Plaza Lifestyle Centre . . . whirlpool, gymnasium, superb treatment area, beauty salon, fast tan sunbeds and steam baths'.*

Hah!

And then, trembling slightly with both fear and triumph, Ellie goes to the fridge and takes out a circular box of cheddar triangles.

This is not a game.
She is such a fool.

20

Oh dear, the power of suggestion. Ellie's attention is entirely concentrated on the mysterious details which jealousy notices with such fatal precision.

Well – so how else are you supposed to behave when you suspect your husband is having an affair but you've no proof whatsoever?

Do you pay to have him followed? Do you bug his phone? Do you check on his every movement? Or do you look for tiny, everyday clues, like the speed with which he gets through his cornflakes, wondering why he's in such a hurry and did he used to eat quickly like that, with one eye on the clock?

Ellie hides the magazine for a start, feeling guilty as if it is proof against herself for her nasty, unwarranted suspicions. The pages are sticky in her fingers. She hides it beneath her side of the mattress so that it's handy to reach for first thing every morning. She needs to see it. She needs to stare at the pictures and work them out.

At night she lies alert beside him. She doesn't go to sleep until Malc does, and if he's restless she wonders why and if he drops straight off to sleep she muses over what he's been doing which could lead to such terrible exhaustion.

It is rumoured that Maria Williams is having an affair which has been going on for years. The reasons Maria showed Ellie those photographs are quite clear in Ellie's mind: Maria would not have gone to the trouble without a dubious motive . . . she's that sort of person. Seeing the glossy pictures of an event she would liked to have attended, noticing how everyone at the Grosvenor was enjoying themselves, old pals together, must have riled Maria beyond endurance. Getting in with what she likes to call 'the right set' has always been important to her. So she would not have come round to share them with Ellie out of any sense of kindness, or interest. She came round with one purpose in mind, and one alone, to warn Ellie about Malc's affair.

And to gloat over Ellie's reaction.

Does it take one to know one, Ellie ponders – one cheat to recognise another? But then again, maybe Maria is wrong. Maybe she's jumped to the wrong conclusions and is only out to cause trouble – putting jealous thoughts into Ellie's head.

'I have given up smoking, Malc,' she tells him that night when he gets home – late, and he hasn't rung to inform her. 'I gave up before lunch. I have thrown my last packet away.'

And it sounds like another gift she is trying to give him, like the blasted results of the cordon bleu. He is not particularly interested, merely polite, distracted by some letter he has to write. He says, 'Well done, Elle. Try and keep it up because you'll feel so much better in the end. Apart from the money.'

'Has the craving stopped for you now?'

My God what answer does she want and what is she really meaning?

Malc says the worst thing she can imagine. 'It all depends what I'm doing and what mood I'm in. It's really the extra energy that I notice most, Elle. Smoking makes you feel tired all the time, apart from the fact that it's so disgusting and you can't go anywhere and do it these days without making somebody else feel sick.'

'Did my smoking disgust you then, Malc?' And she realises with horror that she is following him round.

He stares at her as he passes her by, en route to his study. 'I don't think I even noticed you smoking, Elle,' he says. 'It's so much part of you.'

Oh my God.

She stands at the door of his study, looking in, almost twisting her hands behind her back in her awful, sickly anxiety. 'I have also rung a fitness place. I've got an appointment in a fortnight's time.'

I'm going to be nice. I'm going to be nice and healthy and fit and young again. For you. Just wait for me, Malc. Just give me until the week after next, for Christ's sake you owe me that!

Dear God she could do with a fag.

She chews on her lip, tearing at herself.

She knows she is annoying him. When she swallows the sound she makes is so loud he must be able to hear her. She knows he wants to be left alone to get on with his letter, she can sense the irritation he is trying to conceal with breezy politeness. His mind is on other matters and here he is, coming home tired, being swamped by mundane matters that interest him not a jot.

She is behaving like a child, pestering for a sweet from a father. But what does Ellie want Malc to unwrap and pop into her waiting mouth? Some words. Some words spoken sincerely, that will reassure her and take Maria Williams' cheesey, rubber-gloved fingers out of her mouth for once and for all. She feels like a person in terrible pain, a bottle of painkillers in her hand but the blasted lid is child-proof and do what she might she can't twist it off. Eventually Malc, sitting at his desk with the paper out before him and Ellie gabbling on behind him, turns round and asks, 'Is there anything wrong, Elle?'

She smiles and screws up her nose in the way of Mary Beth Lacey. She shifts her feet a little. She shrugs her shoulders and departs.

'Maria Williams knows nothing at all about you and Malc or your kind,' says the voice when she reaches the kitchen. 'You are not like her and neither is Malc. He would not go off behaving like that, breaking the vows he made in church, lowering his standards, just for a bit of fluff.'

'Maybe it's more than a bit of fluff then,' says Ellie. 'Maybe it's something more serious than that.'

'So you have convinced yourself that something is going on, have you?' asks the voice. 'You have swallowed the bait strung out for you by that vindictive woman next door in the same pathetic way that you picked up her challenge to race with her washing!'

Ellie sits at the kitchen table with her head in her hands. She is so confused. At home all day like she is, with no friends, no work, no diversions, how else is she expected to react? She tries to calm herself down with logic. What is the very worst thing that could happen . . . what is the very worst scenario?

Malc could go off with somebody else and leave her alone for ever.

Ellie can't take that one any further. There doesn't seem to be anywhere else for that one to go. It goes all the way already.

It could be that Malc is just having a fling. That snakey lady coiled up in his arms could be merely a one-night stand.

It could equally be that he was dancing with her because there was no way out of it. To leave her sitting alone at their table might have been impolite. It could well be that their conversation went no further, at the Grosvenor that night, than to comment on the lighting, or the heating, or the flowers. Hell, Gabriella de Courtney could be a married woman with children of her own for all Ellie knows.

Ellie fights her despair.

There have been no telephone calls to the house, after all. She has not picked the phone up only to have it put down. She has not sniffed perfume on Malc's suits or shirts or underpants . . . not that she's thought about it until now. But if there had been perfume, strong perfume, surely Ellie would have smelt it. Or anything else for that matter.

If Malcolm Freeman has been seeing another woman on any regular sort of basis then Ellie would know and there's an end to it.

She makes him a cup of coffee and takes it in. He has informed her that he has already eaten.

'Where did you eat, Malc?'

She has interrupted his writing again. 'Sorry?'

'I asked, where did you eat tonight?'

Malc frowns and shakes his head. 'At the Royal.'

'Was it a nice meal?'

'What?'

'Did you have anything nice?'

'Well, it was all right. Put it just there will you, love. That's fine.'

She tries to read what he's writing over his shoulder but she can't see from here and she doesn't want him to know what she's doing. 'Will you be long, Malc?'

'No, just another few minutes.'

'I'll wait for you then. I won't go up.' There is no upstairs in the bungalow, but they still call going to bed going up.

'No, you go up, Elle.' And as he looks at her again, his irritation shows, like small lines of writing across his brow. 'You go up and I'll follow as soon as I'm ready. Okay?'

'Okay, Malc.'

'Only I'm busy just now, that's all.'

'Okay, Malc.'

'Right then.'

Ellie has a bright blue bath and she fills it to the top. She wishes her body was younger right now. She imagines what Gabriella de Courtney's leg might look like, getting in. She bets she keeps her legs waxed all the time, even in winter. Ellie splays her toes and makes herself bear the feel of the plug-chain between them. It slithers. It's cold. She shivers. Malc used to stroke her feet for her once – she thinks that her feet are probably the most sensual parts of her body. She wonders if Gabriella's breasts are bigger than hers – they must be firmer – and she wonders if she has pink nipples or brown ones, or if her tummy button sticks out or goes in. She thinks it's funny how men know more about women's bodies than women do. Does Malc know about Gabriella's?

She could be dead, lying here motionless like this so that the water stops lapping her and circles her throat like a hot clamp. What would Malc do if she died, if she drowned in the bath tonight? She tries to let herself float, she's sure she'd rise to the top if she wasn't getting so fat or if she wasn't so full of smoke. Perhaps that's what makes her tummy look so fat . . . old smoke . . . but surely it doesn't get down that far.

People don't just throw their lives away for a moment's pleasure. Not in Ellie's world they don't. She powders herself and puts on a clean nightie. She brushes her hair so it shines. She slips under the duvet and feels like the Sleeping Beauty, waiting alone for a hundred years. Only as she waits and he does not come the hundred years pass and she turns from a princess into a cadaver. There are no rosebuds to cover her, only a shroud as she waits for the pathologist's hands.

She is still and cold like a cadaver.

She has left off her bedsocks.

And her heart feels as if it might have died; the tick of the clock assaults her ears.

'Are you awake, Elle?'

'Yes, I'm still awake.'

'Can't you sleep?'

'You'd never leave me, Malc, would you?'

He jokes, 'I thought there was something the matter with you tonight! I thought you were behaving strangely this evening. Go on . . . go into the kitchen and have a fag!'

'You'd never leave me though, would you, seriously?'

'Whatever has made you start talking like this?' He is undressing. He is annoyed. He looks white and slender, like marble, from behind. He ruffles his hair before getting into bed like he always does and it is his hair that makes him human in the night light. She looks at his feet, they have always been hers. She feels him beside her, so familiar, and there is a long, long moment while they wait to see which way he will turn.

Once they slept with babies between them, warm and milky and gurgling with life. They had to face each other then, when they had a baby in bed. 'If there was something wrong, Malc, you would tell me, wouldn't you?'

'Ellie, for goodness sake, if there was something wrong you would be the first to know!'

And he clicks off his light and turns over.

I have asked him, Ellie tells herself. I have asked him and he has answered.

And he is absolutely right.

I might not have been the first, *but I do know.*

But then comes another morning, and another, and here is Ellie on that terrible carousel going round and round and round, going through the whole thing over again, quite dizzy by now, a wild-eyed sleuth searching for clues.

He is slurping his cornflakes.

Why?

Because he has always slurped his cornflakes, you stupid bat.

There is nothing else for it. She is going to have to go and have a look at this wretched woman Gabriella.

21

Would a woman like Gabriella de Courtney want Malc?

It is one week after Maria's visit and should she tell Malc that she's been to the Royal Albert Waterside Art Gallery this afternoon? Ellie removes *The Deesider* from its mattress home and leaves it open on the kitchen table, quite casually, but in such a position that he cannot possibly miss it the minute he gets in.

He's late, it is dark, and her eyes are sore from peering out of the window.

'Maria brought them round,' says Ellie easily, puffing her face free from steam as she checks the pie in the oven.

Malc sits down. He keeps his coat on. She watches him out of the corner of her eye. Ellie doesn't like chaos but she senses there's some kind of chaos here in her kitchen. Does it come from her, all red and flustered, with pastry annoying her under her nails down where she can't quite get at it, or does it come from him? She is suddenly conscious of the past they have shared together and it is like a tight ball of hempy string, used often and re-wound again, hairy, with knots in. It used to be strong and dependable . . .

Would a woman like that want him?

Not as he used to be, certainly.

'It looks as if you are having a good time. Maybe I ought to have come after all. I will, next time, if you like.'

Silence.

'That's if I'm invited.' She laughs hysterically, aware of her tight faded smile.

Silence.

'Maria says she's got some gorgeous dresses in at the moment and I said I'd go and have a look next time I pass by. Maybe I ought to buy something fancy because I haven't got anything suitable for an event like that one. I never thought I'd need to wear a dress like that but now I don't know. I thought that I might pop in. Next time I go by. And she looks nice, Gabriella de Courtney. She looks like an interesting person.'

Silence again while she circles him; she waits with dull eyes and dull ears but can only hear the squeak and the clank of the Williams' wrought-iron gates closing.

Malc moves for the first time and he brings his hands together, spreading his fingers as if to take some ache out of them. She watches him swallow before he brings himself to say, 'She is an interesting person, Elle. You'd like her.'

'Huh . . . you thought that I'd like Maria Williams, but I didn't.'

'Ellie.' Malc clears his throat, and then he asks her hoarsely, 'Hell, d'you fancy a drink?'

'I'll get it, Malc. You just sit there. Tea won't be long.' She ought to be laughing at that . . . after all these years of convincing Malc to call it dinner. 'And don't you want to take your coat off? It's hot in here what with the cooker . . .'

It looks as if he's bowing to her when he shrugs himself out of it and Ellie can't see the expression in his eyes. His coat smells of frost – she is grateful to be handed it – there are sparkles of crispy night air on it that look like sequins when she holds it up to the light of the hall.

She plods back into the kitchen in spite of knowing that a monster waits in there. She puts his glass down in front of him, solid and heavy with golden fire inside it, and she pours herself a sherry from the kitchen cupboard.

'Ellie, I have been wanting to talk to you, but you've been so peculiar lately that there hasn't been a right time.'

Ellie calms the rattling of the saucepan lid before she sits down.

'I don't know how to start.'

Ellie felt proud to be married, yes she did, even though she was seventeen and everyone was against it, even though she'd had no choice and it was a shot-gun wedding. She'd felt proud in her heart, proud to be wanted. Proud to walk down the street, pregnant, with her man.

'Things have been happening,' Malc says.

And Ellie could tell that all her friends were jealous because she had found a man for her very own.

169

'I can't tell you exactly when it first started.'

They had broken the bank to buy the tiny ruby. They shouldn't have done that. They bought that ruby and never caught up.

'The first time we met was at Speke airport. We were booked on to the same plane; it was the afternoon I rang you to say we'd been held up by fog and I didn't know whether we'd get off until tomorrow.'

There had always been a kind of worship in his eyes. He'd given up his classes and they'd decorated the bedroom. They'd cleaned up the whole house and decorated that, too. When Mandy was born she'd come into a palace . . . new cot . . . new pram . . . and a tiny white chest of drawers with rosebuds down the sides.

'It was obvious the plane wasn't going to take off so we went to have a drink.'

Oh, she'd been so frightened of the birth. The midwife had tried to push Malc out, but knowing of her terror he had bravely refused to leave the room.

'We were instantly attracted to each other. That's the only way I can say it. I can't think of any other bloody words which will explain.'

They hadn't planned a second child straight after. Malc had been determined, even then, to carry out his plans. 'We'll not stay in this bloody slum, not a moment longer than necessary. You're worthy of more than this, Ellie.' But yes, there had been an odd sort of pleasure in parading the pram in front of her mother . . . look, Mam, look, I might not be able to pass exams but I can have beautiful babies!

'I wish you'd say something, Elle. This isn't easy. I don't enjoy causing this sort of pain, you know.' And Malc hides his face in his hands.

'What are you telling me? I don't know what you're telling me.' In the small space between them is all the emptiness in the world.

Malc lifts his face again and Ellie sees his anguish. She asks him again, 'What are you telling me, Malc?'

'That Gabriella and I want to be together.'

'That you don't want to be with me any more?'

'I never thought I'd ever listen to myself talking like this.'

'So what do you want to do?'

'I would like to go away, just for a little while.'

'With her?'

'With Gabby, maybe, yes.'

'And leave me here?'

'We would see each other, Ellie. Whenever you needed to do that we could see each other.'

'In case I'm lonely, d'you mean?'

'Don't, Elle.'

'I'm sorry, Malc, I didn't mean it like that. I didn't mean to sound feeble.'

'It might only be for a little while. It might not work out between us.'

'Would you come back then, Malc? Once you'd tried things out?'

'Ellie. The thing is, I don't think we love each other any more. I don't honestly think we have loved each other for a very long time, and I've thought about this, and thought, and thought, and I've come to the conclusion that since I've had this new job everything has suddenly become much clearer. We were jogging along in a rut, Ellie, rubbing along together out of necessity and habit. We hardly had time for feelings. I know this is a shock . . . shit, I know what you're feeling, Elle, honest to God I know what you must be feeling just now. But when you are able to start thinking about all this more clearly, I truly believe that you might find yourself realising that I am right. We didn't have very much, Elle, and apart from the memories, we don't have much now. Do we?'

'You want me to answer? Is that what you've paused for?'

'I want to know what you're thinking.'

'Why, Malc? Why do you want to know that? Are you hoping that I'll take away some of your pain by saying that what you are doing is all right?'

'Sod it, Elle, no, I don't want that. That's not what I'm asking.'

'What do you want? Why did you tell me? Why couldn't you have carried on with your sordid little affair on the side, why couldn't you have just carried on screwing the bitch in secret without bringing me into it?'

And this is the first time Ellie has imagined Malc in bed with his arms wrapped round somebody else. *Somebody else knows what he feels like and somebody else knows what he says.*

'I had to tell you, Elle.'

'Because you are leaving?'

'Yes, because of that.'

'So you would have kept me in the dark if it hadn't got this far?'

'I would have tried to spare you.'

'Spare me?' Ellie screams.

'Please, Elle.' His head is going into his hands again but she won't let it, she jerks it up with shocking words. He can't be allowed to escape like that.

'What's she like in bed then, Malc? Hot, is she? Juicy and eager? I expect she does things that I won't do. I expect she gobbles you off . . . that's the expression, isn't it? Does she suck your cock for you . . . or perhaps you have this secret urge to go up women's arses. Perhaps that's what she does for you . . .' Even as she rages comes the agonising awareness that spite and fury are such temporary shields.

Malc holds out his hands like a preacher, but they are more like the solid buffers of a train. 'Don't make this worse, Elle, please. I beg you, don't make this worse than it already is.'

'Could it be worse? You say you know how I'm feeling now. I doubt that, Malc. I doubt that you'll ever come even close to knowing how I am feeling just now. I think I knew. Maybe that's just my pride protecting me, Jesus, I need something to protect me, but I think I knew you were off fucking somebody else.'

'Does it matter whether you knew or not? Does that feel important?'

'You fucking bastard. And why tonight? Why did you pick tonight to tell me? Did you plan it with her? Did you decide this between you and are you going to ring her up in a minute, one of those quiet phone calls you make from your "study" when the door is closed! I suppose they were all to her, weren't they? All those late evening phone calls! Oh, what a pathetic, blind cow I am! Did you laugh at me, Malc? I must have been so fucking funny. Did you say to Gabriella, "Oh, don't worry about Ellie, she can't even get one clue in the

Telegraph crossword, we've nothing to worry about from that quarter".' Ellie cannot stop now. She cannot even consider stopping because what will happen when she stops?

'Elle, you know very well it could never have been like that.'

'Do I? How do I know that? You tell me, Malc. How do I know?'

'I have never been that sort of person . . . the kind of person to be deliberately cruel to anyone else.'

'I never knew you, Malc. I never even knew the slightest thing about you.'

'We did know each other once, Elle, but that was a long time ago.'

'Before this raving bitch came along. Before you went sniffing between her legs.'

Oh God, how these words are hurting her. They are vile, they are filthy in her mouth. She spews them out because she must, she vomits them into the horror. She cannot rid her tongue of the taste of them.

Malc closes his eyes with pain so Ellie seizes on that. 'Oh, it hurts you does it, to hear me slagging your filthy piece off in front of you? Noble, good-thinking Malcolm Freeman, towering high on his pinnacle of love, is that it? Looking down to the depths of the sewer which is his crappy old wife Ellie! God, you disgust me. God, you really, really revolt me. I shudder when I think of you together. That's what I do, I shudder.' And Ellie shudders.

'I'm going to go now, Elle.'

What does he mean – go? 'But you haven't had any tea!'

Malc stands up. 'I'm not hungry.'

'But where are you going? And at this time of night! Don't go now, Malc. Stay for the night. Stay and let's talk. We can't leave it like this, don't leave me like this. Don't go out, Malc.'

Malc looks like a wounded soldier, brave, strong, but one of his legs is probably full of shot and he's bleeding somewhere you can't see.

'I will come back and see you in the morning.'

Ellie makes frantic gestures. She whines like a dog, 'But I have made this pie!'

'It will be easier for us to talk in the morning.'

'And there's episode four of *White Gates* on at nine twenty-five.'

'I'm not going to hurt you any more than I have to in all this, Elle.'

He can't leave without his coat. Ellie rushes into the hall and grabs it, clutches it against her, refusing to give it up.

Malc stands there staring at her for a moment, his car keys in his hand, his scarf, she notices, he never took off. So he'd never meant to stay.

'I'm not going to give you your coat, Malc, because I think this is silly. I think you should stay. We have to talk. You can't just leave me.' Not like this. She screams in her heart. *You can't just leave me like this!* You can't just walk out and drive away and leave me with all this pain, and all empty, on my own.

'I don't think any amount of talking would get us anywhere tonight. You are too het up. We are both too upset.'

'Don't go, Malcolm.'

'I will phone in the morning to see how you are and then I will come round if that's what you want.'

'Don't go, Malcolm.'

'About half-past nine. I will phone. On the dot, I promise you.'

'And what will I do until then?' He is halfway out of the door and the pie is burning.

'Try and get some sleep, Elle. I want you to try and sleep.'

'D'you think I should fill a bottle?'

'Yes, fill a bottle, and take a book with you.'

'I haven't got a new book. I never went to the library this week.'

'Well, a magazine then. Hell, Elle, there must be something in the house that you haven't read.'

'I don't think I'm going to be able to sleep, Malc. I didn't mean those things I said.'

'I will phone at half-past nine. I promise.'

'Don't go, Malcolm.'

He closes the door very quietly. Like a frightened man who's got a stolen diamond hidden in his pocket.

Ellie creeps after him and opens it. She begs into the screaming cold night on a little whisper. 'Don't go.'

174

She watches the puffs of the jeep's exhaust, like fleecy pieces of candy floss, sticky, sweet, gone before you can taste it.

She lets the door close behind her and drops to the floor, cuddled up tight on the welcome mat and hugging her knees like a little child.

She licks her knee, tasting herself. She digs in her teeth and makes a red mark. She rocks herself while she hugs his coat, 'Oh don't go, Malcolm. Don't leave me all on my own. Mam, Mam, help me, kiss it better, Mam, kiss little Ellie better, Mam. Make it stop hurting . . . no, no, no, no, take it away make it stop God. *Jesus tender shepherd hear me.* I'll be a good girl, God, and I'll do anything You say only please take this away and make it stop.'

22

There has to be humiliation first. Nobody likes it. Nobody wants to know about it but it just has to happen, that's all.

In order to see it through it is quite important to remember that humiliation is something the victim allows to happen. In Ellie's case she begs for it to happen, and when it comes it is awful.

Never does Ellie Freeman want to endure another such night as this first one. She takes a barrel of biscuits to bed after downing her hitherto untouched sherry and Malc's abandoned scotch. She carries the whisky bottle to bed with her as well as a hot water bottle, and there she lies, dizzy and wide-eyed, propped on her pillows with the bedside light on, and the curtains undrawn, and the bedroom feels as empty and huge as an aircraft hangar without doors.

From that night onwards, throughout the rest of her whole life, the taste of scotch will become the taste of anguish.

Disbelief is the first line of defence, and that is a thought process requiring intense concentration for the super-bending of facts, the distortion of expressions and the turning round of conversations. He cannot have meant what he said. Malc is attracted to this evil woman because he is not strong enough to resist her. The last thing he really wants in the world is to go off with somebody else, to leave his home and his wife. And it won't take too long before he comes to his senses.

And that scenario requires an imaginative response from Ellie, because what will she say and how will she behave when he comes back, cap in hand, guilt-ridden and sorrowful?

She will be quiet, understanding, dignified but hurt. Extremely hurt. But at this point in time she would take him back, most certainly.

Unsophisticated and still very immature in a strange, little-boyish kind of way, Malc has misread this woman's intentions towards him. Feeling uncommonly pleased with himself, no doubt, for attracting such an obvious creature, his response is, perhaps, an understandable one.

She's read about men of Malc's age in magazines. They cannot be trusted. They are afraid of getting old, and of losing their appeal and their sexuality, their identity even, and they are striving to find themselves before it's too late.

And they often make fools of themselves in the process – hell – she peers at the centre spread in *The Deesider* which she has beside her in bed, in Malc's place. He could be this girl's father!

Anyway, Malc loves her, for hadn't she seen love in his eyes this evening, even as he was unfolding his tale of horror, even as he was, with every word he uttered, destroying her? Yes, she had seen love on his face and it was love that had caused him his torture. If Malc did not love her he wouldn't have bothered to be gentle. He would not have put up with her fishwife reactions, he would have stormed out of the house earlier and he certainly would not have planned to ring her tomorrow.

And Ellie knows Malc in a way that this unscrupulous, hard-faced creature never could and never will. Ellie knows where his strengths lie, and his weaknesses. If she is calm enough and cunning enough to fight this battle correctly she reassures herself that she has all the weapons.

All the weapons except two . . . novelty and beauty, which Ellie thrusts aside.

Malc, after all, is a creature of Ellie's creation. Not in a million years would this malicious Gabriella de Courtney have looked at him twice just a year ago, in his overalls, with his hangdog expression and his going-to-nowhere eyes. But the other man is still there, forming the core of him, deep inside him, no matter how urgently he struts along or how effortlessly he conducts conversations or how charming he sounds on the phone. Oh yes, the old Malc is still there all right . . . the Malcolm who is unquestionably Ellie's.

And, if necessary, if she has to, she will call him back. Like a spirit.

She has the power.

Already there are silly little things which gnaw – she hasn't locked the doors and she hasn't turned the heating off – Malc's last jobs of the day.

Ellie slurps scotch from the bottle, wiping the trickle off her chin with the back of her hand like a hard woman. She reaches confusedly for a fag, her hand hits the biscuit barrel and she brings that into bed with her instead and cuddles it.

She's glad she hadn't confessed to Malc that she'd gone to the gallery. Already she regrets her loss of dignity and that revelation would have made her feel worse. Unable to smoke, a whole week seething under a million dark suspicions, Ellie could not endure remaining at home doing nothing with the minutes ticking so slowly by. She felt that if she paced the house any longer – with the magazine pictures the centrifugal force of her universe, the black hole – she would lose her mind. Her appointment at *The Plaza Lifestyle Centre* wasn't until next week and she hadn't got anything to do. Her hands were not steady enough for the patchwork and nor were her nerves.

So she slapped the pages closed, stuffed them back under the mattress again, slammed the door and backed out the car. No sign of Maria, thank God. That snake-in-the-grass next door must have gone to work.

She drove through all the old streets, moving slowly down Nelson Street and noticing, for the first time, the holes in the road. Dusty red brick, aerials and drainpipes, the rooftops made patterns against a darkening sky. She had no fear that she might be seen and recognised – not that it mattered – for during the day there was nobody home. Her heart lurched when she passed number nine and saw new curtains up in the front room window; someone had placed a cupboard thoughtlessly so that its plywood back showed through the net. Someone had gone and spoilt it.

At that point in time she couldn't quite understand what was making her so nervous – was it this slinky woman cuddled up so safely in Malc's arms, or was it the stabbing jealousy of knowing that Robert Beasely was there making merry among them. Or fear . . . of loss, the lonely feeling of exclusion from something, being locked out without a key and nobody willing to let her in, or even to tell her the correct address.

Elspeth Freeman was the only one not invited to the party which was going on with such hilarity behind that damn green door.

Perhaps her fears would come into focus correctly if she could get a look at the woman in the pictures.

Ellie parked down an old dock road where tramlines were still embedded in cobbles. They were still headed in the same direction, still knowing where they were going, only not understanding that there was no longer any point. Ellie felt like a stranger, yet on familiar ground. All the big warehouses round here had been knocked down, and in their place rose weird, wooden, multi-layered structures, some octagonal, held together with pieces of glass, with little square pent-houses set on the tops. The cranes had gone, the containers had gone, the chains and the ropes and the hoists had gone.

But they had left some of the bollards and painted them glossy black. Now they looked like something to do with No Parking, and there were little signposts bristling with infor-mation that pointed her towards the gallery. She followed them with great interest, meandering down dark passageways lit by Victorian lighting, and in dark overhangs were shop windows displaying artistic wares, pewter vases and what looked like pieces of driftwood. There were very empty-looking shop windows and deserted-looking shops. She peered inside one – it was mostly carpet.

They had not been able to conceal the smell or the sound of the Mersey . . . they had not been able to pick it up, stuff it, label it and stick it at the back of the dockland museum.

She had nearly smashed straight into the gallery doors. There was so much glass she got it mixed up with the space. She found herself walking like a blind person, her hand stretched out anxiously before her. And there were so many levels of paving, so many fountains and statues, that the whole effect was confusing.

Sudden, total silence greeted her as the door swung closed behind her. She was a huge, childish painting, red and raw from the cold, a roughly-done intruder scribbled in sticky crayons. Ellie had never imagined the paintings would be so large. They dwarfed her, she felt like a crumb on the floor as she stared up at them, overawed, and you never saw the same sort of force coming out of real people as you did from these oil ones. And Ellie had never noticed that the sky or the sea were full of such colours. But they were, really, if you looked hard.

Ellie walked from room to room, her feet echoing hollowly. Everywhere was fresh new wood, so bright it was almost dazzling. And all the roof was glass sky. There were people sprinkled about, standing back or reading catalogues but they were unimportant. She stopped rushing because you could not rush in here, you had to walk slowly and with respect and, this was the queerest sensation, you had to look up.

So where, in all this, was Gabriella?

Women in uniforms like long-distance coach hostesses sat reading on chairs in the corners of the rooms. In the foyer was a counter selling postcards and knick-knacks like tea towels and miniature jars of jam. Beyond that was a café and over the wood you could just smell the coffee. Ellie sensed that soon she would find a room which said Private.

She did.

She loitered, pretending to be waiting for someone by looking bored and checking her watch and tutting tiredly every so often. You could see the door from the café, so she went inside for a while and sat down, ordering nothing but easing off her shoes.

And then Gabriella de Courtney came out with a man. Ellie wouldn't have recognised her from the photographs but for the hair; there was so much of it. It wasn't long, not hanging down, but sticking out wildly with bows here and there like an exhibition dog. And yet Ellie knew that every fuzzy strand was meant to be as it was, that every tweak and every tickle of it was just right.

And it was fawn.

And she was wearing just about the ugliest 'suit' that Ellie Freeman had ever seen. If you could buy suits at Woolworths, then Ellie would be quite certain that this one had come from there. It was a kind of mustard-coloured linen, and crumpled, and there were seams in Gabriella's stockings. Gabriella was long, lean but busty with a multitude of scarves flung round

180

her neck, and she had the most excited eyes that Ellie had ever seen.

The man was but a shadow by her side. Gabriella saw him out expertly and then, with long determined strides, went back through the door marked Private.

Well – and what had Ellie expected?

Not this feeling of exhaustion, certainly. Ellie gained nothing from her visit to the gallery save for the loathing directed at herself for succumbing to the urge to go there, and an unexpected, deeper sinking of the heart. If Ellie was utterly frank with herself, and she was, she understood this second feeling and froze in her tracks. Ellie realised instantly that she did not know this bold woman, and that if she ever became her enemy she would not know where to attack.

What the hell should she do? Ellie swigs at the whisky again, and searches her befuddled mind while she blunders through the bedclothes for a lost bit of biscuit. No, she's glad she didn't let on that she'd been there. That would have been a grave mistake.

Gabriella de Courtney is no beauty . . . not in the way that Ellie sees beautiful. And yet. . . ?

The voice speaks to Ellie. 'Take your money away. Withdraw it.'

And Ellie snaps back, 'What good would that do? Canonwaits don't need it, they are doing perfectly well on their own without my help.'

'Well tell him, then,' says the voice. 'Pull the rug out from under the bastard. He'd never have got the job in the first place if you hadn't paid for it. Take him down a peg . . . that'll do the trick.'

Ellie muses with difficulty. Her head swims round and round. In the end she moans, 'He would hate me if I did that.'

'But you'd have him back.'

'And we'd be just as we were in the first place.'

'Was that really so terrible?' asks the voice, nagging on at her like an old watch.

And Ellie has to answer honestly that it does not seem quite so terrible now looking back on their life in Nelson Street from this awful, painful perspective. They had never had to endure anything slightly like this. There were times, many times, when she'd felt she was on her own, and that Malc was just beating time beside her, but that loneliness had been nothing at all compared with this.

She sobs to herself, drunkenly. 'Oh God oh God oh God.' She sweats in the bed because of that damn central heating, but she hasn't the strength to get up and go and turn it off. The idea of opening the window does not occur to her fuddled wits.

She contorts her face and twists her mouth to get it round the name, 'Gabby!' What an ugly sound – Gabby Gabby Gabby Garbage Gutters and Gizzards.

Oh, what is Malc doing now? Ellie reaches clumsily for the clock; she delves in the mess on her bedside table to reach it and she shudders when she sees the time – half-past three in the morning. What is he doing? Lying beside her contented in sleep, or making love? Is Gabriella de Courtney twisting one elegantly manicured finger through the thick bushy hairs on Malc's chest? Or a more intimate place? Or are they talking together, discussing her ... and if so, *in what way does he discuss her?* And that thought is so totally distressing, so painfully enormous is the sense of betrayal that Ellie cannot endure it. So she hugs it to her, stabbing herself with her own knife, making a vast space so that the humiliation has all the room it needs to come in and settle comfortably.

She reaches for a fag again and, finding none there, weeps with the pain of deprivation.

And it is not so much a sleep that Ellie finallly sinks into when the hands of the clock go round to five, it is more of a red-hot blast of oblivion, a ride on the choppiest sea in the world, seared by a scorching sun. With biscuit crumbs in her bed and the neck of a bottle gripped tight in her hand, she tosses on waves tinted puce with nightmare. She is granted just two hours of this before she wakes up, weak and exhausted, and the remorseless battering of merciless reality takes over from sleep.

Ellie Freeman, millionaire twice over, hauls herself out of her messy bed and gazes apathetically at the ruin of herself in the mirror – and she'd thought Maria Williams had an eye-infection! Extraordinarily, she has survived, but in order to continue she cannot be idle, sober or alone for one minute. She showers, she drags on some clothes and, after backing out the car, sets off through the freezing rain with shaking hands, a trembling lip and grim determination, in the direction of Robert Beasely's house.

She would not pass a breath-test if she was stopped.

23

'I am sorry, I didn't quite catch . . .'

'Ellie! It's Ellie.'

It's not yet seven o'clock and here she is on Robert Beasely's Victorian doorstep, trying to explain to Bella who she is and why she's here and why she has to be let into the house immediately. Bella Beasely, who has risen to answer the frantic ringing, wears a pale blue, three-quarter-length towelling dressing gown with a large collar and a hood. Ellie wants one. In the middle of all this horror, Ellie knows that she wants one, and she's tempted to ask where Bella bought hers.

'But it's only seven o'clock in the morning!' She can't work out who Ellie is. She is still half-asleep. 'Nobody's up yet!'

Robert's children James and Victoria are up, they are coming downstairs in fluffy jumpsuits, hanging over the banisters while they peer through to see what is going on.

Bella Beasely has thin wrists and an intelligent-looking, sensible black-strapped watch.

Ellie says, 'Perhaps I ought to have telephoned before I came over.'

Bella runs her hands through her brown curly hair and agrees. 'That might have helped – this is a bit of a surprise. And you say you are a customer . . . a customer of the bank?'

'Yes, but I'm more than just an ordinary customer. Robert has been helping me with my investments and now I have run into some terrible trouble and I need his advice very badly indeed.'

'So badly that you couldn't wait for the bank to open, it would seem.'

'I don't see Robert at the bank,' says Ellie sharply. And then she watches as some half-dawning recognition crosses Bella's face; the eyebrows rise, just slightly, the teeth catch the bottom lip and the eyes, vaguely irritated up until now,

184

move to take her in all over, making sense of a story she has once been told.

Bella knows about Ellie. Robert has told her.

Ellie should not feel betrayed by this because it is natural that Robert would tell his wife such an extraordinary story.

But how did he tell it?

Ellie peers through the door and sees James and Victoria sitting listening on the bottom stair. Bella follows her glance, shrugs her thin shoulders indifferently and says, 'Well, you'd better come in so I can close the door. I can't leave you waiting out here. Call Daddy, James, will you please, and tell him that it is important. There's someone called Ellie here to see him.'

James rushes up the stairs in an exaggerated scramble. Victoria, with her long brown hair and her pear-shaped face, sits on and stares. The door closes and the light through the glass casts various-coloured reflections on an otherwise colourless carpet.

It is the house she thought it was when she drove by last Christmas Day with Malc in the new Cherokee.

Bella is clearly embarrassed, and harassed. 'You'd better wait in here,' she says, opening the door to the first room on the right. 'And would you like some tea while you are waiting? He shouldn't be long.'

Ellie nods and passes through, smiling at Victoria who creeps away warily on bare feet. Ellie supposes she probably does look a bit frightening this morning, to a child. The room is airy and square, a sitting room with lots of tall bookcases in it and a fireplace with a fancy tile grate. She doesn't sit down on either of those huge, squashy sofas, covered in parrots and jungle leaves, but she tries to pull herself together with the help of the mirror, a mirror like the one she was going to have . . . in her Georgian house, one day.

The Beaselys are getting Christmas cards already. Oh God – Christmas! Ellie stares hard at herself. She looks as if she's been through some terrible, long, debilitating illness. Even her clothes don't appear to fit properly and she has buttoned her shirt up wrongly. Her hand shakes as she tries to right it and she attempts to settle her cardigan more squarely on her shoulders - slipped like that it looks as if she's slanted all over, as if she is having a stroke. Her face she can do nothing about. It looks ravaged. She feels ravaged, yes she feels raped and ravaged and attacked and abused.

This isn't how she had dreamed it would be when she first came to Robert's house. She had hoped she would be invited. And then she wonders painfully if Gabriella and Malcolm have been here already.

'Are you sure you are feeling all right? Can I get you something else, like a Paracetamol, or a glass of water?'

'I am not feeling all right,' says Ellie, accepting the tea with a shaking hand. 'But neither Paracetamol or water will help me.'

'I am sorry,' says Bella, hovering by the mantelpiece. 'Whatever is wrong, I am sorry.'

'I had to come here. I couldn't think of anywhere else,' says Ellie.

Bella Beasely says nothing at all, but raises her eyebrows and frowns slightly.

'I have had no sleep,' says Ellie. 'No sleep at all. My husband announced that he was leaving me yesterday. His name is Malcolm Freeman, perhaps you know him?'

'If I do I can't remember,' says Bella, seating herself in a position prepared for flight on the edge of the chair nearest the door. Ellie remains standing, although her legs feel stiff. She doesn't know if she can bend herself sufficiently in order to sit down.

'Well, he spent last night away from home. With his new woman . . . Gabriella bloody de Courtney.'

She sees Bella start a little. Her countenance darkens before she lightens it with that weak smile again: she has either heard of the slut or she knows her. Bella says, 'I really don't know what to say. It must be terrible for you.'

'Yes.' Ellie attempts to sit down and succeeds. Seeing how much the cup is shaking, Bella rushes forward and places a table in front of her. 'Thank you,' says Ellie. 'You are being very kind.'

'Not at all,' says Bella, agitating for Robert to come down and help her out here. 'Perhaps he'll come back,' she says, rather hopelessly, into the awkward silence.

'He'll come back. It's just a matter of when, and it's just a matter of how to cope with the hell of it while he is gone. He doesn't love her, you know.'

'Probably not,' says Bella Beasely, who runs creative writing groups for sex offenders. It seems to Ellie that she is probably more at ease with sex offenders than she is with someone like her. At least you know what sex offenders have done, while with an abandoned woman you can only guess what terrible wrongs she might have committed to have driven her husband away.

Hearing a sound that Ellie can't hear, Bella gets up in haste and flashes a quick smile across the room before she rushes out. Then Ellie hears them whispering together before Robert's worried face appears through the door and with it the anxious word, 'Ellie?'

She wants to run into his arms and be hugged.

She wants to tell him everything, all the cruel, wicked things that Malc said, the fact that she got herself drunk last night, the feelings that are raging inside her, the fears, the powerlessness of her situation. He is strong while she is weak, he has the answers while she has not.

But Robert does not look as if he is willing to let Ellie Freeman run into his arms. They are crossed, for a start, and so are his legs when he sits down, gravely serious.

'Bella tells me that you and Malcolm have had a disagreement.'

'He's left me,' Ellie sobs, and struggles around in her handbag for a tissue.

'How did you know where I lived?'

Ellie shakes her head, bewildered. 'Oh, I don't know, Robert. I have always known where you lived. I think I looked up your address right at the beginning. He walked out of the door on me last night.' She can hardly speak for the crying, but Robert doesn't come over, he leans further forward instead as if he can reach her that way. 'And I don't know what to do.' Ellie is shaking like a jelly now, almost completely out of control.

'This is obviously a very traumatic time for you.'

Ellie stares across the room with her eyes and her face

awash with tears. Her mouth drops open. She can't speak so she nods.

'I think you might have done better to remain at home until you felt more able to cope with the situation.'

Ellie bites a terribly trembling lip.

'It was quite a surprise to be woken up like this, I must admit.'

In the silences that follow Robert's short, sharp sentences, the sound of Ellie's breathing takes over.

'Rushing out of the house like this, acting so impulsively, is not going to make you feel any better.' And when Ellie doesn't answer Robert says, 'Is it?' And then again, 'Is it?'

'N . . . n . . . no.'

'I would like to be able to help you in some way, Ellie.'

Out of a mouth that is full of wet cardboard Ellie manages to gasp, 'I need someone to help me and I couldn't think of anyone else.' And her voice rises into a desperate sob.

'Neither Bella nor I are at home during the day. Our schedules are pretty heavy.'

'What?'

Robert hurries on, 'I've got to say it, Ellie. I am surprised you came here.'

'I wanted to talk to you!'

'But you could have telephoned the bank,' and then, slightly more gently, 'couldn't you? You could have waited.'

'Well yes, I suppose I could have.'

'But you decided you couldn't wait.'

'I have had no sleep,' moans Ellie, rocking herself backwards and forwards.

Robert Beasely sighs and lets his shoulders sag. It is funny to see him here in his house with his personal effects around him . . . photographs, pictures, ornaments, table lamps, books . . . 'You had better tell me what happened, seeing as you're here.'

Ellie replaces her cup on its saucer with caution. She shakes her head vaguely. 'There isn't very much to tell, really. He just said he wanted to move out for a little while, that he wanted to be with her.'

'Gabriella?'

Ellie pounces. 'You know her, don't you?'

'Yes, we know her.'

'Do you know her well?'

'She used to be a friend of Bella's, actually.' Robert's discomfiture is pronounced – his throat does three quick swallows. 'And this is all pretty difficult. I wish that my wife . . .'

'A close friend?'

'No, not a close friend. More of an acquaintance, I suppose.'

'I saw the photographs of the Grosvenor dinner, I saw how you were all together. I didn't really realise until then that you must know Malcolm quite well.'

'There are times when we bump into each other. At functions, naturally.'

'Do you like him?'

At once the question sounds childlike and Robert answers, 'Well enough.'

Ellie bites her lip. 'Do you like her?'

'Who?'

'Gabriella.'

'Ellie, really, I am just not prepared to say whether I like her or not. And this conversation is getting us nowhere at all. It is all getting just a little bit silly and I am still very confused over the reasons why you decided to come here.'

'I thought . . .' Ellie starts.

'Yes?' Robert leans further forward.

'I thought . . .' The sounds of morning are going on in the rest of the house, footsteps crossing bedroom floors, the creaking of central heating, the shrill squeal of a child, the running of taps. Ellie remembers how silent the bungalow was when she left it . . . and the awesome silence of last night after Malc went.

'What did you think, Ellie?'

She can't hold his eyes. 'I thought you might be able to help me.'

'Well, I certainly would if I could, Ellie, but I can't see how.'

'I needed to be with somebody.'

189

Robert withdraws. 'Well, I can understand that . . .'

'I needed to be with someone I trusted.'

'Am I supposed to be flattered by that?'

'Bella . . . she seems like a very nice person.'

'What's all this about, Ellie?'

'I have always wanted to come here, you know.'

'I can't imagine why.'

'Can't you, Robert?'

'Sometimes, Ellie, I find it quite hard to understand you.'

'Perhaps you have never known anyone quite like me before.'

And then he smiles, makes a joke of it, relieved to be able to do so. 'I certainly agree with you there!'

Ellie does not smile with him, but she's stopped crying so that's a small start. She says, 'I should not have come here this morning, should I?'

And Robert shakes his head and says, 'No, not really.'

'It wasn't on, was it? It was the wrong thing to do. You are not here for this sort of thing, are you?'

'I am interested in you, Ellie. Yours is an interesting situation, and we have been able to do so much with the . . .'

'Fuck off.'

'I beg your pardon?'

'I said fuck off.'

'Ellie, now this attitude is really ridiculous. You are overwrought and exhausted, you don't know what you are saying or what you are doing.'

'I know exactly what I am doing.'

'Well if you do know, then it was quite inexcusable for you to come barging into my house, waking my wife and my children at dawn, causing all sorts of problems . . .'

'I see that now. I see that I shouldn't have done that.'

But Robert Beasely is uneasy. Maybe he thinks she is suicidal and needs professional help because he asks her, 'What do you intend to do now? Can I suggest that we make an appointment for later on this morning? I think I am booked until half-past eleven but after that, if you care to ring up, Janet can probably fit you in and we can discuss the wider issues of this . . .' He wants Ellie out of the house.

190

'Don't talk any more.'

'What?'

Ellie gets up. 'Please don't talk any more. I don't want to hear you talking.'

'So you won't ring up? You are determined to carry on behaving badly.'

'No, I'm going now. I won't hold you up any longer.'

Robert Beasely messes up his hair in frustration. 'Listen, Ellie. I know I have upset you by my reaction but really, you have to understand that your personal problems are not in my brief . . .'

And then Ellie roars with laughter. She feels quite fond of him again in a removed kind of way. He has made her smile . . . he has given her a taste of those other feelings which she feared she would never know again. She will be able to laugh one day . . . Laughter still lives . . . nobody's killed it. And if there's laughter there'll be joy, too, and contentment, wonder, and that ordinary, soft kind of sadness which can be dealt with gently.

Ellie makes for the door. 'Please apologise to Bella for me,' she says sincerely. 'What on earth must she think of me, letting myself go to pieces like that?'

'Oh, don't worry about that.'

'All right then, I won't. I just don't want her thinking that I don't know how to behave.'

'Bella wouldn't dream of thinking that.'

Ellie turns to face him at the door. 'One thing,' she says, 'and I'd really be grateful if you'd answer this honestly. Did you know that this affair was going on, Robert?'

He answers her directly and quickly, so she knows very well he is lying. 'Hand on my heart, I had absolutely no idea.'

'And has Malcolm ever been here to your house?'

'Here? Why would he come here? I don't know Malcolm that well, Ellie,' and Ellie knows that this time, he is telling the truth.

'Thank you for that,' she says.

And when she looks back as she gets into her car she sees a child's face staring out through a window of the room she's just left, and she knows that either James or Victoria hurried in after she'd left to see the freak, the extraordinary creature their mother must have been tutting about while her husband 'dealt' with the mess in the front room.

24

The enemy is advancing. It is hurtling towards Ellie and threatening to strip her, threatening, as the surgeon did her mother, to take everything away.

Ellie drives: if she drives very fast indeed she just might be able to leave some of her own humiliation behind. She drives on and on, trying to work things out, attempting to come to terms with her extraordinary isolation.

There is nowhere to go and nobody to go to.

If Ellie had worked in a factory like Margot, or in the organised bustle of a hospital canteen like Di, her situation would most likely be different. Her lonely job in the Arcade working for Mrs Gogh, sometimes helped by a young YTS girl on a Saturday, was hardly conducive to making friends and getting to know people. And Nelson Street had changed so much . . . everyone in it staunchly withstood being moved into one of those barrack-like flat complexes set on a hill like a fortress strung with white flags of surrender – nappies – and painted blue and yellow. They signed petitions and held protest meetings objecting to the move. Men with forms had been dispatched from the council, they bobbed up with irritating regularity over the years like outbreaks of fleas and vermin; they called themselves inspectors and they tried to declare that Nelson Street was insanitary and unsafe. Rubbish. Once, in spite of the protests, they almost succeeded. The bulldozers ranged against the mutinous residents across the wasteland behind the advertising hoardings, giant, grey and massive like regiments of battle tanks. They squatted there for weeks, gathering litter and old coke cans in their huge destructive claws and the people of Nelson Street put boards across their windows, had posters printed and went by night to unlock the petrol caps and pour water into the great beasts' engines. Old people's eyes went bright, they grinned gummily and said it was just like the war.

They planned to line themselves up across the road, and some of them said they would rather die than be shifted.

Then the council ran out of money. The whole thing spluttered out and with that went the staunch sense of pulling together against the odds. The odds of life retreated beyond the narrow frontiers of Nelson Street and became invisible, like the germs; they were no longer something you could see, attack, or range yourself against. The odds turned into silent vigils outside barbed wired gates, blue hands rubbing together over braziers, desperate conversations in front of glass partitions, and after that the loneliness of closing your door against the world and fighting an unseen enemy alone.

Nobody could win this battle. People started leaving Nelson Street and those who came to replace them were younger and angrier, super-defensive so that catching eyes in the street was like giving your terror away.

No, Ellie has no friends down Nelson Street.

Di had asked her once, 'Come to aerobics with me. You need to get out and about a bit for just a couple of evenings.'

Ellie had answered, 'I'm never that keen on leaving Malc on his own.'

'Well, why doesn't he go somewhere – take up a hobby or something? He's such a slob, Elle.'

She always enjoyed defending Malc. There was a kind of safety in doing it. 'He's tired out, Di. He has to work very hard and it's physical work, remember. He's worn out by the time he gets home.'

'But he wouldn't mind if you did something.'

This was a difficult argument to answer because Ellie suspected that if she went out, Malc would probably not even miss her. That might be so, but she didn't like doing it, she just felt guilty about it, that's all. And secretly she was afraid that she might be the most unhealthy person there if she went to aerobics and they would all see how short of breath she was, although Di smoked like a train and still managed it somehow.

Very occasionally, if there was absolutely nothing on telly, she might persuade Malc to take her to see a film, but the last one they'd gone to see was *One Flew Over the Cuckoo's Nest* – so you can tell how long ago that was.

And then of course there was always the club on a Friday night. Sometimes they went there on Saturdays, too. And Ellie felt satisfied with Di and Margot. She knew she would never find such close, true friends as them, and it did not occur to her that one day she might want to.

Malc was exactly the same. He didn't have any friends except Dave and Dick; the people at Watt & Wyatt were only workmates and somehow for him, that made them separate and different.

Ellie winces as she drives along, remembering the cordon bleu and the poetry. Perhaps she is not the sort of person whom anyone would want as a friend. Perhaps she isn't interesting enough or doesn't have sufficient to give – too satisfied, with a closed mind – because even with Malc as he was, there had been something comforting about drawing the curtains in number nine, lighting the fire and settling down for the evening with a book, the telly and the *Mirror* crossword. She used to start it and Malc always finished it, but he had never demanded a harder one, never suggested that they might tackle a more difficult paper. Perhaps Malc had been satisfied, too, in a moaning, miserable, hopeless sort of way, and maybe Ellie had secretly known that.

She calls on God as she drives along. Many times. And loudly.

She is terribly hurt because Robert was so appalled to see her, and worse than that, because she has got that relationship so wrong. Ellie sees herself as pathetic. A kind word, a few lunches, that genuine interest which Robert had shown . . . oh, what an easy conquest she was, and buoyed up by the belief that somehow her money made her different. At one point, and she can hardly bear to admit this to herself as she drives along the grey, wet link-road, at one point she even believed that in a guarded, subtle kind of way he had fancied her, and oh God she had flirted with him, too, smiling a certain smile, positioning herself in a certain kind of way, making her eyes go wistful, trying to be interesting and seductive. Oh God oh God, at forty and Robert was what –

thirty-two, thirty-five, something like that. She can hear him now, going home to Bella, that able, sociable creature with her television relative and her artistic sister. She can hear him accepting a drink and starting, 'You're not going to believe this but such an amusing thing happened to me today. There was this peculiar woman . . . it's a bit sad, really.'

Ellie swerves and almost goes into the back of a lorry. The driver behind overtakes, winds down his window and shakes his fist at her. Ellie, on top of all the other pain – it fugs the air, it mists up the windscreen – on top of all this other pain Ellie Freeman has still got room to be hurt by a stranger waving his fist.

She slumps at the wheel and drives on, automatically turning for home. Well, where else can you turn? She rummages in her bag for a fag and, remembering she's given them up, accelerates, accidentally knocking the wiper switch as she goes so it feels as if she drives through a storm.

She hears the telephone ringing when she's got her key halfway in the lock. She has made up her mind not to answer it. Let him worry. Let him not know how she's thinking or what she is feeling. If she can only make Malc suffer just a modicum of what she is suffering.

She rams in the key, flings open the door and races across the hall to pick it up. 'Malc?'

'It's me,' says Malc. 'I tried earlier but got no reply.'

'I've been out,' says Ellie, but Malc does not ask her where. So he does not think he has those rights any longer? No one has those rights over Ellie any more. She has relinquished them involuntarily, she feels desolate and despairing.

'How did you sleep?'

'I hardly had any sleep at all.'

'I've been thinking,' says Malc, and his voice is curiously distant. 'It might be a good idea if you went to the doctor's and asked for something to help you.'

'Sleeping pills?' Does he hate her that much? Is he angling for her to take her own life?

'Just for a little while, until the worst of this is all over. And maybe he could give you something to help you through the day.'

This! From Malc – who used to pour scorn on Disprin, who chose to stand out in the yard breathing deeply if he got a headache rather than take anything 'those bastards are pushing out'. This must be the de Courtney woman's influence – she looks like the type who would fly to a bottle for comfort.

'I would rather try not to do that,' says Ellie with dignity. 'Not unless it is really necessary.' Hah! Give him something to worry about, let him think she has not hit rock bottom yet.

She can tell that Malc is checking his watch when he says, 'Now, Ellie, what about me coming over?'

'Yes, that might be a good idea.'

'What time would you like me?'

Ellie's day is hardly hemmed in by appointments, she's hardly got to fetch her diary to check it. 'Any time. Now?'

'Right away?'

'You might as well.'

'Right. I'll see you in about forty minutes, then.'

Where is he speaking from? Work, or the home of the slut? It must be from Gabriella's because it's not ten o'clock and he wouldn't go into work for an hour, not if he's planning to leave so soon. And if it's HER house he's ringing from then SHE is probably listening.

'Is she listening?'

'Who?'

'Gabriella?'

'Don't be silly, Ellie.' And she has the feeling that is the way she is going to be spoken to whenever she expresses herself honestly now. 'Don't be silly, Ellie, don't be silly.' Without a man, immediately she is relegated to the status of child.

Will their conversations over the coming weeks get longer and longer or shorter and shorter, until they stop having conversations at all, just like it used to be? Until they merely grunt acknowledgements while passing? Will she pass him? Once he's gone, if he goes, will she ever pass him, or, in the end, will he be just one more stranger in the umbrella and pinstripe horde?

And is Gabriella de Courtney uneasy about Malc coming over? Did he have to argue with her in order to get his way – oh, Ellie does hope so.

She ought to get the house straight, she ought to have it fresh and smelling nice. And herself . . . she doesn't want Malc to see her looking like this. She has always been the strong one – she led, Malc followed. She'd held him for years by being like that; it would be folly to change that now, just because of her need.

'A brick', that's what she was, and she can be a brick again if she works the cement in hard.

So Ellie turns herself into a whirlwind, and right deep inside this flashing, spinning vision of washing-up mop and hoover, down in the breathless vortex, is the hope that if she plays this one right he might agree to come home.

And then this whole nightmare will be over.

She always was a creature of hope. Malc's leaving hasn't changed that, nothing had ever been able to change that.

So it's a clean house that Malc comes home to, and a kitchen that smells of lemon and a wife who smells of tears. But it's all shipshape on the surface and what shows is what matters now.

When he comes into the house – he does not ring the bell, he uses his own key – Ellie sees, with some satisfaction, that he has not slept well either. They are two tired people sitting down at a new kitchen table with a new kind of strangeness between them. It manifests itself as politeness. Ellie asks to be excused as she goes to fetch the milk from the step and she casts worried eyes at next door in case Maria Williams saw him coming home.

'I am going to turn the heating to the automatic timer again, Malc,' she says, 'because I know I'll never remember to turn it off every night manually.' She wants to hear him say, 'Don't bother,' and she wants to hear him say, 'This isn't going to last long enough for us to change our old habits,' but Malc just looks surprised, astonished to find that her mind is still on such mundane matters.

'And that is something else we are going to have to discuss at some stage,' he says. 'Money.'

'Money?'

'Yes. I want to reassure you straight away that money is one thing you don't have to worry about.'

198

Well, and isn't that sweet of him?

'I am going to try and make it possible for you to stay here and that your standard of living does not drop. I want you to be able to keep your little car . . .'

It sounds as if he is never coming back.

'And all the time you are going to be living somewhere else?'

'Yes, at the moment it looks like that, yes.'

'With her?'

'That's how it's going to be, yes.'

'Does she have a house of her own?'

'Gabriella has her own flat.'

And now comes the appalling realisation that he is going to remove his things. 'So we are going to have to decide which belongings are yours and which are mine, aren't we?' says Ellie.

Malc seems surprised to hear Ellie being so practical. 'I wasn't going to bring that matter up yet.'

'Why not? It is something I am going to have to face at some point, isn't it?'

'I have a small case at Gabriella's. I will collect some more clothes before I leave this morning, but I don't want to hurt you any more than I have to.'

'Yes, I remember you saying that last night, Malc, but please don't expect me to be grateful for that.'

'I don't. I don't want your gratitude.' And here is his hang-dog expression again.

She is genuinely curious. 'What do you want from me, Malc?'

'I would like us to go through this thing with the minimum of bitterness, so that afterwards we can face each other with some dignity left. And in order to achieve this I want you to tell me how you are coping. I want you to feel free to contact me, to talk to me whenever you need to.'

Ellie remembers sitting here in this same chair a week ago, before Maria Williams came round with that magazine. She sat on the same chair but she was a different person then. And incredibly, Malc thinks she is that last-week person; he is talking to her as if she is, reasoning with her as if she still has a brain in her head and human thoughts and emotions. He does not see the animal with the sore, yellow eyes, the bared teeth and the hackles that bristle around her neck. Nor can he hear her panting, or the soft pad-pad of the desperate animal who has to kill or be killed. With a kind of sickly sweetness, hiding her scent, she responds, 'I think what would help me more than anything else just now would be to meet this Gabriella of yours.'

Right now. Let's see if the bitch is up to this! This challenge of Ellie's is bound to shake her. Rigid.

Malc answers quickly, 'I don't think that would be a very good idea.'

Ellie smiles. How pathetic, he is protecting the cow. But she is determined to be persistent. 'I can see that she might feel uncomfortable about talking to me in the circumstances. I can understand that she might need some time to think about it.'

'Oh, I don't think Gabriella would mind. In fact, she has told me she would like to meet you, very much. It's me, Elle. I don't know if I could handle that – not now. Not yet.'

Incredible! What sort of hard-faced woman is this, and can it be true that Gabriella is eager to meet her? Ellie presses her challenge. 'You told me to tell you honestly, you said you wanted to know how I felt.'

Malc says, 'But I just can't see how any good could come from a meeting between you.'

'Perhaps no good would come from it, but I would have satisfied some need in myself. I want to know what she's like, Malc. I want to see how she feels about this.'

'Well, why don't you just let me tell you?'

'Because that wouldn't be the same thing at all.'

And Ellie knows that all he honestly wants to discuss are the practicalities of all this, the money, the 'arrangements'. Oh, men are all the same. They say they want to talk but they don't. They are happier with car engines and football scores, the latest price of redwood shutters and, just recently, the movements of stocks and shares.

There seems to be no room anywhere in all this for talking about Malc coming back. He is too busy smoothing his path clear for leaving, and to do that successfully he has to make certain that Ellie will be all right. She can see how wary he is, listening carefully for the slightest crack in her voice that will warn him that she's changing back into the violent creature she was last night.

She keeps that creature hidden behind her wounded smile, but it's still there . . . and it's breathing softly . . .

'If that's what you're sure you want to do.'

'Yes, I am quite sure about that, Malc.' She expects Gabriella to back down.

'When would you like this meeting?'

'Oh, as soon as possible I think, don't you?'

He looks at Ellie suspiciously. 'You're not going to make a scene or anything like that, are you, because that won't work with Gabriella. Nothing like that will work.'

'You are being unkind to me, Malc.'

He shakes his head wearily. 'I am just worried, that's all. You seem too calm and collected this morning.'

'And after last night you expected to find me still wild?'

'I honestly didn't know what to expect.' He gives one of his little-boy smiles but the mischief is absent. 'I was ready for anything.'

'Were you ready to find my dead body on the floor?'

'Oh Ellie, don't!'

'Because that's what I felt like doing when the jeep pulled away.'

'I know you are not that foolish. You never were that type. You were always strong, Ellie, much, much stronger than me.'

'This has never happened to me before.'

'It has never happened to me, either, Elle. What I am doing is not easy.'

Poor Malc.

He wants her to help him! Just as he has always done, he wants her to help him! It is the extraordinary realisation of this that gives Ellie her new feeling of power. It is the combination of that and her reaction to the humiliation she suffered earlier this morning, sitting in the drawing room of Robert's house, and the way he and Bella had said, in so many words, 'You are not one of us in spite of your money, so go away.'

201

Funny where power and strength can come from. Funny the places where pride can be born.

Ellie paces the kitchen while she waits for Malc to select his belongings. She would be happier doing this for him . . . she knows what he needs far better than he does. She closes her ears to the sounds from the bedroom of wardrobes opening, drawers closing, halving a life – hers. When he comes back he sits down heavily, confronting her, ready for anything. He has left his case at the door but she can smell suitcases and empty cupboards because losing has a smell of its own.

Immediately she asks him, 'What are we going to say to Mandy and Kev?' She half-expects him to say that nothing is yet that certain, and it's not worth upsetting them.

'I thought I would write them a letter,' says Malc.

'Have you thought about what you are going to say?'

'Yes, I have.'

'Are you going to tell me? Are you going to let me see this letter?' It will be the first letter Malc has ever written to his children. Ellie's the one who writes, and she signs his name for him.

'I would rather not, Elle.'

'Will there be things in it that you'd rather I didn't know?' He doesn't answer so Ellie goes on, 'And you are asking me to be honest!'

'Don't attack me, Elle.'

'I have a right to know, Malc, so that I can respond.'

'The children were always yours, weren't they, Ellie?' Malc says dryly.

'*Is that how you felt?* Why did you never feel able to say anything? Oh Malc, I think this idea has been arrived at fairly recently because I never saw any signs of it before. In all those years there was never a clue.'

'What could I give them that you weren't already showering on them?'

Ellie says, 'They would have liked to have known you, for a start!'

'I was always around.'

'But never quite there, Malc, never quite there!'

'You didn't like it when I started taking Kev to watch

Everton. You said it was no place for a child – remember? You said he was far too young. Football yobs – remember that? You accused me of turning him into a soccer yob.'

'I wanted Kev to know there was more to life than football. I was terrified that he'd become obsessive like some of the other lads in the street.'

'And did you think I wanted that?'

'What was I to think? You were always so scornful of anything other than sport. It seemed as if anything different Kev took an interest in was a threat to you!'

'And could he have threatened me so easily, Elle? Even then was your opinion of me so low?'

'You refused to come up to the school!'

'Oh, come on . . . The one time I went with you, whenever I began to answer the teacher's questions you butted in and answered yourself, as if I was too slow, or as if I might say something that would disgrace you!'

'Oh, Malc, how can you say that? And I didn't notice you once turning off the telly so they could sit in the warm to do their homework. They had to go upstairs and spend hours shivering in freezing cold bedrooms.'

'I brought home electric fires for their rooms!'

'Yes, but they never worked properly, did they?'

'I didn't hear you make a fuss! You never said about that!'

'No, of course I didn't, because you were always so snappy and bad-tempered I never liked to! You had more time for that snotty-nosed brat next door than you ever had for Kevin.'

'Johnny Malloney? If you think back you'll notice that it was Johnny Malloney who had more time for me!'

What on earth are they talking about? What on earth have they got into?

'Oh Malcolm, I didn't imagine I was going to have to sit here and listen to you feeling sorry for yourself.'

'I didn't expect that I was going to.'

'There was obviously so much going on inside that head of yours that I never suspected, so many resentments – and now you are bringing them out and turning them on me like secret weapons!'

'"You don't want to turn out like your father, Kev." Just how many times do you think I heard you saying that, Elle?'

'But not in any kind of seriousness. Christ, come on now Malc, you know that!'

'You admired me, did you? Is that what you're going to say next?'

'For a lot of things – yes – I admired you!'

'So that's why you used to tell Mandy, "Get your exams, get on. Work hard, you don't want to end up stuck in a dump like Nelson Street with a life as dead-end as mine." Yes, you were always so full of encouragement and admiration for me, weren't you, Elle?'

'I wanted the children to be able to fulfil their dreams, Malc. And I used every device I could find to fire them!'

'I was the perfect example of what they must never allow themselves to become!'

'I never spoke to the children about you.'

'No but you used me relentlessly for illustration!'

'And myself!'

'What did you have to feel ashamed of, Elle? It was you who fought the battles, you were the one who defeated the odds in spite of the trials ranged against you, you were the plucky one, I was the defeated.'

Ellie is shocked. 'Is that what it felt like?'

Malc nods. 'Yes, that's exactly what it felt like.'

This is so unfair because Malc is exaggerating. Anyone could talk like he's talking now and it had never been quite like that. Ellie admits to herself that there might be some truth in what he says . . . but it hadn't been anything like that. And now his face is colouring as he rises up on the strength of righteous resentment.

'You have absolutely no idea what getting this job did for me. The fact that I was chosen over the heads of hundreds of others, the fact that I was expected to work well, the respectful way I was treated. Right from the beginning they made it clear that I was an important part of the company, included in all the decisions, listened to. The fact that I can drive, Elle! For me it was like a cripple suddenly finding he had a pair of legs, and walking. As long as you live you will never know, Elle, what getting that job did for me, and I will never be able to truly explain it . . .'

Ellie is silent, staring hard at a flower on the wallpaper just above his head. Tears are threatening to fall, and she has promised herself that she will shed no tears.

'. . . and Gabriella sees me in a way you could never see me. It is in her expectations of me, Elle. She expects me to be successful, she expects me to cope. She is proud to be with me, she doesn't look for the stain on my tie or the untied shoelace.'

This is unfair. 'I was never aware that I did that!'

'You never said, but I felt you looking. I always felt you looking.'

Ellie says quietly, 'And you don't think I could change?'

'Ellie, I don't need you to change. Not any more. Not now.' And he looks at her sadly, considering whether or not to go on before he says, very gently, very carefully, 'And you could never fit into my new way of life. You are a threat to me, Elle, with your old-fashioned ideas about what is correct and what's not, your peculiar notions of how to behave and what knife to use and all those words . . . supper, drawing room, napkin. It doesn't matter, Elle, don't you see that? I am not accepted because I know which tie to wear or what words to say. I made it because I am me, and good at my job, and because my ideas are good and because I am dependable and because I can see a good deal, act fast and clinch it. It is nothing to do with the way you hold your knife, Elle, not any more it's not. I'm sorry, but it just isn't.'

'Common,' says Ellie bleakly.

'Yes, exactly, common. It has no meaning any more. Not for me.'

She wants him to leave immediately. She wants to make arrangements for the meeting with Gabriella bloody de Courtney – the whore is bound to bow out of that one – and then she wants him to go. She is too hurt to stay awake any longer. She has to find sleep, she whines for it as a baby whines for its bottle. And the memories she is desperate to push away, the memories of this morning's total humiliation, are bounding towards her like snapping dogs.

But Malc is leaning across the table and he is saying, 'I didn't come here this morning in order to hurt you. I didn't want us to talk this way, not yet, probably not ever.'

'I want to have a bath and wash my hair now, Malc.'

'Well, the water will be hot if the heating has been left on.'

'Yes.' Ellie sweeps back her hair with her hand. 'Yes, I suppose that's one blessing, isn't it?' She smiles weakly.

Malc gets up, looking more defeated than she does. 'I'll ring you. I will speak to Gabriella and then I will ring you. I'll try and arrange it for soon, if that's what you're sure you want.'

Ellie is not sure of anything any more, but she sticks to her guns because she has to stick to something and she doesn't want to fall apart completely, not yet.

'All right, Malc.' She lets him out with his case. 'I'll wait to hear from you then.'

As he goes he tells her, 'I'm sorry, Elle.'

And her answer is gentle. 'And I'm sorry, too.' Because through all the years I have known you I have never seen you looking so small and I have never heard you sounding so bloody pathetic.

25

After her meeting with Gabriella de Courtney Ellie Freeman goes to bed and sleeps for two days and two nights . . . forty-eight hours of oblivion . . . and when she wakes up she does not get out of bed. She stays in it for a week.

Dwelling on the matter.

She refuses to answer the phone and she puts the chain on the door. The milk stays on the step, thickening up and getting sour.

She has created a monster, a monstrous man desirable to women, women like Caroline Plunket-Kirby, Gabriella de Courtney and probably Miss Bacon, too. She was afraid of them, as alien to them as ice is to fire, and yet the unsophisticated, the inexperienced, the boring Ellie Freeman must have known whom they'd welcome into their beds.

With her money she has formed him and with her influence over the years she has moulded him. And, what's more, she had picked out the material in the first place; she had decided on the best bit of clay around twenty-one years ago and picked it up quickly before anyone else could grab it.

He is strong. He is earthy. He is muscled, bronzed and lean now. He is quick-witted and glib-tongued, yet kind, charming, and he knows how to look after a woman.

And the Malcolm Freeman of Nelson Street, whom Ellie had met by the coke pile all those years ago, was never more close than when Ellie saw him crossing the colossal space of Gabriella's carpet to fetch the ice for the drinks.

The boldness was back in his eyes and there was one loose curl over his forehead just spiralled enough to get your finger in.

Yes, Gabriella had been keen to meet her and so Ellie was deprived of even that little victory.

Their arrival had been heralded by a great flap of security. You had to speak into a grille before the front doors of the flat block were opened . . . you had to insert a card to operate the lift and then you had to pass over a bleeping device before you even reached the penthouse. During all this palaver Malc smiled at Ellie sheepishly. Ellie smiled back with a smile that was crimped on to her face. Try as she might, she could not remove it; she was lacquered into it with misgivings and terror.

She had removed the short, sharp barbecue skewer from her handbag just before Malc arrived to pick her up, thinking better of it, or chickening out more likely. She had been planning, in the secretly desperate hours of night, to place this skewer under a cushion on the de Courtney woman's chair at the first opportune moment. She had also removed the handbag-sized Waspeze spray with the eye warnings on it, the sachet of Weedol and the loaded Stanley knife. These things were to do with dark night thoughts and she normally kept them in a multi-pocketed velvet roll called a stocking tidy but which she now referred to as her 'comforter'. Sometimes she brought it into bed with her and stroked the velvet while she moaned to herself with her eyes closed.

No, she would fight the lion unarmed, she decided, with the laurel wreath of a headache tightening her brows.

'You look very smart,' said Malc when he arrived to fetch her.

'I like to try,' said Ellie briskly.

'I'm in the bath, darling.' called a voice which controlled the smoothly opening door – a remote control device with which she was also able to turn on the cooker and draw the curtains. 'Won't be a mo. Make yourselves at home.'

And although Malc smiled apologetically you could see he admired the bitch's nerve. He made the excuse, 'She probably thinks you'd be more relaxed with me on your own for a while, just until you get your bearings.'

Oh, how kind.

'She's spent all evening preparing something special. She really does want to be friends.'

Oh. So she's not deliberately trying to squash me, thought 'silly' Ellie. She has not asked me here for that. And while she glided round the elegantly furnished sitting room, taking in the pictures, the rugs, the window blinds, the raised areas and the lowered areas, Malc watched her and said, 'This flat is Gabby's pride and joy. She was lucky to get it – over a hundred people had their names down for it even before it was built.'

'It's certainly got a lovely view,' agreed Ellie, going to the window and peering out into the darkness, looking down on the strings of fairy-lights, the flickers of distant, slow-moving ships and the private glows of yachts tied up in the marina.

'It cost her the earth, but she says she was paying for a dream so she didn't mind.'

'That's right,' said Ellie. 'You wouldn't mind paying for a dream.' She turned towards Malc, resting her back on the window ledge. 'And if you stay with her do you intend to live here? What about a garden? What about those green fields you so badly hankered after?'

'That was your dream remember, Elle, never mine.' Ellie frowned, because this was not true. He had never asked her what she wanted, and it was always Malc who was so keen on having a garden. Malc continued, 'We'd stay here because we both love it. I think it would kill Gabby if she had to move. She's always telling me how she feels part of it all, you see, with it being in the same block as the gallery which she had a large hand in designing.'

Ellie mused, and took her eyes round the apartment again, more slowly. So this was Gabby. This was Gabby's dream – the dream of today's woman, sophisticated, labour-saving, up-market, somewhat pretentious, but it smacked of desire and freedom. For who but a dreamer of freedom would choose to position themselves beside a river, beside the sea, so they could lie in bed and watch the ships sail in and out to faraway places, exotic lands and strange mysterious traditions?

Protected from reality by chrome and laminate and bollards painted black. Protected from freedom by a fine strong man who was old enough to be her father. This Gabby was just like a little girl, really.

Ellie said, 'It is slightly dangerous to satisfy a dream so young.'

'Gabby is twenty-eight.'

209

'And that's not young?'

'She is old enough to know what she wants, and to go out and get it.'

'Like you then, Malc?'

But he didn't know if Ellie was mocking him or not, so he didn't reply.

'For someone of her age she has a prestigious job.'

'She has never wanted any other. She had to work extremely hard, push herself forward and convince all the old fuddy-duddies that she could take on the whole enterprise and follow it through. There's five years of her contract to go but she says she feels she hasn't even started yet.'

'She certainly knows exactly what she wants, doesn't she?' Ellie was impressed and she could see why Malc would be. Impressed and staggered by such forceful energy.

What drove her?

'I expect she had a good start . . . the right schools . . . well-connected parents?'

'Gabby achieved what she did without any help, although yes, she comes from what we'd call a privileged background. They didn't want her to follow an artistic career, though. They're all mixed up in the law and they'd hoped she'd follow them into that.'

Ah!

'I suppose that eventually she'll want to get married?' Well, Ellie had to know! And she would also dearly like to know what Gabriella was going to get out of this meeting. Did she want to gloat? Was it that simple?

'We haven't gone into that yet, Elle. Gabby is a very independent person. Her independence is important to her, she's never accepted any help from her family.' And he said this with pride, as if somehow this factor in Gabriella's personality was in his, too! And Ellie thought that the need to live up high, on the top of something, looking down on the rest of the world as it blundered by, was probably all part of the need to conquer alone.

But Gabby wasn't alone any more. She had Malc with her. And they were both dependent, if on nothing else, on the structure that held them up here.

210

'I expect only nice people are allowed to come and live here?'

'Well, for the money you have to pay for one of these apartments you'd hardly get your riff-raff. This is one of the most expensive pieces of real estate in the city.'

'A long way from Nelson Street, Malc.'

And he nodded thoughtfully as he brought his wife her drink.

Ellie had tried very hard to look presentable this evening. She had gone to Maria Williams' boutique for the first time ever . . . 'Glamour Puss' . . . in the centre of town.

'Anything special?' asked Maria in a bright brittle voice. She must have known something was wrong because Ellie's face was still puffy and Malc's jeep hadn't been parked outside the bungalow for two nights. Ellie could have told Maria that Malc was away, that wasn't so unusual, except for the fact that he kept popping back during the day to see her.

Ellie was terribly tired and way beyond playing games. 'No, nothing special. It is just important to me that I look nice.'

'Well, about how much do you want to spend?'

'I don't care what I spend,' said Ellie impatiently. 'As long as I get the right look.'

'Well then, let me recommend . . .' and Maria began to pull dresses out, brightly hanging each on the changing-room rail before launching into a fanciful description of every one.

With her dulled senses Ellie was confused. What sort of image did she want to create, what sort of impression did she want to make on this scheming termagant who had taken her husband – and more than that, did it honestly matter? She thought that it probably did, and it was that which kept her inside the shop and prevented her from running out into the street in tears, flapping Maria off her as you'd flap at a persistent wasp.

Ellie knew that whatever she bought she was not going to look good. You couldn't look good when you felt like she did inside, dreary and frightened, abandoned and ugly. But she would do her best, and it was important that she choose something comfortable. She pushed away Maria's bows and sequins, she turned her back on the balls of netting and the

211

petalled skirts, and in the end she chose quite a simple blouse and skirt in wishy-washy blues all run together, made out of silk. It was the rubbery texture of the silk and the smooth coolness of it that attracted her. She might not be able to appear smooth and cool, she might not be able to ripple elegantly over the bulging difficulties of life, but her outfit did.

'I think you have made a very sensible choice,' said Maria, eyeing the price-tag with pleasure. 'That'll take you any-where.'

What on earth did that expression mean?

She'd already decided to wear the pearl earrings which Malc had bought for their anniversary, and the silver bracelet he had chosen with love last Christmas.

And then she popped into the hairdresser's before going home and just had a simple cut. Her hair was very depressed, the hairdresser, Simon, said. She could have told him that.

Malc had been as good as his word and it was only the next day he phoned to ask if Friday would be all right. 'Friday night,' he said, 'and Gabby says how about a meal?'

And if Ellie was taken aback by the nerve of the woman, she didn't show it. She responded with pluck. 'That sounds nice, but where?'

'Here at the apartment. Well, it'll give us a little more privacy, we thought . . .'

'Yes, lovely,' said Ellie, astonished, gripping the phone with a shaking hand.

'Nothing formal,' said Malc.

'Well no,' said Ellie.

'No fuss, I mean,' said Malc. 'It's not necessary. I'll pick you up about eight.'

Like a date, really.

'You still want to go through with this?' he finished tentatively.

'I have to meet her,' said Ellie staunchly.

'Well, that's that then. That's organised.'

She felt he expected her to say something else but she didn't know what there was left to say, so she just said goodbye. She always tried to say goodbye first on the phone;

she always tried to get up first in order to end their meetings. She was desperate not to be left hanging on, clinging and unable to let him go – like that first time – when she'd tried to hang on to his coat. And he couldn't know that the minute the phone went down she slithered to the floor, weeping copiously into the receiver.

A pale blue light shaped like a Canterbury bell came down on the end of a long cord and dangled over the table, which was laid on the raised platform beside the vast picture windows that overlooked the river. There were various salads set out in chunky white bowls looking healthy and clean. Wine was cooling in a silver bucket. Outside, on summer nights, Ellie imagined they'd have dinner on the balcony. There were urns out there, and plant pots, and white iron chairs, and what looked like a very complicated barbecue. If you looked down to your right you could just see the angular patterns of the gallery roof, like a complex design of wooden pyramids leading off round the corner. You could smell Gabriella's bathwater, heat and body, hot hair and essence of roses. You could also smell the food, something spicy and dark, something well under control, simmering sensibly, coming from the kitchen.

Gabriella entered straight from the bedroom. She was wearing a kind of karate suit, the trousers and jacket fluttered several feet behind her and it was the smooth way she walked that made Ellie think of the adverts for sanitary towels they'd started to put on the telly. She was also wearing a turban and Ellie, on first sight, thought she had washed her hair and forgotten to take the towel off, but this was not so.

She walked straight up to Ellie, opened her arms and tried to kiss her.

Ellie sat very still and allowed Gabriella de Courtney to waft round her. Malc got up from his chair – did he always get up when she entered a room? – kissed her and caught her hand. They had eyes only for each other.

They were in love!

And this was the only sort of woman with whom Ellie could not deal. She wanted to curl up like a child. She wanted to suck her thumb. She wanted to call out, I don't want to be your enemy, I want to be you, to be yours, I want for you to be my mummy.

'I am so glad you came,' said Gabriella, terribly directly.

'I felt that I ought to meet you,' Ellie replied.

'I liked you the minute I heard that,' said Gabriella, coming to sit down beside Ellie so that the white leather sank with a little puff. 'And I know that in spite of all this we can be friends.'

Ellie's heart was banging in her face, shooting colours there, and terrible, uncontrollable pulses. Malc fetched Gabriella a drink and while she sat there waiting for it she held out a hand pointed like a snake's head and stared at Ellie with interest. She said, 'Put the veggies on darling, they're all ready in the kitchen,' and Malc almost bowed to her before drifting across the carpet and out. Dark and lean and suave in his chocolate-coloured jacket, his roll-neck sweater and his perfectly creased trousers.

Gabriella leaned forward and the leather puffed again. 'And now we have a chance to talk.' Her breath smelled of toothpaste. 'You must be feeling very lonely and confused just now. It was brave of you to come here. You're a strong woman, Ellie, aren't you?'

Ellie sat back. Her stomach bulged silkily; she should have worn the shirt outside, she should not have worn a belt and tried for a waist.

'Darling, how rude of me.' Gabriella leapt up. 'You must be gasping.' And she came back with a carved wooden box full of expensive cigarettes.

'I don't,' said Ellie, waving her lifeline away. And then she said, 'I have come to tell you that I'm not giving him up. I have come here to tell you that, whatever the cost, I am determined that Malc will come back to me.'

Gabriella looked flabbergasted. 'You can't mean ... whatever the cost?'

Ellie sat forward and the leather groaned. 'I do mean it. I mean exactly that.'

'But I thought we could make this a pleasant evening ... getting to know each other. It is important that we do that, you know, Ellie.'

214

Not only was Ellie having to fight the enemy, sitting here so silver and white, so beautifully poised beside her, she was having to find the courage to attack the fears and insecurities of a whole lifetime. All the Plunket-Kirbys of the world were ranged against her in this luxurious room, all the Miss Bacons, all the women that she would have loved to have been but could not understand, let alone defeat. Di, Margot . . . even Mrs Gogh, any of those she could fight and win with a fist or a sharp nail or a shrill, screaming, hair-pulling scuffle. She wanted smooth, clever words, and disdain. She wanted a silvery laugh, a dismissive smile. She wanted half-closed eyes and a silky haircut like all the women on telly, like all the women in magazines with their perfect, plastic faces. She forced herself to repeat the words she'd rehearsed fifty times. 'We may well have a pleasant evening, once you understand my position quite clearly, but it is important that you get this fact into your extraordinarily well-wrapped up head. Malc and I have been married for over twenty years. We have two children who mean a great deal to both of us. You don't want him . . . you have your pick of men, you are clever, pretty and vivacious. I am getting older, I am set in my ways. I do not have a career or an absorbing interest. I am not particularly talented in any way. But I am half of Malc and Malc is half of me, we have grown together like two old roses in a garden and our roots are intertwined. I love him as he is, no matter what he does or what happens to him or what mistakes he might make. I love him . . .' and then Ellie ran out of words and sat back, gasping, tempted to beg for forgiveness.

Gabriella's slightly pointed face came towards her with its mouth just a little parted. She said: 'How terribly interesting! You are all the same – you people, you are all the same! The minute you see something you consider yours by right slipping away from you, you rise up and fight, never considering if it's something you really want, or something you wouldn't be better off without! Look at yourself! There is nothing there to attract a man like Malcolm. Habit – security – some false ideas about safety and growing old alone, lonely! That's why you want him . . . and to save face. You never wanted him before he left you – admit it! Why can't we both be honest and both come out of this victorious. You don't want him and I do. And perhaps the most important factor of all is that he doesn't want you!'

Ellie did not reach out and rip off Gabriella's turban, she did not grab for a handful of hair. She resisted and said, 'He has been hypnotised by you and everything he thinks you stand for, that's all. Once the novelty has worn off – and it will, oh yes it will – he will move on. He is not like you, Gabriella, he doesn't come from the same kind of background as you . . .'

'Oh yes, that's right darling, bring up that old chestnut. Malcolm has told me how important you consider background and breeding. Honestly, it's people like you that keep the class thing going, forever harping on about it as if it's static, as if it's something that hasn't been changing! Open your eyes, Ellie, for God's sake, look around you! While you were stuck in your rut down Nelson Street the world was turning. You were left behind, dragging your old ideas along with you, huddled up behind your net curtains, looking out at the world you could never have, and cursing it for leaving you out! I wouldn't be at all surprised to learn that you actually resented Malc's getting out and getting on. I wouldn't be surprised at all.'

'You are wrong, Gabriella.' And Ellie swallowed a hiccup of fear.

'Everything that Malcolm says about you is true!'

'What does he say?'

'That it was you who always kept him down. That you allowed yourself to get pregnant in order to trap him. That he was forced to give up night-school because of you and your feeble moanings, and that you have no ambition, none whatsoever. He says he has to drag you along to places and that you don't know how to change . . . Now, are you sure you still want him, at any cost?'

'You think so little of me and yet you expected me to accept this situation, to come here tonight and make friends?'

'I couldn't believe what Malcolm was saying. I thought we could solve this in a sensible, forward-looking way. And I had to meet you, Ellie, for all sorts of most important reasons I had to meet you and judge how much you really cared.'

'Malc is finding his feet in a new world. The things he says are defensive, he is trying to justify his years of failure to you and to himself at the same time, can't you see that? Anyone can look back and find excuses; there are always people to blame for not being who we would like to have been. And there is truth in it all, yes – anyone can bend the truth to their own advantage when it's convenient to do so. It's so easy to do that. I wasn't innocent, Gabriella, and I admit that, but neither was Malc. Who is?' And she thought that the Stanley knife blade would have made a nice, neat scarlet cut in the fluttery hollow at the base of Gabriella's very white throat –

When Malc returned they both sat back and answered his tentative smile. 'Everything okay?'

'Fine, darling,' said Gabriella, claiming him quickly. 'We've had a little chat, haven't we, Ellie? We've got quite a few issues sorted out.'

'I have said what I came to say,' said Ellie stiffly, reeling from the pain of discovering what he'd been saying about her, and yet proud of herself for not breaking down, for not reverting to type.

'Put some music on, angel.' Gabriella was uneasy with the silence; it sat on the room greenly and steamily along with the smell of broccoli boiling. So they talked about this and that, and then they eventually moved to the table. Ellie couldn't remember what they ate . . . something with kidney beans in and lots of tomato purée.

'Do we want to continue the discussion you were having before dinner?' asked Malc, when they'd finished.

'No, not really. I would like to be taken home now,' said Ellie.

'That's silly,' said Gabriella. 'You disappoint me, Ellie. We can't back away from it now.'

'I am not backing away,' said Ellie. 'I want to take it home and think it over.'

'That sounds fair enough to me,' said Malc quickly, and Gabriella gave him a little frown.

'I still feel we can come together if we work at this hard enough, darling,' she said. 'There must be common ground somewhere.'

'I want to go home now,' said Ellie. 'I don't want to talk any more.' But in the car she said to Malc, 'I wish you hadn't said those things about me.'

And he told her, 'It was unfair of Gabriella to repeat them.'

'I haven't got anyone to tell my side to,' she said.

'No, I do see that,' said Malc.

'You really consider that I held you back, don't you?'

'You always seemed quite happy with life as it was.'

'Well, you weren't making any alternative suggestions, Malc. What else was there to do but just keep going and make the best of it?'

'You were able to put a brave face on it. Sometimes, I used to come home and feel I was dead, Elle.'

'I know,' she said. 'I know.'

'Well, if you knew, it's just a great shame neither of us were able to say anything about it. Day after day after day,' said Malc, tightening his lips and turning into the cul-de-sac with his indicator ticking.

'But I just don't see how it was all my fault.'

'Well, it wasn't, Ellie. We both know that – but it doesn't matter now. That's behind us, and we've got to look forward to the future now. Somehow you must find a future for yourself with some brightness in it, like I have.'

'With somebody else?' asked Ellie.

'Not necessarily,' said Malc. 'It's not so terrible to be alone.'

Oh, isn't it, Malc, she asked into the darkness, soundlessly.

And that was that. She had confronted the monster: and what on earth had Gabriella got out of it? Surely she had not derived that much pleasure from showing off her gracious apartment?

So Ellie goes to bed and she stays there, sleeping for forty-eight hours, and pigging it for the rest of the time, raiding the fridge for the last of its contents, heating up odds and sods from the freezer, going over her situation again and again, working it all out.

Sometimes calmly, sometimes in a frenzy. But she doesn't drink and she doesn't smoke. Drink just makes her feel ill, but giving up smoking is something quite different. By depriving

218

herself of her nicotine habit she feels she is controlling the pain. If she can conquer that, she can conquer anything. It is one, pathetic little strength a non-smoker would not understand.

And then, after seven days are up, Ellie Freeman comes to a decision. She rises from her bed and makes two telephone calls.

26

The first telephone call Ellie makes is to Gabriella. She apologises for her intransigence and tells her she wants to be friends. Surprisingly the conceited Gabriella is not surprised. And oh yes, deep in her heart Ellie would so like a friendship to be possible.

'I think you are right, Gabriella, there *is* some common ground and it is essential that we find it.' Icy shivers run down her spine as she speaks, and yet she does not hate Gabriella. She cannot. She is not able to hate her.

'Malcolm has been terribly worried about you, darling. He's been trying to call you up every day, he's been on to the neighbours, he was going to give it until the end of today and then he was going to contact the police! But I knew you would get in touch, I even expected to hear from you earlier. What on earth have you been doing with yourself all this time?'

'Just getting my head together, that's all.'

'Well, I'm so glad you called me. And now, how about lunch?'

The second phone call Ellie makes is to the bank, and when Robert Beasely comes on the line she does not beat about the bush. She tells him she's going to move her accounts.

'This is silly, Ellie,' is his immediate response. 'You shouldn't make any serious moves while you are so emotionally charged. We've got to talk about this. I realise now that I over-reacted when you came round last week. Bella is still going on at me about it, but I was taken aback at the time and I possibly wasn't very helpful. We must talk, Ellie.'

'I am not interested in talking to you any more, Robert.'

'A decision like this should not be taken on the strength of personal feelings!'

'Tell me a decision that is ever taken for any other reason?'

'Ellie, listen to me for goodness sake! How about lunch?'

There is a serious sense of loss because she must stick to

her decision, but now look . . . everyone is wanting to have lunch with her. Ellie is suddenly in demand!

And then she goes to the *Plaza Lifestyle Centre* and spends the rest of the day there. With her eyes on the weights of the weighing machine and her pencil poised on Ellie's chart, Janey, her white-coated trainer, tells Ellie, 'Frankly, for your height, you are enormous.'

She knows she has gained a stone already. 'That's all right,' she replies with confidence. 'I don't mind being enormous. I haven't come here to lose weight, but to tone up and be pampered.'

'Being fat isn't going to make you feel better.'

'I want to feel I have weight behind me.'

'Well you certainly have got that.'

She is stripped of most of her body hair – she enjoys the pain because it is all external. She allows her pores to be steamed and opened. She drifts, whale-like, in shallow lukewarm water, being pummelled by spurting, surging jets; she spends an hour sandwiched between infra-red rays; she stands and smiles while a rubber belt tones up her bottom and she submits to the expert hands of the concentration-camp-faced masseuse, feeling greasy and malleable and groaning. Then she swims for an hour.

And when she strides out between the swing doors she gasps the fresh air and she feels alive. Vibrant.

She returns to the bungalow as dusk is falling; she stares at it hard from the road, before pulling her car up the drive. She nods and gives a little smile. 'You'll do for now,' she tells it.

Maria Williams pops her head out of her kitchen window; the curtains billow like long, pink and white checked hair around her inquisitive face. 'Everything all right?' she calls, and Ellie thinks of Di's cuckoo clock, so terribly predictable, so obscenely insistent.

'Oh go away, Maria, and mind your own business for once in your life.' And then Ellie lets herself into the silence which is her house.

Never mind that – what on earth is wrong with silence? It allows you to imprint yourself upon it and the larger you are

221

the better! You can only get lost in silence if you are small and frightened, just like the dark.

Ellie knows that outside this body of pain there is life, if she can only find it.

Mandy phones and Ellie has a pleasant conversation during which she assures her worried daughter, 'Really, Mandy, I am all right. I wasn't – I've been to hell and back, but I think I am going to pull through.'

'What on earth's the matter with Dad? What d'you think has come over him?'

'He's found his wings and he's trying them out. He'll soon discover that he's being a cuckoo and the little bird he has chosen will find him out.'

'You sound very positive, Mum.'

'Well I'm trying to be, Mandy.'

'Kev has taken it very badly. I spoke to him yesterday and he says he's not ringing because he doesn't know what to say. He's not ready to talk about it yet.'

'I can understand that. Tell him from me that that's fine.'

'I'd come down and see you if I could, only this Christmas I'm going to have to be on duty and Kev's been invited to go to this castle in Spain.'

'I will be perfectly all right, Mandy. You are not to worry about me.'

'I am worried, because you sound too good to be true. Why don't you come up here? You'd enjoy it – there are lots of merry people about and loads of organised things to do. I'll pay your fare if money's a problem. It would help to take you out of yourself.'

'I have been out of myself. For a whole week I have been out of myself, and now what I'm attempting to do is to get back in. Money is no problem, either, as your father is being very generous, but it's nice that you asked me, Mandy, because now I know I am choosing to be alone.'

'Well . . . if you're sure?'

'I am sure.'

'I've had a right go at Dad.'

'Don't fight on my behalf, Mandy. There is no need for you to do that.'

'I am not fighting on your behalf, Mum. I am fighting on mine. I am absolutely disgusted with him – he is making himself ridiculous and I wanted him to know that!'

Di rings. She says, 'Oh Elle, I heard what happened, love. Come over here and stay with us for a while. Dave says you'd be very welcome, just until Christmas is over.'

And Ellie has just finished reassuring Di when Margot rings in a terrible state. 'The fucking evil bastard! Milk him for every penny he's got! That bitch only wants him for his money, she's that type, you can tell that! Get round there and scratch her eyes out – I'll come with you. I wouldn't mind coming with you if you wanted some support. Or I could send Dick along with some of the boys . . . put the frighteners on.'

'Do you know her, Margot?'

'I've read about her in the paper and I know her type.'

'Let's just wait and see.' Ellie tries to placate her.

'But you don't intend to take this lying down! Men can't be allowed to get away with this sort of thing . . .'

'I am not lying down. I have done all the lying down I intend to do.'

'What's happening, then? What are you doing about it?' Margot is frantic on the phone.

'I am letting time pass. I am allowing the world to go by.'

'Well, I am going to ring you every day and I want you to come over here whenever you feel like it . . . even in the middle of the night. I am leaving my back door unlocked. My house is yours now, Elle, just for as long as you need it. And the spare bed is aired and made up.'

Ellie eats sardines straight from the tin as she talks, licking every finger clean as she goes along, separating flesh from bone. She keeps a six-pack of crisps in the hall now, where once she kept her cigarettes.

She spends that evening perusing the local papers, which get scattered with pieces of Cadbury's fruit and nut. She doesn't let any of the chocolate escape, she rescues the wayward splinters on the end of a wet finger.

It is a week before Christmas now, and the following day Ellie puts on her hat and coat and drives out to Huyton. Ellie views Christmas with disfavour this year, she really hasn't the

223

time for it. The exhausted Christmas shoppers are out with their anger and their dull eyes, dragging their children along by the arms and manoeuvring uncomfortable bags and bundles. Carols trill from hot store doorways where men stand dismally and wait for their wives, looking resigned; sexless Rudolphs perform mechanically on platforms of plastic snow. Ellie's mission is so urgent that her coat is unfastened despite the weather but the bank is easy to find. And this time she will see the manager at the new bank for exactly what he is, as unreal as the welcome smile on the cashier's face, as false as the rubber plants, as pretentious as the circular column in the centre of the room – just one more prop in the money game, just one more smooth invitation, as tight and as sly as those chains they use to secure their pens to the counters.

And that's fine – just so long as she knows and understands. So long as she's a player, not a silver boot to be moved at will from the Waterworks to the Old Kent Road. She will pass Go on her own, thank you very much, and collect the rewards herself.

Charming? Yes.

Interested? Yes.

Helpful? Yes.

The new manager is also inquisitive to know her reason for moving such a vast investment portfolio, but it's perfectly all right to be restrained in her replies. You don't have to sell your soul to get help, not when you're paying for it like Ellie is. And yes, he will write a letter to the Avery Road branch of Barclays, and yes he will organise everything, but Ellie must write one herself, telling the bank that that's what she wants to do.

Ellie deals with him cursorily; she doesn't even bother to remember his name. She's got his card in her handbag and that's as close as she needs to get. 'And just as soon as the transfer's been made I shall be needing to make several extremely hefty withdrawals, so I want you to free this sum of money and put it on deposit in a separate account by the end of January at the latest.'

Whatever his name is doesn't argue; it has something to do

224

with Ellie's forthright attitude. He thinks she knows about money – he thinks that she understands!

And here, down this side street, is the agent she's circled in the newspaper. It is a small branch in a large string and there, in the window, are the empty flats . . . The insides are now finished to specification – they had to be re-done because the original contractor tried to cut corners and the prestigious developers couldn't have that. There are three apartments left – only three available – and it is first come, first served. Ellie had noticed the three vacant flats . . . you couldn't help but notice, on her fateful meeting with Gabriella, on her first visit to the Waterside. And Ellie is first come, and her money is virtually here in her purse – cash – no problems with mortgages or selling her own house first.

She hovers at the window, staring in, feeling the blackness well up again and fearing that, this time, she might not be able to push it back. No, she can't get this far and retire defeated. Her heart takes a tumble when she sees the Georgian house up for sale in Ridley Place, right opposite the library – it is like being mocked by a dream and she nearly cries out in pain. It wants doing up, it is quite badly distressed like Ellie herself; it has been used as offices for the past twenty years and will need complete renovation.

The desecration of the house began the year that Ellie was married. That's when it lost its beauty and got stuffed with files and folders, when its fireplaces were ripped out and filing cabinets were thrust into place. That's when the myriad dusty inconsequentials of life got to its pelmets and cornices, reached its noble attics and its dark, dank basements. And there it was, darkened by Ellie's reflection, rising in sad magnificence between the jaunty, strutting apartments in the estate agent's window.

Well, why shouldn't she buy that, too?

'And move into it?' asks the voice.

'Well, no – I couldn't move in immediately. I'd have to do it up.'

'And risk having a house like that and ending up living in it alone?'

'Why not? And anyway, I am certain my plan is going to work. If I wasn't certain I wouldn't be doing it.'

'How could you do up a house like that? You've got no idea about materials or styles or good taste.'

'I could get help, couldn't I? I could pay for expert advice. And I've plenty of money to pay for the upkeep.'

'Somebody would find out.'

'How would they find out? Nobody knows me in that area. And I could always sell it again if I wanted to. I might never get another chance.'

Ellie goes inside on rubber legs and the door chinks closed behind her. The girl is no good, she cannot be bothered to talk to the girl; she wants to speak to the manager. His eyes open wide when she tells him.

'Are you representing a company, madam?' he asks with disbelief.

'No, this is a private venture and it is important that my business here remains absolutely confidential.'

'Naturally you will want to view.'

'No, I do not need to view. I want those three flats. I am prepared to put deposits down this morning and no, I am not interested in bargaining or obtaining surveyors' reports.'

'If I may say so, I think that in the case of number twenty-eight Ridley Place, that might be slightly foolish. The house needs a great deal of work done to it before it can be used as a private residence.'

'I am fully aware of that, and that is my business,' says Ellie. 'All I want to do is make sure I clinch this deal before Christmas.'

'If you would care to give me your solicitor's name and address.'

That's easy. That's in her bag, in the secret little pocket that Malc never knew was there – not that he would have bothered to search her bag anyway, not since he gave up smoking. She's only used the solicitors once, and that was to make her will. They are a firm in London. They do not know her and they never wished to, and nor does she need to know them. Theirs is a sensible, business-like arrangement and Ellie is grateful for their discretion.

She clinches the deal with a handshake and heads back to her car with the brochures in a carrier bag.

'You don't need to put them in a carrier bag,' she tells the flustered manager who is a lean and predatory young man and overcome by the affluence of his dowdy customer. He will go back home tonight and tell his mother, 'It's true what they say, people who have real money don't go round advertising it.' 'It's not as secretive as that!' says Ellie.

But he insists. It is a bakery bag with pictures of cottage loaves on the front, and when she gets to her car she finds crumbs in the bottom of it.

Crumbs in the bottom of the bag, and she has just promised to spend one and a quarter of her two million pounds with nobody to advise her.

No wonder she drives jerkily.

She cannot go straight back home, not until she's seen it. She drives back into the city, against the traffic, and she manages to park beside a meter right outside number twenty-eight.

She calls to the house from the cosy, dry-mouthed heat of her car. Tears start in her eyes. She calls to the house with hope and it answers. She can feel it . . . it leans towards her massively in all its proud dereliction. It has unwashed windows and no proper curtains to call its own. Its door is faded with peeling paint and all the little scrolly bits on the walls are chipping away. Spiders and woodlice have no doubt made hay on the windowsills, there is no aerial on its many chimneys, and no smoke comes out of them, nothing to say that anyone is home. It has been unloved and neglected.

It is gently solid. It is waiting. It promises her everything she craves for.

She feels nothing at all about the flats except a satisfactory sense of achievement. They are merely a means to an end, while the house . . .

Among her Christmas cards comes one from Bella and Robert Beasely, and a note scratched quickly on the bottom informs her that in February he is moving on – a job at head office – an important promotion. He is able to communicate with her now that Malc has gone. She smiles. The pain of humiliation is still there but she's pleased to hear he's leaving. The fewer people around here who know what she is about the better!

Ellie is going to have a very happy Christmas alone in her bungalow with lots of books to read and lots of food to eat, her speculations and her brochures. Over the whole of the Christmas period Ellie will gain another stone, her hair will take on some of its old gloss again and her investments will multiply – just because they exist and are being managed astutely. Ellie must not worry about money any more. She has more important matters on her mind.

Because, after twenty-one years, Ellie has fallen in love again.

With a house and a sense of purpose.

27

Although it doesn't appear so from the inside, the Royal Albert Waterside apartments development is shaped like a lantern. Designed by an architect obviously disdainful of superstition, there are thirteen apartments in all, four on each of the first three floors with the penthouse alone on the top.

The apartment on the ground floor, thinks Ellie, will do very well for the Skinners, because although it has only four bedrooms and there are nine in the family (on and off), it is far more spacious than their back-to-back in Nelson Street and Ellie knows they will make do in their own particular style.

What should she write to these London solicitors, Barker, Base, Trial-Cody, what do they need to know about the Skinners? That this bright and breezy family, so plagued by colds and catarrh, are needy and deserving is perfectly clear, and that she, Ellie, feels a need to help those still in the place from whence she has come is also quite understandable.

'Some sort of agreement for life,' she writes, needing expert clarification although she is certain that some such legal procedure must exist for her purpose, *'and naturally I do not want anyone ever to know who their benefactor might be.'*

Well, naturally.

Everyone down Nelson Street, while liking the Skinners and sympathising, despaired of them at the same time. You could not pass number forty-two without smelling something akin to unchanged bedding, something that smacked of smoked haddock wrapped up badly and left in a dustbin, and something else . . . much more elusive . . . the smell of jumble sales in village halls run by women with blue hair. Hair . . . that was the underlying smell that was so hard to find and define. Hair and heads.

They were a much-visited family – by social workers, debt collectors and people bearing hampers and second-hand bicycles from various civic charities. They were also blessed with a vast and endless extended family network . . . and these relatives used to arrive in a glorious selection of unusual conveyances. The Skinners themselves owned an ancient tip-up truck, which remained parked most of the time, resting on its heavily punctured tyres like a geriatric gasping for breath.

As, one by one, the Skinner children slipped into their teens in their chained and leather-jacketed way, they began to acquire an individuality and they began to be known by names.

'That bloody Marvin's bike nearly knocked Mrs Davis down again. She went spare, poor old girl, but he says it's the brakes, he can't get the parts for the brakes. He shouldn't be on the road . . . he's got no licence, no insurance . . .'

'Did you hear the girl Dorry coming home again last night? It must have been after four because Fred thought it was his alarm and reached to turn the bloody thing off. After four, and what is she, thirteen? She can't be any older than thirteen because . . .'

'I've been round there to complain about our back bog window again. That's the third time it's gone in a month and what if anyone'd been sitting there – well, it's not funny – it'd give anyone a heart attack, and that cheeky bugger Marcus came out with his arms crossed, in that way he has. He swore it wasn't his football but her at thirty-eight insists she saw him climbing over the wall after it.'

As for the parents, Duane and Jackie Skinner, they were, 'Never in, and she's every bit as bad as him. Only ever interested in a good time, only ever has been, and hasn't she heard of contraception? Every year since they've been here she looks as if she's pregnant, she walks as though she is even when she's not, and when have you known that house without a baby bawling outside?'

'Duane Skinner has never done a full day's work in his life, and he's not ashamed of the fact, oh no, he boasts about it down at the Queen's Arms, but he's got plenty of money when it comes to the booze. They're never without the things they consider essential.'

Ellie had chatted with Jackie Skinner on several occasions, on her way to work and back and once, one Christmas, she had nervously packed up a box of reject toys from Funorama and taken it round on Christmas Eve. She'd told Jackie Skinner, 'No one'll miss them and they might as well come here as go back to the factory and be thrown into some furnace.'

'The kids'll love these.' Ellie had watched how Jackie Skinner seemed to turn into a child herself as she rifled through the box . . . you'd think she was staring at a treasure chest full of gold. Their house was a riot of decorations, some already torn loose from the sellotape and wafting about the room; a real Christmas tree stood at a precarious angle in one corner with a baby pulling at the chocolate baubles that decked the lower branches, and even the motor bike that made progress through the narrow hall well-nigh impossible had its handlebars twisted with tinsel. 'They're all new!' exclaimed Jackie Skinner over the toys, her huge blue eyes bright with excitement, 'and I can't find nothing wrong with any of them.'

'Well, I just thought . . .' began Ellie, feeling embarrassment because her last-minute idea had been so well received. 'I'm glad you like them. I quite often get the opportunity to pick up odds and ends, and now that I know you don't mind I'll make a point of looking out . . .'

'Oh, I'd be ever so grateful.'

'Well, then,' said Ellie, feeling terribly pleased.

And then there had been that cold frosty night, eerily silent, when Ellie had been unable to sleep for the slap slap slap of Jackie's mules as she wandered up and down the street. Ellie had caught sight of her last thing, when she'd been putting the milk bottles out on the step. She'd felt concern even then. Poor soul, wrapped in a blanket, traipsing up and down looking all huddled and worried.

Eventually the weary slapping got too much for Ellie. She'd drawn on her dressing-gown, clutched her hot water bottle to her, picked up a torch and gone out to see.

Jackie Skinner shuffled eagerly towards her. 'It's Duane,' she cried. 'We had a row earlier and he just went off . . . said he was never coming back. I've been up the Queen's and I've been down the Boot but nobody there has seen him.'

'Oh, Jackie my love.' Ellie shivered in the piercing cold. 'Don't you think you ought to go and wait indoors by the fire? It's brass monkey weather out here and you rushing up and down isn't going to help. I'll come and sit with you for a while if it's company you're wanting.'

'I can't go back in. It's no use, I have to stay on the watch.' And Jackie Skinner, thin yet pregnant, had worn a look of such total despair it made Ellie shiver more than the cold. Her metal curlers seemed shot with the frost, and the hairnet full of holes let through clumps of peroxide hair the exact colour of the lifeless stars.

'Well, I'll walk with you for a while then. Hang on a minute and I'll go and brew us a cuppa and bring it out.'

'Ta, Mrs Freeman.'

'Oh no, you must call me Ellie.'

'That's a pretty name. Is it short for Elinor?'

'Yes, yes it is,' lied Ellie. She hated her real name of Elspeth.

So they huddled there talking out on the step, drinking their scalding tea, and they weren't halfway through it before the lean, lank figure of Duane Skinner, meandering from side to side, came out of the shadows and slurped towards them.

Jackie Skinner had instantly returned her cup to Ellie's frozen hands and with a wild yelp of joyous recognition, she and her slippers and her dowdy blanket had gone shooting off up the road; where the two met the shadows came together, and stayed there resting in each other's arms. Who was supporting whom was hard to say . . .

And the next morning, to Ellie's amazement, came this Thank You note through the door, and a tiny little lighthouse with *A Gift from Blackpool* on it.

Yes, Ellie considers that Duane and Jackie Skinner, so hopeless and so hopeful, are a most deserving couple. And she'll be doing the rest of Nelson Street a favour, also, because everyone will be thrilled to see the back of them.

Dwarfy Sugden is a different proposition entirely. He lived with his tiny, twittering, bird-like mother until she died . . . he never married, never had a girlfriend – and it was whispered that he took women's underwear off lines. He was called

Dwarfy, Ellie supposes, because the man was so huge, in width as well as in height. 'Never all there, never quite right in the head,' is what people used to say about Dwarfy, and he did not come from Nelson Street but from Gatby Terrace, which ran along beside the coalyard.

Ellie has always suspected that Dwarfy knew exactly what he was at, that his performances were all acts, designed either to draw attention to himself or in order to get away with murder.

His expression is that of a martyr. He wears his hair long, like a Red Indian, over the collar of his old Army greatcoat, and he walks, sometimes, when it suits him, with an exaggerated limp. To hear Dwarfy approaching in the dark is to hear a dragging, hollow sound, and his shadow rises and falls against redbrick walls in the street-lights.

Dwarfy Sugden is a lurker in dark doorways, and a flasher, and the police, considering him harmless after all these years, have given up trying to contain him. Keeping him locked away is no answer, and there is no corrective treatment yet for his numerous and distressing little problems.

Ellie thinks that the first-floor apartment might well suit Dwarfy. It wouldn't really matter where he lived because he would always need to roam about, oh yes, to try and restrain Dwarfy would be a cruel thing to do. There are lots of dark corners, alleyways and angles around and about Gabriella's Waterside apartment block. And he would soon fill those vast bedrooms with the strange collections with which he fills his barrow . . . Too much space would not intimidate Dwarfy, he would utilize it or ignore it, in his very own individual manner.

In her carefully composed letter to Barker, Base, Trial-Cody, Ellie stresses the sadness of Dwarfy's predicament, living all alone and on the breadline like that, with nobody around to talk to or understand him. *'I think he would enjoy living near the water,'* she writes. *'He would enjoy all the activity. He could find a seat, eat his dinner and watch it all go by and I think it would do him good.'*

Ellie smiles happily to herself as she considers the most suitable residents with whom to fill her last vacant flat.

Ellie was at school with Fern and Blanche Peters; she has

shared the odd fag in the bike sheds with them in her day. They weren't there for long and she doubts that Malc would even remember them, for they were quiet and drab, stooped a little and had thin, pointed features. They didn't stand out, in fact they always seemed to be trying to get away and not be there. Someone said their childhood was very sad but nobody knew any of the details. It was true that Fern had a terrible stutter and used to flinch a lot, while Blanche had a knicker-wetting habit, even at fourteen.

They were close, as sisters, even then. They always went round together.

Ellie doesn't know them to speak to any more . . . well, they are rarely about in the day, they hang about Lime Street station and the gambling arcades in the city. But she knows where they live, still in their old home in the high windy tower block on Sefton Hill. And Ellie only knows that because Margot mentioned it years ago: 'Couple of old pros, you'd never have thought it, would you, not after what they were like at school. Weren't you in the same class as that Blanche once, Ellie?'

Ellie did not like to admit that once she'd gone round with the Peters sisters. She answered, 'Yes, I remember Blanche, and nobody wanted to sit next to her because she stank.'

Margot looked affronted. 'Well, let's hope she's got her act together by now. She must have done, surely, to be doing what she's doing. Men wouldn't like . . . And there's all sorts of trouble in the block because of their drunken parties and that parade of sordid louts who line up outside their door. It's terrible, Edna Rawlings at number eighty told me when I was speaking to her yesterday. The Peters sisters live next door and she says that some nights they get no sleep at all. And then there's always the fear of fire . . . it's not so much Fern and Blanche, it's the people they attract, you see.'

'These are old acquaintances of mine who need a hand up in the world because of an appalling childhood,' Ellie writes now. *'So you can see how absolutely essential it is that nobody knows who owns the apartments, and that all sorts of precautions must be taken in order to keep my name out of it.'*

Ellie has not bothered with decorations this year; hers is a different kind of Christmas but the excitement she feels is that of an expectant child ... she almost feels that she still believes in magic. There is great and enormous pleasure to be had, over the quietness of Christmas, in going back to the solicitor's letter and amending it, just ever so slightly. Sometimes Ellie gets up in the night, opens a packet of cream crackers, covers them with cheese spread and pores over the letter with a pen in her hand, for hours. She is pleased with it by the time she comes to send it. She thinks she has conveyed just enough to get her false motives accepted, and she has stressed, again and again, the importance of remaining an anonymous benefactor.

With only good in her heart.

Every week Ellie keeps her appointments at the *Plaza Lifestyle Centre* and comes out feeling better than ever in spite of her increasing size. Janey, her trainer, says she can't understand it. 'I wish you'd take home one of our special diet sheets,' she whines, but Ellie is perfectly happy. She even has a go on the weights in the gym, and has been into Liverpool to buy outsize clothes to accommodate her new and expanding figure – she's found a special shop that deals only in size sixteen and up. She chooses very loud colours, and she is especially fond of a cape which she thinks makes her look like Margaret Rutherford. When she is wearing it, she flies along on top of the world.

She buys magazines like *Homes and Gardens* and *Country Life;* she dreams about her Georgian house. She tries not to go near it again as she doesn't want to go in and tempt fate until it is really hers. When the right time comes she wants to go round it and savour it all on her own.

By the end of January, Ellie has paid the four deposits – one for each flat and the other for number twenty-eight Ridley Place. One evening she takes a chance and goes to the Waterside but cannot get in. She sees that the strips across the windows outside saying *For Sale* are missing, and the bold *Sold* signs in bright red already replace them. She rubs her hands with glee and chuckles fatly to herself.

And then she decides that the time has come to accept Gabriella's kind invitation for lunch, and she agrees to meet

Malcolm at the Canonwaits offices in order 'to get things straightened out'.

'How are you?' asks Malc on the phone, as he always does.

'I am perfectly happy, Malc, much to my own surprise. At last I seem to have found a new interest.'

'Oh, that's marvellous! And might I ask what?'

'Furnishings and fabrics,' says Ellie brightly.

'Oh, you mean you've gone back to your patchwork quilt.'

'Something along those lines, Malc,' says Ellie, tucking into a jar of peanut butter with her finger, and her eyes are twinkling. 'Something like that.'

28

Interestingly, over the last few years the Skinners have obviously acquired a selection of animals.

The tip-up truck has come to rest on the newly-laid cobbled area outside the Waterside and a grey-furred dog, a cross between a lurcher and an Alsatian, lollops out of the truck's driving seat, slides between the dangerous metal slithers of the half-opened door and lazily cocks its leg against one of the glossy bollards.

Inside in the hall, past the front doors – which have been propped open by a stout iron washing-line post – is a home-made hutch with God knows what living inside it; only its smell is relevant here, and the structure is held together by ugly pieces of four-by-two with nails spiked ferociously through them.

Ellie follows Gabriella inside. It is the second Saturday in March and they have just finished lunching together. Since January this has become a regular habit. This time Gabriella chose a seafood restaurant with sawdust on the floor, rigging strung across the ceiling, and decking the walls were lobster nets with strange pieces of cork and coloured balls hanging inside. Throughout their meal a muted quartet in pirate costume sang sea shanties to an accordion. Gabriella has asked Ellie back for a coffee and it is her very first chance to see the result of her carefully planned action at first-hand.

'Absolutely ghastly things have been going on,' confided Gabriella when they arrived at the restaurant and first sat down. She leaned forward and fiddled nervously with pieces of hardened candle grease. 'And nobody can quite under-stand how it's possible. We have written a joint letter to the developers . . . not only the residents of the Waterside but the residents of all the other new houses and maisonettes overlooking the river. Well, we were all given to understand . . . The owners of the Marina are on our side, too. You just wouldn't believe the trouble it's all caused.' Gabriella looked around furtively before she confesses, ashamed of her weakness, 'I haven't been sleeping.'

'What has happened?' Ellie looked suitably shocked. She had been wondering when Gabriella was going to mention it.

'There were three empty flats,' said Gabriella, trying to explain without losing her cool. 'They were behind all the others in being sold because the contract for the interiors had been given to another firm . . . I don't know why . . . and that firm tried to cheat the developers by cutting down on the cost. Anyway, the long and the short of it was that these three flats were not completed with the rest and it was only just before Christmas that they were put up for sale. Everyone believed, quite naturally, that they would be bought by right-minded people.'

'Well, naturally. They must have been expensive.'

'Oh, they were. Very expensive. They were advertised in all the right places, you know, magazines and supplements, but everyone knew they'd be snapped up quickly.'

'There wasn't a waiting list, then?'

'No, funnily enough, the developers were embarrassed about the mess they'd got into with the interiors so it didn't work quite like that. They had to take them off the market, you see, and I suppose they didn't want to be plagued by unhappy customers . . .'

'Who did buy them then?' asked Ellie smoothly, picking up a bread stick and snapping off the end.

Gabriella chewed at a raw carrot and stared challengingly at Ellie. 'There's an obnoxious family on the ground floor – the weirdest, dirtiest old man you ever saw on the first, and a couple of whores have moved in at the top.'

'I don't believe it! How could people like that afford the Waterside?'

Gabriella shook a well-groomed head. She wore a crisply-fresh cotton headscarf on the back of her hair, and huge anchor earrings that tugged at her tiny earlobes. A diamanté fish sparkled on the breast of her wide-ribbed jumper. She looked slightly French this morning with those black fish-net stockings. 'That's what everyone's asking. That's what we've asked the developers, too, but they say they've washed their hands of the place, it's not their concern any more. They swear that they don't know, either. All the properties are out of their hands and all the agreements have been signed. We're still looking into it all, of course.'

'Well of course you would, you'd have to,' said Ellie, who spread over the whole of the little wooden chair so that the embroidered hem of her scarlet smock swept the sawdust.

'I must say,' said Gabriella, coming out of her misery for a moment, 'you look absolutely wonderful.'

'I feel good at the moment, yes, I do,' Ellie smiled.

'Living alone must be good for you!' joked Gabriella, watching as her seafood platter came over on a round wooden breadboard. The waiter wore blue and white knee-length breeches, and from there he was bare all the way down to his thonged sandals.

'There is something to be said for it, although I am not used to it yet, not after twenty-one years of marriage.'

Gabriella stared at the sucker of a squid and stuck it hard with her fork.

Ellie said, 'But I have put on weight.'

'Yes, I can see that,' said Gabriella, 'but it seems to sort of suit you, you know. You look better for it.'

'How's the gallery going?'

'Have you ever been in to have a look round? Have you ever seen it?' Gabriella's eyes lit up and Ellie could see that what Malc kept telling her was true, that along with her apartment, and Malc, this was another pride and joy.

'Once, a while ago, but I wouldn't mind going again.'

'We'll have coffee at the flat and go there this afternoon then,' said Gabriella happily. And then she amended that to, 'If Malc's not back.'

'He used to play squash on a Saturday,' remarked Ellie.

'Yes, he still likes his squash – and I encourage him to go. I don't want him going all middle-aged and unhealthy on me!'

'Quite,' said Ellie, looking at her pink seafood bisque.

And then they had gone on to talk of other things, mostly to do with Gabriella – the people she knew and the places she'd been, and Ellie took the opportunity of asking her, 'Did you ever know the Beaselys?'

'I knew Bella Beasely once, but not very well – horrid, intense sort of person, bit of a do-gooder. She tried to lure me into helping with her frightful prison activities once, asked me to display some of their work in the gallery! It was all pretty embarrassing as you can imagine. One doesn't really know what to say, does one? We fell out over it in the end.'

'So you don't keep in touch?'

Gabriella shook her head and rinsed her mouth with a sparkling white wine. 'No, we were never that friendly. Why, did you know them?'

'No, not really, but I thought Malc did.' Ellie was just testing, testing for safety.

'No, I don't think he did. They weren't friends, if that's what you mean.'

Ellie was relieved to hear this. In spite of what she considered to be his great betrayal, she was certain that Robert Beasely would not have been so unprofessional as to give her secret away to anyone other than his wife. Now, living and working three hundred miles away, no matter what happened he'd never be tempted. Yes, Ellie was quite safe.

'And what are your plans for the future?' Ellie enquired innocently. 'You must have already decided what you want to do when you've finished here.'

'That all depends on how this goes,' said Gabriella seriously. 'If I make a good job of this the world is my oyster. If not, I've had it, I suppose you could say.' She laughed and dabbed her mouth and her anchor earrings rattled nautically. 'But that's not very likely. Everything is going wonderfully well. We're having a big open day in April, important people coming up, you know the sort of thing, sausage rolls and canapés and, if the weather's nice, tables outside, music and displays.' And then she said, 'You must come! Remind me to give you a VIP ticket.'

'That would be very nice,' said Ellie.

'And what about you, Ellie? How are you honestly feeling, about Malcolm and me? Is it still as hurtful, is it still just the same?'

240

'It is hurtful, to be abandoned. Yes, that is hurtful.'

'But that's only if you're determined to see it in that light. The word abandoned is surely quite wrong. He hasn't abandoned you at all. I would think that since you've been living apart you've had more meaningful contact than you've had for years! And you're both able to get some of those old resentments out.'

'It is quite different meeting someone occasionally from living with them day after day, year after year.'

'Yes – much more valuable in some ways, because after so long surely it's impossible not to take the other one for granted! And that's awful,' said Gabriella sincerely. 'That's terribly wrong.'

'But it's also to do with trust,' Ellie added.

'Trust!' shrieked Gabriella daintily. 'Trust is the most unfair demand you can make on anyone, because how can you honestly promise always to be trustworthy, never to let them down, never to fall short, never ever to betray.'

'Well, I suppose you are right – maybe you can't.'

'Of course you can't, and it's wicked to expect it.'

'So Malcolm will never be able to trust you, is that what you're saying?'

'I would never use trust as a basis for anything, no. Malcolm and I are two separate individuals who happen to be sharing a home and a bed, and it's important we remember that, and respect that. Anything could happen to either of us at any given moment in time, and I don't see why we should turn our face from the world and feel guilty. Trust is a threat, and it almost begs for betrayal.'

And Ellie feels a great deal better when she hears that, since she is beginning to suspect that Gabriella trusts her! She is freed by the naïvety of her enemy's words.

Poor Malc. Hung up with his old-fashioned, working-class values, he will be shattered. Ellie must hurry up and rescue him, but dammit she's going as fast as she can!

So, after lunch they move on. Ellie Freeman owns three flats in this block . . . and it *is* a block, whatever the residents might prefer to call it. So it is with a proprietorial interest that she enters, and far more confidently than when she came here

241

the first time, tripping along behind Malc all decked out in her new blue silk and scared half to death at the prospect of meeting Gabriella.

'Isn't it . . . it can't be . . . Jackie Skinner!'

'Mrs Freeman!'

'Oh, please call me Ellie! I have always told you to call me Ellie. What on earth are you doing here?'

Jackie Skinner is pregnant again but not in maternity clothes, oh no. Her badly stained shirt gapes open across her stomach and the zip at the back of her skirt has been left undone. Standing squarely, she takes a lank strand of hair and hooks it behind her ear, looking vague and harassed as always when she says, 'I live here now.'

Gabriella stops and turns round. 'Do you know these people?'

'Yes, of course I do. It is extraordinary! Jackie lived in the same street as us. You were there for, what must it be, at least ten years, weren't you, Jackie?'

Jackie nods eagerly. The gap between her two front teeth is very wide. She is taking a plate of green things to the creature in the hutch and a good inch of ash hangs from the fag in her mouth. Gabriella thinks about it first and then says slowly, 'Then Malc must know them, too.'

'Of course Malc knows Jackie. Why, hasn't he said?'

Gabriella turns round and makes for the lift entrance. 'No,' she casts back over her shoulder, 'he hasn't said.'

Jackie calls out, 'Pop in on your way back out, why don't you? We can have a fag and a gossip.'

'I have given up smoking,' says Ellie with pride.

The lift is still working but there are two half-bare children playing on the floor with a box of broken cars between them and where has that puddle of water come from? Ellie watches as Gabriella, stepping cautiously, decides whether or not to turn them out. 'You see!' she spits at Ellie with her eyebrows fiercely raised. She decides against it and the lift rises, the children play on undisturbed, and the whole party reaches the third floor with an expensive chunk and a click.

Gabriella pauses for a moment before she exits, and looks nervously around her. 'He sometimes waits up here,' she says, obscurely.

'Who?'

'The vile old man from the first floor. This is where he waits sometimes and I don't know why or what he is here for.' This top landing is pervaded by the stench of rancid chip-fat, and Ellie hurries after the retreating figure of Gabriella as she dashes up the small stairway to the safety of the penthouse.

'I can see what you mean,' Ellie tells her, as the door closes behind them.

'It's not that I'm a snob,' Gabriella says quickly, making for the kitchen. 'As you well know, I have firm beliefs about people's rights to rise in the world, about the divisions between us being all in the mind.'

'Yes, I remember, you said that before,' nods Ellie.

'But some of these people are mentally ill,' says Gabriella, removing her earrings with care. 'They must be to behave like they do! I mean, that mother hasn't the first idea about looking after children . . . they could be caught in that lift, it could nip the ends of their fingers off! And I daren't come home on my own at night!'

'Why ever not?' There is not one item out of place amidst all this white and chrome; there is nothing in here that does not match exactly.

'Because of HIM! That's why.'

'Who?'

'That man on the first floor! I can't begin to tell you what he looks like.'

'Poor old thing,' says Ellie, and Gabriella looks at her sharply.

'If it happens again I'm going to ring the police whatever Malcolm says. It might be no use but nevertheless they should be informed. Malcolm is much too patient and easygoing about all of this and sometimes his attitude makes me furious!'

'If what happens again?' Ellie watches as Gabriella plugs the percolator in and prepares two china cups. But she knows, oh yes, Ellie knows.

'He stands there behind corners with his horrid prick out, and it's really just not on. I have never been a nervous person,' and they move into the sitting room. The central heating is on

243

so there is no need to light the gas fire. Gabriella fiddles with a pile of artistic magazines before she sits down. 'I am not easily given to hysteria, but honestly, Ellie, it's not just his prick, the man is so sinister and ugly . . . limping along with his long hair swinging . . . and the bent wheel of that damn barrow squeaking!'

'You sound as if you're describing someone else I used to know!'

Gabriella sits on the edge of her chair. She says wearily, 'They say that his name is Sugden.'

'Not Dwarfy Sugden, surely!' Ellie is relieved to be able to let her face move into a laugh, but it has to be a sympathetic one, and it is.

'When did you know him?'

'Well, there was a man like that used to live over the back of Nelson Street.'

Gabriella does exercises with her neck. 'But this is incredible!'

'Not really. I suppose most of Liverpool knows Dwarfy Sugden – that he lived not two blocks away from me must be purely coincidental.'

'For God's sake – the local tramp, the local flasher! And he has managed to move in to the Waterside apartments along with the most problematic family in the city and two old tarts and their entourage!' Gabriella leans forward and narrows her eyes; it feels, for a second, as if she considers the possibility of this dire situation being Ellie's work before she instantly dismisses it. 'How, Ellie? How have these people moved in here? Who is paying for them and why? Why would anyone waste their money like this?'

'Well, it certainly seems a peculiar way to spend a fortune, and you're talking about somebody with more than enough to throw around. Sounds like the act of a lunatic to me.'

'Or some charity that nobody's heard of.'

'Or some political body trying to cause trouble. There was a big fuss when this development was first talked about . . . you know the sort of thing, locals being pushed out, toffee-nosed yuppies with more money than they know what to do with moving in. You were around at the time, you must have known all about that. I remember what this area used to look like . . .' Ellie rubs the possibilities in.

'But nobody's going around with this sort of money, nobody's prepared to spend these sorts of sums in order to prove a point, surely! Why would they need to do that, to take it this far? That is absolutely ridiculous!'

'Goodness knows,' says Ellie, 'but it must be terribly difficult for you. And, when you think about it, it can only get worse. Perhaps, if it's upsetting you so much, you should think about moving out?'

'Never!' Gabriella's voice is sharp. 'Never in a million years! I had to contend with a hundred others, I had to have my name pulled out of a hat to get this penthouse. It would take more than this to drive me out, and the rest of the residents feel exactly the same. These people,' and Gabriella's nose wrinkles up, 'are going to have to learn to fit in with the rest of us. They are not going to be allowed to remain here and pull everything down to their level!'

The coffee plops in the kitchen and as Gabriella gets up, Ellie says, 'They're off to a good start, though. It looks as if they are already doing quite well.' She makes sure that her voice is most sympathetic. She does not allow herself to smile until she's quite sure that Gabriella has left the room.

29

This habit of categorising people, summing them up and working them out – well, Malc might disapprove and scoff at Ellie for doing it, but you've got to admit that it works. Here is the fearful Gabriella, who represents all the human attributes that Ellie can't understand, reacting in the same way as anyone else, and pathetically predictable when it comes to stressful situations.

It is all extremely pleasing, and Ellie feels her self-confidence soaring. She's getting on with Gabriella rather successfully, too, these days. She even suspects that Gabriella quite likes her, as she is always wanting to be with her and meet for lunch!

How is Gabriella going to react when Malc makes a fool of himself? One thing is quite certain – the slut will goad him into it. She can't help herself because she is frightened – threatened and surrounded as she is by the sounds and sights of the underprivileged and defeated. Everything that she stands for and all that she hopes for, is threatened.

Ellie visits Malc for further practical discussions. She takes her car into the city, but before she goes to the Canonwaits offices she drives to Ridley Place to see how the contractors are getting on.

As always, when she approaches the house her heart lifts. She is unaccountably upset to see the skips outside and all the splintered old pelmets and floorboards, although she knows that this has to happen before any progress can be made. Nor does she quite trust the builder. Although she likes him, she would feel far happier if she were strong enough and skilled enough to carry out the whole process herself. She realises that she has personalised the place, and that she identifies with it, and she knows she would not want Pete Sparrow poking away with his pick in any of her little nooks and crannies.

He is too rough with it. She doesn't like to see old skirting boards being flung so carelessly out of the windows. She considers the whole process would be more bearable if it were done in private, behind awnings.

'How's it all coming along, Pete?'

He pokes at his cap. 'Fair and nicely, Mrs Freeman. We're down in the basements now. We've cleared all the rubbish from the attics down and soon the men'll be in to deal with the rot.'

'Good.'

Ellie is not even slightly concerned about protecting her identity here. Liverpool is a large city – there are hundreds of people with the name of Freeman. If her name did ever get back, if anyone gossiped, nobody would dream of associating this grand house with her. She does not move in Malc's circle. She does not move in any circle – as far as Ellie is concerned, she is going in a straight line.

She does not make a habit of talking about herself and nobody asks.

She resents the presence of the builders, their knapsacks and their thermos flasks, and the hammering sounds that come from every part of the house, and although she puts a smile on her face she always tries to find an empty room and then she closes the door – if there is one – and she sits in it. In three or four weeks' time the necessary destruction will be finished and the pain will be over. The constructive process will begin and Ellie will be able to take a more active part. She can't wait; she has so many ideas and plans that they topple over in her head at night. They bombard her, they set her brain on fire, she is afraid that she might die or go mad before she can accomplish anything.

She compares Gabriella's dream and her own with interest, for they are surprisingly similar. It is just that Ellie prefers the old and the solid while Gabriella goes for the flimsier, less permanent structure. Gabriella likes to look out of her window and see an array of fascinating life floating by, while Ellie isn't bothered so much by what goes on out of the window, it is what is inside that is all-important to her. But to both of them their homes are extremely important.

247

Perhaps Ellie is just more frightened that hers might be taken away, while Gabriella is more confident and doesn't need such firm foundations.

'Gabriella is more trusting, actually, than I am,' muses Ellie to the voice, 'in spite of her protests to the contrary.'

And when she feels a tiny prick of conscience the voice reassures her, 'That's her lookout, nothing to do with you. You press on, you're doing all right.'

'I am still afraid of her,' Ellie confesses.

'Well, so long as you're not showing it, that's what matters,' the voice replies firmly.

The Canonwaits offices are vast and impressive, and convey solidity and purpose. When you look out all you can see is grey sky and seagulls. She passes along glass-walled corridors that divide enormous, whitely-lit spaces in which the machinery of money whirrs round, armies of people sit at desks and the sound that dominates everything else is the tringing of telephones and the clacking of Faxes. Paper is piled up everywhere, crying for help; it fills wire bins and it litters desks and gets spiked on sharp little hooks. Malcolm's office is right at the end. It is one of the few rooms in this building which has four walls and a door, apart from the lavatories.

'Ah . . . Ellie,' he says, as if she is a rep. He just manages not to stand up and hold out his hand. He looks tired, dazed by the suddenness of events, most probably.

'You're looking tired, Malc,' Ellie says as she sits down.

'That's no wonder. Gabby's told you about what's been going on?'

'She told me last week when I had lunch with her, yes. Are things no better?'

'Not really,' and he passes his hand across his eyes in that tired old gesture. 'We can't get anywhere with the developers. All they'll give us is the name of a firm of solicitors in London and they are as tight as a duck's arse. It's Gabriella, really. I'm not around most of the time, so it's she who has to put up with most of it. All that happens to me is that I slide on motorbike oil whenever I go into the hall and now, to cap it all, the bloody lift isn't working.'

Ellie smiles sympathetically. 'It looks as if some of your old life is dogging your footsteps, doesn't it? I couldn't believe it when I saw Jackie Skinner, and old Dwarfy Sugden. It really is very strange.'

Malc seems to be overwhelmed by gloom. 'And it's not all that easy, being hassled by an ancient prostitute on your own staircase when you come home late from work.'

'No,' Ellie agrees quickly. 'That can't be very nice at all.'

'Last week there was a pool of vomit outside their door.'

'Oh God Malc, that's disgusting!'

Malc rubs his eyes again, tiredly. 'The cleaners can't cope. The whole place is beginning to smell of Dettol.'

Ellie leans forward in great concern. 'So what are you going to do?'

'Well, Gabriella says we have to strengthen the residents' association. We have to act together in order to get this sorted out and I agree with her. That is the only way.'

'And what do the other residents say?'

'They're as pissed off about it all as we are. Two of them have put their flats on the market but they're not getting anywhere because of the state of the place whenever a likely customer comes round to view. The trouble is,' and here Malc smacks his forehead, 'the really awful part is that none of them ever seem to go out! Apart from Dwarfy Sugden, but even he is never very far away.'

'Has anyone tried speaking to the Skinners, reasoning with them, explaining?' asks Ellie. 'I mean, the Skinners are really not bad at heart.'

'Of course we have tried – over and over again! Every tactic has been tried from anger to quiet, sensible requests, but you known Duane Skinner – he smiles in that toothless way of his and apologises profusely, promising that everything's going to change and the very next day, there's another incident. Last week, for instance, there was a trail of dogshit right across the hall and the Commodore's wife slipped in it and broke her ankle.'

'Surely they can sue them for that!'

'Sue them? The Skinners might live in one of the most sought-after premises in Liverpool but they don't have two halfpennies to rub together, they are still on social security. What would be the point in taking a family like that to court? And lo and behold the very next day one of their damn kids rescued a stray puppy, so now we've got that to contend with.'

'Well, what about the police? They're bound to take action. Prostitution, for a start – that's not legal, is it?'

'It's perfectly all right as long as you don't advertise and conduct your business in the privacy of your own home.'

'But the nuisance, Malc! You can't cause nuisance to your neighbours.'

'Oh Ellie, the police are in and out of there all the time. Gabby woke up to the sound of a police siren at quarter to four this morning. She's on pills now to help her sleep. She says that her nerves are shot and she's terrified about the big open day at the gallery.'

'Well, I don't know quite what to say.' And then she adds, 'Except that they didn't seem as bad as this when they lived in Nelson Street.'

'It's quite different now,' says Malc, slightly snappily, 'and what makes it worse is that Gabby's got more at stake here than anyone else. That's why she wants me to lead the residents' action group, so that something will be done, and quickly.'

OH YES OH YES OH YES . . . Ellie feels like a witch, a wicked, wily, warty old witch with the brew bubbling at her fingertips. How easy it all is – why hadn't she realised how easy it is to manipulate and stir and make things happen? Gabriella, my darling, you are even more predictable than I ever hoped you might be. You disappoint me, my dear, you are making this all so terribly easy.

She tries not to smile as a witch might smile. 'And are you going to do that, Malc?'

Of course you are! Of course you are – but let me hear you tell it!

'Well, everyone sort of expects a lead from us, what with Gabriella being so involved in the place and us having the penthouse,' Malc says dismally.

Well, they would, wouldn't they?

'But how do you feel about doing that, Malc? I mean, you

250

know the Skinners, you know poor old Dwarfy, it's a bit like turning against your own people, surely.'

'I don't see it in that way at all, Ellie. Everyone has rights, and these unsavoury people are threatening ours!'

Ellie raises her eyebrows but holds her tongue. She is not worried about her 'tenants', she is not worried about playing games with people who are already the pawns of society. They are quite safe, safer than they have ever been: they cannot be evicted from their homes no matter what the action group do, Ellie has made quite certain of that. And if, by some terrible chance, something were to happen to them, Ellie is quite prepared to bail them out.

'And now, how about you, Elle? We've spent the whole time talking about me and my problems when the whole point of your coming here this morning was for us to get to grips with yours. How is the financial arrangement working? Are you finding yourself able to cope?'

'If I'm careful,' says Ellie, wrapping her new canary yellow coat around her. 'But I never was one to go overboard.'

'And the car – is that still going all right?'

'Yes, it's a reliable little runner.'

'And how about next door? Is she still pestering you?'

'No, I am quite settled in and Maria hasn't been a problem since I told her to mind her own business. She turns away when she sees me and sticks her nose up in the air.'

'And that doesn't upset you?'

Ellie can't tell him she is never in, that she is either out shopping, ordering gorgeous wallpapers and chintzes, at the *Plaza* or round at her new house.

'I have changed, Malc,' she tells him. 'I am much more easygoing than I was before. Having nobody to rely on now, I have found new depths in myself.'

'I have to say, Ellie, that I honestly do admire the way you have dealt with all this.' And for the first time since he has left her she senses his vulnerability, in the way the Arcade was always so vulnerable – grand and imposing though it was – to the sharp stones of little boys.

Ellie's got quite a few stones in her pocket.

'I am an accepting person, Malc, and I think I have

adjusted, eventually, to most of the events in my life . . . given time.'

'You were always the stronger of the two of us, Elle.'

'Yes, you often used to say that, didn't you?'

'There was only one time when I felt you really needed me, and that was before Mandy was born . . . the time when you were so frightened, living with Mum and Dad and me away three nights a week at night-school.'

'I made you give it up, though, didn't I, and for that you have never forgiven me.'

'You forced me into taking the Canonwaits job, too, remember. Without your nagging I'd never have gone for it, never have reached the heights that I have unless you had persuaded me. So you are wrong – any old resentments of that kind are behind me now.'

Elle gets up to go. She jokes when she says, 'So really, apart from the little problem of Gabriella, you could say that things have never been so good between us!'

'You could say that, yes.'

His sexy smile is back and she wants him. She knows that everything is going well with Canonwaits because she receives the quarterly reports and reads them avidly. She knows that this end of the operation lies entirely in Malc's hands and that Murphy and Ramon now work from London. So, if it wasn't for the personal problems that are building up around him at home, Malc would be a contented, fulfilled man. Ellie knows and understands why she lost him; she lost herself, too, for a while back there and she learned a painful lesson in the process. She is angry with him for not having patience, for not caring enough to wait for her, but she loves him enough to forgive him.

She shouldn't have asked him to be leader.

He has always hated being leader and it is perfectly natural that in his hour of need he would lock on to someone as fiercely determined as Gabriella.

And Ellie has always loved Malc.

And she has always known that in spite of those little moments of hatred, those hopelessly depressing times when they had not known how to talk to each other, touch each

252

other, or how to break free from the situation, she has always known that he loved her, too.

Even in their desperation they had been like two little children hugging each other in a storm, crying in silence and not knowing where to shelter.

That's what Ellie wants to believe and she's damn well sticking to it.

30

Now Councillor Mrs Rene Cash is left-wing, and it is
possible to go further than that and state, tentatively, that she
could well be one of the most left-wing people in all the world
and to speculate as to what she might be doing in this country
in the first place.

A sweet, timid-looking woman, frail and prone to dressing
in muted colours, she is, in spite of her violent political
leanings, extremely fond of animals, so much so that when
one of her pets dies – so far a dachshund, two budgerigars and
three feral cats have suffered this fate – she has it stuffed for
posterity. She is kindness itself to her constituents; she
maintains an almost constant open house and never feels
prevailed upon nor taken advantage of.

It is the steely glint in her eye and her fanatical refusal to
take more than four hours sleep a night that singles her out
from the other widows who live quite quietly in her small
verdant cul-de-sac. Councillor Mrs Rene Cash's lights go
out at two, and they are back on at six; her neighbours say they
could set their clocks by her regular habits. So when she
stands up in her place in the council chamber all the men have
to be quiet in order to hear her still, small voice. No one could
be so rude as to bray at or bully this violet-smelling, very
English, white-haired old lady.

Ellie rings her up. She has been waiting to make this
telephone call for weeks. She knows very well the
Councillor's views on the development of the old docklands –
indeed, there is nobody in the nation who is not perfectly
aware of her views, and those of the little committee she
chairs which meets round at her bungalow for tea and biscuits
every other week. In televised debates, Councillor Cash
dominates the proceedings with her well-timed silences and
her glances. She has been known to quell, with one well-
directed look over her thin half-lenses, men like Dennis

Skinner and Arthur Scargill, both of whom, viewers must assume, she considers to be virtually National Front.

Indeed, in his time Arthur Scargill has been reduced to pleading, 'Oh please, Rene, give me a break.'

The telephone is answered by a sweet treble voice which courteously asks her who she is and how she is and what is her purpose for calling.

Ellie gives a false name and a real address . . . in one of the most deprived areas of the city, rented, dubiously tenanted, and therefore not traceable by any perusal of the voters' register. Over the wires she can feel Rene Cash soften towards her.

'They are clubbing together with all their might and all their power and all their clever ways of speaking in order to push these poor souls out,' sobs Ellie convincingly. 'They are holding the first residents' action group meeting on Tuesday night and I know it's all going to be done behind closed doors – the press will be excluded as usual and nobody is going to know what's going on.'

'And might I ask what your personal interest is in this, my dear?'

My dear?

But it's all right coming from this ancient quarter.

'I have lived in this area of Liverpool all my life. I have seen what has happened to it. I have even been homeless in my time,' cries Ellie. 'I know what it's like to feel despised and persecuted, and to feel there's no place to rest my head. These people might not be the world's best examples of humanity, but they have fallen upon some good luck – for once in their lives something good has happened to them, but now it looks as though it is all going to be taken away.'

She knows that a telephone recorder is going – you always know – and she also senses that notes are being assiduously taken.

'Can you tell me who is going to be allowed to attend this meeting?'

'All the residents of the Waterside Apartments, the residents of the new houses alongside the river, and anyone connected with the marina. I suppose that would include anyone with a permanent mooring – or their representatives.'

'Have you any idea what is going to happen at this early stage?' asks Councillor Mrs Rene Cash, encouragingly.

'No, but I assume the objectives are to pick an action group and vote on some ways and means of tackling their problems. They consider that the whole nature of the complex is under threat, you see, from the very people to whom it belonged in the first place!'

'Quite so. I understand. And can you furnish me with any more details of the intended victims of this grubby little back-street campaign?'

So Ellie does the telling while Councillor Mrs Cash does the recording and the note-taking and her tiny white head whirls round with ideas and plans, just as Ellie's whirls with well-justified high expectations.

'I don't want to become any more involved in this than I am already,' confides Ellie. 'I am in a dangerous enough position as it is . . . if anyone should find out that a warning was given . . . and this is all supposed to be terribly confidential.'

'Mum's the word,' says Mrs Cash. She does not ask Ellie where her information comes from. She isn't remotely interested in motives – results are what matter. 'Rest assured, when I give my word you can trust it absolutely.'

'So someone'll be there on the night?' asks Ellie, in need of reassurance.

'Someone'll be there,' and Ellie marvels that a voice so calm and controlled can sound so quietly sinister.

Councillor Mrs Rene Cash is a woman of action – not words. She works behind the scenes, she enjoys great influence, and once she scents her prey she is like a bloodhound and will never give up.

The press like her – she is worth cultivating. When she rings up she is put straight through to editors. They have achieved some of their biggest scoops from her mild suggestions in the past. She has a nose for news on the make, for situations that are on the simmer, coming up to the boil.

Poor Malc.

Especially when you think where he comes from.

Ellie is in her element now, not least because she can start making constructive suggestions to the builders who are at the point of restoring twenty-eight Ridley Place to its former glory. She spends whole days there with a flask and a packet of sandwiches, a fruit cake and some Nice biscuits. She discusses every pro and con with Pete Sparrow, who seems as enamoured of the house as she is, who doesn't mind dwelling on detail and who has 'done up one or two of these fabulous places in my time'. Ellie asks where, and goes round to check, and she is gratified by the results she sees.

Neighbours passing by start popping in to see what's going on. They are not like the Heswall neighbours; they are more interested in what's being done to the house than in what sort of person might be living in it. People come and go . . . houses like this will last hundreds more years, especially when they're being rejuvenated as thoroughly and as splendidly as this one. The callers have fascinating suggestions to make – like where she can obtain some proper old baths and where she might find a match for these old mouldings. Sometimes Ellie sits on a sawing block alongside one of these passers-by and chats about this and that for hours, sharing her flask with them.

Nobody bothers to ask her where she comes from or where she is going. Nobody seems to be put off by her accent. And, to be fair, Ellie is quite an imposing individual these days with her charts and the stub of pencil behind her ear, her gaudy wraps and her cocky hats, and that way she has of tearing from room to room, whistling to Pete Sparrow with two fingers in her mouth.

She is large.

She gets asked to dinner by the retired Brigadier and his wife at number twenty-six. She accepts without qualms, she arrives without fear, loaded with old photographs she's found in a backstreet photographers, and they spend a wonderful evening getting quite drunk and discussing architecture and how Liverpool used to be in its heyday.

'Of course I used to like pop music,' confides Ellie. 'I missed out on the proper stuff somewhere along the line. Sometimes I get my old records out and I play them, revelling in the nostalgia.'

'Oh, so do I!' shouts the Brigadier's wife, Norma. 'It's John who likes the classical stuff. You must make him take you with him next time he goes to the Phil.'

'I would be hugely honoured to have you accompany me,' her husband confirms.

And so that's how Ellie starts going regularly to concerts. She does not worry about being recognised, for no one would ever expect to see her here, and she wears her reading spectacles which even Malc has never seen, and low-brimmed hats which she can pull down further if she needs to.

'When do you think you will finally be able to move in?' asks the Brigadier, his eyes moist as they always are when they come out after listening to the music. He has explained to her that sometimes he feels so sad he can't bear it – 'almost suicidal in fact' – but at other times he feels quite warlike. 'It'll be nice to have a neighbour again.'

'They say three months, but you can't trust builders,' says Ellie, greedily finishing off the large box of Milk Tray in the taxi.

She enjoys the peace and quiet of being at home in the bungalow. She actually enjoys the silence and she's getting braver, beginning to believe that if she stops plotting and planning for a moment she might not cry. She suspects that the locals are talking about her in the butcher's and in the newsagent's, and wondering where she goes in the daytime, but that doesn't worry her now. She has not touched the housework in weeks; occasionally she pulls out the washing machine, but not often and germs must be breeding some-where but she's too big for them to bother her. This year the garden will go wild; she will probably get complaints from Wilfred as the seeds blow over the fence.

She is a woman in waiting.

Malc telephones her directly after the Tuesday night meeting and Ellie is slightly surprised, but not totally.

'It all seemed to go very well. They picked me as Chairman. Well, Gabby put me forward, actually – I don't think there were too many other contenders. It's all a little bit tricky.'

'Were there lots of people there?'

'Yes, of course, everyone is very concerned. They all

wanted to have their say. Everyone was repeating what Gabby and I are always saying – how amazing it is the way standards can fall so fast.'

Ellie looks around the bungalow, at the basket of unwashed clothes by the door, at the gathering dust and crisp packets overflowing the bins, at the bits of fluff on the carpet and she agrees, yes, how fast it can happen.

'Once the rot's set in,' says Malc.

Ellie smiles. She is not a slob and the state of her house is nothing to do with that. She does not love this place – bad things have happened to her in it. This bungalow is nothing to do with her now; it is part of her old life, part of what she used to be and it is not necessary for her to keep it clean nor to look after it. It is just so low on her list of priorities that nothing about it matters: her heart moved out of here long ago. She asks Malc, 'So what did you decide, or is it too secret to tell me?'

'Well, the first thing is to draw up a list of rules, and to get the Skinners, Dwarfy and the Peters to sign it, legally. We're having the list drawn up properly, so that we can prosecute if the terms are consistently flouted.'

'But they haven't got any money to pay fines with.'

'Then they'll have to go to prison, won't they, until they learn how to behave. We can't all live our lives without a sense of social responsibility, Ellie.'

'What sort of rules?' Ellie is interested, but she mustn't appear too keen.

'Oh, about stopping children from playing in the lift, keeping the sound down after midnight, keeping the hallways clean and the steps outside, not repairing motor vehicles on the premises . . . the normal, acceptable code of life. And no pets. Hell, Ellie, it's reasonable to expect at least that degree of normality from them, whoever they are!'

'I agree with you, Malc.' And she thinks about Dwarfy Sugden, and whether his barrow would come under the heading of a vehicle or not, and of whether he has any idea of the time, before or after midnight. Surely you have to be sane in order to sign an agreement . . . and how sane is Dwarfy?

And how literate is Duane?

259

They should not have to sign this agreement . . . it would be dangerous for them to commit themselves to a list of rules they could not possibly obey and so Ellie is going to get a letter off to her solicitors, instructing them to inform her life-tenants of that fact, post-haste.

She does not have to, though, because before she can get her thoughts together there is interference from another quarter. Councillor Mrs Rene Cash has lived up to her reputation: she has come up trumps.

The banner headline in the local morning paper screams up at her. It is better than she dreamed it would be: '*GET BACK TO YOUR SIDE OF THE TRACKS*' . . . *Waterside residents warn locals.* And it's a quote, given by the Commodore during a heated speech of denouncement which he is surely now regretting! The report is careful to quote other passages from several similar tirades during which the action group commit-tee had no idea that a tape recorder was playing quietly under the reporter's mac. They had no reason to suspect that a reporter would be there at all, lurking sneakily among their number . . . Ellie supposes he put his name down as a boat owner and in all the excitement nobody had bothered to check.

And then, a little further down, Councillor Mrs Rene Cash comes in with a pertinent quote of her own. '*It is always interesting to observe to what depths people will sink in order to protect their own privileged order. And it will be interesting to watch the future developments of this undoubtedly distressing situation. Some of us feel extremely uneasy about the present élitist state of the dockland and the way it has been allowed to distance itself and its luxurious amenities from the common people to whom it once belonged.*'

And there's worse to come!

The following morning the Waterside apartments are featured across the middle pages. Ellie takes the paper back to bed and snuggles between the covers with a coffee and a plateful of buttered toast. She licks her greasy fingers. There are pictures of the Skinners, beaming snottily on the cobbled area outside the apartments, managing to look pathetic and needy but likeable enough when posed like that. The dogs,

260

and two of the most extreme children, have been excluded from the picture.

And there is Dwarfy Sugden, managing to look more normal than Ellie has ever seen him, sorry for himself with his greatcoat done up and the contents of his barrow covered over, and his hair tucked neatly into a band. It is, after all, only when he slinks about in the darkness that Dwarfy becomes menacing. Fern and Blanche Peters can never look anything other than what they are, but it is obvious that they are enjoying the drama and having their photographs taken. They beam from the pages, saucily, with a terrible kind of gloating knowledge in their eyes, like lust.

The city takes sides – and those daring to support the action group tend not to be the nicest of people. They don't come over well in interviews with their three-piece suits and their public school accents. They are too defensive, too open to attack from sharp-voiced, carefully classless interviewers who have dealt with their type before. There is simply no safe place for them in society any more and they should not appear in public like that.

It is all much too delicate.

It is not long before the national tabloids pick up the story; their reporters dig around a bit and find out all about Malc who has been appointed spokesman for the detested Waterside Action Group. *WHOSE SIDE ARE YOU ON, MATE?* is the best they can do, but it is enough. It is hurtful, and it touches on all sorts of difficult areas which Malc would rather leave dead and buried.

So would poor Gabriella.

She distances herself for the sake of the gallery, just as Ellie guesses she might.

And next time Ellie bumps into the Brigadier he tells her, 'A rum business,' as he puffs off down the street with his deerstalker at a jaunty angle and his carrier bag full of empties. She knows what he is talking about, he does not have to stop and explain, because few people are talking about anything else.

261

31

It takes time, but eventually the people with banners disperse and go away.

'I told you they would, Malc,' says Ellie. 'This sort of thing is invariably a nine-day wonder.'

But fighting his way to his car through a crowd of hisses, day after day, has clearly taken its toll on Malc.

'We haven't given up,' he insists, looking bleary-eyed and defeated. He slams his fist into his hand. 'Hell, we can't give up. Look what they're doing to the place! But will anyone listen to our point of view? No, they bloody won't! All they're concerned about is protecting the rights of the downtrodden and the rejected. Downtrodden my arse! I'd like to get my bloody hands on the bastard who put them here in the first place, I can tell you.'

Sadly, what Malc says is perfectly true. The two swing doors of the gallery have been gritted up – they won't swing closed – with a mixture of playdough and mud concocted by five year old Barry Skinner, who sits on the patio area stirring it tirelessly, and sometimes licking it off a wooden spoon, as a more privileged child might taste cake-mix. Bright red graffiti depicting the tool of a giant has various mis-spelt expletives trailing drippily along the decorative wall below the eye-catching obscenity. All the miniature flowerbeds, so carefully and correctly designed, have been desecrated, like graves, so that only stalks remain and a scattering of sad petals. The cleverly angled paving area is covered with old chalkmarks . . . no . . . not hopscotch or anything so reasonable as that . . . but fourteen year old Charlene Skinner's crude attempts at pavement artistry.

And there, over by the edge of the water beside the seat where a bin has been thoughtfully provided, is the week-old litter scattered by Dwarfy. It contains not only his sandwich wrappers and the remains of his extraordinary consumption of high alcohol lager, but the cast-offs from his daily barrow scavengings which range from old clothes (which could well have come from washing lines) to firewood, from gigantic cardboard boxes to foil containers as though he has raided some Chinese restaurant or market.

The most enormous dog turds of every consistency imaginable have been deposited in the most unlikely places, and the Skinners have discovered the ideal spot in which to empty their hutch-leavings . . . in the hole in the wall in the little alley beside the gallery turning – a hole which houses the heating controls and ducts for the entire complex.

And there, dominating the attractive cobbled area directly outside, rests the Skinners' tip-up truck, hopelessly wheel-clamped, with one headlight spiralling out on wires, giving it the look of a puzzled drunk who has come to rest in the gutter and has no intention of ever moving on.

'This is ridiculous, Malc,' says Ellie. 'Surely anyone who came to look would see this and understand your point of view.'

'They don't want to see it, so they don't. Principle is all they are interested in and there's all sorts of high moral principles at stake. And now, before tomorrow's celebration of the arts day, Gabby is having to pay a firm of clean-up contractors to come and shift all this mess. The council refuse to do it. It is nothing short of scandalous.'

Ellie has come to see if she can be of any help, but Gabby is busy in the gallery and Malc is at the flat, unshaven, tired and angry, holed up there like a hostage. 'I thought you were another of those bloody hacks,' he said, when he opened the door with caution.

And when she assured him there were no cameras about he offered to show Ellie round to prove his point.

'It is cruel what they have been saying about you,' she told him, as they wandered around in the bright spring sunshine. 'I don't know how you can bear it. Bringing up your past like that, even finding old friends who knew you . . . and highlighting the fact that Warren and Mickey are still inside doing time.'

'Oh, that's nothing,' says Malc bitterly. 'It was when they

discovered Mum was an alcoholic, and compared that with my persecution of these people, saying it was a psychological thing and I secretly wanted to get my own back – now that really hurt.'

'It must have done,' says Ellie. 'And calling your dad an old lag.'

'You wouldn't believe what these people are allowed to get away with.'

'And has it affected you at work at all?'

'Luckily no,' says Malc morosely. 'Ramon and Murphy look on it all as some sort of joke. They tell me to see the funny side, but to me there doesn't seem to be a funny side.'

'And Gabriella? How's she coping with your unpopularity? How does she like being shacked up with the most hated man of the moment?'

Malc is silent for a while, considering whether it's safe to confide. They come to rest on a seat overlooking the liverish water. Yachts bob up and down at their moorings and little flags clack. A breeze lifts Ellie's hair and she pulls her beret down further. She unwraps a ham and tomato roll and offers a piece to Malc. He ignores her. Malc seems to shiver so Ellie says, 'You should have brought a coat – it's not that warm yet.'

'This whole situation has put a strain on our relationship, Elle.'

'Well, it's bound to do that.' She keeps any suggestion of triumph well out of her voice.

'And yet it was Gabby's idea that I should lead the action group. I wouldn't have done it, but she insisted.'

'You blame her for your predicament?' Ellie throws some pieces of bread to the seagulls. Their beaks are sharp and vicious and their eyes are blackly vindictive.

'When I look back I can remember feeling some surprise that she didn't take on the job herself. After all, she's quite capable.'

'Perhaps she was astute enough to recognise the pitfalls. It hasn't hurt your job, Malc, but unpopularity of this kind would certainly have affected hers.'

'I suppose you are right.'

'You didn't have to take it on,' says Ellie, taking another

large bite and watching as a ship glides by in the hazy distance. 'Did you?'

'Gabby is a very complicated woman, quite different from you, or me for that matter, Elle. The little things upset her, like being woken by the Peters' racket in the middle of the night . . . getting shit on her shoe . . . the way Jackie Skinner has started collecting her mail and shouts out after her, and Dwarfy quite seriously frightens her. But, overall, she is more accepting than I am, determined to sort this out, oh yes, very determined in that respect, but in another way it doesn't seem to touch her, can you understand that? She never seems to get completely involved. And as far as these newspaper attacks go, well, she says it is not her affair and that I ought to be able to deal with it.' And then Malc seems to make a decision and says, 'I think the pressure has got to her, though, Elle. Her eyes are often far away as if she's thinking about something else.'

'Perhaps she's heading for a breakdown,' says Ellie.

'Oh no, it's nothing like that.' Malc kicks at a pestering gull.

How would you know, Malc?

'She is probably concentrating all her attention on tomorrow. I've seen it advertised everywhere. Let's hope the protesters keep away, for her sake.'

Malc looks at her. 'It was kind of you to come and offer to help, Elle. You've always been like that, haven't you?'

'I like to do my bit,' says Ellie. 'And I had to see you because I was worried about you.'

'Well, Gabby's got everything organised. There's not an awful lot for her to do now, really, other than wait and see how it goes, and entertain the big-wigs tomorrow.' And then he considers again when he says, 'She likes you, you know.'

'Who?'

'Gabby. She likes you. She says she admires you. She says I was lucky to have you.'

'Does she?' Ellie feels unaccountably pleased and moved to say, 'Well. There's something about Gabriella that I like, too. Her sense of purpose, her drive, her enthusiasm for life and her ability to grab an opportunity when she sees it. But she's quite hard, Malc, isn't she? She wouldn't allow much to get in her way.'

265

'I don't know whether that's a good thing or a bad thing,' says Malc.

'Oh, but it's good.' Ellie is quite certain. 'I wish I'd been born with her confidence, but I think it comes from the belief that you're better than anyone else, a belief that's probably learnt in childhood.'

'I wonder if you can acquire it later in life?'

'Not in the same sort of way. Unless it's bred into you you're just pretending – putting on a brave face, that sort of thing. I mean, look at you. You've done well, you are a high achiever, but you are still terribly vulnerable at heart, Malc, aren't you – in a way that Gabriella is not.'

'It's nice, sitting chatting like this, Ellie. I wonder why we didn't do more of it.'

'We didn't have much to talk about, I suppose. Either that, or we didn't consider each other worth talking to.'

'You make it sound so bleak.'

'Well, wasn't it?'

'I wonder, Elle. I wonder what's going to happen in the end.'

'We will just have to wait and see, Malc, won't we.'

'You seem happier, more contented than you have ever been. I have never seen such a dramatic change in a person over such a short space of time. From that frightened woman with no idea what to do with herself, all wrapped up with the family, going to those dreadful classes, forever cooking and cleaning the house, just waiting for me to come home . . . and now look at you!'

Malc says this with pride, as if he has had something to do with it.

'I think it's my size that gives the impression of super-confidence,' says Ellie, 'and the bright colours I have started to wear. Bright colours suit me and yet I never dared try them before. I was worried in case you wouldn't approve, I suppose. You always used to call women who wore bright colours hard. You seemed to prefer the subdued and the flimsy, superficially of course.'

Malc turns right round on the seat and stares hard at her. 'What do you do all day, Elle? I can never really work that out.'

266

'Oh, this and that,' she says flippantly. 'It's surprising how quickly time passes,' and she brushes the crumbs from her coat before moving on to the crisps.

'And you have settled down in the bungalow?'

'Oh yes, although if circumstances were different, if there was enough money coming in, I would keep an eye open for a different kind of house and I would move back into the city. I can't get used to the quiet and I still don't like Maria.'

'What sort of house?' Malc has never asked this before.

'A Georgian house I think, like those near the library. They do come up for sale every now and then and we might be lucky . . . someone could find themselves in a hurry to sell, we might get a snip.'

'We?' Malc frowns.

'You asked me a hypothetical question and I answered it hypothetically. Why, don't you like Georgian houses?'

'Well, yes, I do. But they are very expensive.'

'Well, as I said, it's just a dream.'

But Ellie knows that Malc is working out in his head just how much he earns and what it would stretch to. He is not considering returning to her, he is interested in doing the sum, that's all.

Three Skinner children have started a game of football and although the ball doesn't actually hit Malc and Ellie, it comes dangerously close; it is unnerving, you cannot relax or concentrate, you cannot take your eye off the heavy ball.

'Can't you find somewhere else to do that, for God's sake,' shouts Malc, all tensed up again and pulled into a narrow straight line. 'You can see there's people sitting here trying to enjoy some peace and quiet.'

'Don't you start on us, mister, we'll get the papers on you!'

'Bastards,' mutters Malc, getting up.

'Leave it, Malc,' says Ellie. 'I've got to go now, anyway.'

But Malc is making a calculated approach for the ball, trying to work out where it's going next, rolling up his sleeves in his urgency.

'You take our ball, mate, and I'm telling my da on you.'

The children are small – the eldest can be no more than seven or eight, and the holes in their jeans could be caused by either fashion or neglect.

'I used to watch for hours while you played football down Nelson Street, Malc, bouncing the ball from wall to wall while the women cursed you and the men joined in on their way past.'

'Well, this isn't Nelson Street, Ellie, is it?'

'No, it's not, but the children are still children.'

He turns towards her, distracted. 'So you think this is acceptable, then? You think I should just go and bloody leave them to carry on and break some more glass?'

She does not want to see him made a fool of. He is no longer quick enough to dominate the game, he will not catch the ball and somebody has to stop him. It's funny, because she feels some old resentment welling up from somewhere . . . she is the mother again, responsible, and Malc, in spite of everything that has happened, in spite of all the growing he has done, is still the child in need of protection. This feeling reduces her. It pushes her back into pastel clothes. It shrinks her to the smallness of a woman with a washing basket bending over with pegs in her mouth. It sends her scurrying to cookery classes to pamper the man, to placate him, to satisfy the little-boy moods.

She feels herself holding her breath again in that same gasp, waiting to see what will happen to somebody else, just as if she's a springboard with no feelings of her own on which he is going to bounce down. Diminishing her.

'I'm going, Malc,' she says, making for her car. She doesn't look round to see what has happened, she doesn't want to know any more! Hell, it is no longer her problem. 'I'll see you tomorrow,' she flings over her shoulder, 'and let's hope the weather stays fine.'

There is no reply, just the sounds of scuffles and snorts and bouncing balls and one, high-pitched, little-boy laugh, with fear in it, and triumph, too.

Ellie expands again as she drives to her new house and begins to supervise the unloading of the wallpapers. 'Mornin' Mrs Freeman. You're late today.' She places each boxful in the appropriate room, sighing over every roll as she unpacks it gently. The walls are pale and smooth, waiting for covering. The skirting boards and the woodwork are undercoated

268

already and there is a pleasing smell of fresh wood and turpentine, a relaxing sense of space and unclutter in every room.

Ellie absorbs the silence.

Pete Sparrow's footsteps are hollow, his fag is attached to his lip. 'We're nearly there now, Mrs Freeman. Just another month and you'll be in, lock stock and barrel, right on schedule.'

Ellie nods to Pete Sparrow and smiles. 'You've done a good job, Pete, and I'm grateful.'

'You and me both, Mrs Freeman. We did it together – remember?'

Waiting. The house is waiting.

32

Ellie wakes up to find an April morning at war with itself. It could rain, it could blow, it could even hail beneath that suggestion of sunshine. For Gabriella, this morning, the decisions she is going to have to make must be daunting.

Ellie smiles up at her multi-cobwebbed bedroom ceiling.

In order to savour this day of triumph Ellie is going to dress with care. She picks her way across piles of old magazines, empty boxes of chocolates, brochures and face-mask packaging on her journey from bed to wardrobe. Bright, she thinks to herself, bright to the point of dazzling, and sod the weather. She doesn't often feel the cold now, not like she used to, for the layers of fat keep it at bay: she carries her own warmth inside her. She's never worn this one yet – the skirt and jacket go together and are of the same material, a kind of harsh gabardine with a sheen. The suit is safari-style with epaulettes, and coloured the most violent purple. The shirt she's going to wear is the crisp cotton red one. She gets it out of the drawer and sniffs it. Lovely. It is just back from the laundry.

She never bothers about her shoes. Strangely, she never gives a thought to those and most of the time she trails around in the same old knee-length boots because they are comfortable.

She's going to look quite artistic, she thinks, as she admires herself in the mirror – quite one of the gang. These bungalow rooms are almost too small to accommodate her now . . . she needs to stride out and stretch, she needs to move quickly, and this house is designed for a small neat woman, with small neat ways, who goes slowly. Not Ellie.

She prepares breakfast – cereal and a fry up, followed by toast and marmalade. Breakfast is her favourite meal now she can linger over it and enjoy it, now it's not over and done with in a hurry. She loves the sense of non-panic these new mornings induce in her. She is not up and moving around in a desperate rush on behalf of somebody else . . . that sense of panic used to grip her and last, sometimes, throughout the whole of the day. Start as you mean to go on, thinks Ellie, spreading the butter and enjoying the sensation of the soft, yellow uncurling of it . . . steadily and with purpose. And she covers her two eggs with a slurping layer of tomato sauce.

When she finally arrives at the Royal Albert Art Gallery the roads are already crowded and glossy-caped policemen are directing the traffic into nearby car parks. Coaches sit there waiting, filled with the restlessness of schoolchildren and recorders, some dressed in peasant costumes with handfuls of bells and posies.

Are they going to need their macs or aren't they, and where are the public lavatories? These questions haunt the teachers' faces.

There is bunting strung from building to building, darkening the thin streets, and banners which say, LIVERPOOL'S DAY FOR THE CELEBRATION OF THE ARTS. Someone thrusts a programme through the Metro window and Ellie almost tips up her bag in her effort to pass over one pound.

A uniformed band tunes up under an awning on the patio beside the water, and rows of spindly-looking green chairs are lined up before it, but no one is sitting down yet as the weather is far too uncertain. Two containers to be used for props are hidden away round one corner, and they look stark and out of place, as if someone has forgotten to clear them away. There are booths selling prints, pottery, jewellery, embroidered linens and wooden, home-made toys. Behind each booth are craftsmen demonstrating their skills. There are no hot dogs or fish and chips for sale here, only baked potatoes, wholefood pizzas, pastas, and rolls sprinkled with sesame seeds.

The Skinners' dog looks suspiciously round as it cocks its tatty leg over the wheel of the baked potato cart.

Ellie gives in her ticket and passes through the VIP barrier into the gallery foyer. It is quieter in here, and sherry is going round on a tray. There are little dips along the counter where the postcards and tea towels usually sit. Malc edges his way through the whispering crowd towards her.

'How's it all going?' asks Ellie, chewing a celery stalk.

'Fingers crossed,' says Malc, as though he is up to no good. 'No disasters yet, but then it's only just begun.'

'How's Gabriella?'

'Very calm. She's used to handling this sort of thing.'

'Aren't the public going to be allowed into the gallery? Have they got to stay outside?'

'Oh, no. Once this reception's over the barriers will be removed and then they can file round if they want to, but most of the real entertainment is going to happen outside.' Malc looks out dubiously. 'There are lots of covered spaces in case it rains. Nobody needs to get wet.'

'Gabriella's contractors did a marvellous job. There's no sign of litter or graffiti, no broken windows as far as I could see, no half-built go carts and no broken bottles. No old prams, either. It all looks remarkably well organised.'

'Well, as I said, Gabby's used to this sort of thing.' And Malc looks pleased.

'No press, either?' Ellie sniffs one of the dips to see if there is garlic in it or not.

'Only those expressly invited here for the right reasons. Gabby was very careful when she sent the badges out and she wrote a special letter to all the editors.'

'Very sensible – she seems to have thought of everything. Even the flowerbeds have been replanted, I noticed.'

'Well, we know that won't last long. They'll soon be got at again, no doubt.'

But it doesn't look as if anything will be got at today; it looks as if Gabriella's quite safe. Men with walkie-talkies lurk on corners, sneaky-eyed and watching for trouble. The St John ambulance is parked down a side street. Two men with guard dogs patrol the old dockside and there are barriers up to stop people falling over into the water. The fountains on the patio outside the gallery play freely and happily, the water around them fresh and clear; someone has scooped out the old bus tickets and dog-ends, and all the statues have been freed from encumbrances such as toilet rolls and parking cones.

'Drink up,' says Malc. 'When the mayoress arrives there'll be speeches and then all this'll be cleared away. Hang on, I'll get you another.' Neither Malc nor Ellie have been able to break free from the habit of grabbing anything that's on the house.

'Ah, Ellie! You came then!'

'Of course I came. Did you think I might not?'

Gabriella smiles. 'No, but then one never knows. You are looking extraordinarily wonderful!'

Ellie glances around her, brushing her chin free of vol-au-vent crumbs. 'Do you know all these people?'

'Most of them.'

'They must think very highly of you . . . all that you've done since you came here. And you must feel very satisfied.'

Gabriella smiles again. She looks very sophisticated today in a way that Ellie could never achieve and, strangely, although she admires it, she no longer wants it for herself. Gabriella is wearing a black silk dress which would be severe if it wasn't for the blazing jewelled belt and the array of silver chains and necklaces. Her fawn hair is full of lights. 'It is my job. It is what I was trained for.'

'If there is anything you want me to do don't hesitate to say.'

'Thank you, Ellie.'

And then Gabriella has gone, drifting off cloudily into the crowd, and Ellie catches occasional sights of her, gesturing here and chatting there, all done with admirable grace and elegance. Ellie takes her flopping cardboard plate back to the counter and fills it with Twiglets and Niblets before they come to take them away.

It is a little bit over the top for outriders to precede the mayoral car, but presumably a way must be cleared through the crowd. Somebody blows a trumpet and everyone falls quiet to see where the sound has come from. The double doors to the gallery are opened wide and propped back, and outside, the crowd pushes towards the barriers. A red carpet has been laid out and a large space cleared in front of the building, with chairs lined up and loudspeakers ready for the speeches.

Ellie has a perfect view.

It makes an attractive setting, with the fountain playing like that and the intriguing structure of the gallery rising behind, woodily oriental like a Chinese pagoda with many roofs. The lady mayoress struggles from her car, clutching her hat and smiling bravely like the Queen Mother. Her eyes follow the carpet up the steps to the paved platform area. The wind blows her skirts, but not enough to cause undue concern. A barge hoots eerily from the river and the crowd gives an uncertain little series of claps.

'Well, it looks as if we're going to be lucky,' starts the lady mayoress, staring hopefully at the sky and testing the microphone. She is having trouble removing her gloves, and her handbag is thrown, like her chain, over her right shoulder. 'It would make a change, wouldn't it,' she says to the crowd in a friendly way.

And then she is introduced, rather needlessly, and her speech begins. Gabriella sits on one of the chairs beside her, and several other important-looking people wearing badges, whom Ellie has never seen before, sit on the others. Ellie, still indoors, is thrust against the windows, but it's warm in here so she's all right, and every now and then somebody smiles at her as if they might know her and she smiles back.

Gradually her eyes, along with a thousand others, are drawn by a movement towards the fountain. They watch the Skinners' dog sniff round the base of it, and then take his grizzled head over the top; he seems to wait for a while, assessing the likely depths of the water, but you can tell that the Skinners' dog has been here before.

'And so we all began to think about the purpose of our national treasures,' the lady mayoress is saying.

The Skinners' dog moves forward, his two front legs on the low brick circular wall of the fountain. Perhaps he's going to have a drink. His tail is low between his legs.

'. . . and to whom they really belonged, whose real right it was to possess them . . .'

He is paddling in the water now and all eyes are on him. His bony ribcage drips, and the underside of his pronounced grey snout goes beard-like with water. His eyes appear to be leering, swivelling round redly in his narrow head. He is not a dog that anyone – even the strangest child - would automatically want to pat. Perhaps he is going to have a swim.

274

'. . . and then, of course, it was a question of where to find the money. Here the businessmen of Liverpool came into their own, and we must never forget the great debt of gratitude we owe to well-known names such as . . .'

The dog is clambering up the slippery sides of the plinth on which rests the black marble porpoise. His sinewy wet limbs must be surprisingly strong because it is quite a steep slope, and small; surely it is hard to maintain a grip with such wet, leathery paws. His mottled grey balls hang low, emphasised horribly by the wetness of his undercarriage, and appallingly scrawny, like a pair of misformed Spanish castanets.

'What's that long red thing, like a carrot, sticking . . .'

The child is quickly hushed but there are a few nervous titters.

'And so this is the first real occasion on which we have all been able to come together in order to really enjoy this magnificent collection for which we have to thank . . .'

The dog is humping the porpoise. His grey arms cling to the smooth-seagoing shape of it, his back legs tremble under his terrible efforts and there is something distressingly human in the way he batters the front of himself manfully against the chill, black back of the rigid creature beneath him. The porpoise continues to spurt water from its mouth, an uninterrupted flow of clear, cool, almost jellified water, while it is jabbed at ruthlessly from behind.

'Ey-up.'

The crowd collapses with laughter. It would be silly for the lady mayoress to attempt to continue. She backs away from the microphone with a resigned smile. 'Let the show go on!' she shouts shrilly, like a good sport, over her shoulder as she is ushered indoors for a glass of sherry.

The wave-tops turn green, they are blustery and threatening. Little girls jingle their bells and dance between bursts of rain, white teeth chattering. One set of steps has been converted into a stage and people stand watching beneath umbrellas, but the actors have to shout to be heard and this creates some difficulties. Someone has to stand at the gallery door to prevent people carrying food from entering. A Punch and Judy show attracts a large crowd, as does the old fishing smack in the marina on which a white-jacketed pianist is playing a white grand piano.

It is all looking good.

'Bugger you, you bastards, coming round here as if you've no homes of your own to go to.' The squeak of Dwarfy's returning barrow can hardly be detected above the noise and, huge though he is, his burly figure can hardly be seen down there among the people. It is as if he has not been informed about what's going on. He looks about him blearily, wondering if he has returned to the right place, or if his new home has been taken over while he's been gone.

He puts down his barrow and wanders across to the source of the loudest noise. The bandstand is still fairly deserted; the chairs tremble in the gusts of wind as there is no one to hold them down except a few old couples, resting. Dwarfy picks up the first chair and throws it. It lands in the water.

'Hey!' The bandleader turns around and pauses, red-faced, in his conducting. 'Hey, you, stop that! That's vandalism that is!'

'Don't you come here accusing me of vandalism,' Dwarfy mutters, moving to the second chair, his mettle up now. 'Coming here uninvited . . . making this bloody row.' And Dwarfy flings a second chair, and a third, staring belligerently at the chubby bandleader as he does so.

One of the eagle-eyed guards moves in, whispering to his walkie-talkie. 'Now listen . . .' He tries to reason with Dwarfy but Dwarfy is not putting up with that. He picks up a fourth chair and he flings it. The guard tries to restrain him, looking over his shoulder nervously for support.

'Move away from here, there's going to be trouble.' The bandleader ushers the old people from the few chairs they occupy. They leave the scene muttering angrily and join the edge of the gathering crowd. Two guards stand and watch Dwarfy now, deep in discussion, their hands on their hips. Dwarfy keeps his eye closely on them while he continues flinging the chairs. He has a rhythm going, and when one of the guards approaches from the front and another from behind Dwarfy roars, opening his terrible mouth wide like a yawning hippopotamus – great strands of saliva seem to hold

276

it together. He attacks them by whirling round – the chair is his weapon, he has it by its two back legs: 'And if you come any nearer to me you'll end up in the water, you can bet your life you will.'

'It's a shame,' calls a troublemaker from the crowd.

'Leave the poor old guy alone, you're making him worse,' cries a do-gooder. 'Can't you see he's barmy?'

'But he's throwing the chairs into the water!' One of the guards protests, tries to explain.

'He wouldn't have done if you hadn't got his back up.'

They try and argue but it is no use – the crowd has already taken sides and Dwarfy senses this and carries on like a programmed automaton, wild-eyed, mad-haired, disposing of as many chairs as he can while he has the chance. Getting chairs into the water is now the most important thing in Dwarfy's life and he goes about it singlemindedly. They don't sink, but bob around on top of the waves with their legs in the air. A group of women lean dangerously over the edge, down the steps beside the water, trying to prod them nearer with sticks, to grab them to take home.

'Well, they're all right for the kitchen.'

'Better than anything I've got.'

In spite of the high levels of security the police will have to be called. In the meantime, there is a nasty scuffle during which Dwarfy has to be subdued, grounded and handcuffed, and there is an unseemly wait for the police van, when Dwarfy screams out all the obscenities which he has ever heard in his life. The crowd grows larger, surly and more voluble. Certain well-known troublemakers push themselves to the front.

Some people leave.

This could turn into a nasty incident. The bandleader decides to play on, for he knows that music is a calming influence, and it is to the strains of *Tulips from Amsterdam* that Dwarfy is pushed in the wagon and carted away to spend an uncomfortable night in the familiar police cell, where he worries himself sick about his cart, weeping, 'One of those buggers'll whip it for certain, and then what'll I do?'

Inside the gallery things are slightly calmer.

All Gabriella has to do is demand the handing over of the

crudely-done cards . . . *Promotions, parties, strip-o-grams, escorts, anything considered for the right price* and insist that Fern and Blanche Peters leave the premises forthwith. 'It's against the law apart from anything else,' she tells them firmly and they quail and quake before her icy smile. All she has to do is apologise over the loudspeaker to those members of the public who have been unfortunate enough to receive one. All she has to do is prevent Jackie Skinner from sitting on the seat in front of the nude Botticelli and feeding the latest baby . . . her dirty bra strap is worse, actually, than her exposed breast with its crusted nipple. All she has to do is to persuade the insolent Marcus from stealing a part from the 'World of the Machine' room, explaining as nicely as she can in front of the crowd that that particular spanner is essential to make up the structure's armpit, with Marcus protesting, 'It'd be a bloody sight more use on my bike.'

Ellie moves colourfully around the afternoon, watching, listening, missing nothing and enjoying every moment.

When Ellie goes to bid her farewells, feeling the pleasant exhaustion of total satisfaction, Gabriella says sweetly, 'But darling, you must stay for the fireworks! There's a party of us going to watch from the terrace, it'll be a marvellous end to the day.'

Ellie declines. 'I can only stand so much, at my age,' she smiles.

'Oh, come on,' Gabriella insists, 'you've got more energy than the rest of us put together.'

'How do you feel now, Gabriella? Relieved, I expect, now that it's nearly over? And did it go according to plan?' In spite of all she must have endured, she does not look even slightly flustered.

'Not so much according to plan, but more as I suspected it would,' and Gabriella gives a wry smile.

Can nothing defeat the woman? Surely, inside, she is screaming?

'Well, I for one thoroughly enjoyed myself in spite of the setbacks,' says Ellie.

'Yes, you look as if you did. I'm glad,' says Gabriella, moving off through the lingering crowds to find Malc.

Well, she's hardly likely to give me the satisfaction of breaking down in front of me, says Ellie, consoling herself as she drives home, smiling nearly all the way.

Poor Malc. She imagines the rest of his evening.

33

Gabriella's hold on Malc has been loosened. She seems to be letting him go. One day he phones to ask if he can come to the bungalow, 'to take a look at the garden.' Ellie is quick to refuse – she doesn't have anyone visit her any more. Di has asked several times, so has Margot, and Kev wants to come and have a look, but to everyone Ellie makes the same excuse: 'I'll come to you, I'd rather. You know how I love to get out.'

To Kev she says, 'Go and stay with your father. It's much nicer there, and you could learn to sail.'

The bungalow is shrivelled up like a sun-dried chrysalis, or a scaly old snakeskin; there is no real room for anyone in it. The furniture has not seen polish for months, the curtains have a tie-dye effect with damp-looking stains from being so rarely drawn, and all the surfaces are covered with that vague suggestion of frost, a kind of ashy-white dust which shows up badly when the sun shines in. It's beginning to smell of litter and every now and then – she doesn't know why she bothers – Ellie goes round with a black dustbin bag and gathers it all together.

She's got far more to do with her time than cope with nonsense like that, and she doesn't want a cleaner, she doesn't want anyone coming in and wanting to chat. The bungalow is a place to sleep, a place to eat and a place for telephone calls – not a place to be living in.

Ellie spends almost every day round at twenty-eight Ridley Place. She has to be there to see that the curtains are hung properly, the carpets are laid and the brand new furniture is exactly what she ordered – not only furniture, of course, but lamps, rugs, new bedding and towels. Everything's new, even down to biscuit tins and cruets. She has great fun with the kitchen, she keeps it old-fashioned in the most modern way and the firm which installs it wants to come and take photographs for an advertising feature. Brass-bottomed pans hang around her wonderful black Aga, great oak settles squashed with cushions sit either side of the scarred old table and only the best Worcester china is displayed in her glass-fronted dresser.

Eventually there comes a day when even Pete Sparrow considers it finished; it is the day he comes round, not for his last cheque, because Ellie is holding that back in case of mistakes, but for his scarf and his bobble hat.

He smacks his lips together with a fag gripped between. 'This is a special, a one-off,' he tells Ellie and the Brigadier, who are sitting having coffee in the drawing room. Norma is on the floor rifling through Ellie's record collection, drinking coke with a straw. 'And I am dead chuffed with what I've accomplished here.'

'You have every right to be chuffed,' says the Brigadier, dunking a dark chocolate digestive.

'But I couldn't have done it without her,' Pete Sparrow goes on, looking at Ellie with undisguised admiration. 'She's been a pillar of strength to me and a rich source of inspiration. She has a natural touch, she knows what's right, down to the last bath plug, down to the last toilet chain. She knows it's the details what really count.'

'Well,' says Ellie.

'And I think you're wasting a great talent,' Pete goes on. 'I think you'd be wrong to stick at one.'

'You think she should go in for this sort of thing in a professional way?' asks Norma.

'She'd be snapped up. They'd only have to come and see this and they'd snap her up. There's not many people who know . . . natural-like. Most people have to be taught it and then there's always something a little bit missing.'

Ellie flushes with pleasure.

'You know what proper people like,' says Pete Sparrow, moving reluctantly out of the house of which he has become so proud.

But it is really that evening when she is on her own that Ellie experiences that sensation of sheer pleasure. It is softly, calmly, summer – with a gentle green light filtering in and a nightingale singing. There is dew on the grass of her small garden, black soil, old roses are starting to grow again now the rubble has been cleared around them. The stout walls filter the sounds and only seem to allow the right ones in . . . this house knows Ellie and she is at one with it. She sits and she sips a glass of sherry, at one with herself and happy as she can never remember being . . . not so totally . . . no, not ever.

She has decided to have a small house-warming party, nothing much, just drinks and nibbles – mostly the neighbours. Her shoes are off and her feet are up on the sofa. She is deciding whether or not she can stay the night; it seems such a shame to leave it. She has bought some invitations and she fills them in as she sits there, reluctant to do anything much except lie back and savour this swelling feeling of joy.

She feels lazy.

Lonely? No. Isn't that funny, she's not even slightly lonely. She frowns when she hears the doorbell go, she has to put on her shoes and go all the way downstairs, and it can only be a salesman, or Norma who's forgotten something, or other neighbours coming round to introduce themselves. Ellie's not in the mood for talking.

She is in the mood for feeling.

She opens the door and there's Gabriella. Ellie jumps. Her face whitens. It is hard for Ellie to take this in – for this is another world intruding – it is as if someone from *Neighbours* has strayed into *Coronation Street*, it is worrying, disorientating – and Ellie is lost for words.

'Aren't you going to invite me in?'

Gabriella is all eyes . . . admiring eyes . . . very wide, very blue, very certain.

'How did you know about my house?'

Gabriella just smiles and exclaims, as she mounts the stairs behind a breathless Ellie, 'My oh my!'

There is nothing for it but to show her into the drawing room and Gabriella, in a red towelling jumpsuit and trainers, settles down, her eyes wandering around the room, absorbing every last delicate detail. She shakes her head amazedly and asks for a drink.

'What?'

'I'll have the same as you.' She nods towards the glass which Ellie has forgotten.

Ellie is in a state of shock. She moves, but she doesn't know how she moves; she thinks, but without direction or logic. When she looks back she will remember every second of this unexpected encounter, every glance, every meaningful look, every slant of the light, the way the rug curls up at one corner and the creases in the magazine.

Gabriella de Courtney relaxes by stretching her legs and allowing her arms to rest along the top of the sofa. She gazes at Ellie very seriously. 'Much as I am enjoying the game, tempted though I am to allow it to go on, for it is compelling in itself – it is quite, quite fascinating – nevertheless I feel it is time that we stop playing and count up what we've got.'

Ellie manages to squeak, 'I do not understand you.'

Gabriella gives a small laugh. 'Oh, Ellie! Please give me the credit of allowing me some intelligence, some sense of foresight, some desires and motives other than the ones you have been insulting me with up until now. Every dog has its day and I have allowed you yours. You had to be allowed one small moment of triumph – a day neither of us is quickly going to forget.'

'I still don't know what you're talking about, and I don't understand how you knew about my house!'

Get out get out get out you are spoiling it. You look good in it but you are ruining it! Ellie's hands are sweating . . . she has been caught . . . she is going to be punished. She wants to run away but there is nowhere to go and Gabriella is staring at her steadily as if she knows.

'Well, sweetie, I have to confess that I did not fall out with my intellectual friend, Bella Beasely, over the small matter of prisoners' art. It was, to be truthful, much more mundane than that. I fell out with that sharp little lady because I was fucking her husband. It's surprising what men tell you in bed. It's astonishing to discover all the small matters they like to confide while they're . . .'

'Robert told you about my money?' The pain of this is double-edged, sharp and rusty, it cuts her jaggedly and withdraws, bringing a tinny raw slice of Ellie with it. It is a

283

betrayal of enormous proportions. Ellie remembers the discomfort on Bella Beasely's face when she'd gone round for help on that terrible first morning and mentioned Gabriella's name, and Robert's unease . . . Ellie has to smile, because there she'd been, fantasising, dreaming that he might fancy her. Oh God, take it away . . .

Gabriella is going on quite unperturbed. She probably knows how Ellie feels – she seems to know everything, doesn't she? 'And as far as finding out about your house, that was quite simple. I only had to follow you from Malcolm's office one day and you led me straight to it.'

Ellie steadies her hand as she reaches for her sherry, as the awful truth dawns. 'So Robert told you about the money?' she repeats.

'He told me about your money before I even met Malcolm, right at the very beginning before it all started. And all about your clever little scheme – it was rather sweet, we thought. I recognised the challenge immediately. One million five hundred and twenty-five thousand pounds. Well, that's a staggering amount, Ellie, especially for someone who's never seen a fifty-pound note in her life.'

'But you didn't tell Malc?'

'Why would I tell Malcolm?'

Ellie shakes her head. 'I just thought you possibly might.'

Gabriella fills her hand with peanuts from Ellie's new glass dish before she sits back once again.

'No, I didn't tell Malcolm. I wanted to see what you'd do with it. I was extremely interested to know what you'd do with it. I knew you'd try and buy him back but I wasn't sure how. There was a point when I thought you might offer it to me – fair exchange, so to speak, but that was before I met you. That was before I gave the matter much serious thought.'

'And then what?'

'Then I realised that you would never do that. Then I threw in the bait, told Malcolm that the penthouse was mine and that my job meant more to me than anything else in the world.'

'But it did! Anyone could see that it did! And the penthouse was *you*, Gabriella. It was perfectly and completely right for you!'

'Oh Ellie, sometimes you really disappoint me. How do you know it was *me*? I am a total stranger!'

'But the penthouse is yours! It has all your things in it!'

Gabriella smiles, the frightening smile of a person who knows and enjoys power over another human being. She stares at Ellie through patterns of cut glass. 'The penthouse goes with the gallery. Whoever runs the gallery lives in the penthouse. It's not mine, it has never been mine. I furnished it because I was the first person to live in it.'

'But Malc said . . .'

'It is very easy to get Malcolm to say anything. He was very easy to catch. He is like Plasticine – like ready-made pastry. You know that, Ellie, as well as I do.'

There is more pain in Ellie than hatred. 'I thought those were your precious things.'

Gabriella uses a conciliatory tone. 'It was important to bring you to the apartments, to let you see the empty flats and make you believe that to leave there would destroy me. I made sure, I emphasised over and over again how important my job and my apartment were to me. And you soaked it up . . . you are frightened of women like me, aren't you Ellie? And when you are frightened of people you do tend to make them up. It is important to humanise them, to give them all sorts of little vulnerable defects . . .'

'How do you know that?' asks Ellie, barely audible.

Gabriella is cool, calm and collected while Ellie feels she is growing a hump on her back and she might well be dribbling.

'Everyone knows that.'

'What are you going to do?'

Gabriella flashes an even more piercing smile. She takes her time before she answers. 'I could have told Malcolm you had won the money and were keeping it quiet soon after I met him. I could have told him you paid for that job of his, but that wouldn't have worked.' Gabriella smiles at Ellie, quite fondly. 'He would probably have loved you all the more for that. I could have told him it was you who bought the empty apartments, who moved the Skinners in and those other unsavoury people, but he would probably have laughed and understood – I certainly did. No, I had to wait until you did something that would turn him against you for ever, with no turning back, and I didn't have to wait very long. Oh Ellie, women like you are so pathetically predictable.' Gabriella sits forward. 'Ellie, Malcolm would never forgive you if I told him it was you who informed the newspapers and brought all that embarrassment down on his head. It slayed him, Ellie, he was tortured by it, and he struggled, most of the time without sleep, to get through it. You hit him where it really hurt . . . he turned, very publicly, on his own kind and he got pulverised for it.' Gabriella retrieves her arms and sits back, positioning them behind her head. 'And do you know something, Ellie? I don't think he will ever quite recover from that. From that plan of yours. From what you did to him.'

'I wanted him back,' sobs Ellie, inferior, helpless. 'I only wanted him back.' But her words fall and evaporate before Gabriella's ironic, interested gaze.

'And you can have him back, my dear. I certainly don't want him any more.' Gabriella gazes around the room again, making her eyes go wider and wider. 'But this house will do me, this house and whatever you have left in that bank of yours which I am sure is still considerable.'

'My house?' Ellie is completely lost now.

'Darling! I certainly can't stay living in the penthouse, not now, dear, not after what you've done. There's no hope of getting the buggers out, you made quite sure of that, I suppose.'

'And you could make Malc come back to me?'

'I'd only have to chuck him out and he'd come back to you tomorrow. Malcolm is not a man who can live well on his own. He is a man who needs to feel the strength of a woman behind him, as you well know, Ellie, as you and I both well know.'

'You never loved him?'

'He was good for a fling, as most men are. I do not intend to spend the rest of my life shacked up to any single one of them. Don't look so tortured, Ellie. I am offering to let you have what you want! And you have me to thank, really, for taking Malcolm off your hands so that you could exercise your own tiny wings for a while, so that you could sort out all that destructive stuff between you. I can see you both being really happy together. Happy ever after!'

The poison in Gabriella's words brings a flush to Ellie's cheeks. She asks, 'And your job at the gallery?'

'You are naive enough to think that that could be under threat. I am a professional, Ellie, and one small setback is not going to undermine my whole career! Especially if I am independent, with money behind me.'

Mortified by her own stupidity Ellie pleads, 'What about your family? They have money! You turned it down to be independent.'

'Ellie, my family might be the right sort of people but they are poor as church mice. I'd have to wait years before I inherited anything worthwhile from them.'

Ellie shakes her head despairingly. 'All those terrible lies! And your acting was so good!'

'I only acted out your own fantasy for you. You had it all going in your mind's eye anyway. I became the person you wanted to see, that's all. It didn't require much talent to convince you.'

'What would Malc say if he knew what you'd done – that you'd used him like a piece of old carpet and that you'd throw him out tomorrow if it suited you?'

'It does not matter to me in the slightest what Malcolm thinks of me. The only person to whom what Malcolm thinks matters is you, I'm afraid, sweetie. Now, before I go I would be thrilled if you could show me round. There might be some changes I'll need to make, and there's no need to eye the poker like that, Ellie, you're not the kind of person to go in for violence. If you were, you would have resorted to that before now. Oh yes, there have been times when you have been desperate enough. I do understand you know, Ellie.' And her tone is one of mild reproach.

Meekly, obediently, Ellie gets up and shows Gabriella round. She insists on seeing everything, so Ellie has to open the airing cupboard and display the sheets, let down the attic steps and take her up there, too. And all the while Ellie is trying to come to terms with the painful fact that she has been used, that Gabriella is the one who directed and manipulated her from the start, that even her emotions have been directed, from a cool, safe distance, by Gabriella. As if Ellie was a rag doll.

287

How Gabriella must despise her.

And here was Ellie, feeling huge and grand . . . brimming over with all sorts of silly little hopes. Yes, if she could, if she dared, she would kill her.

Down in the kitchen Gabriella pokes and pries and comments, she even remarks on the length of the handles of Ellie's wooden spoons and the sharpness of her knife collection.

'I suppose you had decided on a way of tackling the neighbours, if you had managed to lure Malc back as you dreamed you would, persuading him, eventually, to sell that dratted bungalow to buy this?'

'I was going to confide in the Brigadier.' Ellie admits that much to her. 'He's a broad-minded man, he would have helped me. Given time, I would have worked something out.'

'Oh yes, I'm sure you would, Ellie. I have so enjoyed watching your little game . . . women are so much more devious, so much more imaginative than men, darling, aren't they?'

Gabriella's darting eyes miss nothing. It is dark before she is ready to leave.

'You approve then, do you?' asks Ellie.

'Yes, top marks, I approve!' Gabriella rubs her hands together. She looks just like Miss Bacon did when Ellie handed in a neat piece of work.

Ellie is humbled and totally humiliated by the elation this approval still gives her.

At last Ellie can show Gabriella out. The quiet, placid life of the square goes on behind them, soft lighting through curtains, a shadow bending, and on the road the occasional purr of a car, the closing of a door, the soft casting of a headlight. In the porch-light Gabriella's features are pointed and hard. She should not stand directly under lights like that, and mosquitoes are clustering in swarms round her. But Ellie doesn't want to attack her, there is something about Gabriella she fears and admires and needs to keep intact. But she shakes her head softly as she closes the door.

Gabriella slams her car door, rams in her car keys and revs away triumphantly into the night.

The stairs are tiring. Ellie has been up and down them too many times today. Her legs are aching because she has a great deal of weight to carry. There is something to be said for bungalows.

34

Sometimes.

You feel so tired.

You can hardly move.

Now – heavy like a slug, sticking to every stair, a silver trail of misery behind her as she winds and mounts, the peace and quiet she'd so enjoyed two hours ago has turned into silence, a frightening wall of darkness on to which she is too small to make an impression. It engulfs her and she is terrified again.

Ellie has always been afraid of the world.

Everything in her life has always told her she is unimportant.

Her simple invitation cards laugh at her now and she smiles back at them as she pushes them into a neat pile, willing, as always, to share the joke, to laugh at herself. Well, you've got to laugh, haven't you? If you can't laugh . . .

Ellie weeps. Her large body shakes and she weeps horribly.

'What you've got to do is list your goals. See . . . there's five pages of space for your goals.' Ellie remembers how she'd laughed, how they'd all laughed at Margot's list of goals. Margot had been given this book called *Plan Your Own Destiny*, and in it were suggestions, in case the readers were too uninspired, thick or too downright boring to have any ideas of their own. Ellie remembers some of them . . . to become a qualified commercial pilot, a wealthy inventor, a ballet star, a golf professional and then, coming down to earth with a bump, it was kindly suggested that some people might have smaller goals than that: '*You might just want to be a housewife fattening a family budget with extra income earned through successful spare-time activities.*'

Well! Now then!

'*Which role have you chosen for yourself? Success or failure? A continued average, humdrum, aimless, muttering, run-of-the-mill existence as just another member of the common herd. . . ?*' The book crossly suggested that some of its more recalcitrant readers might even have chosen that!

'*Take off those blinkers!*' shouted the book, while exhorting you to, '*Figure out your circuit and rev up your generator.*'

Margot, using the correct jargon, shouted back, 'You've gotta believe, you've gotta dream!'

Margot had put down her goals – to get to be Secretary General of the United Nations within five years, to learn to play the violin like Yehudi Menuhin, to get hung up in chains wearing a school angel costume and be whipped by Dudley Moore, and to be able to say the word 'Peugeot' without having to stop and think about it.

'Here, the trouble with yours is that they contradict themselves,' Di had said seriously, drawing a wet, circular explanation in spilt rum and coke and drying her finger on a sandwich. 'I mean, if you got to be Secretary General you wouldn't have time to practise the violin, it wouldn't matter if you could say Peugeot and you'd probably be so busy shagging your way to the top that you wouldn't have the energy to dress up and do that with Dudley Moore. You'd probably get to bed and only want to sleep. Your phone'd be ringing all night long with very serious problems for you to solve.'

'And you can't just sit and wait about for your dreams to come true,' Ellie remembers saying with urgency. 'That's what the book says. If you want to be Secretary General you'd have to go to the library tomorrow and look up everything about being Secretary General, and then you'd have to start climbing up towards that goal. I mean, you'd probably have to learn some languages for a start.'

Oh, God help me. Because Ellie never had any goals of her own – hers were always for other people: please let Kev get into Cardiff, please let Mandy pass her maths, please let Lil stop drinking, it's going to kill her in the end. Please let Malc find something to make him happy, something to put that gleam back into his eyes again.

And none of Ellie's goals would last as long as a year, let alone five. They changed too frequently, for she was too unambitious, she would never have time to do all the homework the book suggested, she could never be bothered to get up in the night and record her dreams.

And yet some people know exactly what they want – like the bleak-eyed girl she'd met in the park in London. Like Gabriella . . .

Love and envy . . . am I unnatural, Ellie wonders. My God, am I unnatural to be feeling jealous, not of Gabriella, who possesses Malc and is casual enough about it to be prepared to give him away . . . *but of Malc for having Gabriella?* And should I be hurting because Gabriella thinks so little of me, just as I was beginning to believe that she liked me . . . After all these years, a woman like that . . . I had come so far that I honestly thought she liked me!

And was proud of that.

Oh God, help me.

Selfish, Freda would say, if she suspected that Ellie had dreams of her own and was nurturing them. 'You're selfish, you are! Think about other people for a change, instead of forever pushing yourself forward!' She always said this when she considered that Ellie was showing off. 'Look at me, what d'you think would've happened to us if I'd fooled around dreaming all day?'

And in Mr Wilkins' study, after her terrible experience with the love of her life, Miss Bacon . . . 'Elspeth Thwait.' He pulled his glasses off his nose with two exacting fingers, he wiggled the golden hooks off his ears. 'I have been watching you for some time now and I can see that if you are not very careful you will go off the rails completely. You have got yourself in with the wrong set of people. You are not one of them, Elspeth, you are no tearaway, and in your circumstances you cannot afford to be. The sooner you get a job and start earning to help your poor mother, struggling on as she is like a martyr, the better. It is essential that you remember that . . .'

But her love for Miss Bacon had given her wings, had given her so many new and wild desires that she hadn't known where to put them, so she put them 'down there' and screwed with Malc in the central heating shed. Over and over again, wilder and wilder, faster and faster, rougher and rougher as if, in that way, she could rid herself of the fury, could drive it out, exorcise it.

Oh, but she'd been wanting something far wilder than that. Something . . . oh, too far away, too huge to describe. Too far to touch.

Strange . . . she'd found some of it here in this house, in the feelings she'd experienced while doing it up. It was in the choosing, in the wonderful sense of energy; she'd been all-powerful in some little way, all-powerful in her ability to take part in a unique act of creation.

It was beautiful. Yes, very beautiful. And it came from her, nobody else really, unless you counted Pete Sparrow, but he'd been happy to keep quiet and go along with Ellie's ideas.

Gabriella might have manipulated and directed her, Ellie might have been just a tiny, boring counter in Gabriella's wicked game, but the house is Ellie's and Gabriella has not contributed one thought, one idea – not one suggestion has been hers.

Yet number twenty-eight Ridley Place is Gabriella's now. She's bought it. She hasn't needed money, yet she's bought it.

Gabriella has the power, the goals were hers. Don't do this to me, Gabriella, pleads Ellie the beggar into a wonderful embroidered cushion, which is soaking wet with her tears.

I cannot let it go. If I let it go then the part of me that I have lost for so long and only just found will go with it, and I might as well curl up and die.

But she has no alternative. Malc is the prize. Malc has accumulated, over the years, into the snowball and now, at last, Ellie can win it back . . . She hears the rattling, clanking money machines and the wistful lament of the music. Hasn't she been pushing her money in the slots, standing there, eyes glued to the whizzing oranges and the plummeting pine-apples, hasn't every single thing she has done since winning her money been to do with getting Malc back?

No, actually, it has not. And, strangely enough, this is the only part that Gabriella would truly understand.

Ellie worries because of the way her thoughts are taking her; they are dangerous thoughts and selfish ones. She sits up straight and wipes her nose. 'What about this house?' she sniffs. 'I dreamed of us both living in it – that's why I bought it.'

'No, that is not true and why are you telling lies?' says the voice very firmly. 'This house was always yours, Ellie, only yours. There is nothing of Malc's in it; even the wallpaper in the dining room is vaguely pink, and Malc hates pink. The mattress on the bed is hard, and you know how Malc detests hard mattresses.'

'But it is a double bed – a bed for two people, and his wardrobe is there, waiting for him, still empty.'

'And you are a very large person with lots of new clothes.'

'Am I large enough? Won't I be lonely?'

'How long is it since you have been lonely, Ellie?'

'But it's nice to have someone coming home.'

'Is it? I can't answer that one. Nobody can answer that one – it's a little bit like Mr Wilkins ordering you to take your eyes down and look at yourself, to look at yourself and see what you must always be . . . no flying for you, Elspeth Thwait. It has been decreed by some greater being than you will ever be.'

'I know the feeling of being great, I was touched by it once.'

'AND YOU WERE TOUCHED BY IT AGAIN WHEN YOU CREATED THIS HOUSE.'

Ellie would scratch its eyes out, but the voice does not have eyes. Ellie thinks she is going mad, her brain is redhot like the hard round elements on her old electric cooker in Nelson Street. If she is touched by water she might spit.

Ellie gets up and slides the music on to the CD player. She pushes the button so that it floods the whole house, for hidden speakers have been built into every room. She stares at her reflection in the gigantic mirror above the fireplace but she's not going to laugh at the face she sees there, not this time. She goes softly up the stairs. She moves round the house from room to room, dimming the light in each as she goes and drawing the curtains against the sweet-smelling summer night, enjoying the swish of them, taking courage from the thick richness of them.

There are no germs here and the place is too big for dust and cobwebs ever to dominate it.

And anyway, Ellie has a cleaner now, a nice energetic

young man called Sam who comes in a van decorated with mops and has just started his own business. She was going to invite Sam to her house-warming party – Sam, Norma and John, Pete Sparrow and his men and their wives, all a little odd, all rather eccentric people. How lovely it would have been if she could have invited Di and Margot, too. How perfect that would have been. She could have confessed everything she had done – how they would have enjoyed that! And she could have helped them out financially if she'd given that matter some thought; there is no need for them to hate her automatically just because she's come into some money. Some businesslike arrangement could have been made . . . there is always a way.

Ellie supposes Gabriella will have a party soon after moving in. She hopes that her rival will not change the house too much . . .

Ellie fingers all the surfaces with love. Perhaps she is wrong to invest so much emotion in a place, because that, after all, is what it is – bricks and mortar and nothing to get sentimental about. Anyone could have done it, let's face it . . .

But not quite like this.

No, the house is nothing to do with bricks and mortar, as a painting is nothing to do with paints, as a poem is nothing to do with words and Ellie knows that really.

She reaches Malc's photograph and tries to go past but she can't. His face stares out at her sadly, for it was taken in unhappier times. Were there unhappier times? She has to sit down and clasp it, she even sits on her bed. She is aware that she is acting, like playing a part in a film, but when you're unhappy you need to follow a pattern or you end up on the floor screaming 'Mummy!' It's not nice, really . . . and when did Mummy honestly take away the pain?

There was love between them, once. Yes, there was love, whatever love is. And then it was over and dead. Malc knew, but Ellie clung on to the thing that was left. Her reaction was something to do with the fear of loneliness, of being frightened, a child again in the big wide world. Ellie never mourned, she just clung on to the process of mourning.

So now she smiles softly, sadly, because there is terrible sadness in wisdom come late.

It isn't like that any more. Oh yes, the fear is still there, she can feel its beating wings sometimes, she can sense the cavernous depths of it, she can gauge the vaulted heights of it. It goes on and on to the stars, if she lets it.

Because it *is* nice to have someone come home.

But not if you're not there to meet them.

The decision is easy, really, and she could have taken it years ago. Ellie puts the photograph down . . . not face down because there's no need to go that far . . . but just as it was, there on her bedside table. She goes down the stairs and sits on the sofa and looks at the list of guests she has made. It's silly . . . she is certainly not going to have a party, her first party, without her friends.

So she takes a new card out of the box and twists the lid off her fountain pen – she won't have biros now, it's just a little quirk of hers, like keeping the immersion on all day and knowing there is always hot water. The card shines up at her with a vacant whiteness, waiting for the dark blue words, and there is a dotted line for the names she must write, like the dotted lines in the book that waited, all those years ago, to receive Margot's goals. Actually, Margot would probably have made an extremely good Secretary General.

'Malcolm and Gabriella . . .'

Like a signature.

The ink flows smoothly as if it has been waiting. It is all so simple, really, and yet so violent, relinquishing so much anguish in those two linked words.

She has written them out and written herself in. She has got herself back, her reassuring, funny, confused, pathetic, emotional but basically likable self: she can never again be truly alone. Not in that enormous sort of way.

Later that evening Gabriella tells Malc about this absolutely amazing house she has found. 'And we are going to have to think very hard about our on-going relationship,' she says briskly.

While a fat woman in a moonlit garden leans towards the first of her summer roses.

296